The   l

By

Doreen Demerjian

Copyright © *Doreen Demerjian,* 2024

All Rights Reserved

Dedicated to GOD

&

All Those Who Do HIS Work, especially Healthcare Professionals, EMS Workers and Veterinarians.

Literary license has been taken with some characters, events and customs to fit the storyline and create dramatic impact.

Table of Contents

Chapter 1 3

Shipwrecked 3

Chapter 2 17

The Search 17

Chapter 3 28

Reunion 28

Chapter 4 40

Wounded 40

Chapter 5 49

Dr. Chikaris 49

Chapter 6 52

Kitchen Surgery part 1 52

Chapter 7 63

Kitchen Surgery part 2 63

Chapter 8 74

Afterward 74

Chapter 9 77

The Morrow 77

Chapter 10 79

The Lords Esper 79

Chapter 11 95

Training Day 95

Chapter 12 102

The Feast 102

Chapter 13 137

After the Feast 137

Chapter 14 145

Horse Thief 145

Chapter 15 149

The Problem 149

Chapter 16 152

An Invitation 152

Chapter 17 155

The Solution 155

Chapter 18 167

After the Betrothal 167

Chapter 19 169

Next Morning 169

Chapter 20 172

The North Pasture 172

Chapter 21	176
In the Chapel	176
Chapter 22	184
We Meet Again	184
Chapter 23	192
Onboard to Jaffa	192
Chapter 24	195
Heart to Heart	195
Chapter 25	197
Jaffa	197
Chapter 26	211
Richard	211
Chapter 27	224
Castle Whetherly on Moon Isle	224
Chapter 28	226
Ellette	226
Chapter 29	232
The Search	232
Chapter 30	245
The Sea Stallion	245
Chapter 31	272

Lady Emlyn and Raoul the Duc de Marche 272

Chapter 32 290

The Path to Emlyn 290

Chapter 33 301

Emlyn Found.. 301

Chapter 34 308

After the Battle... 308

Chapter 35 312

Richard Again... 312

Chapter 36 315

Hugo and Emlyn... 315

Chapter 37 323

The Return of the Duc de Marche 323

Chapter 38 325

A Means to an End... 325

Chapter 39 327

Dyfen and Emlyn.. 327

Chapter 40 339

Aftermath 339

Chapter 41 343

Leaving it Behind... 343

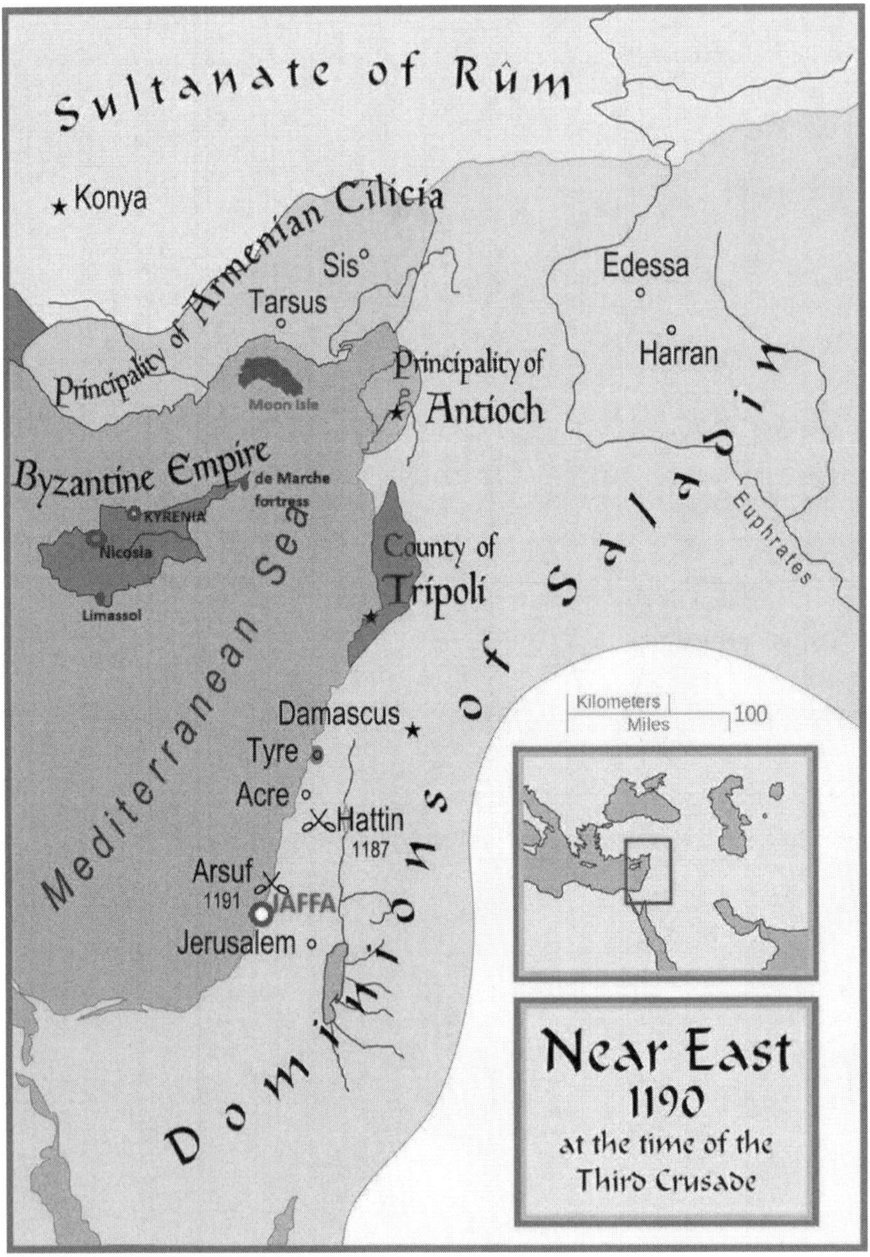
Sultanate of Rûm
Konya
Principality of Armenian Cilicia
Sis
Tarsus
Moon Isle
Edessa
Harran
Principality of Antioch
Byzantine Empire
de Marche fortress
KYRENIA
Nicosia
Limassol
County of Tripoli
Mediterranean Sea
Dominions of Saladin
Euphrates
Damascus
Tyre
Acre
Hattin
1187
Arsuf
1191
JAFFA
Jerusalem
Kilometers
Miles
100
Near East
1190
at the time of the
Third Crusade

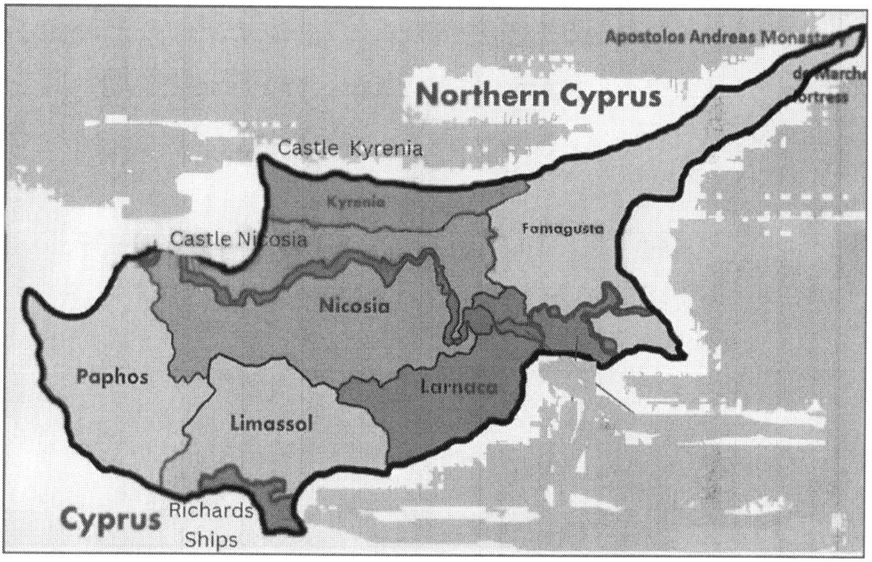
Apostolos Andreas
Northern Cyprus
Castle Kyrenia
Kyrenia
Famagusta
Castle Nicosia
Nicosia
Paphos
Larnaca
Limassol
Cyprus
Richards
Ships

Chapter 1

Shipwrecked

Cyprus Island - Third Crusade Year 1191

Emlyn Elora Esper stood on the white, sandy beach looking downward into the blue-tinted bottom of the sea as she had done countless times before. She could see her reflection rippling as the wind blew the shallow water into tiny waves around her legs, ankle-deep in the surf. The wet sand conformed around her feet and felt like soft, caressing pillows. The breeze pushed her long, dark-brown hair backwards from her light olive-complected face.

It was a cool and sunny morning, the aftermath of the tremendous storm that had crashed upon the island the evening before, leaving broken trees in its wake. The air was rife with the smell of salt. She could taste it on her tongue as the spindrift infiltrated the air.

She cast her gaze down the beach, hoping to see her mare, Firah, who was last seen jumping the pasture wall in terror of the approaching storm. The beach was a favorite place of theirs, and Emlyn thought of finding her here, now that the weather had settled. She had brought rope just in case. It lay in the sand next to her shoes, which she had cast off upon arriving.

As she stood listening to the rhythm of the waves crashing onto the shore, a piercing, shrill, dissonant sound broke the peace. Her head came up, and her large, hazel-green eyes looked out over the water.

The echo of distressful shrieking drew her eyes further out to sea. A look of alarm spread over her face. Firah? She squeezed her eyes together, looking out to the east, trying to pinpoint the origin of the sound. It was hard to tell because of the rising wind. She turned her head, gazing out over the horizonless sea with its crashing waves rolling onto the shore. Had Firah been swept out to sea in the storm?

She continued squinting her eyes to adjust to the sun's blinding rays. Something big was moving toward the shore. It was loud and becoming louder. She could hear shrill shrieks emanating from the big spikes of ocean water surrounding large, thrashing bodies.

She stood transfixed, bracing herself, unsure of what was approaching. She could see it was followed by dots of wreckage in the background.

Two blurred objects rose from the water, sloshing, still crying out loudly. Emlyn moved out of the way before she was nearly run over by two soaking and loudly neighing horses emerging from the surf. Their powerful hindquarters propelled them onto shore, still calling out as they emerged. Each was telegraphing its position and condition to the other. Was she being visited by Poseidon's own sons, Arion and Pegasus?

Two young stallions stood pawing the wet sand. One was the color of gilt silver and the other black as night. She was struck by their majestic beauty. Their wet bodies shone in the strong morning sun, and their surprisingly blue-colored eyes were wild with panic and confusion. As they gained traction onto solid ground, they became calmer. She had never seen blue eyes in a horse before; now, each stood looking out over the sea with a steadfast look of intelligence and purpose.

She backed away, giving them a chance to become more secure in their newfound safety from the water. The horses began to circle, whinnying in comfort with heads up, continuing to scan the liquid horizon as if looking for someone. Suddenly, their ears straightened, and they both turned their heads in the same direction. Wreckage was floating toward the beach, being pushed closer with each wave. The horses stood rooted to the ground and watched, focused on a moving pile of flotsam.

Emlyn strained her eyes but could see nothing unusual, although she knew something must be out there. The horses were so focused on approaching planks of wood floating toward the shoreline that she was able to move up next to them without their notice. All four ears remained erect while manes and tails whipped wildly in the wind. Their eyes never wavered from an object headed towards shore. As it moved closer, the horses started calling to it. Bellowing neighs that came back to them on the wind, stamping their feet in impatience as they danced in place.

The wreckage scraped the beach about one hundred yards down from where they stood. The sand grabbed it, anchoring it to shore. The stallions took off, making a beeline toward the rubble, heads down and haunches pushed forward. Reaching it, they both pushed their noses into a muscled body resting on a studded door. Emlyn hurried after them, slowing down as she drew near, careful not to startle the horses.

She saw movement. Finally, a form rolled off the door onto the sandy beach. "Shhh, shhh, my sons," it emitted half choked. "We are safe now. Thanks be to our merciful Lord," the raspy voice croaked. A strong, long-fingered hand made the sign of the cross, then reached up to touch each big, soft muzzle. The horses knew the voice, recognized the decidedly masculine hand and nuzzled the darkly tanned fingers in response. *Poseidon has come for his sons*, she thought, half dreaming. All thoughts of Firah now forgotten. Lying on his back, Poseidon turned his head toward her.

He noticed a sea blue and ivory-clad figure of a young woman slowly moving toward the three of them. Her long, heavy, dark hair was tied at the nape of her neck by a blue and ivory, fine linen scarf. She wore a loosely fitting kirtle and was without shoes. Her feet were delicate and tanned, he noted. She was no stranger to the beach. The sweeping wind sent her hair and clothing billowing, outlining her long, lithe body. Her willowy form was graceful in movement as she neared them. He scanned the beach, searching for her attendant or escort. He saw no one.

"Hail! Are you injured?" She shouted to be heard above the sound of the surf.

He lay there quietly, recovering his strength and regaining the ability to reason. They had reached land. The others on board? Where were they? Alive or dead? He knit his brows with worry and felt for his belt to make sure he still had custody of his pouch containing coins and other necessary articles. He relaxed when he felt it still fastened to his sash.

He last saw the captain at the firrer of the Carlyle trying to steer the ship to safety. Fortunately, the round ship was hugging the coastline, so land was near. It had been listing to port, taking on more and more water. When it became clear it would not survive the rough seas, he had made haste to warn the others to abandon ship and then had run down to the cargo hold to release his two stallions, Zakar and Arazi, from their slings where they were whinnying in rising panic. Once released, the horses held their heads high above the water as he led them up the specially designed ramp to the flooded main deck. He had insisted upon bringing it to make it easier for horses to gain footing. He thanked the Lord that he had been adamant it be loaded.

His five Irish Wolfhounds that followed behind had found it hard to keep their footing on the slippery deck surface. Now that they had all reached the top deck, he saw that a section of the gunwale was missing. He had steered the stallions in front of it and, with all of his might, had pushed them by their hindquarters over the side and into the sea, jumping in after them. The dogs had followed him over the side, one by one. They would all be safe as long as they stayed ahead of the heavier wreckage that was fast overtaking them from behind.

Once overboard in the tepid coastal waters, he had tried to climb onto Zakar's slippery back as the silver stallion paddled by him but fell off twice. He was left behind to drag himself up onto the first object floating by big enough to support him. It appeared to be what was left of one of the ship's doors. The wood was now nearly black, soaked with seawater, the large decorative studs prominent enough for him to hold onto. The dogs paddled furiously to keep up.

Safely ashore and exhausted, he looked up at the two young horses he had raised from foals, now nuzzling his legs, urging him to stand. Twin brothers. Good, they were safe. He wondered where the dogs were.

Emlyn was about ten feet away by now and thoughtfully eyed the castaways as the three celebrated their reunion. Observing the man's gentle demeanor with the horses caused her to lower her guard and move closer to them.

She could see that he was well-built with deeply tanned skin the color of gold. His long, brown, wet hair pulled up into a single thick braid trailed down to his midback. It was shot through with blond strands errantly surrounding his face. His gaze shifted from the horses to her. She saw eyes the color of an aqua-blue sea shimmering up at her. His almond-shaped eyes squinted as they focused upon her face. The color reminded her of the waters near shore when lit by the sun just before dusk. The warmth of his complexion set his blue eyes ablaze.

He possessed a long, straight nose, and a strong, well-defined jawline. He wore a small silver earring dangling from his right ear in the shape of a cross. It was inset with a very fine Persian turquoise at its center. He had the style of the Orient about him, but his features were those of a Saxon.

She noticed he had lost a leather boot, and his wet clothes were hanging closely to his long, lanky, muscled body. He was tall with wide shoulders, perchance in his late teens or early twenties.

She could see a long, brown leather cord hanging around his neck where his linen shirt had fallen open at the laces. His hand rested upon a nugget-sized stone similar to the one in his earring, attached to the cord. The aqua-blue of the stone echoed the color of his eyes, she thought. There was also a stream of blood running down his left temple.

His tired eyes were locked onto her face as if trying to evaluate the level of danger she presented as he absent-mindedly stroked his jawline, dragging his right thumb down across dark, prickly stubble. She noted how strong yet sensitive his fingers looked.

Seeing her approach, his eyes settled on her face, watching as she moved toward them. She stopped to rub the horses' shoulders in a circular motion. He continued to scan the beach for a guard or escort, unable to believe she had come alone. His face was drawn with worry, and his features reflected his exhaustion, yet he could not relax his vigilance. The horses accepted her, he thought to himself, still stroking his jaw unconsciously. A good sign of trust.

Now, she was standing in front of him and began to kneel, permitting him to observe her at close quarters. Her sleek, dark hair blew behind her in the wind. Dark limbal rings around the corneas of beautiful hazel-green eyes created a sense of deep drama in a distinct and charming face.

"You are bleeding. Let me see to that," she said in a smooth, even voice. Her hand reached to untie the kerchief from her hair, allowing it to blow wildly around her.

He put his fingers to his head and felt blood.

"It is nothing; I feel no pain," he said while trying to avoid her hands and wincing at the same time.

"Let me stem the flow, then do what you will," she insisted. She had already folded and placed the cloth around his head, tying it into place. "At least, the cut has been cleansed by the sea."

When the back of her fingers brushed against his brow, she felt a tingling sensation down her spine and then a feeling of calm overtook her. Her eyes focused on his face in surprise. She searched it for a reaction. Did he experience the same sensation? She could well imagine this to be how his horses felt under his touch.

With her nearness, he could smell the faint scent of Damascus rose as if it were part of her, emanating from the fabric she had placed over his wound. He closed his eyes for a few seconds and breathed in, feeling at peace.

He opened his eyes, embarrassed. Collecting himself, he was eager to change the focus from himself. "How is it that you come to the beach unescorted? Does not your family fear for your safety?" he asked with a hint of suspicion.

"I am here in search of my mare who fled her pasture this morning because of the storm. I had hoped to find her here, a favorite place of ours, but, alas, she is not here. I did not wish to wait for my...uhm...escort, so I hurried ahead. He should be here presently," she fibbed, not wanting this stranger to know she was alone.

He studied her, noting the fixed set of her jaw and the defiant look on her interesting face, "You fled your escort? Fled without your shoes... hmmm... your would-be protector is not an agreeable man then, I take it."

"I did not say, fled," she stressed. "I said, I did not wait. And my shoes are over there," she said, pointing behind her in annoyance. "I removed them when I arrived at the beach. My companion will arrive shortly," she repeated.

"But is it wise to search unaccompanied? You could come to harm. Are you not afraid for your safety?" his eyes tried to read hers as he spoke in that low, raspy voice. The whiteness of his teeth contrasted against the gold of his skin.

"Are you telling me that I have need to worry for my safety? That you are not to be trusted? Normally, a brigand would not take such matters into account," she pointed out. "And no, I do not fear you because you show more concern for my safety than do I. I hardly think I have much to fear in you," she said, searching his face.

"You question neither my motive nor my honor? You dismiss me? I am insulted, maiden," he joked. "I am rather certain I look fearsome at present."

Emlyn laughed with him and felt very at ease with this stranger.

"My intent is not to insult but rather assure you that I feel myself in no danger. Although I do not question your ability to overcome a threat if you considered it necessary."

He became serious. "I am well able to protect myself. It is your welfare I speak of. Any type of man could come ashore after such a storm. It is not safe for a maiden to be on her own. Where is this escort? Should he not be here by now?"

Emlyn, who enjoyed being on her own without a man overseeing all she did, was beginning to get angry. How dare this stranger to her home chastise her. "My escort," she began, "must have been delayed and is of no concern to you."

"Well, what of your missing mare then? Describe her," he asked, changing the subject to something less heated.

'She is an Andalusian. Dappled, gray in color, almost black at the hind. A dark mane and tail with a fine head. She answers to, Firah, and I am Emlyn, Emlyn Esper," she stated, bowing her head. "My father is Lord here. Master of Kyrenia. You are on the north coast of the Isle of Cyprus; in case you have reason to wonder. And what may you be called?" Emlyn asked, looking at him expectantly.

He slowly rose onto one knee as if she had said nothing. Dragged himself to a standing position by grasping a handful of long, white mane from the silver gilt stallion. He could feel his strength returning now that he was no longer fighting the waves. The warm air relaxed him.

She kept her distance, focusing her eyes upon him as he arose. He ignored her question, but she did not seem to notice.

"Your stallions inspire wonder. I have not seen their kind before. They are quite handsome. What is their pedigree? "

She had broached a topic he loved to speak upon, and forgetting all else, he answered in earnest.

"They are of the ancient Nisean breed that Armenians have bred for generations in their southern foothills. The mount of kings throughout history. They are rare and have seldom been seen outside of that area, most likely why they are new to your eyes."

"I have heard of Niseans, but surely they are not so tall?" Emlyn questioned with interest.

"Commonly no, they are not as large as these," he said as he lovingly stroked the black neck of Arazi. "My family has bred horses as far back as can be remembered. Niseans are a tough breed capable of surviving harsh living conditions. Many have blue eyes and metallic-looking coats, as do these. They are known for their loyalty, endurance, speed, and intelligence that borders on intuition. For all these reasons, they are highly prized by most, but to me, they are like my sons and beyond price."

As he finished speaking, they both turned their heads in the direction of the sound of steady hoof beats and could see a dark horse galloping wildly towards them in a terror-stricken state. Wet sand was flying in its wake.

Emlyn recognized the horse immediately. "Firah!" she shouted; her voice lost in the loud surf. "Oh my Lord, this is my mare, and she is headed for the rocks!" She was referring to a rocky section of shore that last night's storm had buried in sand, making it barely visible. "She is not going to stop!" Emlyn was gasping, trying to catch her breath, she was so overcome with panic.

The tall stranger unexpectedly jumped onto the back of the black stallion which stood nearest him and began to canter down the beach toward the errant Firah.

The mare was about four hundred yards away and fast approaching. He and Arazi covered the halfway point in seconds before quickly turning to face Emlyn. They started a slow canter toward her until Firah caught up.

Emlyn watched in awe. The excitement of the moment energized both rider and horse. The fleetness of the black stallion was remarkable.

Firah was quickly approaching, and as she drew nearer to Dyfen and Arazi, Dyfen sent Arazi into a gallop, keeping abreast of the mare as Firah and Arazi raced side by side down the beach. He used his right knee to signal Arazi closer to Firah.

As they ran neck and neck beside one another, manes flying in the wind, he leaned over, grabbed a handful of Firah's mane, and carefully moved his body onto her back while running down the shoreline. The weight of his body seemed to calm the mare, who was slowing down as Arazi started to fall back. Dyfen loosened his grip on the mare's mane, and she started to slow down to a canter and then to a trot. He guided her around the rocks and finally came to a walk just before reaching Emlyn.

The mare was wet with sweat, and a white, foamy lather covered her body. They circled around and then walked into the surf to cool Firah down. It was necessary to reduce the lactic acid buildup after such a labored workout. Otherwise, the mare would suffer severe muscle pain.

Emlyn stood on the shore with his stallions while the stranger made sure her horse was uninjured. He was standing in shallow water next to Firah, running his hands up and down her legs while cooing to her in his low, raspy voice in a foreign tongue. Emlyn waded into the water with rope, ready to take charge.

She took a step toward them, rope in outstretched hand and stumbled. Dyfen reached a strong arm out, caught her about the waist and gently pushed her upright. She could feel the steeliness in his forearm.

"Hah! Have a care; I can only attend to one damsel at a time," he said jokingly.

She blushed with embarrassment. She felt his muscled arm ease away from her while she regained her balance. She shoved the rope at him.

Taking it, he slowly looped it loosely around the mare's neck, all the while talking to her in low tones.

Emlyn headed back to shore, feeling humiliated.

He led Firah out of the water and handed the rope to Emlyn. "She is tired and shall not cause you any trouble. Poor frightened girl," he cooed, stroking the dappled mare's arched neck.

He walked over to his own two steeds.

Emlyn took the rope and placed her arms around Firah, relieved that she was safe but ashamed that she had little to do with saving her. Hugging her closely, she sighed into the mare's neck. The two stood together on the wet, sandy beach. Emlyn's wet clothing clung to her lower body, drawing attention to the outline of her shapely legs under the clinging kirtle.

The two stallions watched the mare with interest. "Enough!" Dyfen said sternly, reading their minds. There are too many distracting females here, he thought.

By now, Emlyn was soaking wet and emotionally spent. She thought about the extraordinary display of horsemanship she had just witnessed and found herself captivated and drawn toward this young man who had such a winning way with horses. She still did not know his name and saw he was preparing to leave.

He effortlessly hoisted himself onto the silver stallion's back; his legs came round to hug the horse's flanks. Kicking off his one boot, he circled the horse a few times, pointing him westward where he had seen the tide take the dogs.

He turned the horse to face her and gently squeezed Zakar's sides as he pulled back on the mane, signaling the horse to walk backwards while he spoke.

"So, we are in Kyrenia. I know of it. My name is Dyfen, Dyfen Whetherly," he said, returning to the conversation before the escapade with Firah. He had a worried look on his handsome face. "I must take my leave to seek my brothers and my five dogs, who are family to me. I must know that they are safe. With God's blessing, they have reached land unharmed."

"My prayers are with you, Dyfen," Emlyn responded. "May merciful God grant them safe passage to land. I am returning home and will entreat my father to send men out seeking survivors."

He nodded his head to her in thanks and pulled Zakar's mane to the left, turning him around and headed down the coast. He held his hand up in goodbye to her and rode off. The black stallion cantered closely behind.

Emlyn shouted and waved her arms after them.

He heard her call as he rode on. The wind made it hard to hear, but it sounded as if she had shouted, "Beware or be aware …." and the word "church," he had not heard the rest. Beware of what? He wondered. No time to worry about that now. He had to find his brothers, Isley and Dover, or his mother would have his skin. Hopefully, they were with the dogs.

Isley, a year younger than Dyfen and one year older than Dover, came to stay with the Whetherlys on Dyfen's sixth birthday; Dyfen liked to joke that he had received a pony and a brother as gifts and was not sure which he held more dear.

Isley's father had been a close friend to Lord Whetherly. They had been warriors together in the Holy Land, where Geoffrey Standen had died in battle. The two friends had promised to take in each other's family if one of them fell. Lady Standen had died the prior year, birthing a stillborn child. So, Isley had been orphaned upon his father's death.

Braxton Whetherly brought the five-year-old son of his friend home to Moon Isle, where Dyfen's mother took to Isley immediately, and loved him as her own. He was a quiet, studious boy who minded well. He and Dyfen were inseparable from the start, with Dover tagging after them as soon as he could keep up. She raised all three boys as brothers, teaching them to protect and stand together as one. Isley was as devoted to Lord and Lady Whetherly as any true son could be.

Dyfen had seen his youngest brother, Dover, taken overboard by a large wave that broke over the bow of the listing Carlyle just after he himself had leapt in after his horses.

Onboard, Isley still stood clutching the gunwale to maintain balance when Dyfen's eyes met his for a second. Isley understood the unspoken request. He rolled his eyes upward and threw himself over the side after Dover, letting out a yell when he hit the sea with a big splash. After that, Dyfen lost track of them both as the tide took him away.

Emlyn watched Dyfen and his stallions disappear into the white, beachy horizon. She slowly turned back toward the path from which she had traveled down to the beach. He is headed toward the old church, she thought to herself. She shuddered as the dark image flashed in her mind. She sped up her pace, collected her shoes, and, with Firah in tow, hurried home to tell her father what had transpired this morning. Explaining to him how she had come to the beach without a chaperone once again would be something she was not looking forward to.

Chapter 2

The Search

Dyfen gently squeezed his knees, and Zakar instantly responded by picking up speed. Arazi ran abreast of them as they cantered down the beach on the edge of the pounding surf. The trio slowed down to avoid wreckage that had collected on the beach. The shoreline was dotted with color as Dyfen noted clothing and other brilliantly colored fabrics strewn about.

He had been riding for nearly fifteen minutes without coming across evidence of survivors. The coast was narrowing into a small cove when Dyfen caught sight of a familiar figure up ahead.

Isley had removed his soaked, heavy outer clothing, which was in a pile at his feet. His linen shirt sleeves were hanging in tatters around his muscled wrists. Dyfen approached his brother on horseback. Arazi had reached him first. Isley extended his strong arm out to stroke the plush nose of the black Arazi standing before him.

Isley Standen's thick, long, brown hair tied loosely at the back was covered in sand. He lifted his hair and shook the sand out, throwing granular missiles in every direction. His finely chiseled features were grim as he pushed himself into a standing position and looked around.

"Isley!" Dyfen pulled Zakar up and swung his right leg in a forward dismount.

Isley turned his head. "Dyfen! Glad to see you made it with the lads," he cried joyfully as he now greeted Zakar.

Dyfen and Isley stood about the same height and had similar athletic builds. Anyone could easily mistake them for true brothers.

Isley answered the unspoken question. "Dover is here somewhere. I never actually saw him, although I heard him call out my name a few minutes ago. Damned if I know from where."

"Have you seen Cydryn and the pack?" Dyfen asked worriedly, scanning the horizon. "I expected to find them with Arazi and Zakar but they were nowhere in sight when I finally reached the beach. They aren't here with you?"

Isley rubbed the side of his face as he responded, "I have not seen the dogs since leaving the ship. I saw Cydryn jump overboard after you. And as we know, where Cydryn goes, the others follow; I thought the dogs would be with you. They probably ended up down shore a bit," he said reassuringly.

As his brother spoke, Dyfen saw that his hand was bleeding as he moved it across his face.

Isley noticed Dyfen looking at the injury. "I pushed some wreckage away with that hand. It's nothing," Isley commented in a matter-of-fact tone. "What happened to your head?"

"I am not sure. I must have hit it on something." Dyfen unconsciously moved his hand to his temple, and he felt the wound under the cloth. The blood had coagulated.

"Where did you find that?" Isley queried, pointing at the feminine-looking kerchief around Dyfen's head.

"Something I discovered on the beach. Must have been from the ship," Dyfen mumbled.

He untied the kerchief from his head, walked over to the water, and rinsed it in the surf. Walking back, he grabbed Isley's injured hand and wrapped the kerchief around it, fastening it on top with a knot.

"There, that should keep it clean for now. I don't think it will require stitching."

"Is that your professional opinion?" Isley joked. "Uncle August would be proud of you," he chuckled.

August, the younger brother of Braxton Whetherly, was a warrior and widely known as a skilled surgeon. He had convinced the men to transfer remains from the battlefield to his makeshift dissection table, where he studied the inner workings of the body. His growing understanding of anatomy assisted him in performing successful surgeries in the field hospital they had roughly constructed, and his reputation grew among the men. Braxton often jested that his brother's skill in battle was motivated by his need for bodies to dissect.

Upon returning from the Holy Land, August enlisted his young nephews as assistants, aiding him in dissections as he documented his findings for his growing library.

"Now, where did that damnable brother of ours go?" Isley asked as he held up his good hand to shield his eyes from the sun.

Dyfen squeezed his eyes shut as if the thought gave his head pain.

"Damn him," Dyfen exclaimed out of frustration. "Let us seek him without delay. The sooner we find him, the sooner we can look for the dogs," he said, anxious to know that they had survived.

The two of them walked around calling for Dover. "Dover! Do-Ver!" Nothing. Not a sound but the surf.

"Here are footprints leading up this hill," Dyfen muttered, looking at some impressions in the sand. "The bugger probably climbed up there. When I find him, I will throttle him to be sure. Remind me of it," he directed Isley.

"Not if I see him first," Isley sighed. "Dover is the most exasperating lad. I am surprised father has not strapped him to a stable post long before now to keep his arse out of trouble."

Dyfen smiled, "You think that would make a difference? Ha! He'd probably bring down the stable roof, trying to free himself. Most likely, taking out half of the horses while doing so. No, our brother needs someone to mind him at all times. It is the only way to make sure he is not a danger to others. Lord knows I have long stopped worrying for his safety."

"He could not have gotten far. I will take these steps to the top of the cliff. After I find him and choke him senseless, we will meet you back here and figure out what to do next. The horses are yours to tend to, Isley. They are worn and need fresh water and to graze. I will search for Dover while you take care of their needs."

Isley smiled. The two brothers were always threatening injury to one another. Or at least most of the time, Dyfen was trothing oaths to God Almighty with his intent to pummel Dover on sight. He had every intention of fulfilling these oaths when he uttered them, but somehow, action never followed. Dover had an excessive amount of Whetherly charm and usually talked his way out of his well-deserved punishment, much to Isley's chagrin. It was difficult to face Dover and maintain anger.

Dyfen now turned to follow the wet sandy prints, which started at a flight of stone steps carved into the side of the hill. Each step was long but not deep as they wound around the slope. He backed up, craning his neck to see where they were leading and what lay above. He could see the dark outline of a stone church perched on the edge of the cliff, arched stained glass windows facing the sea. Its segmented, copper, gilded dome had a blue-green patina. The words Emlyn had shouted in warning came to mind. This must be the church she had warned of, he thought.

Dover must have climbed up to view the disposition of the Carlyle and to spot survivors. Not an entirely poor idea, he thought, but if he had ascended the steps, he should be able to see us. I would expect him to call out to us. He would be happy to see that the horses had made it to land and his brothers as well. The only ones missing were the dogs. The thought of the missing dogs bothered Dyfen, but he shook it off, focusing on locating Dover.

The hill was steep, and the narrow steps had some thorny weeds growing in cracks, making it hard to find a place to set his bare feet. They spiraled upward at a steep plane, twisting toward the back of the hill. Finally, the last step came into sight, and Dyfen grabbed the ground and pulled himself to the top. He was at the back of an old stone church located in a clearing surrounded by fir trees which loomed up around it. Shadows of the firs fell over the ground, cooling the clearing by blocking the sun.

Dyfen looked toward the church. It was a solid stone structure containing a fanned-shaped, conical dome, which is typical of Armenian religious architecture. His mother had described her church to them many times when she spoke about her youth.

There were two smaller apses on the northern and southern sides of the building. A large cross sat at the top of the dome. Another weathered cross sat atop a spire on the largest apse at the east end. There was a carved wooden door on the west. The windows were similarly arched and bore jewel-toned, stained-glass panes colored cobalt blue, garnet red, emerald green and gold. They must be magnificent from the inside, Dyfen thought. I wonder why it has been abandoned?

He cautiously walked around the building to an overlook of the coast. Looking down, he saw that Isley and the horses had moved on. He turned toward a small, overgrown cemetery and saw the back of a tall man in a dark muslin cloak a hundred feet away. His head was covered with a hood. A monk? At an abandoned church? he wondered.

As he moved closer, he picked up a stout stick to protect himself, just in case the man before him was not friendly. After Emlyn's cryptic warning, he was unsure of what to expect and, in truth, was rather on edge. He moved stealthily forward. When he was close, he called out, "Hail." The figure turned toward him quickly, taking Dyfen by surprise.

Dyfen had the stick raised, ready to strike, when a sleeved arm moved upward to intercept the blow, pushing back hard on Dyfen's forearm, deflecting the stick away. Dyfen twisted his body to the left, clutching the stick with both hands now and came round ready to strike when the hood fell back, and he saw his brother's face. He dropped his arms. "Dover! What in the devil's hell are you doing dressed as a monk?" He eyed his brother with suspicion.

"Well, brother, your love for me is as strong as ever, I see. You were just about to land a blow to my head," Dover said dryly, glancing at the stick still in his brother's hands.

"I came looking for you. I followed the tracks from the beach. I had no idea who you were, you sodden idiot! How could I know it was you? Some ill could have befallen you. And here I find you dressed in a monk's habit," Dyfen shouted. "and I was warned about this place," he muttered under his breath.

Dover found his brother's exasperation comical. "Why do you worry, Dyfen? You know how providence favors me," Dover said, smirking, looking straight into his brother's eyes with his own equally startling blue ones. It was widely known within the family that good fortune was a friend to Dover. Others may suffer from accidents and consequences but he never seemed to fall victim.

At seventeen years of age, his version of the Whetherly eye color was more allium than aqua in color, and his hair was black as night, echoing that of their mother. Black eyebrows arched over his long almond-shaped eyes. Where Dyfen's complexion had a golden hue, Dover had a ruddy, healthy glow along with a long, straight nose and a generous mouth. A family resemblance was evident, but their looks were completely individual.

"True, you have the luck of the devil himself, Dover. But there will come a time when that luck turns on you," he warned.

"Well, that time is not now, brother," Dover leaned back on one leg. "Did you happen to see Isley anywhere? The sea pushed me onto the shore. I rested a bit. I called his name but received no answer. Seeing the steps, I followed them up to this higher vantage. Did he make it ashore safely? The waves were rough. I was worried for both of you and more for the dogs and horses."

Dyfen reassured him. "The horses made it ashore and were waiting for me when I landed. I found Isley here recovering on the beach. He injured his hand. Otherwise, he seemed fine, but you know Isley, even if he were near death, he would not tell it. The dogs, I have no knowledge of although I am hopeful that they reached shore. Five dogs the size of wolves running the countryside should be easy enough to find. We will seek them next." Dyfen stared at his brother with a calm, patient look and asked, "Well, pray tell, where did you find that cloak?"

"It is a monk's habit, and I found it lying on the ground. Whoever it belonged to, I imagine they no longer had need of it, and seeing that I did, being soaked to the bone and the wind quite cool up here, I put it on. Damned warm too. Very serviceable although lacking in a fashion entirely."

"I cannot imagine anyone less suited to wear a monk's habit," Dyfen joked.

"It was here, and I had a need. I was trying to decide what to do when you attacked me," Dover commented. "I feel incomplete without my sword and dagger. Lost in the wreck. We must gain replacements as soon as possible," Dover advised.

"With any luck, we may see our own again if our chests wash ashore," Dyfen replied. "I saw many while riding here."

His brother was not listening. He was too busy considering the stone building in the churchyard. "Looks like a weapons house," Dover observed. "Let us see if any weapons were left behind."

"After that, let us have a fast look in the church," Dyfen said. "Since we are here, we might as well give it a quick visit in case whoever left that habit is still here. It is in quite fair condition, so it could not have been here long," Dyfen observed. "I wonder why this church is thought of as ominous," Dyfen mused.

"Who said it was ominous?" Dover asked.

"Ah, no one. I just assumed it must be since it appears abandoned. Why else would cause a church to be left like this?" Dyfen responded gruffly, dismissing his brother's question.

They approached the single-story stone building in the churchyard and pushed the door open with some effort. It was dark inside, but through filtered light from the open door, they could see swords and daggers covered in dust that had been abandoned by their owners, pinioned in racks. "I wonder why all of these weapons were left behind by their owners," Dyfen said, throwing his stick away and picking up a sword from the rack. He gripped it by the hilt, feeling it for balance, then brought it to eye level, scrutinizing it for straightness in the dim light, eyeing the fuller. Dover did the same. They found three that would do, the third for Isley when they rejoined him. They left, grabbing the best three daggers they could find on their way out. "These will do until we can reclaim our own things; God willing, our chests made it to shore and did not sink to the bottom of the sea," Dover mumbled.

They headed for the church door. A high wind had the treetops swaying, and the sky had turned a slate grey. The air held the sweet scent of cedar as it blew around them. The smooth stone walkway made the distance on Dyfen's bare feet easier.

As they approached the church door, Dyfen became alert. He motioned to Dover, who nodded in response. "Let us be cautious, Dover. Someone left that robe you wear, so let us be watchful until we know there is no need to be. We are strangers here and may be seen as threats."

They held their swords at the ready, just in case, as they moved toward the wooden, carved, oak door with oversized iron hinges in the form of crosses. Dover put his hand on the dove-shaped brass handle and pulled the door open slowly. It let out a loud and long squeak, and then silence befell the dark interior as the wind fell off.

It was cool and dark inside. The interior smelled faintly of old incense and smoke. Colored shafts of sunlight fell from the stained windows encircling the dome high overhead and fell onto patterns on the limestone floor.

Once inside, the brothers looked down the nave toward a white marble altar where a wooden cross still stood. They each fell to a knee, placing a hand on the hilt of their swords. They bent their heads in reverence while crossing themselves before whispering a prayer ending in "amen." They crossed themselves again and stood up.

A stone arch stood solidly at the entrance of the nave with dusty, old Armenian characters carved around its curve. From that point on, an aisle was formed by tall stone pillars with carved khachkars on each of them.

"Well, brother, are you able to read what it says? You were always better at this than I," Dyfen asked, looking at Dover expectantly.

"Unfortunately, Isley is not here. He would be able to read this in a trice," Dover mumbled. "The carvings are pretty dust-covered, but I think it says.," he squinted hard, craning his neck leaning backward, "Surb T'adsu yekeghets I, Church of St Thaddeus," Dover translated, breathing out.

"Mother would be proud," Dyfen beamed, smiling.

"She would be at that," Dover smiled back. "You must remember to tell her those lessons were not in vain when we return home," he laughed.

"Pray, why must I tell her?" Dyfen asked. "It must be yourself to tell."

"I do not want to appear immodest," Dover joked.

Dyfen cast him a look questioning his seriousness. "Our mother knows you all too well, Dover. Modesty is a stranger to you." Dyfen placed his hand on his brother's shoulder in affection.

"Ahhmm, yes," Dover deflected and started walking down the nave toward the apse. Dyfen followed him. There were two very large khachkars, with fine, intricate interlacing standing on each side of the apse. They looked up at the sky-colored dome overhead. Sun streamed through stained glass, making the entire eastern dais glow, imbued with a holy light of peace and serenity. A large silver cross hanging on the wall shimmered with the reflected colored light.

"This is fully beautiful," Dover exclaimed while they stood looking at the altar basking in the beauty of its white marble with rose-pink veining. "This church is in fairly good shape for being abandoned," he jokingly remarked as an understatement.

Dyfen smiled. "It is," he said, casting his eyes downwards. He noticed two scorch marks behind the altar. "Look at this, Dover. There are two black marks on the floor." He moved his bare foot over them. "As if someone stood here with soot on their boots."

"I ask why the door remains unbolted?" Dover questioned, looking perplexed. "If none come for services any longer, one would think it would be locked."

Dyfen agreed with his assessment and decided to explore further. "I will have a look around," he said as he headed back down the nave while Dover stayed studying the craftwork that surrounded him.

Once Dyfen reached the atrium, he turned down a short hall to the left and pushed open a door into a room that appeared to be the vestry. His eyes traveled around the dusty room. Dark, heavy paneling was lit by three arched windows on the far wall. His eyes came to rest upon an old document that lay furled on top of the oak table situated near the windows. He walked over and carefully started to unroll it. He picked up a heavy, ornate silver candlestick on a shelf nearby and used it to pin down the top of the scroll. He held the bottom in place with his hand. Dyfen gazed at a beautifully drawn map of a city called Ayrivank on the Sea of Gegham.

Chapter 3

Reunion

Down on the beach, Isley had led the horses up an embankment to a small grassy knoll overlooking the shoreline. As luck would have it, there were pools of water left from the storm that were suitable for drinking. Arazi and Zakar were calmly grazing while Isley examined his surroundings. The horses stood near each other, long necks down in the long, lush grass. He would be able to see Dyfen and Dover when they descended to the beach.

"Well, my lads, eat up because you will need your strength. We will be leaving here as soon as your master returns with Dover," Isley stated. "If he can find him," he muttered in an aside.

The horses raised their heads and turned to the left. Their ears were erect, listening.

Isley looked in the same direction and saw a company of riders cresting a distant hill, traveling toward them. Five altogether. Arazi let out a loud call to the approaching horses. Now what? he thought.

There were four men and a woman.

"Hail!" called out the rider in the lead as they drew near. Once in front of Isley, he dismounted. Arazi moved nearer to Isley, followed by Zakar.

The dismounted man stepped forward. "I am Rylan Esper. This is my daughter, Emlyn, and my son, Eryk," he gestured to each as he spoke. He looked nearly forty years of age and of medium height. His shoulder-length brown hair was shot with grey and had a uniform wave. His hazel eyes proclaimed him as a father or close relation to the girl that came with him. He had a cleft in his chin thinly veiled by a goatee. His general appearance was that of a distinguished, broadly built warrior. On his chest hung a large, gold medallion with a fivefold cross over a sword hilt.

Eryk Esper looked much like his father with the same brown hair, broad chest, and cleft chin. His eyes were light brown, and he was a bit taller.

The young maiden was close enough for Isley to see that she was strikingly handsome in a quiet way, with dark brown hair pulled back at the nape and braided at the temple. Her elongated, hazel-green eyes had dark limbal rings and long, dark lashes, marking her appearance as interesting as well as attractive. She had a slightly olive cast, which seemed to glow in the strong light of day, and a slightly upward turn to her fine nose. Her full lips were stained the color of beet juice. He studied her with curiosity. She rode astride like a man. A maiden with her own mind, Isley thought.

All four men wore dark tunics and leggings. Their tanned boots were so excellently crafted that although obviously worn, their quality was still apparent.

Rylan Esper continued with the introductions, "May I introduce our neighbors; Sir Gracyn Rend," as he gestured toward the other older man. Nodding towards the younger man, "and his son, Hugo."

Both men were wolfishly lean and tall. Gracyn had a pocked complexion and piercing black eyes, long dark hair and a mustache and goatee. He looked formidable. His son, Hugo, had a strong facial resemblance to his father, but his face was unblemished, and instead of rendering him milder in aspect, his strong jaw and keen slate, grey eyes gave him the look of a man not to be trifled with. His long hair was blond and wavy, unlike his father's dark color.

"Gracyn, ...Hugo," Isley tilted his head at each when speaking their name. Giving each a level gaze to take their measure. They gave the same assessing gaze in return. Hugo had a very intense look about him, Isley noted.

"I observe that Dyfen found you." The maiden had moved her horse to face him with her eyes fixed on his bandaged hand.

"I met your saucy friend on the beach this morning with these very stallions while I was looking for my mare. As soon as he was able, he set out to find you, your brother, and his dogs..."

Hugo had moved his steed next to Emlyn's. "Jinol told me you were still abed. Resting," he accused quietly.

Emlyn glanced at her father with a sheepish look on her face, wondering if he had heard. She had told him of her meeting with Dyfen but did not see fit to include she ventured out alone. He was always scolding her for her independence.

Gracyn, who was closest to the two, overheard their exchange. "Your father allows you too much latitude, Lady Emlyn," Gracyn spoke in a low tone. "Hugo, of course, only fears for your wellbeing."

Isley sensed an undercurrent and moved the conversation past whatever was taking place before him. "Ahhhh…. my saucy friend, Dyfen, did find me, Lady Emlyn. How did you come to know him?" Isley asked, wondering why Dyfen had not mentioned the encounter to him and how he had come to be described as saucy.

"You wear my scarf about your hand," She observed. "I used it to wrap his head this morning to stem his bleeding. I trust his wound has healed?" she asked.

Isley started to unwrap his hand to return the scarf to her. "Please allow me to restore it to you, Lady Emlyn."

"Nay, please do not trouble yourself. I gave it freely and did not expect to ever see it again, in truth," she responded.

Isley gave his head a slight bow, smiled at her and spoke. "Allow me to introduce myself. I am Isley, Isley Standen. Brother to Dover and Dyfen Whetherly.

He now seeks our youngest brother," Isley said. "He climbed some stone steps on the beach to a church standing on the hill above. He has been gone this half-hour past.

"We were aboard the Carlyle before it sank, along with these stallions and five dogs. Rather large dogs. Have you seen them?" He looked at them with questioning eyes.

"Oh, Yes! We have most certainly met your dogs," Rylan Esper stated dryly. "Which brings us to why we have come. My men found them running up the shoreline further west, where a few of our horses were grazing. The horses were herded home, and the dogs moved with them as if shepherding them. They are presently in our stable, where your hounds have been terrorizing all since arriving. Five dogs the size of small horses. Well, they eat like horses and have been running in a pack, getting into all manner of mischief. These dogs have stationed themselves in the stable yard and will not leave its confines. They will not allow us to enter where our own horses abide. My stablemaster is beside himself. We had to borrow these mounts from Lord Rend's men at arms who happened to be visiting us," he chuckled good-naturedly. 'We came to ask you to rescue us from your dogs as well as offer you shelter and any assistance we can provide until you depart from our shores. Your brother had mentioned losing his dogs to my daughter earlier this day. She suggested your brother had headed in this direction, and when she recognized these two stallions, we rode over. Most fortunate we discovered you, as Rend here, wanted to fill the dogs with arrows to be rid of them but Emlyn would not allow it."

Isley, looking directly at Hugo, said in a curt and threatening manner, "You sought to kill our dogs? Why would you consider such harsh action once you knew that they had people looking for them?"

"Your dogs were preventing us access to our mounts; why else? They are a menace to our horses and our lives." Hugo had dismounted and approached Isley in a dismissive manner. "The dark grey one is particularly vicious."

Isley immediately recognized Cydryn from Hugo's description. 'The dark grey one.' The smallest of the five but the leader to his brothers Avak, Osyn, Tyber and Aubryn.

Isley met Hugo's gaze. "I know that to be a falsehood," he said with an even voice. "Those dogs would never harm a horse. Their very purpose is to protect horses. You should think yourself fortunate. Lady Emlyn prevented you from acting on your misguided notion. You would have to kill them all at the same time, or the survivors would rip you to pieces. They have been battle-trained and have put an end to many a foe on the field. So, it is providential that there is at least one so compassionate among you." He glanced at Emlyn, who met his eyes.

He continued. "Know this Rend, if harm is brought to one hair on their collective hides, you can be assured there will be most severe consequences for you." Both men held the other's eye.

Their standoff was interrupted by Gracyn Rend, who spoke in a commanding air. "Let us hurriedly complete our mission to find your brother and return to the castle to resolve the situation." He remained mounted and had moved his horse off to the side. "I imagine you will be soon leaving and taking your hounds with you." His eyes fixed on Isley for an answer to his next question. "What is your destination?"

"We are in Cyprus?" asked Isley. He dodged the question gracefully. He did not want to provide information until he had answers.

"Yes, on the northern coast. Kyrenia," answered Eryk Esper

Lord Esper, who had remounted, interrupted. "Let us ride to the church of St. Thaddeus and see about your brothers. It may also interest you to know that other survivors have washed ashore safely, most likely due to the closeness to land of the ship when it went down. Most of the crew, including its captain, have already sought passage on other ships. None suffered great injury; praise be to Our Lord."

Isley was relieved to hear that the others aboard the Carlyle had fared well. He noticed that Rylan Esper had turned his borrowed horse around. A sleek, grey mount with a long flowing mane, outfitted with a black leather bridle and a caucus tribal patterned, felted blanket of reds and blues. Rend's men at arms must be paid handsomely to own such steeds, Isley thought. He noted that Lord Esper sat a horse well in a kindly and regal manner. Hugo, on the other hand, handled his steed roughly and without consideration. His horse bristled at the rough treatment. With everyone on horseback, it was obvious that they expected Isley to accompany them.

He whistled low to the horses. Arazi and Zakar, who had wandered off to graze, came trotting over to his side. He mounted the sleek, black Arazi easily without the benefit of tack, and Zakar followed behind as they rode. They headed in the direction of the old church. He had hold of Arazi's long flowing mane. He could feel the texture of the coarse strands in his palm. The wind blew his hair and Arazi's mane backward in a long flowing stream as they rode.

Emlyn glanced over at Isley, wondering about his party's original destination. Where were they headed with horses and hounds? Dyfen had avoided the question, and Isley had done the same. Her curiosity was piqued.

Isley's face had a set look as he rode. It was composed, but she could see an edge in it. His strong hands held the mane in a comfortable way that showed he was used to riding without the benefit of a saddle or bridle. His horse and he seemed melded as one as the black stallion's long strides put him up front with Hugo, who was a strong rider. Isley never as much as glanced in her direction.

It took them fifteen minutes to arrive. They broke through a stand of trees that opened into a clearing in which the old church stood. The front door was open.

Isley jumped off Arazi before they came to a full stop and ran towards the door, calling Dyfen's name and leaving the others to dismount.

He was met by Dover, who was still wearing the monk's habit. At first, Isley did not recognize him. "What do you have on for God's love?" cried Isley, his face wrinkled in puzzlement. "And where in the devil's hell have you been all of this time?"

"Everyone seems to have an interest in my attire," Dover mused out loud. "It's something I found lying on the ground here," he stated pointing. "Now as to...."

Isley cut him off. "Where is Dyfen? He came up here to find you. Have you seen him?"

"Yes, he is here with me. Dyfen headed toward the vestry. Let us go back and look for him."

Isley looked at him with a troubled glance. "These people, waiting outside, came to me while I was grazing the horses. It seems our dogs have taken over their stable, guarding their horses, from them! Cydryn will not allow anyone to approach, they say. They had to borrow the steeds they ride to find us."

Dover responded, "It is a curious thing for them to do. Cydryn must be transferring his duties to the current stable. Having lost sight of Zakar and Arazi, they must be guarding the stable as a precaution. He and his brothers make menacing guards. If I did not know them, I would not attempt to enter that stable. Many a time they have foiled raiders by being so vigilant. Our horses owe their safety to that pack many times over if you recall."

Isley spoke with a sense of urgency, "I remember that well, but we have no currency here, and for the lads to take over the local Lord's stable…. well, it is not being considered a friendly gesture and has put their lives in danger. We need to call off Cydryn at once. There is a bore called Hugo Rend, riding with us, who sought to shoot the pack down. They were only saved by the objections of a rather attractive maiden named Emlyn. She says she knows Dyfen and of the dogs. You know as well as I what would happen if one of the dogs were wounded or, for God's sake, even killed. There would be no stopping the rest from tearing that person apart. Hugo is an arrogant fool, as you will see for yourself."

They arrived at the vestry and pushed the door open. Dyfen was sitting at a table, looking at a scroll on the table. He was so engrossed that he did not look up when the two walked in.

"Dyfen," Isley shouted. Dyfen flinched and tore his eyes away from the document he was studying. He smiled up at Isley and his brother. "Hail, Isley, you decided not to wait for our return," Dyfen smiled.

"Enough lingering," Dover interjected. "Tell him." He cast Isley a sideways look and didn't wait for Isley to speak. "Dyfen, the dogs have been found, all of them well but there is a bit of a problem we need to attend to."

"What problem?" Dyfen asked.

"Isley has brought the Lords of the land with him, and it seems the hounds have their stable under guard and are allowing none to enter. We need to put a stop to this before catastrophe befalls them."

"I understand it is not acceptable but to call it a catastrophe seems harsh. What catastrophe would this cause?" Dyfen posed.

Dover answered, "Isley says there is an arse by the name of Hugo Rend, who wishes to kill them to access the stable. He would have done so if a maiden named Emlyn had not prevented him from doing so by appealing to her father. They have come seeking you."

"Isley, is this true?" Dyfen asked.

"It is true, Dyfen. The man is an arse, and we are fortunate that Lady Emlyn intervened. There is no doubt at least one dog would be dead, and probably the bowman who did the deed would have been torn apart by the rest of them. After all, we are guests here."

Dyfen became visibly alarmed. "Let us leave without delay. I will kill anyone who harms those dogs." His face was composed but Isley and Dover could see the tension in his neck as he started to move at a brisk pace. They trailed in his wake.

The three strode down the dark hallway and exited the church. Their eyes had to adjust to the brightness of the day, and all were forced to squint for a few seconds. Outside, only Lord Esper and his children, Eryk and Emlyn, stood waiting by their mounts. Lord Rend and his son, Hugo, were nowhere to be seen.

"Hail!" Rylan cried to them as they approached. "The Rends decided to return to Kyrenia Castle." He eyed the three men as they approached. "Dyfen and Dover Whetherly, I presume? This is my daughter, Emlyn, and my son Eryk."

Eryk nodded to each. Emlyn had fixed her eyes upon Dyfen.

"Yes, I am Dyfen and this is my brother, Dover," Dyfen gestured toward his brother, who was stepping out of his monk's cloak. "Greetings, Lord Esper; Eryk." He bent his head to each. Looking toward Emlyn. "Lady Emlyn, once again." He met her gaze with the same serious look he had on the beach, and he seemed rather cool, Emlyn noted.

Her face was flushed, and Dyfen could see her to the best advantage without the wild wind and sinking sand of the beach. She was on the taller side, with the top of her head level just under his nose. Her teeth were strong and white behind full, pillowy lips. The slimness of her waist was accented by a golden girdle hanging loosely above the swelling of her hips. The neckline of her riding apparel exposed a fresh, fullness of bosom in perfect proportion to her hips.

Dover turned to face Lord Esper and Eryk; nodded in greeting and noticed Emlyn beside them. His eyes lit up. He bowed low, sweeping his right arm before him. "Lady Emlyn, if there can be a light on this day, it is most certainly you," Dover crooned. She pointedly ignored him.

Isley coughed, trying to suppress a laugh.

Turning toward Dyfen, Emlyn was put off by his cool demeanor towards her. She glared at him. "Did Lord Standen tell you we have your hounds? Rather, they have our horses. They have laid claim to our stable and will not allow us in. Did you not teach your curs to obey, Lord Whetherly?" she taunted.

"Lady Emlyn, they have been trained to protect horses. Although usually, it is my own horses they protect. The sooner we go, the sooner we resolve the matter," Dyfen said curtly. "I trust the Rends will await our return?" he spoke with an edge to his voice.

His annoyance was not lost on Emlyn, who huffed, "I do not find the situation acceptable no matter the reason and indeed, as you may have heard, it has even posed a threat to their lives," she said. "My own horse is one of many inside that stable."

"I hope that Firah is in good health?" Dyfen queried with a certain amount of sarcasm. "I am pleased she arrived home without incident."

"Yes, Firah is at home and well. My thanks to you, once again, for bringing that about," she said quietly so that the men behind her did not hear her. Once again, in an attempt to avoid a confrontation with her father, who she knew would be angry that she had gone out unattended. He allowed her considerable freedom from the constant oversight of a chaperone because he had confidence in her judgment, but he also knew any type of danger might present itself on their shores. He would be displeased with her decision.

"Not everyone is as patient as I. It was all I could do to prevent Hugo from shooting them down. I intentionally requested him to accompany us to protect them," she said in a low voice. "And now he has ridden back to the castle…" She had no need to speak more.

Dyfen stiffened. "We must leave. Now. Lord Esper, if you would lead the way." He mounted Zakar without hesitation.

Emlyn turned toward Dover. "I am lightest. I will ride with my brother. You may take my horse," she said, handing over the reins of a fine chestnut gelding. Her hand gently brushed Dover's in the transfer. Dyfen, witnessing the exchange, noted a flush move up his brother's reddening neck with interest. Well, little brother, you can be vulnerable to a lady's charms, he thought. He watched Dover assist Emlyn mount behind her brother before he pulled himself up onto Emlyn's horse.

Once everyone was mounted, they started off with Rylan Esper in the lead. He led them down a much-traveled path through a primal cedar forest looming with trees and very little undergrowth. The wooded trail wound and narrowed at a wide fieldstone bridge. The sound of hooves echoed hollowly through the woods as they crossed.

Once over the bridge, the path straightened for a distance, and as the trees parted, a large, grey, stone castle with crenelated battlements came into view atop a high cliff. Arrow loops punctuated its walls. Two high-rising towers were stationed at each end. The castle was perched on the northern coast of the island. On the far side, the sea was visible at the bottom of the cliffs. Flags bearing the Esper crest, a fivefold cross hovering over a downward pointing sword was stitched with golden thread on a plain white background, fluttered from the turrets. The golden threading shimmered in the sunlight, making the crosses seem to blaze. The words "Nostro dux Deus Est" (God is our guide) spanning the bottom edge were in black.

The drawbridge was lowering as they approached the barbican where the portcullis was being raised so they may enter. The guards must have spotted them from the parapet allure.

Chapter 4

Wounded

The wind began to bluster suddenly as they crossed the drawbridge, causing treetops to sway to and fro, and then, suddenly, they became calm. Dyfen could hear dogs barking in the distance. Zakar and Arazi recognized the sound. Upon hearing the barking, the stallions began racing at top speed toward it, through the village marketplace toward the stables. People scattered in all directions. As he approached the stone stable, he saw a large, dark-grey hound on top of stacked hay sheaves in a cart at the entrance. Cydryn's hackles were up, and his teeth barred, daring a group of men standing in front of him to come forward. All but one of them held bows with strings pulled taut. Dyfen, Isley and Dover leaped off of their horses and ran toward the stable.

Cydryn was not the largest of the five hounds, but he was recognized as the leader by his brothers. Aubryn, lighter grey in color was standing to the left of him and Avak, medium grey, to the right. Tyber, the darkest was black with Osyn, nearly white, stood in the aisle in case someone breached the first line of defense. Five brothers.

"Cydryn!" Dyfen commanded. Cydryn stopped barking, hackles on his back disappeared, and he stood looking at Dyfen for direction, maintaining his stance with his tail wagging wildly, excited to see his master. Aubryn, Avak, Osyn and Tyber followed suit. All dogs remained in place, emulating Cydryn.

Outside the stable, Hugo Rend stood in front of five bowmen. His face was red with anger, obviously frustrated with the situation. All of the bowmen stood ready with bows drawn and aimed at the five hounds.

"I am done being held at bay by these mad mongrels. They are a danger to us all. I regret that I left matters this long," Hugo stated hotly. "I have a business to attend to and require my horse. Immediately." He was extremely agitated and had a sharp look in his grey eyes.

Dyfen and his brothers were off to the side. "Order your men to put down their bows at once," Dyfen commanded. He pulled out the dagger he had collected from the church weapon house and prepared to throw it.

"You dare threaten me?" Hugo's eyes grew. "I think not. YOU are in the wrong here," he argued. He opened his mouth to continue speaking when a shout was heard.

"Hugo, No!" All turned toward the cry. Emlyn had positioned herself in front of Cydryn, shielding him with her body. "Hugo, please. Abandon this. These dogs are not a danger. Nothing can be gained from this. Their master is here and has called them down. Order your own men to stand down as well," she begged.

Hugo's men looked to him for direction.

Above the bowmen in the shadow of the stable yard, high upon a wooden beam, a Van cat perched. Its two glowing eyes; one blue and one green, looked downward at the men stationed beneath and leaped at its target, knocking one of the bowmen sideways, causing his arrow to be released.

Hugo heard the man fall and turned to look just before the arrow came flying from behind, barely missing him. It skimmed a barn timber, halting its momentum and diverted it into Emlyn's leg. She cried out and crumpled to the ground. A large, white Van cat scampered off toward the castle as the targeted bowman scrambled to his feet. Seeing what had happened, he began to run.

The dogs gave chase. The bowman was no match for the hounds' long stride. They surrounded him with barred teeth, giving the rest of Hugo's men time to grab him as he struggled.

"You idiot! What have you done?" Hugo shouted.

"I was aiming for the hound, my Lord," the bowman stuttered, "when I was knocked down and accidently loosed the arrow."

"But you did not strike the hound, Manard. You managed to strike the Lady of the castle. You fool!" Hugo roared at the cowering man, "and you were only supposed to do so upon my command. I do not recall commanding you to loose arrows."

"I was attacked from above, my Lord. That damnable feline knocked my hand. It was not my fault, my Lord. I beg your forgiveness," the frightened man argued.

Hugo grunted and shrugged past the man. "Throw him in the dungeon until I have time to deal with him," he barked at his men as he headed toward Emlyn.

They left dragging their prisoner along with them.

Dyfen, Isley and Dover rushed toward Emlyn. Hugo, who had been closest, reached her first and bent down to her.

Dyfen knelt down at her side to determine how seriously she had been wounded.

Hugo, annoyed by what he perceived as interference, pushed him away. Dyfen not to be deterred, resumed his place knocking Hugo out of his way. He was stronger than Dyfen expected based on his lithe form.

Hugo, instead of backing away moved into Dyfen's space and looked him directly in the eyes. "She is not your concern, so be off. You and your wretched hounds. I strongly recommend that you stand aside sir, while I send for help to attend to the lady."

Dyfen stepped up. Angry at the situation. "This is your fault, you arrogant ass. There is no time to find help when help is already present," he snapped. "This wound needs to be taken in hand immediately. Fortunately, my brothers and I have been trained to treat such wounds by our uncle. You may have heard of him, August Weatherly?"

"No, I have never heard of such a man. You are mostly likely lying," Hugo spat back.

Dyfen responded with hard fought for restraint, "Rend, listen to me well. The arrow needs to be removed at once while the injury is fresh and blood untainted. Delay may cause infection of the flesh. There is little time to waste."

Hugo, unconvinced, started to reach for Emlyn again.

Dyfen pulled himself up to full height and stepped in front of Hugo. "Be off and allow us to attend to her. We need to get on with treatment." Dyfen's face was composed with an underlying tension. His body was rigid in a threatening manner. He was anxious to attend to the wound as soon as possible and was frustrated by this churl's interference.

They were interrupted by a pained voice. "Hugo. Please stop," Emlyn moaned.

Hugo's face broke into great concern. "I refuse to leave you in the hands of three complete strangers. Emlyn, we know nothing of these men."

"Hugo, please. I trust them. Just leave. Leave at once and pray do not tell my father." Her discomfort was such she did not think about the propriety of the circumstances. She only sought relief from the searing pain.

"Emlyn, have you lost all reason? I cannot do what you ask and in no way can we keep this from your father," Hugo stated, digging in.

Isley, getting impatient, spoke out. "Rend, the longer you give argument the longer she suffers in the dirt," he stated firmly. "For her well-being allow us to attend to her. We know what to do. Our uncle, who is a skilled surgeon, has taught us well."

Hugo's annoyance spiraled. His eyes flashed while strands of hair that had broken loose flew wildly about his face in the wind. He could feel his body tense but his concern for her welfare caused his eyes to soften and choke down his protest. He noted the five hounds watching the argument progress. They were eyeing him closely. It helped make his decision to concede.

With a shrug he backed down. "As you wish, Emlyn, but you are making a grave mistake and I vow to you that your father will most assuredly hear of this."

He turned, straightened his shoulders, and strode away. As he passed, Tyber gave him a menacing look that prompted him to walk faster.

"That wretch, Rend, is well to be gone," Isley said with anger. 'If Lady Emlyn had not acted, Cydryn would be dead."

"Of course, there was a strong likelihood Rend and his men would have been torn asunder before our eyes by the others," Dover added casually.

Watching him retreat, the three men focused their attention back on Emlyn. Her arm was around Dyfen's neck as he supported her body with his own. He pulled out his dagger, scored the arrow shaft, snapped it and threw it to Dover with a toss. Dover caught it with one hand and pushed it into his pouch. He was surveying the surrounding buildings to figure out where they could best tend to her injury.

"Ahh," Emlyn moaned as Dyfen shifted her. "Shakar," she moaned.

"What are you saying?" Dover asked.

"It was Shakar, the kitchen cat that knocked that man to the ground," Emlyn answered panting in pain.

"If it is a cat you favor, you may want to keep that to yourself, Lady Emlyn," Dover said half seriously trying to distract her. She attempted to smile wanly at him.

Dyfen saw that blood was pooling on the ground near her left foot. "We need to tend to your leg instantly." He motioned for his brothers to support her. Dover and Isley shifted her weight onto themselves, placing their shoulders under her arms, helping to brace her.

The dogs were encircling the group, protectively forming a wall around them.

The horses, happy to be reunited with the pack, leaned downward to touch each dog on the nose in a show of affection.

"Point the way for us," Dyfen directed her, anxious to get started.

"Take me through that gate," Emlyn said pointing to a stone archway with iron bars. "It leads to the castle kitchens. We can ask the servants for what we need." She was trying to maintain an easy manner so no one would witness her pain.

Dyfen swept her up in his arms while Dover ran ahead to open the gate and clear the way. Isley brought up the rear to ensure no other threat approached from behind. The dogs maintained their protective barrier surrounding the horses with Cydryn in the lead.

Dover pushed people who had gathered gently to the sides. "Pray, clear a path," Dover told them as people looked at the parade of dogs and horses in surprise.

The group entered a courtyard with a well near a doorway.

"This door," Emlyn pointed when they reached the kitchen door. Dover ran to the wooden door and pushed it open. There was no one there. Dyfen looked about the room for a table long enough to lay her down on and did not see one. He opted for a chair next to a table by the fireplace.

He carried Emlyn to the wooden chair and gently lowered her into it. She winced a bit when her body met the seat.

The horses stood outside the door with the dogs standing guard. A gaggle of geese had separated when they approached. "Dover grab a couple of feathers from those geese," he ordered his brother. Dover ran out and came back panting with two feathers in his hand. He handed them to Dyfen who accepted them and placed them on the table.

The kitchen had whitewashed walls with a line of windows on the outside wall. The corners of the room remained dark. Herbs were hanging from the rafters drying and their scent wafted and mingled with woodsmoke and freshly baked bread. The newly baked loaves were resting on a larger table in the middle of the room draped with coarsely woven towels.

Trying to lighten the mood and divert her attention, Dyfen looked down at Emlyn with a lifted brow. "My Lady, you risked your life for dogs you named as manner less curs?"

She smiled weakly. Her hair had come undone and the once neatly bound tresses flew freely about. "I only meant to stop them from losing their arrows, not offer myself as a target."

"I now clearly understand why you went looking for your mare without your escort. I have never witnessed Cydryn to hold such animosity towards a stranger," Dyfen said dryly referring to Hugo. Emlyn smiled again but Dyfen could see her pain was getting the better of her. Her shoulders slumped as she gritted her teeth. The men looked at each other with concern.

Dyfen dropped to his knees next to her chair and began to lift the left side of Emlyn's skirt carefully upward over the remaining shaft of the arrow. He pushed the fabric away from the wound exposing her upper thigh. Emlyn coming to the realization she was helpless in the midst of three men, worse yet, men she did not know, began to panic at the impropriety. She began clawing his hands and tried to push her gown back down. He grabbed her hands tightly and placed them into her lap. "Emlyn, stop. You must stop fighting me and allow me to do my job," he said tersely.

He could see the iron arrowhead lodged near the inside of mid-thigh. He gently moved her leg up and down. "I don't think the wound is very deep, thanks to God," he said with veiled relief. His voice was low and raspier than usual.

"Still, the removal will be painful. Where are all of your servants?" Dyfen asked her, glancing around the room. "I thought they would be here to help us."

"They must be at church," she said clutching the sides of the seat attempting to stanch the pain and wishing the servants were here with her.

Dyfen stood up. Emlyn quickly pushed her skirts back down over her leg giving Dyfen a defiant glare. "I require my lady's maid, Jinol. Please bring her to me," she commanded.

"There is not enough time for that now. We would not know where to find her in any case," Dyfen responded in an irritated voice, anxious to begin.

Isely took pity upon her. He could see her fear and her pain was evident. "You may trust us to behave chivalrously, my Lady," he said looking at Emlyn with kind eyes, in an attempt to put her at ease. He was still standing next to her chair with his hand on her shoulder. He could feel her trembling. "You have no need to fear us."

He and Dyfen exchanged worried looks above her head. Dyfen signaled him with his eyes toward a narrow table against the wall with all manner and sizes of knives laid out. Isley walked over to it and picked up a knife with a long narrow blade and a yellowed horn handle. He also grabbed two short, flat, wooden meat skewers and brought them over to Dyfen who nodded in agreement at the selection.

Chapter 5

Dr. Chikaris

Hugo rushed into the castle seeking Eston, the Espers' castellan. He spotted him standing in the great hallway speaking to guards on duty. "Eston!" Hugo shouted as he rushed toward him. "Where is Lord Esper? It is of utmost importance I speak to him at once."

Eston turned toward him. He was a very tall Persian of middle-age, greying hair, and ruddy complexion from spending most of his life out of doors. He had large, expressive black eyes that sat below bushy brows and over a prominent regal nose. He did not particularly favor Hugo on a good day and this day was not particularly a good day.

"What business have you with my Lord Esper, Lord Rend?" he said politely but with firmness as always, finding Hugo a bit of an annoyance.

"Emlyn. It's Lady Emlyn! She has been severely injured," Hugo said in an agitated state.

Eston need not hear more. He pushed past Hugo saying, "Follow me," and he strode away with long purposeful strides.

Hugo rushed after him, keeping up with the brisk pace Eston set, now that he was stirred.

They reached the studded library doors and without hesitation Eston pushed them wide open and found Rylan Esper seated at a table with Eryk intently looking at a manuscript. Both men looked up when the doors burst open.

"What is it, Eston?" Rylan questioned concerned. Eston normally did not barge into a room. Always respectful, he would usually ask permission to be allowed to enter.

"Lord Rend asks to speak to you. Lady Emlyn has met with injury," he said with some urgency.

"Hugo, what has befallen Emlyn?" Rylan demanded as he stood up from the table with Eryk following after.

"She has been arrow shot in the limb. We have the man." Hugo's responses were scattered. He did not mention that the bowman was his own man.

"Where is she and who is with her?" Rylan's voice was becoming more strident.

"I was pushed away by those three strangers, those Whetherly whelps that came to our shores this morning.

"You left my injured sister alone with strangers?" Eryk's voice was one of disbelief.

"They asserted they knew what to do, being trained by their Uncle August or some such nonsense and Emlyn believed them. She ordered me to leave her against my insistence to stay. I could not reason with her. I came to you immediately," Hugo responded.

Eston interceded, "Lord, there is such a man. A skilled surgeon by the name of August Whetherly. I know of him and his brother, Braxton, from my time spent in the Holy Land."

"Eston seek Physician Chikaris and bring him immediately to…. Where?" he stopped and turned to Hugo. "Where are they Hugo?" he spoke with a roughness in his voice.

"They were headed toward the castle kitchens, Lord," Hugo said.

"Take me to her," Rylan commanded him. "Eston, bring Dr. Chikaris to the kitchens. We will meet you there. Eryk, come with me."

Eston took off at top speed. Eryk, Rylan, and Hugo headed toward the kitchens.

Chapter 6

Kitchen Surgery part 1

Dover was stoking kindling into the large stone fireplace, reigniting the embers that lay beneath the ashes. A large metal kettle containing water was suspended on an iron hook over the flame. "The water should be ready directly and I found clean cloth in this basket."

He looked down at Dyfen who was still kneeling at Emlyn's knee. "We are putting all our long hours at the feet of Uncle August to good use. In truth, I never thought we would be using it to perform surgery on a living person."

Dyfen shot his brother an irritated look, hoping the comment would not provoke questions from Emlyn. "Pray, keep your mind on the task at hand, Dover. Bring me a large bowl filled with boiled water, sterilize that ewer on the table and bring that basket of clean cloth you found," he instructed.

Looking down at his dirty tunic, Dyfen went over to a shallow trough near the window and poured some heated water into it from the kettle using a large ladle hanging nearby. He stripped off his tattered shirt and lathered up a bar of soap resting there. He rubbed the lather over his chest, arms and hands then rinsed over the trough. Picking up a clean cloth, he dried himself and grabbed a clean apron from a nearby basket, tying it at his neck to cover his torso.

Watching Dyfen prepare, at another time her focus may have been in admiration of his muscled arms and shoulders but instead she asked the question he dreaded regarding Dover's comment. "What was his meaning? 'Living person'?" She was staring at him, waiting for an answer.

Dyfen bent down to inspect the wound. He hesitated and then said, "Our uncle was a great warrior who became a skilled surgeon. He possesses a keen mind for learning and is well known for his knowledge of anatomy. From the time we were boys, we have spent many hours closeted in his dissection room assisting him and learning about the internal structure of bodies. Human and animal alike. Uncle August carefully documented everything in drawings and writings, all which he has stored in his library. We helped him with those as well, giving us a good understanding of what to expect when we remove this arrow head." He looked back up at her.

"Mother always thought us gruesome and would chide us for our 'preference of the departed over the living' as she called it. This is the first time we will actually use our knowledge on a living human. But I assure you that we are your best option," Dyfen stated with confidence.

Isley tried to help calm her, "Uncle August is an ardent admirer of the great man of medicine, Abul-Quasim al-Zahrawi, the father of surgery and possesses all thirty volumes of his work, Kitab al-Tasrif. Perhaps you have heard of him?"

"He often quotes al-Zahrawi, 'Before practicing surgery one should gain knowledge of anatomy and the function of organs.' Uncle August says that there is no better way to realize that knowledge than to witness firsthand the inner workings of God's creations," he finished, hoping he had built on Dyfen's reassurance.

Emlyn looked at each of them warily, "I am unsure if this is good or sorry news for me. I cannot tell which."

Isley tried again, "Dyfen's hands are deft in tending the wounded. Many a horse and dog have him to thank for their lives. I do not see

The Flaming Soul   Doreen Demerjian

it should be any different in this as well." He later thought that she may not have been reassured to find that horses and dogs successfully withstood ministering by Dyfen.

Dyfen lifted the goose quills Dover had brought and cut the ends. He proceeded to split the shafts to widen them into small tubes. "We have these in case the arrowhead is barbed. Placing them over the barbs will lessen the damage to the tissue when the head is lifted upward," he explained to Emlyn, intent on his task.

Isley took a knife over to the fire and held it there for a minute before dipping the blade into the kettle water. Steam rose. He walked back to Dyfen and handed it down to him. "All is ready, Dyfen."

Dyfen took the knife and gestured to Isley and Dover to follow him into a corner for a consult. The three brothers huddled. Dyfen spoke, "As I recall there is a major artery situated near to where that arrowhead landed."

Isley responded. "Yes, there is. I remember the physiology quite well." He hesitated and then asked, "Do you want me to cut the arrow from her leg?"

"No, I will do it." Dyfen said looking at Isley with an unreadable expression on his face. "You have an injured hand."

"Yet, you have an injured head." Isley gave him one last questioning look and seeing the determination in his eyes, fell silent.

"Right. Now that we have everyone's injuries cataloged, what is your plan?" Dover spoke.

"I will need you both to hold her very still to prevent me from nicking that artery. Performing this surgery on a live patient is going to be very different from doing it on a dead body. I am not sure how she will react to the pain. It is your job to make sure she doesn't move while I have the knife in her leg," Dyfen told them.

Both men nodded. Isley ran his hand over his face and Dover looked grim. They understood the seriousness of the situation.

"We will take care of it, Dyfen." Dover assured him.

"You can trust in us, brother." Isley traded looks of determination with Dover.

Dyfen nodded his head and they split up going back to their tasks.

Dyfen loosened the string on his pouch, reached in and pulled out a small bundle of rolled leather. He pulled at the leather strips that bound it and unrolled it, laying it flat on the table. On the inner lining were small compartments. He pulled a swatch of gauzy cloth from one of them and opened it to expose fine needles made of bone. He reached up and carefully unbound his hair, straightening it from the braid. He carefully grabbed a single hair by its end and jerked it from his head. To Emlyn's surprise he used it to thread a needle, and then placed the threaded needle in the bowl of boiled water. After retying his hair, he pressed his fingers into the hot water to resterilize them.

He picked up the ewer Dover had prepared and held it by the handle with a clean cloth. Grabbing a short stool by the leg, he placed the ewer down. "Emlyn, we require you to pass water into this. Can you do it alone or do you need assistance?"

Emlyn looked at Dyfen and her eyes widened. "You ask me to relieve myself here, into this?"

"Well, I could do it for you but I would think you to prefer your own water to disinfect your wound," Dyfen said calmly understanding the idea may sound indelicate to her.

"Is there no other way?" she countered.

"There is, and we make use of them as well, to be overly cautious considering the peril of putrefied flesh. Emlyn, we cannot be too careful when it comes to infection. I know this seems unpleasant but I would rather unpleasantness in social etiquette rather than the need to remove the entire limb if infection sets in." Dyfen was immovable.

Emlyn hesitated, weighing her options then finally answered, "If you will assist me to stand, I think I can manage it on my own." She struggled to stand, wincing with pain.

Isley and Dover each put a hand under an arm to steady her over the stool and turned their heads out of politeness. Emlyn looked each way making sure their heads were turned then lifted her skirts just high enough to cover the stool, letting them drop over the seat. She lowered herself a bit with Dover and Isley still supporting her. Dyfen had walked away to allow her some privacy. Upon not hearing the sound he expected he turned back to her.

Seeing the look of self-consciousness on her face he said, "Pray, do not feel ill at ease Lady Emlyn. We are familiar with the nature of the body and place no shame on such matters. We afford you as much modesty possible as there is no garderobe in the kitchen."

Emlyn was experiencing so much pain by now that shame did not have the significance it might have otherwise. She released her bladder into the ewer making a tinkling sound on the metal. Upon completion she raised her body lifting her skirt over the stool careful not to knock over the ewer.

Judging that she had finished, Dyfen turned back, grabbed the ewer from the stool raising it to his nose and sniffed. Thankfully, it lacked an ammonia smell that would indicate infection. He placed the urine filled ewer on the floor while Dover and Isley carefully eased Emlyn back into her chair.

Dover scanned the many shelves with their assorted bottles and jars until he found what he was looking for. "A well-stocked larder, I see." He picked up a clay bottle and shook it. Pulling out the cork, he put the rim to his lips and tipped it back. He choked. "Vinegar," he exclaimed while gaging. He set it aside.

"Let me sample this," he said spying another vessel. He uncorked it and this time took the precaution to smell its contents. Smiling, he threw back his head and took a deep swig. "Wine! exactly what we need." He brought the bottle over to Emlyn while handing the water bowl and cloth to Dyfen.

Before handing the bottle to her, he tilted it back and took another long swig. 'Ahhh," he exclaimed using the back of his hand to wipe his mouth.

"Drink this, it will help with the pain. Because this is going to hurt like the devil," he said offering the bottle to Emlyn.

She accepted the bottle and took a mouthful and swallowed. "Could you not bring a drinking vessel?" she asked in mock seriousness.

"No time for formalities, Em," he quipped. "We must make haste. Drink again and deeply." While she did this his eyes met Dyfen's and Isley's.

Dyfen interrupted their silent exchange and addressed Emlyn. "Isley and Dover will hold your shoulders to support you while I attempt to remove the arrowhead. We must remove it as soon as possible to minimize the risk of infection."

He took off his belt and used it as a tourniquet above the wound. "Shout if you need to. It is going to hurt like hell. There is no avoiding it." He was kneeling on the flagstone floor in front of her. He knew the pain was going to be excruciating.

"Let us hope the arrow had a bodkin point. It is slimmer and although it penetrates more deeply it causes less damage to the surrounding tissue. If it proves to be a barbed head, I have these goose quills".

Dyfen tried to calculate how deep the wound was by remembering the end he had broken off. He estimated it to be around ten inches. Along with the four inches he could see, he calculated that it was lodged an inch or so below the surface of her skin. Not too deeply, he thought with relief. Still even if he successfully removed the iron without touching the artery the danger would come afterward in the guise of infection, God forbid. He mentally pictured the anatomy drawings his Uncle August had so carefully created in detail, remembering that the artery ran along the inside of the femur. The arrow must have missed it because there was not enough blood escaping the wound. The trick would be to avoid a nick while trying to make the extraction. Dyfen was fairly certain it had not struck bone but to make sure he pinched the end of the shaft closest to her flesh between his index finger and thumb and tried to twist it slightly. It had imperceptible give to it. Good sign that it was not embedded in bone. He looked up at her face to see if she was still conscious. She was still alert but decidedly paler.

Dyfen arose from the floor and walked over to a lantern he had seen when entering the room. He picked up a stick from a tinder box and used it to light the lantern. He turned back toward Emlyn and set it down on the floor near her feet.

Emlyn had been watching him, following his every move. He was in front of her now. He knelt down, turning his body eastward. His face was in profile as he bowed his head making the sign of the cross. The light from the fireplace illuminated his hair and created shadows on the side of his strong face. His lips moved in silent prayer as he again made the sign of the cross, murmuring 'Amen'.

Turning toward Emlyn, he gently removed her shoe. Setting it to the side, he started to lift the hem of her skirt, anxious to study the seriousness of the injury. Once again, she attempted to push his hands away. He grabbed her hands and firmly set them in her lap. "Lady Emlyn, this is not the time for modesty," he chided purposefully and then added more kindly, "I give you my word that your virtue is safe with us, my lady." The blue of his eyes glowed softy in the firelight.

Dyfen lifted her garment upward over the embedded shaft and attempted to push the fabric back and away from the arrow but its weight caused it to slide forward against the shaft. She winced in pain. Out of exasperation, he grabbed the bottom of the dress and ripped it far enough to expose her thigh, then settled each side of the tear across her smooth flesh. He kept his focused on the wound. Taking the knife, he cut the tie that held her knit stocking in place, letting it fall to her foot. Fresh blood trickled down her leg over the dried blood already there. Her ivory colored chemise was encrusted brown with it.

Dyfen picked up the silver ewer and poured the hot urine over the wound to sterilize it, making sure he covered it completely. It puddled on the floor by his knee. Emlyn let out a slight wince at the sting. He then poured wine over her leg to be sure all avenues of infection control were utilized.

He put the knife point next to the shaft and pushed it slowly downward parallel with the shaft, feeling for the head of the arrow as he went. Emlyn let out a large groan while Isley and Dover held her shoulders against the chair back.

Isley had concern in his eyes. Dover looked down at Emlyn and advised, "Drink more wine. It will help with the pain. Dyfen must widen the wound to cleanly pull the arrowhead out."

Dover offered her the bottle. She hesitated for a second and shook her head 'yes' and drank deeply from it as he held it to her lips. Her hair brushed the floor as she tilted her head backward.

Emlyn coughed slightly as she brought her head up and slumped slightly in the chair. Isley put his arm around her shoulders to sooth her and hold her in place after Dyfen shot them a warning look. "Outstanding idea, get her falling down drunk, Dover," Isley quipped as he centered her in the seat.

"Better to be drunk than face this sober," Dover returned.

"Pray God, both of you hold your tongues. I need to steady my mind to the task at hand and you must make certain she does not move." Dyfen's barked. His words were cut short when a racket arose outside. They could hear Avak's loud bark over the other dogs. Dyfen looked at Dover and nodded his head toward the door. Dover went out the kitchen door and saw Rylan, Hugo and Eryk surrounded by the dogs.

Rylan had his hand on the hilt of his dagger. "Call these bothersome dogs away and allow us to pass. We have come for my daughter," Rylan commanded. He had a murderous look on his drawn face. Dover waved his hand downward and silenced the dogs. They all moved aside to allow the visitors to pass. When the men reached the door, Dover stopped them.

"Dyfen is tending to Lady Emlyn's injury and cannot be disturbed," he warned.

"She is my daughter and I will decide who tends to her," Rylan said firmly and evenly. "Now allow us to pass."

Dover emitted a sigh but, in the end, stepped aside and allowed Lord Esper to come charging through the entry with Eryk and Hugo a short distance behind him. Dyfen looked up and before he could speak, Rylan, seeing the delicacy of the surgery, turned around pushing the other two out before him and closed the door. "We will wait outside for physician Chikaris to arrive," he spoke hurriedly.

Just then, Eston rode up with Dr. Chikaris. Rylan gestured toward the door and Dr. Chikaris went in. He stopped a short distance from Emlyn and observed what was going on.

"Hold her upright and still," Dyfen commanded as he pushed the knife deeper into her leg. He could feel the tip of the arrowhead. Regaining his focus, he pushed two flat skewers down onto either side of the arrowhead. While Isley held them apart, he started to lift the shaft upward feeling for resistance as he went. Sweat started to run down his forehead and between his shoulder blades.

He glanced up as Dr. Chikaris came over to observe the surgery. "By God, we do not need another body in this kitchen!" he exclaimed. "If you cannot help for God's love, please leave us."

The doctor watched for a short time longer as he assessed the situation. Then left. Coming out of the kitchen door he spoke, "Lord Esper. I deem Emlyn to be in good hands. I can attend to her if you wish but from what I witnessed the boy's surgical skills are beyond what I can do for her. We need to wait patiently for Lord Whetherly to complete his work." Dr Chikaris tried to put Rylan's mind at ease. "I suggest you return to whatever you were doing, and I will come to you with news after I perform a follow up exam."

"There are strange men with my daughter, whom from what I could see, is not properly clothed!" Rylan shouted.

"Lord, believe in what I say. Right now, they are focused on saving her life and that only. You have no cause for concern. Eston told me of their relation to August Whetherly, it is a name that is respected as a surgeon and healer."

Rylan looked at Dr. Chikaris for a short time and then relaxed. "Eston," he addressed his trusted seneschal, "provide these men with whatever they ask and let the stablemaster know that he is to do the same." He gestured for all to follow as he retreated through the kitchen gate.

Chapter 7

Kitchen Surgery part 2

A loud groan came from inside the kitchen.

Emlyn let out a prolonged cry from the pain. "Just a little more Emlyn, continue to be the brave maiden you are," Dyfen said gently as he continued to pull the shaft upward with little resistance. "Now brace yourself as the head comes clear."

He gave a short tug and pulled the arrowhead out of her leg and set it on the floor. Emlyn pursed her lips till they were white and let out a long, last groan, feeling the last of the metal clear her leg. "Uhhh," escaped her lips and then her body slumped sideways. Isley grabbed her slight shoulders, keeping her upright in the chair while Dyfen prepared to sew together and bandage the wound.

He wiped the blood with a clean cloth and stood up, stretching the tension from his shoulders as he walked over to the kitchen shelves that lined its walls. He laid the bloody knife on the table and looked at the jars. Pulling out stoppers and smelling the contents, he found what he was looking for. Clove oil. He went back to Emlyn and rubbed the wound with a vinegar-soaked cloth. Drying her leg, he drizzled rose honey into the wound then pulled the needle with his hair threaded through it out of the small bowl of boiled water.

"Emlyn this is the last painful thing I will do to you. I will act as quickly as I can. We must pull the torn edges together for them to properly heal" He rubbed her skin with clove oil to numb the area then he pushed the needle through both sides of the wound. Emlyn closed her eyes but did not cry out. As he was stitching the wound, he commented. "I am usually stitching the wounds of our stable hand, Sarkis, after one of his adventures with Dover," he chuckled. He closed the wound using a whip stitch, cut the thread with his dagger and removed the tourniquet.

"There then. It is done," he said looking up at her smiling. He pushed his fingers into the honey jar coating them with honey. He smeared the thick matter over her wound. "For extra measure of healing," he said, as he looked down at Emlyn's closed eyes. His gaze lingered there for a few seconds. Grabbing a clean, dry cloth that had been boiled with rosemary and sea salt out of his unrolled leather kit, he folded it into a square and sprinkled heated sea salt, Dover had prepared, onto its surface. A smear of honey held it in place. Using long strips of cloth, he gently but firmly wrapped her leg.

The last thing he did was to pull her shift down over her leg for modesty. "You should have a care with this leg for some days to come and give the wound time to heal. Do not rest your weight upon it for those days and have your maid clean it and change the cloth three times a day. I will leave instructions with your servant girl on how to prepare the cloth. In time, the stitching may be cut and pulled from the wound."

After providing these instructions, Dyfen rerolled his leather kit placing it back into his pouch then bent down to pick up the arrowhead and dropped it into his pouch. He halted for a second and addressed Emlyn, "Although the arrow's head has been removed, danger remains present. You must be observed carefully for the length of a day to watch for symptoms of infection. Any sign of redness, swelling or unusual pain, should be reported to me post-haste or to your own physician if you have faith in him. Now, your comfort must be arranged and I will stay nearby to watch over you," Dyfen said looking into her clouded eyes. "I am in your debt. My dogs have great meaning to me." He added softly.

Emlyn, although still under the influence, became embarrassed. "Do not make heavy of this. My pain would be far greater if one of your dogs suffered ill at my home," Emlyn said in a drunken voice. "I once had a dog", she murmured her head falling against Isley's midsection, the side of her face resting on him. Her hair across her face.

Isley exchanged a Now what do I do? look with Dover who turned his head toward noise coming from the outside. Dover opened the door where a commotion was in process as the dogs sighted the servants returning from church. Isley gently pushed Emlyn towards Dyfen and stepped outside to quiet them and to provide the servants safe passage through the pack. "Cease," he scolded and the noise came to a sudden end as the dogs stopped their baying. All five laid down with eyes upon him.

A tall, teen-age boy and three women entered quite shaken by their encounter with the dogs. The oldest of the women, the cook, was heavyset with graying hair and dimpled cheeks. The other two were young girls, apparently the kitchen help. They looked around the room with dismay. The cook sighed, putting her hands to her ample hips, "My Lord," she wailed seeing the blood on the floor, the bloody knife, dirty cloth on the table, the empty wine bottle and her jars and bottles shuffled. "What, pray tell, has happened in my kitchen! "

"We required use of it to perform surgery on your mistress, madam. I apologize for the disruption. Where do we find my lady's maid? It is best Lady Emlyn rest. Did she not come with you?" Dyfen asked, looking straight at the cook,

"My heavens! How did Lady Emlyn come to be in a such a way?" the cook cried aloud. "My poor lamb. Who did this? Your father will surely have his head." She rushed over to Emlyn who was still seated, the side of her head now resting on Dover's hip. She gathered Emlyn up in her arms and immediately started issuing orders.

"Kellis, run and find Jinol. Bring her hither, quick as the devil." She signaled for him to approach her and said something to him privately. Kellis, a gangly youth with brown hair and light eyes, took off like a shot. The two young cook assistants had gathered round Emlyn who was recovering from her drunken swoon.

Emlyn, although in pain reassured the kindly cook, "Thank you, Mim. I am well enough. Please see to it that our guests are fed and taken care of, including the beasts outside. They have had a long and stress filled day.

"Lady Emlyn, we must see to your welfare first," Dyfen firmly stated, watching the flurry of activity in the kitchen.

"I would wait for my maid, Jinol," she answered.

Dyfen understood her reluctance to be out of the company of people she knew while feeling so vulnerable and let the matter drop.

Mim had backed away from supporting Emlyn, leaving her in the care of the young kitchen maids. The older woman pulled an apron over her large frame and began stoking the fire. She turned to open a cupboard door, grabbing three goblets and a cask of mead from a storage area. Setting them down on the table, she grabbed a freshly baked loaf of pain-demeine from under the cloth on the long table. Walking to a small door that led to the buttery, she brought out a wheel of cheese and fresh butter. Rushing around the kitchen, she gathered some fresh figs and a smoked leg of mutton hanging in the smoke room. She created quite a feast in a short space of time. She laid it all out on the table.

While pouring the mead, Mim called, "Come help yourselves lads," as she started chopping meat from another mutton leg to fill a long tray.

"We must make sure our animals are fed first," said Dyfen tiredly. He had been standing near Emlyn keeping an eye on her recovery. His appearance bedraggled from events of the day.

"Ye needn't worry about those two handsome steeds outside the door. Kellis knows to fetch a stable boy for them. They will be tended to," Mim stated. "I told him as well, to send some decent clothing back for the three of you along with boots for you, without." She looked at Dyfen when referring to his bare feet. "Later, we will see about finding your items that have washed up onto shore and set to making them right if we can. You are not the first poor souls the waves have cast upon our shores after a storm.

"If tis safe, I will feed those mangy mongrels meself. I have a liking for dogs." She picked up the tray she had been loading with mutton and started out the door. The dogs all arose and started toward her. She backed up into the doorway. "Although it may be that these lads may not have a liking for me."

Isley had followed behind her grabbing a chunk of bread on the way out. "Easy," he said while taking a bite of the chunk of bread. The dogs relaxed and watched the cook set the tray down by the wall. She walked a short distance and sent a bucket down the well, drew it up and set it down near the tray. All ten eyes were on her but none of the dogs moved.

"Alright," Isley told them while raising his right hand signaling them to relax. Cydryn approached the food and the other dogs followed. They surrounded the tray and started feeding.

"Our thanks," he said to Mim with a nod as she stood happily watching them eat what she had offered.

"My Lord, I have never seen such proud sized curs. Are you sure they are not shaggy horses?"

Isley laughed, green eyes sparkling, "You would not be the first to ponder that. They are quite royal in size, I agree. But each has a great heart of gold. Fearless, loyal and true to those they love."

She joked smiling broadly, "I do love a brawny dog. They offer great protection from an unkind world. Only a witless soul would cross paths with this lot."

Just then two young lads carrying bundles approached, accompanied by a young woman who had a worried expression on her youthful face. They went through the kitchen door avoiding the dogs in their path. The dogs looked up, decided they were of no threat and went back to eating. Isley followed them inside and saw that the bundles contained clothing for them all and boots for Dyfen.

"My Lady!" the young maiden cried when she saw Emlyn propped up in the chair, shoe and stocking on the floor and dried blood on her torn skirts. "What mischief has befallen you?"

Emlyn roused herself when she heard the familiar voice. "Jinol! thanks be to God you are here. I ran into an arrow, it seems. These gentlemen removed it from my leg but I profess the pain is extreme. Not a word to father."

"He knows, my Lady. Lord Rend visited your father in quite a state. He summoned me before Kellis reached me. I am to stay with you at all times, no matter what you ask."

Dover was rifling through the clothing that had been brought to them and finally found items that would do for himself. He addressed the females in the room as he dropped his shirt to the floor, "Maidens, you may all wish to keep your faces to the fore so that we may don fresh clothing." The girls turned their backs giggling. Mim grimaced and went about preparing the day's meal, scarcely giving them a look. She had too much work to do to worry about seeing a partially clothed male.

Dyfen, who kept an eye on Emlyn to make sure she was not in danger of falling, noticed that she had not turned her head. She is too sedated to even see, he thought.

The fresh clothing smelled of cedar. Dyfen pulled off the apron and his stained breeches after he found clothing that looked a good fit. Even the boots seemed adequate. Walking about, he announced to all, "Not a poor fit."

The three men were quite handsome in a disheveled way. Hair askew and faces rough and ungroomed.

Isley had found a tan, cambric shirt with matching trousers. He now loosened the tie that held his long brown hair, ran his fingers through it and retied it at the nape of his neck to try to neaten his appearance. He looked weary from the long day of struggle.

Dover likewise looked more relaxed but still tired. His long, straight raven hair hung loosely down his back and his Whetherly blue eyes twinkled with weariness." I propose we see Emlyn safely to her chamber, then find a place to stay for the evening. Tomorrow morn we will plan our leave."

"If one of you will take up my Lady and follow me," Jinol instructed. Dyfen stepped forward, carefully cradled Emlyn in his arms and followed Jinol out of the door.

He could smell the scent of roses in her hair as it brushed his face. He unconsciously closed his eyes.

Cydryn, seeing his master leave started to follow with Avak, Aubryn, Osyn and Tyber trailing. Dyfen turned his head to see the parade behind him. "Cydryn, come," he commanded.

"Cydryn will come with us, and the rest will go with the horses to stand guard." He knew that the pack would follow Avak if Cydryn was not with them.

Looking at Isley and Dover he said, "Ask if we may bed down in the stable to be near our horses for the night." They both nodded in acknowledgment.

He then turned and followed Jinol through the gates carrying Emlyn with Cydryn by his side. The castle armed guards saw the retinue, recognized Jinol and Emlyn. One guard started to speak, noticed the dog looking at him with a challenge in his eyes and decided to say nothing, allowing them to pass.

Jinol led the way through a maze of cresset lamp lit hallways. Dyfen noted that the castle amenities were modern in nature. It was spacious, light-filled and well appointed. They traveled up a wide stone staircase and down the hall to a partially opened door where Jinol had entered. Dyfen followed her and then motioned Cydryn to lay down outside the door. The big dog decided to position himself across the doorsill.

The suite was a generous size, with a sumptuously appointed solar. The fireplace was overly large accented with Persian blue colored tiles. An olivewood trestle table with chairs surrounding it was centered in the room. Alabaster lamps lit the room. It was obvious that Lord Esper spared no expense for the comfort of his family and valued beauty as well. The temperate climate of the island allowed for large windows to light the spacious rooms, keeping them light and airy. Then, he caught the relaxing fragrance of roses wafting up from a walled garden below. No accident he wagered. Even scenting the air had been planned.

There was an enormous blue and white carpet with purple accents covering the slate floor. To the left, was a doorway he guessed was a garderobe and in another room that shared a wall with the fireplace, he could see a large copper bathing tub. Directly to the right, through arched columns was a large poster bed on a low dais. The posters were carved in a glorious, grapevine pattern twisting upwards. Filling the walls next to the bed was a set of three windows and a door to a balcony which overlooked the garden with the sea beneath. One was able to view the garden and the sea at once. Altogether a pleasant suite.

"Pray, set her on the bed, my Lord," Jinol directed as she walked over to the large, billowy mattress. "I will have water brought to bathe as well as some broth to build strength." She walked toward the chamber door. Cydryn moved to allow her to pass and then resumed his position across the entry.

Dyfen gently laid Emlyn down on her soft, sky-blue and white canopied bed. Heavy drapery hung, drawn back at each carved post. "How are you faring Emlyn?" he asked her in a low voice. His hair fell over his shoulder as he bent to place her down.

"I have pain but am well for all that has happened," she said quietly in a tired voice. "My thanks to you for your attention to my wound."

"It is I who thank you, my Lady. I am overly fond of my dogs, Cydryn, in particular whose life you have protected at risk to your own. I cannot repay your sacrifice, but I vow to die in the attempt. My dogs would not hesitate to lay down their lives for me and I for them. It is a devotion that the depth of which, few can grasp." He removed the leather cord from around his neck and placed the turquoise stone in her palm. His gratitude shown in his eyes,

"Beckon me if you are ever in distress by returning it to me. I will know you have need of me and I will come. Wherever I am."

Emlyn's hand closed over the stone and in doing so skimmed his rough hand for a moment. They locked eyes briefly. Embarrassed, Dyfen broke first and backed away, turning to go, he spoke, "Cydryn and I will remain to watch over you tonight. I will be outside the door. I have given Jinol instructions on how to prepare a salve to reduce pain. Remember, If you experience any swelling or redness of the wound call out to me. I will be awake," he advised her.

"It will be unnecessary for you to stay. Our own physician, Dr. Chikaris, will likely be here in a short while and will attend to me onward. I will be well looked after. You have my thanks," Emlyn said to encourage him to leave. She was tired and wanted to rest.

He paused for a moment but understood her concern. It was unsettling to have a strange man outside the chamber door. "I will go but ask that you allow Cydryn to remain. My mind will rest easier knowing he is here. He is good company and he will find me if you have need."

She nodded her head in agreement, too tired to argue.

As he prepares to leave, he reminded her, "You will need time to recover. Remember to favor that leg to prevent the stitching from parting. I take my leave of you for now, my Lady so that you may rest."

"One moment more," was her answer.

"I ask that you submit to my examination of your own injury," She tiredly quipped with a faint smile on her face. "Please bow your head forward so that I may assess your wound."

Dyfen almost refused but then slowly walked to her bedside and lowered his head with some amusement in his eyes. The blood had congealed and dried.

"My head remains firmly upon my neck so I consider your ministering to be a great success," he chuckled. "I would return your kerchief to you but have since set it to work elsewhere. I hope you do not mind. As a bandage it has come in most useful this day."

"Not at all," she smiled weakly not mentioning she had seen it on Isley's hand earlier. "We have each mended the other this day.'"

"Yes, we have. Our good fortune to be near when the need arose," he smiled back.

Before leaving, Dyfen bent down and whispered in Cydryn's ear. The dog was still and gave Dyfen his complete attention. Emlyn swore he understood what was being said. He did not wag his tail or move his body. Dyfen stroked the large dog's head with great affection. Cydryn's brown eyes closed in happiness. His master gave him one last pat, kissed him on the head and left the chamber.

"Reposez-vous bien, ma dame," (Rest well, my lady.) she heard him say as he crossed the threshold.

Jinol entered the room carrying a tray.

Chapter 8

Afterward

As evening approached, Dyfen had a deep need to be alone to contemplate and take measure of their circumstances. As he always did when faced with a heavy burden, he took the dogs and horses for a run.

Together, they wound their way down to the beach. Zakar and Arazi were free of halters and surrounded by their ever-present hound companions.

Avak took lead position filling in for Cydryn who was with Emlyn. His gray fur parted in the wind as he followed Arazi and Zakar down the sandy path; Osyn stayed to the left of the horses while Aubryn, held his position on the right. Tyber, the largest brought up the rear. Each in their place guiding and protecting the stallions from harm.

A mild, warm breeze rolled in with the waves. Dusk was falling as the party reached the sandy shore. The dogs bounded around tagging each other in joyful play. The horses snorted and pawed the wet sand.

Dyfen deep in thought, removed his shirt and pulled off the borrowed boots before hoisting himself onto Zakar's back. It felt good to feel the air on his bare skin. He squinted his eyes in the failing light. Adjusting his seat, he clucked to the stallion signaling him into forward motion. Zakar started a slow trot down the beach. His brother, Arazi, kept level with him as the troupe moved forward, the waves washing over hooves and paws.

Dyfen's mind was filled with events, current and future. Feeling his head clear in the fresh air, he squeezed Zakar's flanks with his legs and gripped the mane more tightly preparing to gallop. He felt free of all burdens as they picked up speed. The breeze flowed over face, chest and arms. In exhilaration, he let go of Zakar's mane and raised both arms to the heavens shouting a single word. "God!" His voice rang out in the twilight.

The dogs ran around them in a loose pack, falling behind as the horses sped up. Their toothy mouths open and smiling, scenting the evening air. Dyfen felt a oneness with his horse. The gilt silver stallion shone in the dimness as his brother kept pace as if his shadow.

The fiery presence of the sun now, diminished into a glowing circle, sunk into the western horizon while the beach glimmered with a luminous specter. Bioluminescent lit waves rolled onto shore; their sparkle glimmered in the evening light.

In her darkened chamber, Emlyn sat deep in thought. She was absent-mindedly turning a gold ring set with a sapphire blue stone on her finger. She could feel a burr on the setting as she moved it. I must have damaged it when I fell, she thought, removing it and placing it by her bedside.

She placed a hand on the pendent hanging at her neck, as she looked out onto the beach. She never tired at the sight of the glowing plankton that came with the tide each evening. In its dim glow she could see carefree figures racing down the beach until they disappeared into the night. A small smile settled on her lips. She had never seen anything so beautiful.

Later that evening Dyfen, Isley and Dover settled into their straw beds in the stable. They were all tired but out of necessity discussed future plans. The dogs milled around them for a while, receiving pats and fond words before settling down near where the horses were stabled.

"Do we go forward to Jaffa or turn back?" Dover asked with his head supported by his hand, barely awake.

Dyfen laid still. He stroked his right thumb against his jawline and stared into the darkness. His mind turned to his mission and reason behind their journey south and finally said in a wooden tone. "On the morrow, I will go to Lord Esper and request passage to Jaffa, and we will move onward as planned." With that, he turned away.

Dover and Isley looked at each other in the dim light but said nothing and soon fell fast asleep.

Chapter 9

The Morrow

Avak, Aubryn, Osyn and Tyber awoke early, surrounding Dover, Isley and Dyfen with wagging tails and cold noses. The normal morning greeting. Then they spotted Kellis and took off to greet him.

Kellis arrived to deliver food to the stable. Mim had sent baskets filled with large loaves of bread, a bowl of churned butter, half wheel of cheese and bowl of assorted fruits with a large ewer of Ayran. Kellis placed them on the trestle table Mim had set up in the stable yard for them. She also sent several large trays loaded with dried meat and vegetables for the dogs. Kellis took great pleasure in personally feeding them alongside Dyfen. He was pleased that the hounds seemed to accept him. At least as long as he was with Dyfen.

Dyfen put his hand on Kellis' shoulder to make it clear he was a friend. The dogs, understanding Kellis was trusted, leapt with joy at their greetings. He could not be sure if the joy was for him or the food he brought. He hoped it was for both. Knowing the commotion meant Kellis had arrived, the horses began to whinny to be included in the reunion inciting the dogs to take off to say good morning to them.

"Blast, these curs and their early rising time," Dover said sarcastically while pushing himself onto his feet. "Daybreak and time to rise."

Dyfen and Isley looked at him with mock disgust as they had arisen earlier and were already at the trough washing up.

Dyfen shivered as he poured water over his head. It ran down his back and chilled his body even in the mild Cyprus morning air. He quickly dried himself and pulled his shirt over his head.

"I am going to arrange passage to Jaffa," he told his brothers before walking away.

Dover was watching his brother leave with an assessing eye and murmured to Isley quietly "Have you noticed he is missing his stone? He never takes it off. He did not lose it in the waves because I saw it on him yesterday. So where might it be?"

Isley nodded, "Yes, I noticed it missing last evening," and raised his eyebrows. "I was not brave enough to ask."

Dover eyed him in his mischievous manner and called out to his eldest brother.

"Dyfen, ahem, have you lost or misplaced Ell… ah, your pendent?"

"Not lost. I know its whereabouts," Dyfen replied but did not explain further. Then, grabbing some bread and cheese from the table, he left.

"Well, then, as long as you know its whereabout…," Dover responded to himself.

He looked sideways at Isley who was grooming the dogs with Kellis. "What the devil possesses him? You know what that stone means to him."

Isley kept working. "Your father's agreement, I think. I fear Dyfen may be regretting it."

"It is times such as these not being the eldest son has its advantages," Dover mused. "A lack of inheritance and a lack of responsibility to accompany it. It weighs out to my liking. Come, let us attend to our empty bellies."

Chapter 10

The Lords Esper

Dyfen was being escorted into the presence of Lord Rylan Esper by his son, Eryk. They traveled through the main hall with its tapestry covered walls to the map room with its large, guarded door. Before he signaled to open the door, Eryk stopped and turned toward Dyfen, "My father will ask what transpired to put my sister in harm's way."

"She has not already informed him of events?" Dyfen queried.

"She did not tell the entirety of it. We would know naught of her injury if Hugo had not stormed into our presence shouting his outrage. Hugo himself visited us twice and sent a servant thrice to learn of her welfare since morning." Eryk continued with an annoyed tone, "My sister can be very stubborn, but her judgement has normally been sound. In this case, allowing herself to be unchaperoned with three unknown men gave us cause to rethink how sound her judgment may be. I can only imagine that her pain was so great it clouded her mind."

"But in the end, you allowed it. Why?" Dyfen asked.

"Eston, whom father places his complete trust in, knew your father and uncle in the Holy land. He is acquainted with your Uncle August's aptitude for healing. And our own physician is aware of your uncle's deep understanding of anatomy. Hearing that you are his apprentice and then witnessing your ability, he convinced father it was in the best interest of Emlyn to allow you to go on with the surgery. Rend was positively beside himself with it all."

Eryk continued, "When we went to her chamber to check upon her condition, we had some issue with your hound, the dark one… Cydryl," he mispronounced the name, "allowing us access… which was only remedied by his obedience to my sister's command, much to our surprise. She seemed exhausted. Upon seeing her distress, we did not insist on answers to our questions for the time being but did insist she be seen by our family physician. Dr. Chikaris was dually impressed with your surgical skills. A fortunate talent, one does not find readily."

"As you presumed, my uncle has a reputation for his skill as a surgeon. My brothers and I have assisted him many times," Dyfen said looking at Eryk for a reaction. He decided not to mention they assisted in the dissection of dead bodies. His look turned solemn and voice serious,

"She placed herself in front of five bowmen to save my dogs. I offer apologies for events leading to this tragedy but the real blame belongs to young Rend for his part in it," he said bluntly.

"We acted in her best interest by quickly removing the arrowhead in spite of his interference. As far as Emlyn goes, I doubt many men would have done a splinter as much as she did yesterday. She is a singular woman of deep courage. She has my profound gratitude and admiration," Dyfen said with deep sincerity.

Her brother smiled, "Emlyn has always been so. She is kind of heart with little thought to herself. I doubt she has a regret." Eryk sighed. "It was she that stayed Hugo's hand from shooting your dogs while they insisted the stables was theirs to protect. She begged my father to ride to you for help. He has a soft spot for my sister…. and he likes dogs," Eryk stated, exhibiting an unexpected dry sense of humor. He nodded to the guards who presented their swords with bowed heads as they passed through the doorway into the room.

Lord Rylan Esper was seated in an ornately carved chair with tribal patterned upholstery at a long, olivewood trestle table. His head was down examining a map when they entered. A large version of the Tabula Rogeriana by Muhammad al-Idrisi, covered one wall. North was at the top he noticed. It had been copied upside down. The table stood before a large, unlit fireplace and large leaded windows at the top of the tall walls were pushed open allowing both light and a soft breeze to enter the room. Cases with wide shelves lined one wall filled with rolled parchment maps. The stone walls were hung with tapestries of woven maps of Cyprus. Colored maps of various nearby countries were laid flat further down the table. All sat upon a large caucus patterned carpet.

Looking up he saw that the room had a tall, domed ceiling painted midnight blue. It was punctuated with stars painted with gold. Thin gold lines connected them to display constellations. It was a magnificent feature creating a very intimate atmosphere.

"I trust my stable has been liberated from your homicidal hounds?" Rylan queried in a serious but wry manner without looking up. "Cydryn, is it? We had the pleasure of meeting him once again mid-day yester. It would give me pleasure to think of him as the pest who prevented me from entering my own stable but after observing how he watches over my daughter with such great care, I dare say I respect him."

Dyfen chuckled, "Cydryn means no harm but his understanding of his task can result in excitement at times. I go to collect him now and with your permission, I would also like to examine Lady Emlyn's wound once more before we depart, if that meets with your approval."

Rylan Esper nodded his head in the affirmative. "I trust you to look upon her as your patient only. Eryk will take you." Rylan shot Dyfen a look that implied his statement was a threat if not followed. Dyfen nodded his head. He understood.

"Even so, you have much to answer for, Whetherly. My daughter languishes in her chamber recovering from misadventure she suffered on your behalf."

"The bowman was one of young Rend's men. He was dragged off by the rest of his mob without comment," Dyfen responded. "You may want to question Hugo about that."

Rylan shook his head in disgust. "I heard tell that one of the stable cats caused his arrow to move off its intended course."

"Which was my dog!" Dyfen retorted hotly. "And found Emlyn, unfortunately. I imagine you will know the answer to these questions and more once you have questioned Hugo," Dyfen said dodging the subject of Shakar, the kitchen cat. "I am surprised you have not done so by now."

Rylan became agitated. "This is troubling. We need answers from Hugo about this," he stated.

"We have always enjoyed a relaxed relationship with the Rends. We allow them freedom to come and go at will but in truth we know little of them since their arrival a few years ago. They have kept to themselves for the most part but we have found it to our benefit to band together to keep our lands safe from Emperor Komnenus and his men. Now, must I worry that his men are a danger to my family? Must we reexamine our relationship?"

Rylan paced as he spoke. "Eston must see to it that all guards remain on alert for the time being. Out of caution,"

Just then the door opened and Eston stuck his head inside the room. Dyfen noted him to be a very large, fierce looking man.

"Eston, just the man!" Rylan called out.

"Sire, pardon my intrusion. How fares the Lady Emlyn?'"

He had been told that Dyfen had entered the room and had come to inspect the son of Braxton and nephew of August Whetherly. He eyed Dyfen appraisingly.

"We were just speaking of her, Eston. She is faring well by all accounts from Dr. Chikaris. Whetherly here is going up to check on his patient one last time. Tell the guards to remain on alert for any suspicious activity within our walls. Pay particular attention to those who young Rend surrounds himself with and rein in Lady Emlyn's freedom as well. She may no longer enjoy the liberty she has previously enjoyed when we assumed our lands safe for her to roam idly about."

The large man lowered his head in respect to Rylan. "Lady Emlyn's injury will aid in keeping her safe. She cannot elude the guards so easily now." He pulled the door closed as he left the room.

Eryk side eyed Dyfen. "Let us go."

Dyfen was about to exit but stopped. "Before I take your leave, Lord Esper, I came to impose upon your hospitality once again. Your assistance in securing passage to Jaffa for myself and my retinue would earn my deepest gratitude. I have a pressing obligation awaiting me there and have need to leave as soon as it is possible."

Rylan thought for a moment. "It may take a day or two to find a ship provisioned with the ability to safely transport your steeds as well. Most likely that will not be till day after the morrow. In the meantime, all of your personal items found washed ashore were restored as best as possible and returned to you. I had them moved to the stable where you seem to prefer to spend your evenings...."

"Oh, and one more matter. The morrow eve, we planned a small feast in your honor to thank you for your care of my daughter. We look forward in showing you and your brothers that our hospitality extends beyond a straw bed in the stable." he had a twinkle in his eye when he spoke, "Mim is beside herself managing preparations. You must have made quite an impression on her. She seldom tolerates short notice to prepare for such a labor-intensive event without grumbling, but not a cross word has come from her. She is a gem of a cook but can be a dragon when her ire is roused," he spoke with amusement in his eyes.

Then he became serious again. "Of course, Emlyn will be absent based on physician's recommendation. Something I am sure you will agree with. He sees it best for her to rest and stay off the wounded leg so soon after the injury."

"I am in complete agreement with your physician," Dyfen said.

"Our deepest thanks to you, Lord Esper. We look forward to attending your gathering and Mim has our full gratitude for her part in it. She has been most kind to us and our dogs. They appreciate her skill in the kitchen as do we. In fact, I am of the suspicion she takes greater care with their victuals than she does ours." He chuckled. "I have regularly mistaken their meals for ours."

"Now, I must take my leave to look in upon 'my patient." Dyfen tilted his head in acknowledgement towards Rylan, turned and followed after Eryk's who was already headed down the hall.

As they traveled down fresco painted hallways and traveled up a grand staircase, Dyfen conversed with Eryk.

"Eston is quite an imposing figure," Dyfen observed. "I can see that your father has great faith in him."

"Eston is both castellan and seneschal here. So, yes, my father places great confidence in him. He is devoted to our family. So much so, he left his own family in Persia to be at father's side," Eryk replied.

"He is Persian? I would say that to be true by the look of him but question his name."

Eryk smiled. "His real name is Esfahan. But father took to calling him Eston for some reason unknown to all. He is both clever and courageous. He is the reason father allowed you to remove the arrow from my sister. He vouched for you when all of this wretched hell broke loose. Our family trusts him with our lives."

"It would seem," Dyfen mused.

They reached the familiar heavily carved doors to Emlyn's chamber on the mezzanine overlooking the great hall. Cydryn was nowhere to be seen. Eryk knocked on the door and heard a soft voice say, "Enter."

Eryk stepped back and allowed Dyfen to move forward into the room. A guard had arrived and whispered something into Eryk's ear. He turned to Dyfen and said, "I have been summoned elsewhere and must go. I place my sister in your hands and expect you to maintain a respectful and chivalrous demeanor at all times, Whetherly," he spoke solemnly mirroring his father's sentiments and left.

Dyfen bowed his head to Eryk then moved into the chamber alone. The subtle hint of Damascus rose filled his nostrils as he crossed the threshold into the airy blue and white appointed solar.

He breathed in deeply and closed his eyes for a second. He moved across the solar past the arches to the bed where Emlyn was sitting up.

Cydryn, having heard and scented his master, remained on the floor at the foot of the bed, watchful. He stood upon sighting Dyfen who bent down to rub his friend's scruffy back and lowered his head to touch noses. "Are you doing your duty brave lad?" Cydryn wagged his tail and looked at him as if to say, 'Not to worry, I am here.' and returned to his post, circling a couple of times before he laid down.

"I trust Cydryn has been on his best behavior for you?" Dyfen said straightening to stand.

Emlyn had her back propped up against a few large down-filled pillows covering her ornately carved headboard. She had bathed and looked refreshed. Her long tresses hung loosely, resting upon her shoulders. He could see a thread of leather through the strands and recognized his pendent to be resting around her delicate neck.

"Yes, Cydryn has been the most perfect gentleman and guardian. He decided he could better serve by being closer. It was his idea to settle here at my bedside," she said with affection in her voice.

Cydryn looked at her with shining eyes when he heard Emlyn say his name. "We had a rich supper of mutton stew and newly picked carrots last night did we not, Cydryn?" Cydryn seemed to burst with excitement at the mention of this.

Dyfen chuckled, "My Lady, in a mere evening, you have ruined my stalwart boy. He will think me miserly after supping on such as you have provided."

"Well, we must keep him strong must we not, dear hound?" she smiled at Cydryn while she spoke. There was a mutual admiration taking place, Dyfen observed in silent amusement.

"I apologize for the intrusion, Lady Emlyn but I have come to monitor your wound to ensure nothing has gone amiss," Dyfen stated, getting to the point of his visit.

He approached the bed. "How fares the pain?"

"It does throb boldly but I am well otherwise."

"I wish to see with mine own eyes that you are recovering well. Indulge me and allow me to look at the wound once more." He sounded casual but in actuality he was worried that she may have been infected by the arrowhead and wanted to make sure the wound looked healthy. Without waiting for a response, he gently moved the bedclothes down only enough to expose the wounded leg where the bandage was located. He shifted her gown up over the injured limb.

With light hands, he carefully removed the dressing. The flesh looked pink and healthy. He was relieved. Looking up at her said in a detached voice, "It appears to be healing well but I fear you will be left with a scar." He began to restore the bandages. His hands moved deftly over her leg.

"I hope it will be a small one." For some reason Emlyn was uncomfortable hearing about a possible scar to her body from his lips.

"Will you be departing soon?" she asked to cover her embarrassment.

"Yes, we must take our leave soon. Your father is graciously seeking a vessel for us. We hope to sail on the tide within the next coming suns."

He tactfully walked away giving her privacy to straighten her shift. He looked out of a set of triple arched windows down onto a walled garden below. He opened the door to the terrace and stepped out.

The view was beautiful, overlooking the beach below. The waves rolled up onto the sand at the bottom of steep cliffs. The air was mild and smelled sweetly from the riot of roses below in the garden.

Her eyes had not left his face even though it was now turned from her as he looked out over the terrace. She studied his tall muscular frame. His dusky colored skin. The silver cross dangling from his right ear.

He had rebraided his hair and it hung down his back with the glint of his aqua eyes in profile. He was dragging his right thumb down the side of his jaw distractedly as she saw him do on the beach when they first met.

He took a deep breath of fresh air and returned to the room. Emlyn was waiting.

"Of course, you must continue your journey," she said lightly. He turned to look at her. 'I fear I have yet to offer my thanks to you and your brothers for saving me yesterday. You must tell them of my heartfelt gratitude for all they did for me. You will thank your uncle for me too? His teachings did not go untested. I offer my regrets for Hugo's behavior as well. His intentions were well meant. You must not judge him too harshly."

"Oh yes, young Rend. As far as I am concerned, this tragedy is all his doing. He has a nerve about him. I have heard he has inquired repeatedly as to your health. He must consider himself something more than a mere escort or do I imagine it?" Dyfen inquired with a hint of sarcasm.

Emlyn was unsure of how to respond so remained silent.

He turned back toward her. "I will relate your message to Isley and Dover. Both will be gladdened to know your leg is mending well and my uncle will ask me a thousand questions on how I applied my training when I see him next." He laughed.

He then decided to broach a question he had wondered since their first meeting on the beach. "I am curious, my lady," he started to say.

"Why is the church upon the hill deserted?"

"There is quite the tale behind it," was her reply. "It happened one evening's service many years ago as the story has been told."

The Flaming Soul   Doreen Demerjian

"The church priest, his name was Kevorkian, the Holy Reverend Father Kevorkian, was leading the worshippers in prayer when a thunderous storm suddenly rained down upon the church's copper dome, striking it repeatedly with brilliant lightning bolts. Suddenly, all of the lanterns inside went dark and a buckler-sized, ball-lightning pierced the church wall. A soft orange globe of light hovered a short time over the altar before splitting into two, one exited through a stained-glass window and the other passed through the heavy wooden door without a trace. People screamed in terror and a cry was heard from the altar where the priest had been standing. None had witnessed the like.

"No one was injured. The scent of sulfur hung in the air along with a wispy cloud of dark smoke, some say it loosely took the form of a man as it floated outside and dissolved into the night air. Afterwards, there was no sign of the old priest. Father Kevorkian had disappeared. Never to be seen again. The parishioners searched for him throughout the night and the next day without success."

Dyfen widened his eyes temporarily taken aback and then chuckled. "Such events would create pause in any congregation. The parishioners preferred a less literal way of seeing the light of the Lord, I imagine."

She raised her eyebrows in mock amusement looking toward the heavens.

"Afterward the villagers refused to return to the church. They are a superstitious lot. They say the orb came from the hereafter to claim their souls. Father Kevorkian's disappearance was never explained and the church has sat empty ever since. Another priest came to the village but he could not convince the people to return to St. Thaddeus. Today, Father Papakian lives in a small rectory behind the church where Father Kevorkian once lived. Services are now held in a small building converted from a grain storehouse. He set up a memorial stone in the church yard to commemorate the missing priest. Somewhere people can pay their respects."

"And do they?" Dyfen asked curiously.

"Some of the older people do. The younger villagers who never knew him are afraid to get anywhere near the churchyard," Emlyn answered.

"Father Kevorkian used to visit the village to replenish his supplies. Afterward he would visit the castle kitchen where the cook would send him on his way with some delicacies from the day's bake. He was remembered fondly there."

"Castle cooks are popular souls with anyone possessing a stomach," Dyfen joked happy to change the subject. "I know Isley and Dover have a great appreciation for the talents of Mim. Speaking of food, I am told there will be a feast on the morrow eve, but you will not be attending."

"Yes, I have said to father that I will be quite able to sit in a chair by then. Quietly. But he does not agree. Dr Chikaris apparently thinks me ill which I am NOT," she said with a pout.

"You will be sorely missed, but I must agree with your father and Dr Chikaris, Lady Emlyn. Rest is best for your leg these next weeks. Give your body time to mend," Dyfen chided her.

"Now upon examining our work and finding the wound healing well I may take my leave from these shores with a settled mind. I have business in Jaffa that will not keep," he said without meeting her eyes.

"This will be our last visit before we sail. Remain well my lady." He motioned to Cydryn who stood up. The dog looked at Emlyn one last time before he followed his master who strode from the room.

As he and Cydryn left, a figure coming from the opposite direction walked by the guard stationed nearby. With a dismissive wave of his hand, he entered Emlyn's solar. Hugo stood at the entry for a few minutes watching her brush her hair as she stared out of the window. He coughed gently and Emlyn turned around.

"You have come back...." seeing Hugo, she stopped.

"I had to come. To make certain you are well," he was looking at her with intensity but spoke calmly. "Your injury is totally attributable to those washed-ashore sea rats and their stable-stealing, attack hounds," he spat out. More quietly he said, "Although, I recognize my part in it."

"I have passed your chamber innumerable times intending to check on you but for that damnable mongrel...," he spoke with frustration.

Hugo's face looked tired and Emlyn could see he had not slept. His grey eyes had dark circles beneath them. His long, fair hair was unkempt, his clothes rumpled and hung from his body as if he had not eaten in days.

"Hugo, have you not slept? Have you not eaten?" she asked him, so poorly did he appear.

"I have slumbered and eaten well enough." He dismissed the questions. "How do you fare, Emlyn?" he asked gently. "Are you in great pain?" Before she could answer his jealousy got the better of him. "Did that father of swine, Whetherly, take advantage of you under the pretense of attending to your wound?"

Emlyn was shocked at his venom but quickly reassured him. "No, they cared for my wound and showed me only respect. I am very grateful men of such skill were present." She could see him visibly relax.

"You are all too trusting Emlyn. You do not understand the true nature of men," he told her.

"Surely, not all men are the same, Hugo. You cannot know that."

"I am afraid, I do. And because of that knowledge, I must place myself between you and harm." His face told her he was completely serious.

"Your innocence and naivety are endearing but you know not of what you speak." He dismissed her objection.

He moved to her side and took her hand up in his, squeezing their intertwined fingers. "I only wish that arrow had found me instead."

Emlyn was touched by his concern. "Hugo, it was naught but misfortune that I was struck. There was naught you could do to avert it."

"I see it otherwise. The man who shot you was my own man. He was aiming for the hound and hoped to win my favor by killing that devil's cur but was knocked down just before losing it."

"You are saying this was not an unfortunate accident?" Emlyn asked incredulously.

"I am saying that my man hoped to win my favor by killing the hound and instead hit you, Emlyn. "

She gave him a questioning look.

He repeated. "The man who shot you loosed an arrow even after seeing you were in its path. You were shot because I brought him there and did not heed your plea to spare the dogs."

She could hear the determination in his voice as he continued. "I swear by God to protect you. To that point, I ask you to cease wandering about unchaperoned. It is unseemly and it is dangerous. You have developed a false sense of security because your father and brother have forgiven your headstrong, unattended adventures in the past but times are shifting here in Kyrenia. There are more dangers present than ever before."

"What new dangers do you speak of Hugo?"

He seemed irritated by her question. "You have been arrow shot. Is that not enough to prove my point? There are strangers here on our shore. They may or may not be a danger. I insist you accept my protection. You would not have been injured if not for their being here."

Emlyn was becoming confused. "Hugo, you said yourself the man was yours. Am I to fear your men then? The strangers on our shores you speak of saved my life."

He became frustrated. "I am saying that these men may or may not be dangerous but the fact that strange men do come to our shores requires you to be more careful. So, I ask of you to think of me as your champion. Pledge to me, hereafter, that the next time of need you will turn to me and not some stranger. In this way only, will I be assured you will be kept from harm."

He continued, attempting to sound nonchalant. "After the events of yesterday, it is clear that good fortune has its limits. I not only vow to protect you from physical harm but know that I can be a good friend to you as well." He mumbled softly, "More than a friend actually."

"My wish is that you think of me that way as well. I can be trusted with your confidence. I pledge it by Our Lord and Savior." He had crossed himself while kneeling at the side of her bed, his tired face looked into hers with a steely determination. "Ease my mind Emlyn, swear to our friendship," he prompted.

Hugo had always been very possessive of her, she knew. She did not want to encourage him but could see the only way he would leave her in peace was to agree to what he asked. Her mind turned to Dyfen leaving their shores in a short while. She would probably never see him again.

"Very well Hugo, I solemnly avow this to you. In the name of Our Lord and Savior, I swear to consider you my champion and friend."

His face relaxed and he dropped her hand to her relief.

"I have done what you ask, now I beg of you Hugo, please rest and seek nourishment."

He nodded his head tiredly and looked at Emlyn one last time. He straightened his clothing, smoothed his hair then walked from the room.

Emlyn sighed, reflecting on what just had occurred. She made a promise to Hugo expecting never having to keep it, so little did she know of coming events.

Chapter 11

Training Day

It was early morning. Isley and Dover were with the horses in the lush, western pasturelands of Kyrenia Castle watching Dyfen exercise his horses. Word had spread throughout the village of the strangers who had survived the shipwreck with their rare, Nisean stallions. Horses so valued for their beauty and intelligence that they were literally worth their weight in gold. Citizens had come to watch with interest as Dyfen put the horses through their liberty training paces.

He used no form of control other than his words and gestures, relying on trust and a mutual understanding between himself and the horse.

He began by walking through the green grass, horses following in a line close behind him. Zakar in the lead. Dyfen stopped, turned to face them.

He gestured stretching his arms out on each side of his body and said, "Line", the stallions lined up across from him with ears standing upright alertly listening to their master's order.

He then lifted his right knee slightly, speaking, "Left", and the horses mirrored his movement.

He put his leg down and raised his right leg, speaking "Right" with the stallions following suit.

"Fine lads," he told them in a soft voice full of praise and patted them each. Zakar snorted.

Dyfen lifted his hands upright at the wrist showing Zakar and Arazi his palms and spoke the command, "Stay" and turned and walked away.

When he reached a distance he turned around, motioned with his hands, flexing his wrists toward his body, in a signal to come to him. He spoke the word, "Come". Both stallions raced to where he stood running shoulder to shoulder next to one another then lining up in front of him in the position they had stood before.

He crossed his hands over one another and spoke "Switch". The horse switched places but remained in alignment with one another.

By this time the gathering crowd was watching in silent awe as the Nisean stallions responded to Dyfen's hand signals and verbal commands. They had never seen horses respond without being controlled by a bridle.

Dyfen parted his hands outward and spoke the command, "Part" and the two horses turned outward in opposite directions until they heard Dyfen speak the word, "Together".

Both horses turned toward each other until they were about twenty feet apart when they heard the command "Return", they both turned back toward Dyfen returning to their starting positions in front of him.

The townspeople were cheering by now. The stallions responded to the audience with heads held high and tails swishing, acknowledging the admiration.

"Good lads," Dyfen spoke again and said the word, "Relax". Giving them permission to do as they please. Each stallion resumed grazing on the lush pasture grass, ignoring all the people that had gathered.

All of this time the dogs were lying together on the grass watching events unfold. The training was something they had seen many times before with many different horses and did not particularly interest them.

However, the gathering of people did create a watchfulness among them, making sure their family members stayed safe. After most of the crowd had dispersed, two men remained. They spoke to one another in a quiet tone after watching the exhibition. They both nodded their heads in agreement and left, making their way back to the village.

Tyber and Osyn started to wrestle, and the others joined in. Isley and Dover smiled at the rough housing and started back to the stable.

Later in the day, Dyfen, Isley and Dover gathered at Kyrenia castle's great hall for the midday meal. They dined on cold roast, coarse loaves of bread and fresh fruits.

"Did I mention that we are to attend a feast in our honor?" Dyfen asked while swiping his bread in the sauce left on his plate.

"I know of it," Dover said casually, focused on his plate.

"You know of it?" his brother asked quizzically. "I don't remember mentioning it. It had completely slipped my mind."

"I was told by Patrice," Dover answered still focused on his food.

"Who is Patrice?" Isley asked.

"One of the kitchen maids. Fine talent with pies," Dover said, finally lifting his eyes from his food looking in turn from Isley to Dyfen who were both laughing.

"Oh, the pie maiden is a friend of yours. We see," Isley joked. "Why are we not taken aback by this bit of news?" he asked Dyfen mockingly.

"Women cannot help but befriend our younger brother, his charm so irresistible," Dyfen joked.

Dover good naturedly ignored them as he usually did when the two found merriment at his expense.

After the meal, they headed down the hall and found themselves near the map room. Dyfen remembered the beauty of the Tabula Rogeriana Lord Esper had on the wall and suggested, "We are close to the map room, Isley. You must see this copy of the Tabula Rogerian. You will enjoy the beauty of the room and the fineness of Lord Esper's maps. Shall we stop by?"

"Yes, let us do so," Isley replied. "I am very interested in viewing it."

They followed as Dyfen led the way. He stopped at the heavy wooden door he remembered from his prior visit. It was open as the day had become warm. Isley stuck his head in. Seeing Rylan in conversation with Gracyn and Dr. Chikaris, he spoke, "Lord Esper, may we trouble you for a favor?"

"Of course, Lord Standen, what is it you wish?" Rylan asked, looking towards him.

"Dyfen was conveying the beauty of the room and the quality of your maps," Isley replied.

"Join us. We welcome your company," Rylan graciously invited them in.

Greetings were extended between all.

"Your Rogeriana is extraordinary," Isley exclaimed, marveling at its beauty.

Rylan chuckled with appreciation at the compliment. "Many have said as much. I would attempt feigning modesty but fear I cannot. It is worthy of praise."

Isley laughed with him and sat down in a cushioned wooden chair at the trestle table and looked down at the map unfurled there. It was an old map of Armenia and the city of Ayrivank was marked.

"Ayrivank," Isley read aloud with interest.

When he heard the name, Ayrivank, Dyfen recalled the map he had seen at the old church. Rylan and Gracyn must have been looking at this map and had marked the same city. A strange coincidence.

Dr. Chikaris had recognized the name as well. Upon hearing it, he repeated it thoughtfully, "Ayrivank, I know that name." He bent his head to the side and squinted his eyes trying to bring the details forward. "Interesting story told to me long ago by an aged priest on pilgrimage to the Holy Land.

"I had occasion to treat him. He was an amiable soul with a severe case of gout. As I was preparing a balm, the old man wistfully recalled a legend from his homeland telling of a Holy Relic which could cure all ailments. It has been safeguarded by Christians since the time of Christ, the old priest claimed while lamenting his illness. He began the telling of a long-told tale in his country. From what I can recall, this is what he said:

"According to an old Armenian manuscript, St Thaddeus, one of the original twelve disciples of Jesus, was given a holy relic by St. Peter to carry with him on his mission to Armenia to introduce Christianity to its people in the year of Our Lord, 43 AD. It describes the relic as The Holy Lance, the Roman spear that pierced the blessed body of

Christ as he hung upon the cross. Upon arriving in Armenia, St Thaddeus was able to convert the Royal Princess with his teachings and left the relic in her care. She built a monastery for followers of the true faith to safeguard it.

"The document did not state precisely the location but described a place that exactly matches the gates of the monastery in Ayrivank," Dr. Chikaris told them.

"Since that time, the relic was safeguarded and protected by monks until one hundred years ago when the Cathlicos, who heads the Holy Armenian Apostolic church, sent it to a sister church in the Armenian Principality of Cilicia, for the purpose of curing a brother suffering from madness. A monk carried the relic with him on board a ship which later met with a sudden and violent storm. The ship was blown from its course only to sink off the shore of Cyprus. They say it was a miracle that the monk survived long enough to make it to shore and hide the Holy Lance there before he was taken by the Lord.

"As I said, the old priest was quite advanced in age, so I thought no further of his tale until a few months ago I was treating a patient with a disfiguring disease and repeated the story to him as a way of providing comfort. Hope is a curative in itself at times. But it had the opposite effect on this man, I fear. He became quite agitated and asked many questions. When I was unable to provide answers, I was escorted out and offered neither shelter nor supper. Rather loutish behavior," he ended, somewhat miffed remembering how he had been treated.

"A charming tale to tell around a fire," Gracyn smiled. "Long years muddy a man's mind. As I remember another apostle, St. Bartholemew, also paid Armenia a visit 25 years later in 68 AD and was skinned alive before he was beheaded by the local religious leaders for converting the Armenian King, Polymius, to Christianity.

I guess some in power were not gladdened by it. Did the priest say anything else?" Gracyn asked with curiosity.

Dr Chikaris, tired from the telling, leaned his head back and stretched his arms upward. "No, that was all of it," he said letting out his breath and standing up. "I am afraid I must take my leave. Of course, I must stop by the kitchens and see my good friend Mim. Just to make certain she remains in good health." And with that, he bid all goodbye.

Everyone smiled inwardly as they knew that the good doctor could not resist the cooking of Mim. Many of his castle visits were merely pretenses to stop by the kitchens to visit with the kindly cook and sample the fare roasting on a spit or bubbling in pots hanging over coal embers.

The three brothers thanked Lord Esper and bid a farewell to Gracyn Rend, leaving the two men alone by the fire.

As they walked back to the stable, they discussed what they had heard. "What do you think of the Ayrivank story?" Dyfen asked Isley.

"I think nothing," Isley answered. "The priest was yearning for a solution to his pain."

"I am more surprised at Gracyn Rend's knowledge of religious history," Dover joked. "Do you think the Holy Lance exists?'"

"I have heard a similar tale told before of a Holy Relic," Isley commented. He looked over at Dyfen to see what he had to say.

"What he calls a legend may be just a folktale," Dyfen mused. "Best to forget it."

Chapter 12

The Feast

The next morn was the day of the feast. It was late midday, when Dyfen left the horses grazing in their lush, green pasture with the dogs to oversee them. He returned to the stable to find Isley and Dover rummaging through battered looking chests. They were their own trunks Rylan's servants had recovered from the sea.

Their clothing which had been washed, dried and folded, smelled sweetly of fresh sea air. The Esper servants had done an excellent job restoring leather back to its original suppleness and color. Two parts water with one-part vinegar to get the salt off, then wiped down with plain water and finishing with an application of olive oil. All the chain mail had been recovered and restored as well by rolling it in barrels of sand to remove the rust and applying oil to the mail as a protective cover.

The stable boys went about their duties mucking stalls, filling troughs with fresh water and cleaning and repairing tack. The air smelled sweetly of freshly cut grass.

"Wonderful, our chests were found!" Dyfen exclaimed. "I miss my own boots."

All three men stripped to the waist and began washing in the trough set up for them. They scrubbed their torsos and washed their hair with thick slices of soap and dried off with coarsely woven blankets. As they went about bathing, they captured the interest of some of the castle's young servant girls who were lingering about the stables with no apparent purpose, hoping to capture the eye of one of the men. Dover was the most inclined to provide them with that attention.

"Dover, can we not even bathe without a group of your admirers bearing witness? I look forward to wearing my own breeches once more and would like to be able to dress with some privacy," Isley pulled his linen shirt over his head as he spoke. He looked with irritation toward Dover who was casting smiles at the young maidens.

"Well, yes. I understand the need for privacy, I suggest that you turn your back to them," Dover said as if it were the answer. He looked over at Dyfen who was oblivious to all of it.

"Dyfen, how does it feel to wear your own boots once again?" he asked his brother.

"A relief," Dyfen returned. "They still need stretching but a day of wear should right that. The borrowed boots were made for feet a bit narrower than my own. But nothing is as satisfying as having my own sword and dagger back in their scabbards on my belt."

He dragged his fingers through his damp hair. It fell shining around his bronzed bare shoulders. He spotted Emlyn's scarf washed and folded over the edge of the trough and picked it up.

Isley noticed Dyfen looking at the scarf and asked, "Dyfen, how did you find Lady Emlyn yesterday morning? Was she of good health?"

Dover and Isley looked at Dyfen with interest. He looked past them when he answered matter-of-factly, "She appeared to be well. She said as much at least. She sends her gratitude and regards to you both."

"You seem to have taken a pronounced interest in her recovery," Dover hinted.

Dyfen looked at him with all seriousness. "She risked her life to save Cydryn's. I cannot begin to repay her. I owe her everything."

He went on to change the subject. "There seems to be an uneasiness in Kyrenia since we washed ashore."

"I sense it too," Isley responded. "I suggest we keep alert while we remain here."

Dover showed agreement with his eyes.

Dyfen switched the conversation to a lighter subject. "I have thoughts of Sarkis these last days. I wish he could have accompanied us on our voyage but better he did not consider the outcome. If father had not needed him to deliver those horses to Sicily, he would be with us now."

"It would be good to see Captain Denisot as well. There would be no need to engage a ship if he were here," Isley finished the thought.

Captain Denisot Febrielle and his specially designed tarida, the Sea Stallion, were the normal mode of transport the Whetherly family usually employed to deliver their horses across the sea. He and Sarkis were delivering six stallions to Tancred of Sicily.

Sarkis Najarian, the lead stable hand, had helped take care of Whetherly horses on Moon Isle since he was ten years old when August brought the injured boy home from his last battle. He had been an arrow boy in the army of a Cilician Lord.

The arrow boys were prized targets of the enemy. The goal was to prevent them from collecting spent arrows used to restock enemy quivers. The job was normally performed by the younger boys not old enough to enter battle.

Sarkis had taken a shaft to the hand while attempting to recover arrows embedded in the ground near a dead knight's body. He was pinned to the body while the heated battle raged around him when Uncle August noticed his plight.

Taking pity on the lad, who cowered while struggling to free his hand from the corpse, August impulsively turned his steed, Ishkhan, around and dismounted in a sheltered area. Crouching and protecting himself with his shield, he reached the boy and used his dagger to cut the fletching from the arrow shaft to pull the lad's hand free.

Grabbing him around the waist, they ran towards Ishkhan who stood patiently waiting in the shadow of the trees. The horse saw them coming and readied himself to flee. He and August had been partners in many battles together and the stallion knew his job.

August let out a low whistle and the brave, white stallion ran towards them in a zigzag pattern, arrows glancing off the barding he wore for protection. August boosted the boy onto the horse and clambered up behind him. Ishkhan took off with arrows still dropping around them.

Ever since then, Sarkis had lovingly fed, washed, and groomed the horses of Moon Isle from the time they were foals giving special attention to Ishkhan, now retired. The horses loved and trusted him and the Whetherlys viewed him as family. Sarkis had a special bond with the dogs as well.

"We all miss him, brother. He is worth twice Shariff's weight in gold and it has never been so apparent than now while we are shifting for ourselves," Isley said.

"Shariff would be offended," Dover joked. "And I miss Sarkis more than you two since he is the only one that will take direction from me," Dover smirked.

"You get him into trouble with your 'directions'. I am surprised he still listens to them," Isley jested. "Remember the time...."

"Pray, let us not start reminiscing about the misfortunes he and I have suffered. No one is more aware of them than I," Dover winced.

"The devil knows, Dover. You have not suffered any misfortune. It is you that emerges unscathed and young Sarkis is scrambling for his life." Isley was now tying his hair back from his face.

Dover looked out before him at nothing in particular. "I cannot explain it. He always starts off right behind me but somehow falls off a cliff or some such misadventure that requires rescuing. It is beyond my understanding," he spoke while finishing to dress.

"Tis the way of fate, brother. No man has ever held God's favor as you do. Mother says you were born under a propitious star. I lean toward believing it," Dyfen laughed as he completed tying the end of his braid. "Now, let us go and submit to our host's honoring of us with this feast." he said as they started toward the castle.

"Oh Isley, what thought you of Lord Esper's copy of Muhammad al-Idrisi's Tabula Rogeriana on his map room wall. Did you note that he had it made with North facing upward unlike the original which faced South?"

"It is unusual. Southward facing is the way it was originally drawn in the tradition of Islamic cartographers. The Greeks and Romans also did so to show their capitals of Athens and Rome in relation to the Great Sea," Isley commented.

"Quite interesting. You two will not fall short of conversation this evening. Your love of cartography will be well met there. It is drawn as if God's own eyes looked down on the world. I wonder if father has a copy of it hidden somewhere in his map room?" Dyfen mused.

They arrived at the great hall with its large, burning fireplace casting shadows on the walls and lit cresset lamps lining the perimeter. Immense oriental tapestries completely covered the stone walls retaining heat and diminishing the dampness in the air. There was a large, storied window at one end of the room for natural light and a mezzanine overlooking the left side of the hall with decorative carved wooden panels including a mashrabiya to allow the warm air to pass through. The temperature in the hall was quite warm and Isley thought that he and his brothers had made the right decision not to don their heavy tunics.

Musicians were playing traditional Cilician folk songs in their honor, filling the room with sonorous tones of the duduk as they walked into the hall. The space held a thin haze of smoke and the smell of spices and aromatics mingled with the scent of roasted meats.

It was a gathering of one hundred-twenty or so Dyfen estimated. He noticed Gracyn talking to a striking auburn-haired maiden as soon as they walked in.

"Lord Whetherly," he called as they walked by. "I desire to speak to you later."

Dyfen nodded towards him but kept walking seeking their host.

"Hail!" they heard Rylan call to them. "You are seated at my side, as my most honored guests. Come."

Dyfen moved toward the wide trestle tables which were arranged in a 'U' shape at the end of the room under the storied window.

Chairs were placed on both sides of the arms of the 'U' to make conversation easier leaving the table connecting the two sides with seating only on the outside perimeter to provide a clear view of the hall. He sat at the left of Lord Esper who was seated in the middle of the table in a highbacked, carved armed chair.

Next to him on his right, was an arrogant, jowled-faced gentleman who was elaborately dressed in very fine, grey silks and brocades. He was animatedly speaking to a dark-haired, aristocratic looking man standing at his side whose gaze steadily moved while he listened. He seemed more interested in surveying the hall than whatever was being spoken. His dark eyes darted back and forth searching.

The aristocrat looked to be in his mid-twenties. He was dressed in dark, rich samite silk attire embroidered with silver thread. He was immaculately groomed. His long hair had a surprising light-brown streak traveling through it near the front and was tied back neatly with a thick, engraved, silver band. He was strikingly handsome and emanated an air of ennui.

Rylan stood to introduce them starting with the jowly man.

"Emperor Komnenus, pray meet newly come guests to our island, Lords Dyfen and Dover Whetherly and Lord Isley Standen."

To the brothers he said. "Emperor Komnenus is our most esteemed highness come from the capitol at Nicosia just hours ago, along with his young daughter, Mareya." Dyfen, Dover and Isley politely bowed before the Emperor who eyed them with suspicion.

Emperor Komnenus came closer to the group and spoke, "Allow me to introduce you to His Grace, Raoul de Lusignan, the Duc de Marche." The Emperor motioned towards the handsome, disinterested man and turned back to them. "What brings you to our fair Isle?" Komnenus had a cruel, slack-jawed face. His dull eyes peered out of the puffy tissue surrounding them. He was of average height and had a head of greasy, swept back hair. When he spoke, his voice was officious with a hint of contemptuousness.

"It is an honor to meet you, Your Grace." Dyfen bowed towards the Duc de Marche who appeared bored. He hesitated before answering Komnenus' question. "Our visit is unplanned, Sire. A result of our ship meeting a most violent and sudden storm causing it to be pushed off course and wrecked on your northern coast. We were truly fortunate to make it to shore unharmed. God's will. The good Lord has supplied us with a most generous host in Lord Esper. He has been highly attentive to our desires."

Komnenus studied them critically before finally speaking, "Yours was not the only ship impacted by the storm. Four ships blown off course landed on our southern shores as well. Were you part of this fleet?"

"Nay, the Carlyle sailed solely on its own but I am unsurprised at their plight. The storm arose quickly with mighty winds. We are lucky to have survived. The Carlyle was mainly a transport ship, carrying our horses to Jaffa. Most of the crew made it ashore I hear and are seeking passage on other ships. Our horses swam ashore," Dover commented.

Emperor Komnenus continued, "Three of these ships in the south were shattered upon the rocks with some survivors which we are entertaining currently. The fourth is afloat but unable to sail. They are refusing our kind offer of shelter and supplies." He smiled in an oily and untrustworthy manner. "You must let me assist you in any way I can. I am blessed with a most generous nature, and you need only ask," he finished.

Rylan leaned into Dyfen and in a low voice said, "Our Emperor overstates his generosity. I have word that he is holding those shipwrecked survivors' captive and has taken all of their valuables." His face was serious. "The ship unable to sail is being refused supplies unless they come ashore which you can be certain will not end well for them. He is not a man to be trusted."

"Thank you for the warning. I could guess as much from his demeanor. His gaze never meets the eye when he speaks," Dyfen murmured back.

To Emperor Komnenus he said, "Our deepest thanks for your largesse, Your Grace. We will most assuredly do so if the need arises. Thus far, Lord Esper has well met our needs and we want for nothing as his guests."

"Yes, Lord Esper is the very essence of munificence," Komnenus spoke as if his mind were elsewhere. Coming back to the present, he stated, "Very well then, Lord Esper, my daughter, Mareya; His Grace and his sister, Ruizonn, along with our retinue plan to stay as your guests for the next few days or so. I pray it is of no indisposition to your household. If you will give word to ready our chambers."

Rylan disguised his disdain, for he was wise enough not to offend the rather temperamental Emperor. "It will be done at once Your Excellency." Rylan signaled to his manservant stationed nearby and whispered into his ear. The servant nodded in understanding and left the hall.

The Duc de Marche, who had remained silent, spoke. His voice like velvet, "Lord Esper, will your fair daughter not be joining us this eve? It was my hope to meet once again." His dark eyebrows arched slightly as he spoke.

"Your Grace, to her misfortune my daughter suffered an injury of consequence recently. Our physician has recommended that she remain in her chamber. Therefore, she will not be dining with us." Rylan had a sober look on his face when he responded. Dyfen could sense from his tone that he did not favor His Grace, Raoul de Lusignan the Duc de Marche, but had selected his words carefully.

"Tis a misfortune indeed that she shan't be attending. Please relate my best wishes to her," the Duc de Marche said looking disappointed, Dyfen noted.

"I will, of course, express your good wishes to Lady Emlyn," Rylan stated and turned toward Dyfen and spoke in an undertone. "It is best Emlyn remain in her chamber this night. She is feeling quite unwell."

"More's the pity. I did so look forward to her charming company. She is a delight," the Duc de Marche responded walking away, signaling his man servant to follow.

"She is feeling unwell then?" Dyfen turned to Rylan with expressed concern.

"Nay, she is well enough considering her injury," Rylan replied but did not offer more.

Dyfen allowed the matter to drop but he wondered what was behind the statement.

Rylan satisfied his curiosity without being asked. He spoke without looking at Dyfen, "It is the rare maiden on our island, outside the walls of Kyrenia, who has escaped violation by Emperor Komnenus and his men. Fear runs deep within our people. Ever since his arrival six years ago there are but a few maidens over ten years of age who have not suffered defilement and abasement at their hands. All who could, did flee before the plunder and carnage that emanated from Komnenus and his army. Estates were pillaged and men murdered on whim. Thus far we have escaped this fate due to Kyrenia's strategic position and the strength of our army."

"Eryk and I attempt to keep close watch over Emlyn insisting she be accompanied on outings but as you see, she consistently refuses to obey my wishes. She has always had an independent spirit no matter how we have chastised her. She eludes guardsman assigned to accompany her. I have chastised many men for losing sight of her. I had to finally stop because it became demoralizing to the men at arms. She refuses their protection. A headstrong woman," Rylan finished. "I pity her future husband," he said half in jest.

Dyfen could tell Rylan was both troubled and proud of his independent daughter. "It appears that the Duc has met Emlyn prior to today."

"He has. They met briefly three years ago. Emlyn, Eryk and I were attending the wedding of a distant relative. More for political purposes than familial duty. The Duc also attended. He was quite taken with her as I remember but I thought he would have forgotten her by now. She was a very young maiden," Rylan told him. "She did not return his interest. The Rends were there as well."

He now eyed Dyfen soberly, "You have my trust, Dyfen. You and your brothers have proven yourselves honorable men. It will be with regret that we watch you take your leave. This unheralded visit by Emperor Komnenus bodes ill for all. Having Raoul de Lusignan, the Duc de Marche, here as well doubles the peril. Be forewarned and cautious in your actions while they are in residence. They are both dangerous men to cross."

Dyfen's eyes met Rylan's with gravity as he said in a quiet tone, "I cannot in good conscience take my leave as long as this danger is present upon you, Lord Esper. Knowing the circumstances, I feel compelled to stay. I am most anxious for the safety of all within these walls."

Rylan interrupted him, "You need not worry, Dyfen. Lord Rend holds sway with his lordship Raoul, the Duc de Marche, making our friendship with the Rends our best protection at present. Komnenus would not dare insult Gracyn for fear of rousing the ire of Raoul whose sister, Ruizzon, is at table with the Rends as we speak." Rylan tilted his head in their direction. "It appears that she is smitten with young Rend." He grimaced as they both looked down the table at Hugo and Ruizzon in conversation.

Dyfen eyed the two of them. Ruizzon was animated and glowing as she spoke to Hugo, who was politely listening. Gracyn sat silently by. To Dyfen, Ruizzon was more interesting to behold than beautiful. She had a certain spark about her. Completely wasted on Rend, he thought to himself.

Rylan looked back at Dyfen and continued speaking, "Their father, Clement, is from the Frankish royal house of de Lusignan. They own a tremendous expanse of land in Famagusta, on the eastern part of the island and the family wealth and power extends well beyond this part of the world. They possess ruling principalities in Christendom and the Levant as well. He curries a close relationship with Salah ad-Din who allows Komnenus to remain in power here. His support allows the Emperor to rule as long as he provides no aid to crusaders. He even has Saracen soldiers stationed at Nicosia where Komnenus resides."

Just then, Isley in the seat next to Dyfen jostled his elbow. He gestured for him to look at Dover on Isley's other side. As Dover was leaning back in his chair to survey the room, a young maiden had seated herself next to him and introduced herself, "Hail sire, I have been told that the magnificent Nisean stallions belong to you. Your horses are the talk of the village, my maid tells me. I have a fondness for a good horse. I am a guest here as well. My name is Mareya. My father is His Excellency, Emperor Komnenus. I have been told you hail from Cilicia and were washed ashore in the storm."

Dover turned in his seat to look at Mareya and was not displeased with what met him there. She looked sixteen years of age with long, dark hair worn loosely, encircled by a gold coronet inset with red stones around her head. Her gown was a deep red samite, shot with gold threads. She wore a large gold cross brooch inset with pink cabochon stones at her breast and the same pink stones at her ears. Her skin was the color of ivory sand and her eyes a warm shade of brown accented by thick, dark lashes.

"Mareya you are most lovely," Dover said with great sincerity. His eyes set upon her in a helpless stare. "More to truth, we hail from Moon Isle off the coast of Cilicia, but the horses are rather magnificent if I am to abandon all modesty. Tell me of yourself. I fear I am smitten."

She blushed at his words although it was not the first time she had heard them from a young man. "Do not be so hasty with your words, my Lord. You have yet to know my mind."

"I do not see what is to be gained," Dover said half seriously.

Her eyes grew large. She stood and moved away deciding to share her company elsewhere down the table to where Hugo and his father sat engaged in conversation with the Duc de Marche's sister, Ruizonn de Lusignan, who sat between them.

Dover's eyes followed her retreat and sighed.

Isley looked at him in disbelief. "Brother, what in God's name made you utter those words?"

"Well, it was truth on my part, but I imagine it made her feel under appreciated. I have spent too much time with the horses and dogs of late," Dover muttered with a hint of forlornness. He threw his back against the chair. His appetite was rising as he surveyed the food around him. Servants filled the deep, gilded glass goblets set before them with wine from a large ewer.

The cups of the three brothers were never empty as serving maidens circled their table waiting for a chance to approach with ewers of wine. Each girl would serve Dover first and then attend to the others.

"We are so well attended," Isley noted. "Overly more than even the lords of the manor."

"It seems so," Dover remarked in an unassuming way, smiling at the young serving girl who was nearest. She returned his smile, blushing deep pink.

"Dover, you are the object of much adoration and Dyfen and I the beneficiaries of your admirers," Isley jested, feeling the effects of the never-ending supply of drink.

He turned to survey the tables laden with mounds of fresh apricots, figs, dates, oranges, pomegranates, almonds, walnuts, a variety of cured olives and cheeses all laid out on the table with baskets of flat breads still warm from the ovens.

Rylan had his servant place fresh goblets before them and poured from a decanter placed near his own cup. "This is my own special vintage grown locally in our mountains. The altitude gives it a sweet taste," He spoke proudly. "Tell me if you have ever sampled another like it." Looking at them, he waited for them to lift their cups.

Dyfen, Isley and Dover each put their goblets up to their lips and each exclaimed at the sweet and fruity flavor they discovered there.

"Lord Esper, your wine is truly a treasure," Isley spoke first. "It rivals our own grown at home. Our father's vineyards are well known in the region. We think that wine most excellent, but this is exceptional."

Rylan's chest expanded noticeably with pride. "We use two strains of our Cyprus grapes: a white and a red variety. They are partially dried in the sun then fermented and pressed. By doing this we concentrate the sweetness of the fruit. They then are aged for years in oak barrels I had brought from France. The outcome is most satisfactory." He drained his goblet and titled the bottom in an outward gesture for it to be refilled by the steward then called for silence, "Pray, excuse me my Lords, it is time to offer a toast to our guests." He rose from his seat and faced his guests.

He held his cup high while speaking, "Hail and welcome good lords, ladies, kindred, friends and most honored guests to our humble feast. We are gathered here to celebrate and honor these three visitors to our shores who have come to us over rough seas from Cilicia, our valued neighbor.

"To add to that honor, we are joined by our island's good Emperor, Emperor Komnenus." he held his glass up, turned toward Dyfen, Isley and Dover then turned back.

"We bid you welcome to our home and table. May we share in an excellent meal and find comfort in fellowship. We drink and wish them 'A life of honor!'" he drank deeply from his goblet.

The toast was returned as 'A life of honor!' echoed throughout the hall. "and now Holy Father Papakian will say grace over our table."

A priest dressed completely in black arose from the main table and said a blessing while all bent their heads and made the sign of the cross in the orthodox fashion, touching thumb and first two fingers together to touch his forehead, mid stomach, left side of his chest and then the right side ending with a flat hand touching his breastbone and uttering, "Amen."

The end of the prayer was a signal for all manner of roasted meats to appear at the tables on skewers and platters. Fish of all varieties were served, accompanied by roasted vegetables native to the island.

While dining, Lord Esper leaned toward Dyfen expressing interest in his background. He spoke in Armenian. 'I am told that in actuality you hail from a small island off the coast of Cilicia called Moon Isle or in the Armenian tongue known as Lusni Khgzin. Your family has quite a reputation for the quality of their horses. In particular, I have heard of the outstanding abilities of their war horses. I have always hoped to have such a horse. Only the very wealthy can afford them," he laughed.

"You speak Armenian, Lord Esper?" Dyfen asked interested that he knew his mother's native tongue.

"There is a large Armenian population here on Cyprus as well as Greek, it is a necessity to speak the languages," he replied. "Many Armenian and Greek traditions have come with them," Rylan stated. "And as you know, many French traditions are here as well through intermarriage of the royal houses, just as the Romaioi have done. In fact, our 'good' Emperor's departed wife was a Princess of Armenia, Land of the Cross. The crusaders would have no chance without the support and supplies furnished by the Cilicians, the only Christian nation in a sea of unbelievers since the year 301 of Our Lord." Lord Esper raised his cup to Dyfen in salute, "Many have tried but none have succeeded to take their faith from the People of the Cross," and then added, "by force or otherwise."

"Very true, and they have paid dearly for it as well," Dyfen agreed.

"My mother's family hales from the foothills of Armenia. Her maiden name is Chaverdian and her family has been known for horse breeding for generations back. When she married my father, her parents gifted them the land on Moon Isle to start their own breeding program. It has become quite well known as Cilicia is the hub of all trade, bridging the east with the west.

"We raise our horses as if they are part of the family and they perform better for it. We instill in them confidence and trust in people so that they will always do what is asked of them no matter how frightened they may be. They are warriors in every sense. On the battlefield they have proven themselves loyal, steadfast, and unshakeable amid savage fighting. They can be trusted by their riders."

"None can say otherwise as to the importance of a brave horse with a good mind. Many a soldier has been saved by his mount," Rylan agreed nodding. "Where were you taking your horses before you were waylaid here?"

"My brothers and I were on our way to Jaffa, sire. Lord Spalding Dove is expecting us," Dyfen answered without detail. He glanced upward as he spoke to avoid eye contact.

Unbeknownst to them, above on the mezzanine a shadow sat behind the decorative wooden screen in the mashrabiya watching the activity below. Emlyn had bullied Jinol into allowing her to sit in a chair to watch the festivities.

She still experienced pain in the injured limb but the potion had Mim made took the edge off. She sat in darkness and silence. Emlyn's eyes were focused on Dyfen as he spoke to her father. She could hear nothing above the music and noise of people conversing. She watched his face as he spoke. She noticed how he ran his thumb down the side of his jaw while her father was speaking. The way his face became serious with intentness. The way his eyes brightened and how he grinned when he spoke.

She wondered what the conversation was about and if her name and entered into it. She would ask her father the next day when he came to see her. She even imagined the stranger with eyes the color of the sea had looked up and smiled at her.

As tradition called, for there was an intermission after the meat course and the musicians were playing a lively tune Dyfen recognized as a folk song taught to them by their mother. He turned his head to face forward and saw Dover standing in the middle of the floor calling out to him and Isley. He had a slack smile on his face that signaled that Dover had enjoyed too much wine. Dyfen walked toward Dover to fetch him back to the table and met with Isley who had the same idea.

Suddenly the music picked up and Dover's feet started moving as he clutched Dyfen and Isley by placing an arm over each shoulder forming a line. Dyfen tried to break away but Dover's grip on his shoulder would require making a scene and both he and Isley knew better than to try to reason with an inebriated Dover in public.

Eryk was walking by with Hugo when Isley grabbed them both and pulled them into line. "We are not doing this alone," he said to them. The five of them took a minute to syncopate their step when they were joined by four additional men. The rhythm of the drums and the melody of the tune had their feet stepping in time with the pulse.

People were surrounding them clapping in rhythm to the beat. Some maidens formed a line and positioned themselves facing the men and the lines danced in unison. Ruizzon de Lusignan placed herself in front of Hugo who smiled at her with good nature.

Mareya had chosen to station herself in front of Isley who was secretly delighted. She had a practiced grace in her movements. Her eyes stayed fixed on Isley's. He blushed at the attention shown him. Emlyn observed the boldness of the Emperor's daughter with interest from above.

"I pray to Our Lord that your ways are more winning than those of your brother's, sire," Mareya jested to Isley.

"You speak of the donkey dancing at my side, do you not, Lady Mareya?" Isley's eyes twinkled as he spoke, and his head lightly tilted to the side towards Dover. He was pleased at the attention she paid him.

"The exact one, Lord Standen," she smiled looking at Dover who was so engaged in the dance he was oblivious to what was happening around him.

"I cannot claim surprise my Lady but most maidens ignore his oafish ways and hear only the sweet words he speaks from what some see as his handsome appearance."

"I am not a milkmaiden that he can win favor with mere words and an attractive exterior. I seek more." Mareya was smiling sweetly.

Isley smiled back in return. Dover had met his match, he thought with a wide grin.

When the music stopped, they all stood making merry about each person's dancing ability. "When they returned your boots had they shrunk?" Dover jested to Dyfen.

"Nay, I received a proper boot for each foot even though my dancing may not have suggested as much," Dyfen chuckled in good nature.

As the music started again, everyone went back to their seats or got in line to dance. Dyfen started to head back to the table when he saw Dover pushing Isley toward the musicians. He went over to see what was happening and he heard Dover provoking Isley.

"Oh come, Isley. We have not heard you sing in an age. Indulge us," Dover coaxed.

"Hail, fellow. You there, with the duduk. Let my friend borrow it for a bit. You can take a rest. I will treat you to some excellent wine while you wait."

The musician did not need to offer twice. He pushed the instrument into Isley's hands and left the dais they stood upon. Dover looked back at Isley who stood slightly breathless from dancing, eyeing the remaining musicians with a dazed expression.

"Do you have a tune you prefer, Lord?" the musician holding a dumbeg asked uncomfortably.

"What if he is a poor player and perhaps even tuneless?" the qunan player whispered to the man next to him in a worried voice.

"He is an honored guest of my Lord. Play your own instrument with greater enthusiasm then. Perhaps, he will not be heard," the oud player instructed sternly.

The musicians all returned to their positions and looked at Isley for guidance.

Isley responded by asking them to play a favorite tune of his mother's. He asked, "Are you acquainted with it?"

"We know it well and have played it many times, my Lord," the oud player bowed and answered. "My name is Haig", he held up his instrument as he spoke. "This is Carnig," pointing to the man with the dumbeg, "and Hagop on the dhol." The other musicians merely nodded in his direction.

Isley stood in front of the musicians in a relaxed way and nodded his head and started the first few notes on the duduk. The others followed. The duduk sent out melodious, haunting notes. The great hall had excellent acoustics. After the first bar, Isley put the instrument down by his side and started to sing. His deep and sonorous voice filled the hall. All conversation ceased and people turned to watch him. Maidens turned their heads toward Isley whose tall, strong body was illuminated in the torch lights, moving with the music as he sang. His hair shone and his green eyes sparkled as he sang the familiar words that he had learned from Fairkene, his adoptive mother, whom he loved so well. He honored her by learning her favorite songs of her homeland. The musicians all looked at each other in surprise and, smiling, played with renewed enthusiasm. They brought the song to an end as people cheered in appreciation.

Rylan turned to Dyfen and asked, "Where did Isley learn such a song, he is not Armenian?"

"My mother used to sing Armenian songs of her childhood to us as boys. She raised Isley from a child and he has great affection for her. Even as a boy he would always do things to please her and make her smile. I sometimes think her affection for him exceeds that for Dover and myself. They have always had a special connection," Dyfen smiled with happiness as he spoke of his mother.

As the song ended, maidens surrounded Isley, engaging him in conversation.

Dover moved over to the group and patted Isley on the back. "Well done, Isley. I taught him well. He was an exceptional student," Dover explained to the ladies who were showing their admiration for Isley, transferring the attention to himself.

Isley took the opportunity to make his way through the crowd to where Mareya was standing off to the side talking to her father, the Emperor. She glanced his way and Isley smiled at her broadly as he made a path towards her.

Her father, His Grace Komnenus, was about to object when a servant came to inform him of a matter that required his attention. He turned to leave.

When Isley reached Mareya, she put her hand out for him to kiss. "You are most gifted Lord Standen," she said.

"You overpraise me, my lady. Pray call me Isley," Isley said looking her directly in the eyes as he bent to place his lips on her soft hand. His eyes sparkled at the compliment from this beautiful maiden and his face flushed only partly from the heat in the room.

"Not at all, …ahh Isley. Your voice has a wonderous timbre. I am in earnest," she stated with a blush rising up her neck. She noticed he still held her hand in his.

Mareya gently started slipping her hand from Isley's big grasp, but he was not letting go. "Lord Standen, you seem to have captured my hand," she remarked.

"If only it were your heart, dear lady," Isley said blushing at his own boldness so uncharacteristic of himself, he realized he may have overindulged in drink. His eyes still locked on hers, he bowed his head and loosened her hand.

Mareya turned a deep shade of rose with pleased embarrassment as her hand dropped to her side.

Isley, embarrassed by now, decided to remove himself. "Lady Mareya, I am afraid my head spins a little from drink. Please excuse me, I must leave to take the air." He bowed to her and started to leave.

She impulsively blurted out, "Do you wish for company? I too, would like to take in cooler air."

He was taken by surprise and did not know how to respond. "I would surely enjoy your company my Lady, but I fear it to be improper without a chaperone. I only plan to stay long enough to clear the cloud in my head." He started to leave again.

"Lord Standen, Isley. Wait. My father would never approve even with a chaperone because he does not know you," she stopped and then made a brash decision, "but I will accompany you out of doors for a short while. You must promise to return me before father notices my absence."

Isley could see that he would not be able to leave without insulting her and he liked her too much to chance that.

She hurried on, "I have several chaperones with me. Let me summon my maid who stands just there." She pointed to an older woman standing a few feet away. She signaled the woman to come to her.

"You have wanted of me, mylady?" she asked Mareya. She was a stout woman of uncertain age.

"Yes, Edrys. Please accompany Lord Standen and I out to the garden," she commanded.

Edrys bowed her head and followed behind Mareya and Isley as they left the hall and made their way out to the walled garden. The night air was cool and refreshing after the heat of the hall. Isley could feel his head clear.

Back at the table, Dyfen rose to make his way to the garderobe. He had consumed a considerable amount of spirits and had a need to relieve himself. "If you will excuse me, Lord Esper, I have something to attend to."

On his way to the garderobe, he met Gracyn who stepped in front of him stopping his forward movement and said, "Whetherly, I wish to speak to you."

"Oh yes, I recall. What have you to say?" Dyfen returned in an irritated manner. "I was just on my way to the garderobe and really have no time for a conversation."

Lord Rend seemed not to hear him, "I admire your stallions greatly. They are the best coursers I have seen in many years. Intelligent, energetic with stamina. I see they travel easily under sail as well. What is your price?"

"My stallions are not for sale, Lord Rend. They are my personal mounts."

"Every horse has its price, surely," Gracyn countered smiling in a friendly way that did not seem natural to him.

"In this case, they do not," Dyfen replied shortly. "Pray excuse me as I have important business to attend to". He continued past him leaving Gracyn open-mouthed.

He traveled down a short hall to find the garderobe occupied. Spotting a staircase nearby he traveled up the steps quickly and located the nearest garderobe, opened the door, and stepped inside, closing the door behind him.

In the evening cool of the garden outside the castle, Edrys decided to stroll a few paces away, giving Isley and Mareya a measure of privacy. Isley guessed that this was not the first time she provided the guise of oversight while providing her mistress with some space.

Mareya leaned against the garden wall resting herself against its rough surface and enjoyed the escape from the heat inside. She looked at the man before her appreciatively. He was tall and winsome yet completely lacking in vanity. His long brown hair was tied back from his handsome face. Eyes the color of forest ferns looked at her softly. His mouth was beautifully shaped in a manly way with strong lips outlined against a chiseled jaw. She impetuously moved her face up to meet his and kissed him solidly on those lips, taking him by surprise. She knew he was unsteady with drink but did not care. Isley, startled by the action, moved slightly away from her.

"Lady Komnenus, you owe me no affection. I invited you out of doors selfishly for your company, not to lure you away from protective eyes. Lord Esper's grapes are more powerful than I supposed." He looked at her intently trying to read her thoughts hoping she did not view him as a lout taking advantage her.

She looked up at him with her bottomless, dark eyes and a wave of desire swept over him. He was able to hold it in check until she reached up and wrapped her arms around his shoulders, arching her back so that the tips of her breasts grazed his chest. Isley steadied himself by placing a large hand against the wall on either side above her head. Holding his body back from hers. Hoping he would be able to control his want.

"We must go back," he stated, pushing himself back and away from her. "I need to regain my presence of mind, Lady Mareya. I honor you too greatly to sully your reputation. Let us go, now." With that, he removed her arms from his neck while giving her such a passionate look that she saw pain there. It melted her heart. She had no defense against that unguarded look and knew from it he would suffer if he felt he had compromised her in any way.

She rallied herself out of the moment. "Lord Standen, you are a man of great integrity and kindness. I will never forget your courtly behavior this evening. Although it pains my heart, we will listen to caution and save my virtue," she joked. She lightly touched his face as she walked by him, smiling gently to herself.

Edrys seeing her mistress leaving started back toward them.

Isley took a deep breath, closed his eyes, and bolstered himself enough to follow her and leave this space he so wanted them to stay in. He knew he was smitten.

When Dyfen reopened the garderobe door and stepped out, Hugo was leaning against the wall waiting for him. Looking more himself than he had the day before.

"The facility is yours," Dyfen quipped as he closed the door behind him.

"I am not here for the facility," Hugo snapped.

"What is your business here then?" Dyfen asked.

"I noted your journey toward the stairs and sought to ensure you returned safely from whence you came, this castle is a labyrinth and I feared you might lose yourself within it, Whetherly," Hugo said with a stern expression.

"Do not bother pretending concern for myself, Hugo. Although, I thank you for your attention to my wellbeing, I am capable of finding my path back," Dyfen spoke as he started to move past Hugo who stepped out in front of him to block his path. "Is not your charming auburn-haired companion missing your company?" he shot at Hugo brushing him aside. "Move yourself," Dyfen commanded.

"Ruizzon de Lusignan is none of your concern, Whetherly," he spat. "Move me then, if you think it possible. You have no dogs to offset the balance now," Hugo taunted.

"Enough. Enough of your games Rend. Remove yourself from my path before I do it for you."

Hugo shoved Dyfen backwards into the stone wall and placed a strong left hand at his throat and squeezed. "I move for no man, Whetherly. Especially not you!" He was stronger than he looked, Dyfen thought, and much more fluid in his movement.

"You cannot mean that Rend." Dyfen used his left hand to grab the arm that was choking him, by the wrist. He pushed Hugo's elbow into a lock position with his right hand and pushed it forward making Hugo bend at the waist. Dyfen brought his right knee up into Hugo's face causing him to fall to the floor, saying, "And apparently… you do not."

Dyfen walked off leaving Hugo behind him. He ignored the stairs and headed down a familiar hallway. He could hear the music and cacophony from below. The smoke and smell of roasted game wafted upward into the gallery.

Walking a few paces, he saw a figure seated in a mashrabiya intently looking downward, face illuminated only by the reflection of light from the great hall below.

He nodded in recognition to Jinol who was standing stiffly at the opposite wall and put a finger up to his mouth to silence her. She relaxed her body into the wall.

"Enjoying the view, Lady Emlyn?" he said from behind her.

Emlyn looked up with a worried expression on her face which turned to relief at the sight of him.

"What is so imperative that you would leave a celebration in your honor?" a smooth male voice spoke.

Dyfen was startled. He had just heard that same voice a few hours ago. A figure was standing in shadow across from where Emlyn was seated.

The Duc de Marche appeared very comfortable. He held a goblet in his long, elegant hand. Dyfen noted that he wore his fingernails slightly longer than was customary and that their surface appeared very smooth. Probably polished with levigated clay, Dyfen thought to himself.

Emlyn looked uneasy. Dyfen sensed that she was uncomfortable in the present company. Remembering his conversation with Rylan, decided a course of action to remove her from the presence of Raoul, Duc de Marche was needed.

"Lady Emlyn, you were to remain in your chamber by physician restriction," he scolded her. "Allow me to return you there. I am certain His Grace, Duc de Marche, will excuse you as he cares only for your better health."

He saw her move slightly in her seat. Without turning around, she spoke, "I thank you Lord Whetherly. I admit that I am weary and fully accept your offer."

The Duc de Marche fixed Dyfen with an inscrutable look.

"Please forgive me, Lady Emlyn. It was not my intent to withhold you from rest. I fear my desire to warm myself in your company overtook my better judgement." He bowed low before her.

"You will excuse us then," Dyfen spoke. Ignoring the Duc de Marche, he bent down to pick Emlyn up in his arms to carry her back to her chamber. He could feel the softness of her curves against him as he walked away with her.

Jinol who was trailing behind them looked back to see the Duc de Marche with his eyes narrowed looking at Dyfen's back.

Dyfen pushed the heavy wooden chamber door open with his shoulder and strode over the threshold through the solar, past the arches toward the plush bed with its heavily carved bedposts.

He was still slightly drunk, and the nearness of her scented hair made him inhale deeply as he slowly lowered her to the soft cushioned mattress with its sky-blue and white trappings. Jinol arranged the pillows to make Emlyn more comfortable and settled in the chair nearby.

Dyfen moved in front of Emlyn and looked down into her face. "How are you faring, Emlyn. Are you still enduring pain from your wound?" his voice was low and raspy. His eyes scanned her while awaiting her response when he noted a faint scratch, barely visible at the bottom of her throat, trailing down to her bosom.

"Emlyn, do you suffer from some rash? I note the scratch upon your neck. Is the discomfort causing you to scratch? I shall have Jinol summon Dr. Chikaris."

Her eyes met his gaze but her mind was elsewhere. de Marche had come seeking her, finding her alone in the mashrabiya. He had leaned toward her in the dimness and placed his index finger at the base of her throat and dragged it down to right above her cleavage. His face so close to hers she could smell the strong drink on his breath.

She could still feel the sharpened nail lightly scraping the surface of her skin. "You have a flawless complexion Lady Emlyn. One can barely keep from touching.," he murmured.

"I mean you no disrespect. Future events will prove that is not my intent. I may be placing a wagon before the donkey, that is all." His dark eyes were filled with desire.

She had been feeling uncomfortable with his suggestive behavior and was uncertain as to what action to take, when to her relief, Dyfen had arrived and de Marche backed away as if nothing had happened.

She dared not speak of it to anyone fearful it may lead to a confrontation. The Duc de Marche was known for his skill with a blade. She dared not risk Dyfen's safety nor that of her family. She knew her father and brother would be incensed and take action.

She came back to the present and responded, "I am well, Dyfen. Truly, I am. My good physician left a portion of willow bark and cloves with Mim who keeps a pot brewing day and night. Jinol makes sure my cup is always filled. It helps to manage the pain."

She waved a partially filled goblet from the tray next to her bed. "I fear I may be allergic to some component of it." She forced herself to sound cheerful, worried he would guess the truth. She feigned a shiver as an excuse to pull her shawl over her shoulders to cover the scrape.

"Perhaps I should bring my farrier tools next visit to file your nails," he joked. Looking down at her hands, he saw that her nails were trimmed short but recalled someone else's who were not.

He tilted his head. "How did you say you gained that scratch?" His eyes narrowed in suspicion. Then they grew large with realization as his mind's eye traveled back to a girl he once knew and his chest visibly expanded, the beginning of anger.

"I will have his worthless head! Only God can save him now." Dyfen ground his teeth while he spoke, "Did he lay hands on you?" He looked to her for an answer.

She was almost too frightened to answer. "What could you mean?" she managed to ask. She looked toward Jinol who was too petrified to move.

"That scratch upon your bosom. Where did you say it came from?" He arched his brows waiting for her response.

None came and he headed for the door, his hand on his sword hilt.

"Stop!" Emlyn shouted. "Why do you care so?" she asked. "It is but a scratch."

"I have my reasons," Dyfen looked to her for an answer.

"It was my ring! I gave myself the scratch. The setting is at fault." She had quickly reached for the blue stone ring on the table next to her bed and pushed it onto her finger while his back was still turned.

"Regard this", she held up her hand. "The setting is faulty. Please calm yourself for God's love."

"Let me see that ring, Emlyn." He held his hand out to her. "If you are protecting that son of the devil, I will slaughter him where he stands. I swear it," Dyfen voice was seething and his palm was facing upward ready to accept the ring.

Emlyn pulled the ring from her finger and dropped it into his extended hand.

Dyfen looked at it carefully and saw that part of the setting was uneven. It was possible it could scratch. He handed it back to her.

"You are speaking the truth? Tell me. You swear it to be God's truth?" he was watching her reaction.

She said a silent prayer asking the Lord's forgiveness for the lie she was about to tell, "Yes, it is God's truth! I swear it!"

As she spoke, she saw his eyes were focused across the solar. The echo of fast approaching footsteps could be heard and caused him to stiffen his shoulders. He walked to the solar where he was met by Hugo, who shoved him with full force into the trestle table.

"The very thing I knew you would do Whetherly. The very thing. What brings you to the lady's suite? You have no business here. I want you to leave. Now!" Hugo's words were more hissed than spoken.

"If you have the means to make me, then use them," Dyfen said in an even tone, staring at Hugo's hardened face. His own rage still present from his conversation with Emlyn.

Hugo pulled out his dagger and pointed it toward Dyfen's throat.

"Rend, return your dagger to its place and leave before you hurt yourself."

"Hurt to myself should not be your primary concern at this time, Whetherly," Hugo was smirking now.

"Oddly enough, it is. Based on your past performance I do not expect this to end any differently," Dyfen taunted.

"I underestimated you in the past, that is true. I have since reset my course." Hugo moved forward with the dagger as Dyfen backed up.

"It is to be then." Dyfen stepped forward to meet Hugo's dagger, drawing his own.

"Lord Whetherly. Dyfen. Pray stop!" Dyfen pulled up and looked at Emlyn who was tensely leaning forward.

He lowered his dagger hand with a look of offense on his face. Emlyn feared Dyfen still held residual anger at the Duc de Marche and what that anger would do to Hugo.

"Stop, you say. To me?" He looked crestfallen. He was insulted.

"Yes," she confirmed.

"May I ask why? I am not the aggressor here. Have you forgotten that this bastard tried to kill my dogs? Kill Cydryn! That you suffer now only because of his actions? For any one of those things I could choke the life out of him without a second thought," he said gritting his teeth.

"Hugo ..." she started to say. She recalled their conversation and her promise to him with some confusion and was conflicted on what to say next.

"She fears for my safety, Whetherly. Is it not obvious? Although she has no need to do so, I am gratified by her devotion." Hugo was smirking.

"Dyfen, please go," Emlyn pled, exhausted from the prior drama. She was looking back and forth between Hugo and Dyfen and just wanted peace.

Seeing Emlyn intercede on Hugo's behalf escalated Dyfen's anger for some reason and he brazenly brandished his dagger toward Rend who was standing at ease in front of him. "I promise you, Rend, she is right in her concern for you. You deserve to be punished for all of the troubles you have wrought."

"Oh, Whetherly, you are so mistaken in this," Hugo said grinning, ignoring the point of the dagger swinging back and forth at his neck.

"Lord Whetherly, I asked that you leave," Emlyn ordered again.

Dyfen was burning with frustration but sheathed his dagger and shouldered Hugo out of his path roughly. He cast a glaring eye at Emlyn as he did it.

"I take my leave as commanded. You may keep the company you prefer, Lady Emlyn," he said with sarcasm, bowing to her. His face took on the look of stone as he moved out of the door and down the hallway without looking back. His eyes were on fire as he dwelt on the insult Emlyn had just paid him.

The Duc de Marche was nowhere to be seen.

Back in the solar, Hugo leaned against the wall eyeing Emlyn whose eyelids had closed, reopening them to look at him with an annoyed stare.

He walked toward her, his eyes upon her neck. "How did you come by that mark?" he asked. "Were you alone with de Marche?" he asked.

Emlyn looked confused at this question coming from Hugo and fell back to the answer she had given Dyfen.

"I did it. One of the prongs on my ring twisted when I fell that day in the stable."

She held her hand up with the ring back in place. "It abraded my skin when I attempted to relieve an itch. Those potions must be causing dryness." She could see him relax with the explanation and the visual of the ring. She wondered why he had brought up de Marche. He had not seen de Marche with her as Dyfen had.

He moved out into the hallway where his men had just arrived. He dropped his head and shook it in disgust, "You are late."

Back in the great hall, Dyfen met Isley, who had returned indoors and had been seeking him. He approached the staircase as Dyfen descended. "Is all well, Dyfen?"

"Yes, fully," Dyfen said with a forced smile. "Come. Let us resume our merriment. Where might Dover be?" he said as they walked off together shoulder to shoulder.

Chapter 13

After the Feast

Dyfen and Isley, each suffering from their own frustrations, exchanged stories of the night and imbibed heavily while doing so. Hours later, it was almost dawn when the brothers finally took their leave.

Dyfen, Dover and Isley ambled back to the stable to check on the horses before seeking much needed rest. All were very worn with the lateness of the hour. Isley was quiet as was his way while Dover still chattered about the events of the night. Dyfen barely listened to him while his mind was taken up by his encounter with Emlyn and Hugo earlier in the evening.

When they arrived at the stable Dyfen went over to Arazi and Zakar who whinnied as they caught scent of him. Cydryn and his brothers arose from lying down and greeted Dyfen with whimpers. "Hello, my sons," he told them touching each dog's nose. He grabbed oats from a bucket and hand fed the horses. "How fares our mighty stallions?"

"Have they given you any trouble this eve, my lads?" he asked the dogs. He gently stroked each horse's forehead as they pushed into his hand.

Down the aisle he noticed one of Emlyn's attendants dozing in a standing position against the stable wall and heard voices speaking in hushed tones nearby.

Curious, he walked down the way and was surprised to espy Emlyn in a box stall seated on a stool. She was stroking a darkly dappled mare's neck, speaking in a gentle tone, Firah.

She was wearing a loosely fitting green shift with a scoop neckline. Her unbound hair trailed down her back.

Standing on the other side of the horse was Kellis who had the mare's upturned hoof in his hands examining it.

They both turned to the doorway as the mare looked toward the approaching Dyfen with her ears pointed forward.

"Can I be of assistance?" he asked the groom ignoring Emlyn.

"Hail sire", Kellis greeted Dyfen grinning in recognition. "We thought she had bruised her foot with her escape, but it proves to be something more. She has heat in her hoof and suffers great pain, unwilling to bear her weight upon it.

"My instructions were to send word to Lady Emlyn if Firah suffered injury. I wanted to wait until daylight but…." he offered the apology for troubling his Lady.

"I am sure you did right, Kellis. Lady Emlyn would want to know if her favorite suffered." Dyfen's eyes went to Emlyn, but she did not look up.

"Firah has had much excitement these past few days." He was eyeing the mare critically to assess her level of comfort. "shat geghets'ik aghjik" ("very pretty girl)", he crooned to her.

"Ayo" ("yes"), Kellis returned grinning.

"Kellis, you speak Armenian then?"

"Very little, sire but I do know when a pretty girl is being mentioned," Kellis grinned.

Dyfen returned the grin. "Allow me to examine her then," he said.

He walked through the stall door and moved to stand by the horse's head as Kellis moved aside. The mare was not putting her full weight upon the hoof in question.

Dyfen put his hand over the hoof and could feel the heat Kellis spoke of. He grabbed a lantern off of a hook on the wall and lifted the mare's hoof turning the bottom upward looking for the black areas he knew he would see.

"She has infection within the hoof," he said letting go of it.

"Kellis hold her head up," he directed.

Kellis moved to the front of the horse taking hold of the rope halter.

Dyfen pulled a short dagger from his boot. He placed the tip of the knife into the lantern fire to disinfect it. He turned his back to the horse, firmly grasped the fetlock bringing it between his legs. He turned the hoof upward and rested it upon his knee.

"Hold her steady Kellis," he directed Kellis tightening his grip on the pastern.

"Lady Emlyn, will you please hold this lantern, just here?" he said emotionlessly, showing her the level he needed it held at.

Emlyn lifted her hand and took the lantern Dyfen was holding out. She remained silent and Dyfen did not look at her.

The lantern cast a yellow light onto the hoof, illuminating the blackened spot in the frog. Dyfen inserted the point of his dagger into the infected spot and twisted in a circular motion allowing pus to stream out of the wound.

"There," he said to Kellis as he returned the knife to his boot. "This should lessen her pain. She is feeling much better for it. Kellis, bring a bucket of sea water and place her hoof into it to clear the pus. Dry the hoof with clean cloth and pack it with honey. Wrap it with clean cloth sealing it with bees' wax and repeat this twice each day for five days. She will be fine. Limit her movement to a small bit of grassy land and do not set her to work until she is comfortable putting her full weight upon that hoof."

Kellis picked up a bucket, slightly swinging it as he left for the beach to fill it with sea water.

Dyfen started to walk away exhausted from the night. "Dyfen!" he heard her call his name. "Pray spare me a word."

He slowly pivoted to face her tear-streaked face.

"My thanks to you, Dyfen. This is twice you have helped Firah, my poor girl," Emlyn said softly with glistening eyes. The stress of the evening's events weighed heavily upon her as well.

"Emlyn," Dyfen spoke with concern in his eyes, all sting from the slight he experienced earlier forgotten. "Do not trouble yourself. The injury is very treatable and will heal within days." He tried to comfort her.

"My tears are not for Firah," she spoke with a look of anguish on her face. "I fear I offended you earlier this eve." She looked at him expectantly, searching his face.

Dyfen looked away and causally answered, "You expressed concern for someone you value and greatly care for. It is most natural. As much as I detest the man, I cannot take offense for your desire that no ill befall him."

It had become more complicated than she knew how to explain. In the end, she said nothing.

"Very well then, I have it in my understanding. No need to speak upon it. Rend is most fortunate to have your high regard because it was my intention to do him harm, in that you were very right," he spoke firmly then started toward the door with an air of unconcern.

Seeing him leave, she became agitated and tried to rise from her chair. Her leg buckled beneath her and she cried out in pain.

Dyfen moved swiftly across the short distance to her. "Lady Emlyn. We agreed you would stay off that leg, did we not?" He moved behind Emlyn to support her around the waist with his left arm pulling her against his chest to take the weight off her leg.

From his vantage point above her it was unavoidable to see his turquoise pendent resting between the soft swell of her breasts. Her proximity brought the scent of roses which emanated from her skin. He felt his senses overwhelming him.

Without thought, his right hand pushed her long, silky hair aside while pulling her gown off her shoulder, clutching the fabric in his hand. She could feel the heat of his body on her back.

His mind cloudy from the long day, he lowered his lips until they rested on the smooth slope of her shoulder and inhaled deeply. The scent of her filled his weary head. He closed his eyes and sighed so intensely she could feel his chest shudder beneath.

He felt his manhood stiffen against his will, falling forward with its weight on his breeches, charging his exhausted body. "Emlyn," he spoke softly, his eyes still closed.

 His tongue traveled slowly over her collarbone, his lips moved over the top line of her shoulder, and he felt her body quiver in response.

Emlyn felt his braid brush against her back, tickling as he moved his mouth over her. She heard his earring tinkle in her ear as he moved his head.

Caught up in the moment and seeking relief from the evening's sordid events, she unconsciously grabbed his braid with her right hand and pulled his head further down over her shoulder until his lips touched the rise of her breast. The side of his face next to hers. She squeezed her eyes closed and opened her mouth, breathing shallowly.

As he stroked her shoulder his right hand started moving downward gently tracing the scratch that lay there. The neckline of her gown had gaped so that he could see her erect nipple. He quickly looked away but it was too late.

Dyfen felt his shaft ache. He let out a deep groan. He had not felt such heat and desire in many years. His tired body could not resist the pull and his weary mind did not wish to.

Emlyn could feel his warm breath upon her shoulder. It held the fruity fragrance of the wine he had that night. She felt the roughness of his beard on her bare skin making her body tingle. The scent of his skin was of fresh sea air. Her reaction was not lost on Dyfen. He could feel his own body shiver in response.

"Emlyn," he gasped involuntarily into her ear.

"Dyfen," she whispered in response.

Hearing her voice speak his name sobered him.

Dyfen lifted his head and slowly moved away, pulling the shoulder of her gown into place. The pang of desire snuffed out as he gently lowered her back onto the stool.

As he snapped back to reality he was shocked at his behavior. He was very tired and still under the influence of considerable drink he had consumed throughout the evening.

He averted his eyes as he spoke, "Lady Emlyn, I beg your forgiveness. I am afraid that I have betrayed your trust and the trust your father has so wrongly placed in me." He turned away wanting to escape from her presence.

"I trust you, Dyfen."

"Well, maybe you should not," he advised her bruskly.

Emlyn tried to speak but he cut off her words.

"It is good that we set sail today. You need not set eyes upon me again," his words were uttered in self-loathing. He just wanted to get away. He assumed she wanted the same. His face was a stony look of calm reserve as he quickly left the stall.

She watched him exit, exhaling. Her leg ached and her body and mind were fatigued. She felt more embarrassed by his rejection of her than ashamed.

He had been clearly drunk and very tired. Dyfen Whetherly was obviously quite practiced in intimacy and had behaved out of instinct. She was keenly aware of the many maidens within her own household who purposely put themselves in his path hoping to catch his eye. Only the good Lord knew how often he acted upon those invitations.

She leaned her weary head onto Firah as she stroked the mare's shoulder.

Dyfen closed the stall door behind him and let out a deep sigh. He had behaved as if she were an alehouse wench, he chided himself.

He headed down the aisle with his head spinning. He was drained in both body and mind.

The servant was still waiting where he had last seen him. "Your Lady awaits you. Attend to her," he said curtly to make sure Emlyn was taken back to her chamber safely.

He could not trust himself to do it while still under the spell of drink. Nor could he face her again, in any case. He wondered what had happened to his self-control. Control he had always been able to assert in the past. Gently refusing the advances of maidens desiring to submit themselves to him if he had been willing. He had not been willing though. Which is why he was so troubled by recent events. He shook all thoughts from his blurred mind and continued down the aisle to his straw bed next to Isley and Dover who were fast asleep.

Where there had once been only straw, he saw coverlets with down pillows for each of them, Dover had two. More servant girl acquaintances his brother had cultivated, he thought to himself wearily.

He dropped down without bothering to wash or remove his clothing, resting the side of his head upon his arm. As he closed his eyes something vaguely troubled him about the scratches Emlyn bore but the faint scent of Damascus rose upon his shirt sleeve filled his head. "Lord, God, please deliver me from temptation," he murmured as he drifted off to sleep.

Chapter 14

Horse Thief

Dyfen, Isley and Dover arose groggily the next day hung over, to the sound of Avak, Tyber, Aubryn and Osyn howling. The noise was loud and was emanating from somewhere close by. Isley ran to the feed room where the grain was stored for the horses. He opened the door and four dogs shot out, speeding past him out into the stable yard. Dyfen hurriedly went to check on the horses and only Arazi was in his stall. Cydryn was missing as well.

"Dover! Isley! Zakar is missing and so is Cydryn," Dyfen cried out.

"To arms and follow the dogs! They will not have traveled far," Dyfen yelled as he nimbly jumped onto Arazi's back and gave him free rein to follow the dogs.

They passed the pack who were running flat out in the direction of a far part of the pasturelands. The air echoed with Cydryn's deep bark and fervent growl.

When they reached Cydryn they saw a limp body up against the stone wall of the winter stable. Zakar was a short distance away standing on three legs. His long, graceful, silver neck was down, and he was snorting in obvious pain. A rope halter was on his head and a tribal saddle rug had fallen to the ground nearby.

Cydryn's teeth were barred, hackles up and he had murder in his eyes.

"Leave it!" Dyfen commanded.

Cydryn, who normally obeyed immediately, had to be told again. Dyfen repeated the words louder with more intensity, "Cydryn, Leave It!" The dog stopped growling but did not relax his attack stance.

By this time the pack had found them and stood slightly behind Cydryn with menacing glares at the bundle huddling up against the stones. Isley and Dover arrived on borrowed mounts from the stable.

"Who in God's name is this?" Isley asked looking at the man huddled against the wall.

"In God's own name, I do not know nor do I much care at present. You take care of whomever that is while I tend to Zakar," Dyfen stated tersely, walking over to where his injured horse stood.

His silver coat shimmered in the morning sun showing beads of sweat that had accumulated from stress. The winded stallion's nostrils flared as he regained his breath. He nickered upon seeing his master.

Stroking his neck and murmuring words of comfort to his beloved Zakar, Dyfen stooped down and moved his hands gently over the horse's fetlock joint which was already swollen.

"He has twisted his tendon. I feel heat within his fetlock even now. We need to keep cold water on it to reduce the swelling. Then I will wrap his leg to keep the swelling from moving upward," he said grimly.

"We must tend to him here, in the winter barn. He will not be able walk back to the stable.

"Arazi will stay here as well. I will boil willow bark and rosemary to put in his water so that he remains calm until his leg heals. The dogs and I will remain here.

"Isley, you, and Dover can move into the castle in the meantime to keep an eye on the good Emperor Komnenus. It is obvious that Zakar will not be able to sail until he is mended."

Isley stood over the form the dogs were so focused upon. "Unto God, this bundle of rags no longer breathes. I would hasten to say he has died before we even arrived. Trampled to death," he said. "Dover ride back and take this bag of rags with you. See if anyone recognizes him. Send back Kellis. Dyfen will need him to assist with tending to Zakar. I would like to know how this man managed to waylay the dogs and take Zakar. He obviously was not able to trick Cydryn."

Dyfen was kneeling down before Zakar and pointed to a spot nearby. "He was in quite a lather when I first came upon him. I could see his abductor had a difficult time controlling him. See how the grass nearby has been ripped out by its roots in a large circular pattern? He must have been spinning and twisted his fetlock. He reared. You can see here where two rear hoof prints are the deepest. He has open wounds on his flanks where spurs have been used," Dyfen finished with anger in his voice. "Zakar put up a mighty fight as he was trained to do. I am surprised the thief was able to ride him this far." His face was taut.

Isley stooped to pick up the saddle blanket looking at it carefully as he held it in one hand. "I recognize this pattern. One like it was on the borrowed horse that Lord Esper rode when he came looking for you that day at the church. He said they had borrowed the horses from Gracyn Rend's men at arms."

Dyfen queried, "I wonder. Gracyn Rend was intent on buying Zakar and Arazi. He approached me with an offer last night that I flatly refused. He did not accept it well. Could this devil's son be from his household?"

Dover looked unhappy. He was mounted and getting ready to leave, "Whoever is responsible has caused a delay in our departure. We will not be sailing this day or soon after. Zakar will not be able to walk distances for some time. The swelling in his fetlock may take weeks to reduce."

Dyfen nodded his head in agreement and was glad that he would be away from the castle if they had to remain. Away from being reminded of the pre-dawn moments that took place in the stable.

"I am certain that the good Lady Emlyn will not be saddened to hear of our prolonged stay," his brother mocked still looking grim.

"Dover," Dyfen responded, head down examining Zakar's leg, "I speak in her best interest. Lady Emlyn needs to stay as far the hell away as possible."

"From all of us or just you?"

'Yes." Came the emphatic reply, turning his attention back to Zakar.

Chapter 15

The Problem

Lord Esper sat in the map room looking at the map of the levant his cartographer had newly copied. He was studying the rivers and newly settled towns in Syria with deep interest. There was a knock on the door, and he shouted, "Enter, Eston."

Eston opened the door and put his head in. "Lord, the Duc de Marche wishes a word with you."

"Have him enter, Eston," Rylan responded absently, putting the map aside.

Raoul de Lusignan, the Duc de Marche, walked in with his usual regal bearing and resplendent attire. His navy silks were fastened at the neck with a large, gold broach inset with sapphires and rubies. He had on a heavy gold chain with an eagle medallion inset with the same stones. The middle finger on his left hand sported a large ruby cabochon carved with the same eagle.

"Your Grace," Rylan greeted. "I am honored by your call. What brings me this honor?"

"I would have a word with you, Esper," de Marche stated. "I thank you for your attention. What I must say will not consume a significant amount of your time."

"You pique my interest, Lord Duc," Rylan returned with an intent look on his face, curiously awaiting what this powerful man had come to say to him in private.

"I will go to the mark." He looked directly into Rylan's eyes watching them closely. "It has not escaped your attention that I am fond of your daughter, Emlyn." He hesitated, "It is well past time for me to sire an heir." He revised, "A legitimate heir."

Pausing, he continued, "Your daughter is a most pleasing maiden both in aspect and in manner. In short, I wish to marry her. To be fully clear, I shall marry her," he stated it as a fact not to be argued.

Rylan's mind started to race. He knew Emlyn could never be happy with such a man. His beloved daughter. She would not be pleased. He was not pleased and could not allow it. In the inner circle of nobles, de Lusignan had an unflattering reputation of preferring his maidens unwilling. It was with dread he heard the proposal fall from his lips.

Finally, he spoke the only thing that could think of, "Your grace, I regret that a betrothal cannot be possible. My utmost regret and apologies." He bowed his head. "Emlyn has been newly promised. The contract has been signed by both parties," he said coolly, waiting for a reaction.

De Marche was not phased, "I do not bother to ask the name of this suitor. I care not. Let me remind you, It is an honor I do you, allying your family with my own. I am sure you must see it as well.

"Announcements of the pledge have not been made. I saw no notice posted on the church doors as customary. I would have known of this engagement otherwise.

"I suggest you withdraw from this contract. I am insisting that you rescind your approval, Esper." Raoul had a set smile on his lips, but his eyes were like stones.

Rylan responded with a slow measured speech, "My regrets yet again, Your Grace. I cannot in good conscience deny my given word. It is a matter of honor. Emlyn is spoken for and will remain so. It is done." Rylan stood his ground solidly.

He was worried about what Emlyn would say when she heard of this. He would have to act fast after he ended this conversation with de Marche to procure a groom. A name crossed his mind, he would speak to this man immediately after the Duc de Marche had left. Once Emlyn heard of his reason for committing her to this betrothal, he felt certain she would not object. The alternative was unspeakable.

Raoul, Duc de Marche continued with his demands, "You will renounce this betrothal, Esper. You will tell this…whomever, whatever you consider necessary to accomplish this task. I will generously provide you a fortnight to manage it. You void the marriage contract and, in its stead, invoke one with me," the Duc stated in a steely manner.

"I repeat, I offer your family my name and titles. They come with considerable privilege and distinction. You would be unwise to turn my offer aside. I am sure the Emperor will agree with me upon this if it becomes necessary to involve him. He easily could be moved to take an interest.

"Now, I have another appointment I must attend to. You will consider my request and its consequences," his smile was wide with a hint of menace and with those parting words, the Duc de Marche confidently left the room.

Rylan placed both of his hands on the table before him with braced arms. He must speak to Emlyn right away.

"Eston!" he yelled. Eston appeared in the doorway. He said something to him in a low tone.

Chapter 16

An Invitation

Emlyn was sitting up in bed holding the stone pendant Dyfen had left her, mindlessly running her finger over its smooth surface as she thought of their meeting in the stable. Her fingers felt the coolness of the stone. She was quiet.

"Jinol; consider my wound," Emlyn quizzed Jinol with a certain intensity of purpose. "Do you think the remaining scar will be repulsive? "

Jinol was now perched on the side of the bed surveying Emlyn's leg while she rubbed olive oil mixed with rose water over the scar, working it into her leg.

"You were deeply injured, my lady, but you are young. Mim assured me that this oil will help flatten and lessen the appearance of a scar."

"Do you think a gallant young man would find it disfiguring and hence find me repellent?" Emlyn asked her with a worried look on her gentle face.

"Do you have a particular gallant in mind, my lady?" Jinol asked looking out of the corner of her eye at Emlyn.

"No, no one in particular. But a maiden does tend to dream of her wedding night, true?" Emlyn expressed casually.

"This is the first you have ever broached marriage, my lady. I thought you had naught interest in binding yourself to a man."

"I may reconsider my future, may I not, Jinol?"

"Yes, I am certain, Lady Emlyn. It would bring your father and brother much happiness to know of your interest in becoming wed. Finally.

"To speak of marriage, my cousin has just arrived from Jaffa. She is here to assist my aunt who injured her hand while working in the kitchens," Jinol conveyed.

"She is a servant to Lady Dove and tells of great preparation by the Lord and Lady for the betrothal feast in celebration of their daughter Randall's coming marriage."

"Randall Dove is lovely," Emlyn commented. "She will make a comely bride for any groom."

Emlyn recalled Randall from a visit to Jaffa with her father and Eryk three or so years hence. She was but fourteen as was Randall. "Eryk was quite taken with her even then," Emlyn recalled.

"As I remember, Lord Dove is very fond of the Viking culture. He raised his daughter no differently than her elder brother. Learned in the ways of war. Some may consider this unseemly in a maiden but it permits Randall a wider range of freedom than most maidens will ever know. It left a lasting impression upon me to father's dismay. Shall we be among her guests, I wonder?"

"I am sure of it, Lady Emlyn," Jinol answered. "My cousin spoke of Lady Dove preparing a list of all nobles as far away as Aquitaine. It will be a lavish celebration."

"What of her intended husband?" Emlyn asked, curious to know a suitor inclined to accept such a strong-willed maiden.

Jinol hesitated for a moment, dreading to say, "a Lord from Cilicia, I was told. Pledges were made but a month ago. The eldest son of a Lord Braxton Whetherly."

It took all within her to keep from gasping when the words were spoken. Emlyn felt as if a blow had been landed to her mid-section.

Just then, there was a hard rap at the door and as Emlyn called out to enter, Eston walked in. "My lady, your father asks for your presence in the map room. You are to come immediately."

Chapter 17

The Solution

Lord Esper paced the room in agitation. It was fifteen minutes before the door opened and Emlyn was brought in by Eston. He placed her gently in a chair in front of the table. Rylan leaned to him and whispered in his ear. Eston nodded in understanding and exited the room.

Her father looked at her with a heavy heart. He was not looking forward to this conversation. "Hail, Emlyn. How far you this day?" he said gently looking at her with tenderness.

"What is it, father? Why did Eston come to me in such an urgent manner?" Emlyn asked with concern.

"Emlyn, I lack a painless way to speak this," he bent his head down to focus on the table before him and then raised it again holding her gaze.

"The Duc de Marche came to me today and has asked for your hand in marriage. He is very insistent upon the matter."

Emlyn was taken aback. The shock in her voice communicated her dislike of the idea. "I fear the Duc, father. He makes me uneasy, and I cannot imagine myself bound to him. You did refuse him, I must believe," Emlyn asked expecting him to affirm her words. She gathered the shawl she was wearing closer to her chest. She had made it a point to never be without its company ever since the evening of the feast.

"Emlyn, I cannot merely reject titled nobility as a marriage prospect. I must have a good reason to deny his request. In his sphere, daughters marry to further the family's prospects. He sees himself as a desirable ally for Kyrenia and he is unwilling to accept an unfavorable answer. He told me as much. Not only does he reject 'Nay', but he also expects me to break the contract I have already agreed to in favor of himself. Imagine the colossal confidence the man has," Rylan spoke in frustration.

"What marriage contract do you speak of father? You have promised me to someone?" Emlyn sat stunned and confused.

"Emlyn, I was so taken aback by de Marche's proposal I told him you were already promised as a method to put him off. I did not commit to an actual person. I could hardly think; the man is so intensely overbearing. To offend him would set us at war. A war we may not win due to his powerful alliances. Let me remind you how powerful his family ties are. At some point I must identify the marriage partner. I am considering Hugo Rend to be a distinct possibility. I think Hugo will agree to cooperate. Hugo cares for you. It is apparent to all. None would be surprised by a marriage between the two of you. I could think of no other we can trust."

Emlyn sat speechless. It appeared she was to be married. Hugo's words from the prior day came back to her. His earnest request to be her champion in a time of need. Her pledge to him. She wondered how he would react.

Eston put his head into the room and announced Hugo's entrance, "Lord Rend has arrived, sire."

Rylan watched Hugo as he entered the room. "Be seated, Lord Rend," he said with great seriousness.

"Has some ill befallen Kyrenia, Lord? Your manner is quite grave," Hugo stated his face taking on an equal seriousness.

The Flaming Soul   Doreen Demerjian

"Hugo, I have observed that you are quite fond of my daughter. Would you agree with this?" Rylan queried.

Hugo looked at Emlyn with a questioning look on his face and answered. "Yes. I make no pretense to the contrary. I have always been overly fond of Emlyn," he admitted puzzled.

Emlyn looked away.

"Would you be willing to commit yourself to her? Take her hand in marriage?" Rylan went on.

"Hugo, do not feel the need to agree," Emlyn interjected with some terseness.

Hugo stopped and looked at her steadily. He took a deep breath. She could see his chest tighten and release, and while still holding Emlyn's gaze, he replied,

"Lord Esper, I would consider it my deepest honor to have Emlyn as my wife. Unquestionably and unflinchingly."

He tore his eyes from Emlyn and turned toward her father. "But why do you ask?" He looked confused then a look of shock came across his face. "Has some vile dreg violated her innocence? Did some villain take advantage of her weakened state? Tell me who and I will run him through just before I slit his throat! Whetherly? was it Whetherly? Did that disgusting filth lay hands upon her?"

He stood up and was on his way out of the door to take action before Rylan commanded, "Sit! Back! Down!" And then less stridently, "I have not yet finished."

Hugo retook his seat, but his face was fused with anger.

"Hugo! Hugo!" Rylan shouted to take his attention back. "The Duc de Marche has come to me this day and asked for my daughter's hand in marriage. I could not allow it, for Emlyn's sake, I could not," his speaking was rushed. "The man is a monster. I cannot hand my daughter to such a man," emphasizing the word, 'hand'.

"When he asked, I spoke a mistruth. I told him she was already betrothed. That we had already signed the marriage contract. I did not know what else to say. He was incensed and asked that I set aside the agreement and pledge Emlyn to himself.

"Thus, my need to know. Can I name you? Will you have her with the understanding that you may be challenged by de Marche? I would not ask this of you or anyone unless I was in desperate need," his voice was half apologetic and half pleading. "I am in desperate need."

"Hugo, understand that agreeing to this is no small favor. He may make an attempt on your life. It is not beneath him."

Both Hugo and Rylan were standing now looking at each other.

"Lord Esper," Hugo knelt on one knee putting his right hand over his heart and the left on his sword hilt, "Under God's eyes, I pledge my love for your daughter. I swear to honor her as my wife and I will cut down anyone who tries to interfere with our union, no matter how high or low their station, whomever they may be."

He stood back up and turned to Emlyn outstretching his hand to her.

"Emlyn, on this day I ask you to be mine." Hugo stood waiting for her answer.

"Hugo, I cannot ask you to imperil yourself for my sake," she replied.

"You are not to trouble yourself regarding my safety. We are now pledged to one another. I will have my father here within the hour to finalize the matter. I must take my leave to fetch him. I know him to be nearby on business. I do troth my loyalty and devotion to you, Emlyn and you alone. All will be well." Hugo gave her a gentle smile and left the room.

Rylan gave Emlyn a worried look. "I am sorry Emlyn. We will annul the contract after de Marche is beyond our borders. As it is, we still must navigate the fortnight given to renounce and destroy this imaginary marriage contract. He instructed me to remain silent regarding your impending engagement, which will provide us with time to stave de Marche off."

Emlyn looked stricken. She was fond of Hugo but had no thought of him as a husband. "Father, I do not wish to marry. Not anyone," she had a firm look on her face.

Her father slit his eyes looking away from her. "Daughter, you will do as I say. I have your welfare within my heart. You know not the consequences of being unspoken for in the presence of those who are accustomed to taking what they set their eyes upon. Let Hugo be your shield from the way of these men.

"I will say, if young Rend's affections for you are half of what his father had for his mother you are in good hands," he told her. "Gracyn Rend loved his wife with a deepness most marriages do not enjoy. Hugo was a young man when she passed on. Gracyn still mourns her loss."

"What befell his mother?" Emlyn asked out of curiosity.

"Gracyn only mentioned her passing once, it so affected him, I did not press for details," Rylan stated. "Apparently, the ship Rhosewen Rend sailed upon was lost at sea.

"Such a sadness," Emlyn commented. "Poor Hugo, to be without a mother he so loved. It may be a blessing I never knew my own mother," Emlyn told her father.

Rylan remained silent.

They both sat with their own thoughts when a short time later they heard footsteps and conversation outside the door. Gracyn Rend strode in with an unreadable expression on his dark face accompanied by his son. Large and powerful, he was a commanding presence. He sat down and pointed to a chair for Hugo to be seated.

"I happened to be in the bailey negotiating a price for stores when Hugo came to me.

"Rylan, my son has advised me that he desires to marry your daughter. I am supposedly here to enter into a marriage contract on behalf of my family. Timing is of an urgent nature, he tells me," Gracyn stated looking grim.

Rylan started to speak. Gracyn put his hand up to stop him. "As his father, it has not escaped my attention that Hugo, although impulsive by nature, has exceeded all past brash behavior in his sudden wish to marry. What has happened to precipitate this rashness? I do not wish to cast doubt upon Emlyn's honor, but I must ask. Does she carry his child?"

"Absolutely not!" Rylan, Emlyn, and Hugo all said at once. Glaring at Gracyn who glared back.

Gracyn looked around at each of them in turn. "It is not unreasonable provided the suddenness of events."

"Father, I desire your approval and support, which will be demonstrated by your signature upon our marriage agreement," Hugo told him with all seriousness. "I wish to marry Emlyn. No matter the circumstances. She has my heart."

Rylan interjected. "Gracyn, allow me to explain. This engagement is but a ruse to keep Emlyn out of the Duc de Marche's hands. He came to me earlier and demanded her hand. She does not wish to wed him. I will not force her to accept him, so I told him she had just recently been promised. I lied. I then had to produce a groom and could think of no other than your son."

Gracyn had been listening intently and addressed his son, "Hugo, I thought to align our family with the house of de Marche via Ruizzon de Lusignan. In fact, the Duc and I have discussed it at length. How now, am I to tell him that you are to marry Emlyn? He most definitely will be affronted for multiple reasons. Do you consider the danger you place yourself in?"

"I can attest to his disapproval," Rylan commented dryly. "It is true, there is a high level of danger that comes with this betrothal. I understand if you wish to reject it."

"I am sure disapproval is but a mild term for his sentiment," Gracyn declared.

"Raoul is a passionate man with severe emotion. His anger will go beyond enraged once he learns who Emlyn is affianced to. We have spoken of a betrothal between Hugo and Ruizzon. She is quite in favor of it after refusing her brother's choice for her. So not only do we deny him the bride of his choice but we deny his sister's choice of groom as well."

Hugo quickly let his distaste for that marriage plan be known. "Father, I have no wish to wed Ruizzon de Lusignan. She is pleasant by all accounts, but I do not love her. She is rather trying, if I am to be honest."

"My son, if I had not loved your mother so well, I would not entertain lack of love as a reason to pass such an opportunity to bind our family to one of such noble birth. I understand you wish to marry for love but in this instance the betrothal is a hoax. No marriage will likely come of it. A hoax that will make an enemy of a powerful man. I ask you to reconsider your part in this."

"I have sworn to protect Emlyn and cannot be dissuaded from it. I hope for a marriage but accept she may not desire one. I plan to do my best to change her mind," Hugo told his father stubbornly. He looked toward Emlyn as he spoke to convince her he would go to any lengths for her.

Emlyn sat quietly wishing she could be anywhere but here. If she must choose which of the two to marry, then Hugo would be her choice without question. She had to come to terms with the fact if the Duc de Marche did not relent, she may have to marry Hugo who was risking not only his own life but his father's as well to save her.

Rylan thought the same. "Gracyn, if it comes to making an enemy of de Marche, know that my family will stand with you. I would never ask you to put yourself in harm's way and abandon you to your fate," Rylan promised. "My hope is that de Marche's desire to wed Emlyn is not as strong as his desire to avoid conflict to the north of his family lands. He can play the bully but when he sees it bears no fruit, he will abandon the quest. If he does not then Hugo and Emlyn will marry.

"I have provided a generous dowry for Emlyn and included a provisional clause for annulment if either party so desires before the actual wedding takes place. De Marche need not know of that," Rylan said with gravity. "The endowment will still go to you if we are at fault in voiding the contract."

"I will pretend to take the fortnight offered to consider de Marche's threat and at the end of that time, will refuse him. We have that much time to prepare ourselves for his wrath," Rylan finished with a sigh.

Rylan looked directly at Emlyn. "Emlyn, unless you object, we will finish this now. I have Eston seeking out Seiffert. He has been busy drafting the marriage contract."

"I am putting all in danger with this ruse. It would be simpler if I depart and return when the Duc de Marche has left us," Emlyn protested.

Hugo answered her, "If you leave, he is sure to follow. You will be running from here to there, trying to elude him. Emlyn, you will be without family and virtually alone. I cannot allow it. We are from this moment engaged. At least I can afford you protection with the hope that he relents and departs," Hugo pleaded trying to reason with her. "He most likely will need to depart. He cannot remain here forever. He has obligations that he cannot neglect."

Emlyn looked unsure.

Seeing this, Rylan appealed to her, "My daughter, I will not allow you to leave, and we cannot all flee with you. You must stay in your home and accept the protection we can provide here," he insisted.

Gracyn, who had been listening to all, could see that his son would choose death in battle rather than allow Emlyn to marry Raoul de Lusignan, the Duc de Marche. He was so like himself. He would marry for love at any cost. At any cost, even if his intended bride did not share that love. He was well aware of his son's obsessions. He mirrored his father in that way too. There would be no stopping him.

Gracyn addressed Emlyn, "Accept Hugo as your intended husband and allow us to prepare for what the future will bring. Let us stand together as one family as your father has proposed." Gracyn met her eyes with an assuring look. If this made Hugo happy, he was willing to go along with this dangerous imposture for his son.

Her father was relieved to hear Gracyn's commitment. "One last word," Rylan stated. "Eryk cannot learn of this. He will be told of the betrothal but not of the tale behind it. If Eryk hears of the Duc's threats, he will take it as an affront to our family honor and will provoke de Marche to answer for it. That must not happen. We must avoid a battle with the de Lusignan family unless it is inescapable but if that is not possible, then we fight. I will not allow my daughter to be married against her will but I also must protect my son."

All the while, Emlyn sat silently bewildered by what lay ahead of her. A marriage to Hugo was not unspeakable. She was fond of him, and he had always made it clear how he felt about her. His dedication to her safety touched her. She felt obligated by his valor. He was willing to withstand death and put his own family in danger on her behalf. She must meet his sacrifice at least.

Gracyn's willingness to support his son had surprised her. He had always seemed so stern and removed. He was respected and even feared by his men, but it was clear that he loved Hugo. She was surprised at his selflessness and knew he put himself in harm's way with his support.

Just then, she heard the thud of boots approaching from behind and turned in her chair to see her brother enter the room.

"Well, there seems to be a gathering of which I was not informed. What goes on here?" Eryk quipped. He looked from one person the next and his eyes landed on his father.

"Father, why are you all here? Did something happen?" he asked expectantly.

Rylan hesitated and replied with one last look at Emlyn, "Grand tidings, Eryk. Your sister and Hugo are engaged. We were just celebrating. Come join us." Ryland spoke with a false gladness he hoped no one took note of.

Eryk raised his brow, narrowed his eyes, and tilted his head slightly to the side at his sister. "Emlyn, we have no secrets from one another. Why did you not confess your desire to marry? Why am I the last to be told?" He was slightly incredulous.

Emlyn could hear the doubt in his voice and hurriedly spoke, "Eryk, so much has come to pass of late, I had not the opportunity to share my news. For that I am sorely sorry. Come now, and share your good wishes with Hugo and I."

"I extend my wishes for your future happiness of course. Hugo, I entrust you with my precious sister, confident that you will keep her in good stead." Eryk held out his forearm to Hugo who took it in a firm grasp.

"Emlyn will be safe with me, Eryk. I will strive each day to win her happiness, and I swear to protect her with my life," Hugo committed.

"Eryk do not make widely known news of this betrothal. I ask for personal reasons," Rylan directed his son.

"What are these "personal" reasons?" Eryk asked suspiciously.

Just then Eston walked into the room once again, whispered into Eryk's ear and looked over at Rylan. Eryk immediately left the room following Eston.

With that, Seiffert, the jurisconsult, ushered himself into the chamber carrying a scroll. A few granules of fine sand poured over the document to prevent smearing, were still clinging to the parchment. He blew them off unceremoniously before setting it on the table.

"Here tis, my Lord," Seiffert stated. "It is complete with all you requested. The document has been backdated a week ago last and includes the dowry amount you specified," he paused and resumed, "along with an annulment clause."

Rylan and Gracyn scanned the document together. After each was satisfied, Rylan picked up a quiver, dipped it in ink and signed his name. He tilted a lit candle allowing the wax to fall onto the document face. Removing the signet ring from the pinky of his left hand, he pushed the face of the ring into the hot wax, leaving an imprint of his family crest. Looking at Gracyn, he passed the document over and Lord Rend did the same. It was done. Hugo and Emlyn were engaged to marry.

Gracyn looked at his son. "Hugo, let us take our leave. We will discuss strategy to prepare for future events. The Duc is to visit this eve. I am guessing he will not arrive in a fair mood. Say good morrow to your fiancée."

Gracyn turned and walked out while Hugo went over to Emlyn's chair and knelt down next to it. "Emlyn, I must leave now but I will return. I have something I want to give you," Hugo said gently, smiling at her.

"Hugo, know my gratitude for what you and your father are risking for my sake," Emlyn said with sincerity.

"I am glad for it, Emlyn," he said squeezing her hand as he straightened up.

"Lord Esper, good eventide." With that, he walked out of the room.

Chapter 18

After the Betrothal

Evening came to castle Rend, situated on the northern coast two miles from Kyrenia castle. In the great hall, Gracyn sat eating his evening meal with Hugo before the fireplace with flames crackling and flickering light across the sturdy wooden table. He lifted a jeweled goblet to his lips and looked over at his son wondering what was in store for him.

"It bodes ill that de Lusignan sent his regrets for this evening, Hugo. I presume it is because he is ill-pleased with his conversation with Lord Esper. Once it is revealed that Emlyn is betrothed to you and that you will not release her from it, he will be paying us a visit of a different nature." He paused, then said, "Be on your guard at all times while he remains in Kyrenia. Nothing is beyond his reach. Know him for the danger he is."

Hugo looked at his father and felt a great surge of love. "Father, I know what my rash commitment has cost you. But I had to accept. I scarcely can believe my good fortune. To be a husband to Emlyn was outside my hopes. God's eyes look upon me."

Gracyn was quiet for a moment. "Hugo, you must keep in your mind that Emlyn does not wish to marry. A wedding may not take place."

"Father, I know what was said but Emlyn does not know her own mind. She is fond of me and needs a husband to protect her. In the end, we will wed."

The Flaming Soul   Doreen Demerjian

His father saw in his son a part of himself. The characteristic roughness in him disappeared when he spoke, "Your mother was such a beautiful soul, Hugo. Both gentle and kind with a radiant beauty as well. I loved her to the core of my being. Even now my love for her remains steadfast. I was not her first choice as husband but in the end, she chose me." He stopped and continued with emotion, "You strongly resemble her in your fairness. I know she would have been pleased for you. She would favor your choice, I am certain."

Chapter 19

Next Morning

Emlyn sat in the garden in a comfortable chair with patterned cushions at her back. Eston stood watch at the heavily ornamented iron garden gate. The roses were in riotous bloom against the stone garden walls with their white and pink petals releasing a heady scent. The gentle murmur of buzzing bees lent a peace to the surroundings as the warm sea breeze whooshed over her skin. She could smell the salt air. She heard a sound on the gravel behind her and turned her head. Her eyes met those of Hugo's. He was dressed in a navy colored tunic cut high at the hip with a long tail for ease of movement.

"Hail, Emlyn. Jinol told me where to find you. I hope not to intrude upon your solace."

"Nay, Hugo. You do not intrude. I sit here to pass the time," she told him lightly.

He took a chair next to hers, stretched his long legs out and grabbed the bottom of her seat, pulling her chair closer to his with little effort.

"Now that we are betrothed, Emlyn, I have something I would like you to have." He reached deep into the pouch at his waist and brought out a white, linen cloth.

As he unfolded it, a gold heart-shaped brooch showed itself. It measured an inch and a half in diameter at its widest point and was studded with small, white seed pearls. At its center, the heart had a gold eastern orthodox cross. Hugo flipped it over to show the letter 'R', symbolizing the Rend name on the back. It was subtly beautiful, but Emlyn feared what it signified.

Hugo held it out to her. "Emlyn, this belonged to my mother. She wore it always from the day she wed my father. I never saw her without it at her breast. The letter 'R' on the obverse not only stands for Rend but her first name as well, Rhosewen. I want you to wear it as a symbol of our betrothal. My engagement gift to you, dear Emlyn. I cannot think of another woman who could do it greater justice."

Emlyn looked at the heart and then back at Hugo before she carefully said, "Hugo, it is lovely, but I cannot accept such a gift from you. Our betrothal is naught but a sham you so goodly agreed to, to shield me from that monster." She tried desperately not to sound as panicked as she felt. This was getting too real. "I am not worthy of it," she protested.

He lifted his hand to stroke her cheek as he spoke with a tenderness she had never heard from him before, "Emlyn, you may view this as a sham at present, but I am firmly committed to our union. I hope that you will come to see it as our destiny as I do. I beg you to wear my mother's brooch, as a ploy if you wish to see it that way. As long as you wear it, it will symbolize that you belong to me, that you are mine and under my protection in all eyes, especially those of the Duc de Marche. To keep you from his reach."

He turned his face from hers so she could not see his face as he continued, "You vowed to turn to me in a time of trial. I hold you to that vow. If your mind remains unchanged after the threat passes, we can annul the contract. I will agree to withdraw my claim to you and put an end to this 'charade'."

She could tell he was trying his best to sound casual. Her heart was sore for him.

"Hugo, I will do my best to honor my vow to you even though I fear the risk it poses to your family. If I but knew when I made that promise that the refuge I sought would pose a danger to you..." her voice broke from the weight of the guilt she felt.

Hugo was touched by her concern and to put her at ease he spoke, "Emlyn do not upset yourself. We will see this through together and together decide what its end will be."

Hugo stood up, bent to kiss the top of her head gently. "Fare thee well for now, my heart," he said before taking his leave down the pea gravel path and through the garden gate where Eston still stood guard.

She watched as his strong, straight back moved down the path. The tail of his tunic flowed back towards her. His long, wavy, blond hair tied at the nape of his neck fluttered in the breeze as he moved. He was handsome and courageous to the point of recklessness. Many damsels would be thrilled to be his intended, she conceded, but her mind was elsewhere. On a man bent down before her. Candlelight illuminating his golden flecked skin. His face intensely focused on the arrow shaft protruding from her leg. The man promised to Randall Dove.

Chapter 20

The North Pasture

Dyfen spent the next ten days high on the hills of the northern barn in constant attendance to Zakar's leg and doing little else. He and Kellis took turns soaking the sprained fetlock in cold salt water and rewrapping it. A makeshift stall was fashioned outside so that Zakar could see his brother, Arazi, while he was turned out into the meadow. Avak, Tyber, Aubryn and Osyn kept vigil over the pasture, but Cydryn never left Zakar's side.

It was a sun-filled and blustery day. A few white clouds scudded across the bluest of skies. Kitchen serving boys had just left after delivering the bountiful breakfast Mim sent each day. Food for dogs and men. The pack was putting on weight Dyfen noticed.

"How is our lad faring this day, Kellis?" Dyfen asked as he returned from the pasture seeing to Arazi.

"The swelling has come done greatly, my Lord," Kellis responded still stooped over Zakar's leg. He rose stiffly from sleeping on the stable floor.

"We shall begin to walk him for a little time, twice each day to slowly build the strength back in the leg and help stave the swelling," Dyfen stated as his attention became directed toward two figures on horseback sauntering casually side by side down a trail. He recognized Emlyn and Hugo. Emlyn wore a beautiful silk gown the color of yarrow. Her long hair was plaited at the sides. She was seated sidesaddle on Firah facing Hugo who sat astride a strapping white Andalusian crossbreed. Their conversation drifted towards him.

"I am very happy, Emlyn," Hugo's voice was uplifted. He leaned over towards Emlyn and placed his hand over hers.

"I am grateful Hugo; you must know that. I daresay my heart is filled with..."

He could hear no more as the wind shifted while they walked on. He could see Hugo leaning in his saddle toward Emlyn. He could hear the faint tinkle of her laughter as the horses moved away. He shook his mind loose from the thoughts. He had not seen her since he had ministered to Firah's hoof and had hoped to be away from these shores by now.

"Dyfen! Lord!" Kellis was talking to him. Dyfen snapped back to the present.

"Yes, Kellis. You spoke? I am afraid my mind did wander for a moment."

"I asked when we should begin these strolls with Zakar, Lord," Kellis repeated looking at Dyfen quizzically.

"Uh, at once. We should begin at once, Kellis. Do you think you can manage it? I have something to attend to which requires I travel to the Castle. Walk him ten minutes and not longer. Place him in the outside stall to graze. Cydryn will keep watch."

"Yes, Lord. Zakar and I have become friends. Have we not, brave warrior?" Kellis was speaking to the horse with obvious fondness in his voice. He was pleased that Dyfen trusted him. For he knew that Dyfen had deep affection for his horses and dogs and to be trusted with their welfare had great significance in his standing with him.

Zakar, nickered in recognition of his friend. Kellis laughed and stroked the big stallion's neck as he slowly led him into the morning light, talking to him as he would an old friend.

Dyfen was deep in thought as he mounted the steed Lord Esper had generously provided and started for Kyrenia Castle. He wondered what was behind the conversation Hugo enjoyed with Emlyn. His brow was knit in worry that she might be getting ahead of the healing process. He hoped today's foray on horseback had not upset the wound. That was only part of his worry, he knew. Seeing Hugo with Emlyn in such intimate circumstances made him wonder. He had no trust of the younger Rend's intentions.

While traveling, he saw two men coming toward him on horseback.

"Hail, brother!" rang out. Dover trotted up to Dyfen on the grey gelding he was riding. Isley leaned forward to put a hand on Dyfen's arm.

"We were coming to see you," Isley said. "How fares Zakar?"

"He is recovering," Dyfen said.

"At our morning meal, as we were enjoying the heavenly fare Mim prepared, we were joined by Eryk. He told us of his sister's betrothal to Hugo Rend. So astounded were we by the news that we wondered if he might have a second sister," Dover tried to make a joke. "He is with her all times now. Whither Emlyn travels, there goes Hugo."

"Yet, to some strangeness, Eryk told us that the betrothal was sub rosa," Isley related.

"I can hardly blame Rylan," Dover exclaimed. "Why would he admit to gaining Rend as a son in law?" he chuckled.

Dyfen ignored the banter and merely shrugged. "It is reasonable for a young maiden to marry. It is the natural progression of life. I was on my way to the castle to see to sailing arrangements. The soonest we leave for Jaffa, the better. I have commitments to honor and the moment Zakar is restored we will board a ship and leave this island. I estimate no longer than a fortnight, possibly less."

"A fortnight it is then," Dover commented.

"That should be time enough for you to bid all of your maiden friends, adieu," Isley joked.

Dover smiled, "Yes, well it would probably be best if we keep our departure date to ourselves. At least until I have had time to prepare 'my friends'. They have so thoughtfully provided us with the softest of linens to rest upon and those special pastries from the kitchen." Dover's face was rapturous with the thought. Coming back to the present he relented, "It will be a sacrifice for all of us to be sure."

Dyfen reached over from his mount and gave him a brotherly punch in the shoulder. Dover cast him a mock look of pain as the three of them headed back to the castle.

Chapter 21

In the Chapel

It was the end of early morning prayers. The sweet smell of incense hung in the warm air of the castle chapel leaving a rising smoky haze. Three hanging candelabra hung down the center of its high ceilinged nave. The whiteness of the limestone walls glowed with color as the strong morning sun blazed through mirror image stained-glass windows depicting a knight on a white horse carrying a flag with the Esper family crest upon it, Nostro dux Deus est, 'God is my guide', facing each other on opposite sides of the apse. The altar, a huge slab of white quartz streaked with a thick, gold vein across the front, was supported by two smaller slabs of white marble. Directly behind was an awe-inspiring backdrop of a tall stained-glass window lit with the rising eastern sun. A serene Christ was rising with his hands outstretched to the congregation. His feet were stationed upon a white cloud.

Dyfen, Isley and Dover were standing in the rear waiting to exit after the service. The congregation was conversing with one another as they moved toward the outdoors.

The three headed over toward the Brutia pine doors, to where Ruizzon and Mareya were standing with their servants awaiting their brother and father respectively.

Following Ruizzon's gaze Dyfen saw that her eyes settled upon Hugo who was standing near the altar. Emlyn was seated in a chair next to him. Both were speaking with the Bishop who was resplendently attired in gold and silver threaded silks, a highly jeweled miter atop his head. Nearby were Rylan and Eryk Esper.

Further from them stood Emperor Komnenus and Raoul de Lusignan, the Duc de Marche, speaking in low tones to one another. Rylan had finally formally declined the Duc 's directive to void Emlyn's current marriage contract and named Hugo Rend as her betrothed. The Duc took the news more quietly than Rylan had expected. It appeared that all would be well.

Dyfen noted that de Marche's eyes were upon Emlyn. He lowered his head and said something to Komnenus. Both men now had eyes on Emlyn. The Duc was dressed very elegantly in a dark slate colored silk tunic with high Spanish leather boots. Dyfen noted his Damascus steel dagger hung by his side flaunting papal policy. It made him uneasy as his own arms were in the Armor house outside in the churchyard.

They studied her with a watchful eye that made Dyfen tense. He recognized the look of unmasked desire that de Marche held in his steely eyes. Dyfen turned back heading toward the front of the chapel where now Emlyn sat alone. He walked up slowly toward her.

"Congratulations on your betrothal Lady Emlyn," Dyfen said looking down at her.

Emlyn eyed him carefully. "Oh, word has come to you," she said frostily not meeting his eyes.

"Well my lady, news of such a joyous pairing is of interest to some." He studied her. "I believe all of Kyrenia knows of it."

"I would not think you to be one of them. You have not come to ask after my health since... for quite some time," she finished abruptly recalling that she had not seen him face to face since the stable.

"Has not your physician come to examine you each day?" he asked soberly, noting her icy response.

"Yes, Doctor Chikaris has come daily to examine the wound. What of it?"

Dyfen remained silent. He did not inform her that the doctor stopped by the northern stable every eve to share the bountiful supper sent by the castle kitchen and to share news of Emlyn's progress. He had learned that she was able to walk now although standing for long lengths of time was still ill advised.

The two men discussed Uncle August and his work. Dr. Chikaris was fascinated by the in-depth study of anatomy Dyfen described. They developed a deep rapport over their many conversations. He even consulted with Dyfen before he performed a difficult surgery asking Dyfen to draw the bone, muscle, and vascular structures for him.

"What of your own joyous tiding?" Emlyn said looking up at Dyfen trying to hide the hurt she felt.

"Of which tiding do you speak?" Dyfen asked her with a puzzled look.

She was about to speak again when she felt a heavy hand upon her shoulder and saw Dyfen's eyes travel upward and past her.

"Whetherly," Hugo spoke with great confidence, smiling with a piercing gaze at Dyfen. His hand was resting proprietarily on Emlyn's shoulder.

"Rend," Dyfen returned evenly. "I extend my congratulations to you on your forthcoming nuptials."

"Yes, Emlyn and I are quite overjoyed," Hugo said with a gleam in his eyes. Emlyn did not respond. "You will excuse us, Whetherly, Emlyn and I must take our leave. We have many details to attend to know that we are pledged to one another."

Hugo stooped to pick up her up, placing his hands under her, lifting her into his arms and pulling her close to his chest. He leaned his head down to touch the top of hers. He gave Dyfen a triumphant look as they moved toward the church door. Emlyn looked back at Dyfen, but he quickly turned his head away not wanting to meet her eyes.

Dyfen moved to where Eryk and his father were standing. They were in conversation. He wanted to warn Lord Esper of his misgivings regarding Raoul de Lusignan. "Lord Esper," Dyfen called, "I would have a word with you."

Eryk and Rylan turned toward him.

"Hail, Lord Whetherly," Eryk responded. "I will leave my father to you. I have business elsewhere," he said as he walked by Dyfen. They looked at each other and smiled their greetings.

"Yes, Dyfen," Rylan spoke looking at him expectantly.

"I want to thank you for your generosity in allowing my use of Kellis and the northern pastures and stables as well."

"All is yours as long as needed. And any other need you may have. My gratitude to you and your brothers on behalf of my daughter is boundless. She is healing well our physician tells me."

"He tells me an equal story when we sup each evening," Dyfen responded. "But there is something that I need to bring to your attention."

"Ah. So, you are following her progress. I am not surprised," Rylan said thoughtfully. Dyfen was unsure what was meant but did not ask.

"Lord Esper, I must speak. I have reason for misgivings regarding the Duc de Marche and his intentions toward Emlyn."

"I understand that you do not like the man. I, myself, do not like the man but let me assure you that any misgivings you may have are already being dealt with. Naught to trouble yourself about," Rylan told him.

Dyfen listened and decided not to take it further. He said quietly, "I must congratulate you on the betrothal. As the bride's father you must be well satisfied in the match." He looked steadily at Rylan.

Rylan seemed uncomfortable with the conversation. He let out a silent sigh and spoke, "How is your stallion faring, Dyfen? I trust he is healing well. He is a magnificent animal. It would be a shame if he were permanently disabled." He looked at Dyfen with great concentration.

"Yes, thanks to the assistance of Kellis we are seeing steady progress. I hope to be able to load him on ship in another week. He will need to regain the strength back in his leg to maintain his balance shipboard even with the use of a sling." Dyfen's gaze remained steady, forcing Rylan to look away.

Finally, Rylan made a decision to trust this young man who had done so much for his family. "Dyfen, I know exactly of which you speak regarding the Duc de Marche. Emlyn's engagement is her protection," he said in a low voice hoping that would be enough.

"What do you mean?" Dyfen asked pointedly.

"Her engagement is a ruse to keep de Marche from her. That is our secret, and no one can know. Eryk does not even know," he returned. "de Marche came to me and asked for her hand, it was a command, really. I told him she was already engaged. I had to say something. Emlyn is heavily displeased but as long as she is out of that fiend's clutches, I am well pleased."

"He accepted your answer?" Dyfen asked somewhat incredulous.

"I admit when I revealed Hugo as her intended, I expected him to strongly object but in the end, he said nothing," Rylan stated.

A servant came to him and whispered in his ear. Rylan nodded and said "The morning hour is late. I must take my leave to attend a meeting with the very same, Duc de Marche who remains as my uninvited guest."

Rylan raised his eyebrows as if exasperated. "He has some concerns he wishes to discuss. That cannot be for the good, but I am bound to honor his requests."

Rylan nodded curtly and walked past Dyfen and toward the church doors.

Dyfen turned and looked after him and scanned the room. He was the last to leave. He walked outside and found Dover waiting for him to exit.

"Where is Isley?" he asked.

"Right over there," Dover pointed by tilting his head towards Isley who stood twelve feet away engaged in conversation with Lady Mareya Komnenus. The young maiden was touching Isley on the arm. His face was riveted on hers. "He is quite taken with the Damsel of Cyprus," Dover quipped. "She does not care much for me. I know not why."

"One can only guess," Dyfen jested. His brother cast him a disdainful look.

Isley noticed the two brothers waiting for him, regretfully excused himself and walked toward them. Before he left her, he unobtrusively touched the crook of her arm. He felt a charge of pleasure shoot through his rigid body and he had to force himself to leave her side.

"Dyfen, what have you been up to, brother?" Isley called as if nothing had happened. They were on their way to the arms house to pick up their weapons. They reached the door of the stone building and went inside.

"I would ask of you the same," Dyfen said with a grin on his face. He had noticed the imperceptible tremor that had surged through Isley as he walked toward them. He had never seen his adopted brother in this way, so closely guarded did he normally keep himself. He could tell by the look on Isley's face that he was not going to respond to his question.

Dyfen grabbed his dagger and slid it into his sash, "The Duc de Marche made me uneasy with his unyielding gaze upon Emlyn. He appears to be obsessed and I know how uncomfortable he makes her."

"She has Hugo to tend to that now, her betrothed," Dover said sourly. "I cannot fathom that match. I would swear to Our Lord she lacks feelings of tenderness towards him. He is more the familial friend. I suppose I misread the relationship," Dover mused examining the blade of his sword.

Isley, who was polishing his dagger against his leg responded, "I too, am surprised by the match. Even if Emlyn desired it, I would think Rylan would not approve. He seems to have an uneasy relationship with the Rends." He slid his dagger back into its scabbard.

"It is not our concern. No one has asked for our aid and we will set sail as soon as Zakar is able," Dyfen said roughly not interested in discussing it. He walked out of the darkness into the light. He mounted Arazi in silence. He bent down to pat the heads of Tyber and Avak who had waited outside with the horses then rode off towards the northern barn with the two dogs running behind.

He was lost in thought over the words Rylan had spoken. Why had they not come to him for aid? She knew she could trust him. He was torn in his emotions. He was annoyed and yet relieved.

Dover and Isley watched them go and began the walk back to see what Mim's kitchen had prepared for the midday meal.

Chapter 22

We Meet Again

Weeks after the meeting at church, her leg felt well enough to sustain her weight. It was quite stiff in the mornings but she found walking strengthened it and loosened the muscles.

"You have healed well, Emlyn. It is one of the cleanest surgeries and fastest recoveries I have witnessed in my years of treating such injuries," Dr. Chikaris said with satisfaction, happy to provide good news to the young girl. "You may venture out and even ride at more than a walk as long as you rest when tired."

Dr. Adonis Chikaris' dimpled smile rested on his ageing, yet still handsome face. His hair was rumpled as usual due to lack of time to tend to himself, so busy was he with caring for the ill and wounded. His only indulgence was a good meal which brought him into regular contact with his favorite person in the form of Mim. His current focus was on the scent of a loin roast floating in the courtyard air.

Down in the stable yard, Emlyn was able to mount Firah, with some assistance from Eston who still watched over her carefully, and ride astride as was her usual manner. While Eston was busy talking to the stable master about bringing his own mount for him to accompany her, Emlyn nudged Firah to move off. Once out of sight, Emlyn urged Firah into a canter as she felt the sheer joy of the crisp mid-afternoon air flow through her hair and the warm Cypriot sun on her face once again. They headed north.

Dyfen was hand walking Zakar around the stable yard under the watchful gaze of Cydryn who was lying in the shade. "Well, my boy you have healed nicely. Your movement is smooth and unfettered. I think we are ready to sail, good lad. In two days', time we weigh anchor for Jaffa. We will both need our sea legs," he chuckled, rubbing the horses muzzle.

The horse made a snorting sound and placed his face next to Dyfen's.

The two made a turn and saw Emlyn stopped in the gateway mounted on Firah. She was dressed in a splendid sage-colored, silk gown cut square at the neck.

He unconsciously looked for his leather cord at her neck, but there was none. Instead a pearl studded heart with a gold cross at its center was pinned at her cleavage. He understood the significance. She must be more willing in this supposed ruse than her father knew.

Her face was flushed from the ride.

"Hail, Lord Whetherly," she called to him. Her lips rested in a gentle smile. "I came to visit Zakar. I see he is faring well," she spoke as if the terse meeting at church weeks before had not occurred.

"Hail, Lady Emlyn. It is with joy I see you able to ride and looking so hale," Dyfen replied looking up at her. He could not resist including a jibe, "I note that you travel without escort. Up to your old ways once more. Where is your betrothed this day?" He tried to seem amused and looked beyond her, pretending to seek Hugo. "Will he not frown upon your solo venture out?"

"Lord Whetherly, my 'betrothed' is none of your concern. My betrothed although not fully aware of my whereabouts will not question my judgement," she responded somewhat miffed at the levity in which he referred to her ride out and knowing her response to be a lie. Hugo would not be pleased.

Dyfen became serious. "I protest his absence. I apologize for the jest. It was poorly timed but, in all earnestness, Emlyn, you should not be outside the castle walls without a man to safeguard you."

She ignored him. "I have heard that Zakar was injured while some thief tried to abscond with him." Looking down she saw that Cydryn had come up to greet her.

Her face broke into a smile. She tried to lean over to pat his head but was unable to safely reach him from atop Firah. Dyfen seeing her difficulty, strode over to Firah, reached up and smoothly pulled Emlyn from her seat, setting her down gently onto the ground before him. Her legs buckled a little and he grabbed her by the waist to steady her. Her body slid against his and their faces were but inches apart. They held a gaze which made Emlyn uncomfortable. She recovered her balance and composure. He seemed unphased.

She blushed and Dyfen backed away. "I wanted to prevent a fall. I beg your pardon, my lady," Dyfen apologized. Glancing down, he saw the brooch stationed at her bosom and quickly averted his eyes.

Emlyn looked uneasy and placed her right hand at her bosom, covering the ornament. "I came to call upon Zakar. Is he well?" she closed the silence.

"He is recovering nicely." Dyfen relaxed with an easy smile. "He has been trained to throw any stranger and trample them, if necessary, to escape. He was injured in the process. Cydryn cornered the scoundrel after he fell. He died of his wounds and a certain measure of fright, most likely. Cydryn does not forgive. He is not one to trifle with."

He looked at her while he was telling the tale and could see a shadow pass over her face. "No permanent harm was done," he quickly reassured her. "All is well."

Cydryn watched the exchange and came to stand close to Emlyn sensing she was troubled. She stroked the dog's head while he closed his eyes in ecstasy.

"You have a friend for life, in Cydryn, my lady. He has taken to you in a strong way," Dyfen told her attempting to cheer her.

"It is very nice to see Zakar is well and to visit with my good friend Cydryn," she responded, speaking directly to the dog with obvious fondness.

She had seen Dyfen eye her brooch and felt discomforted. She decided to depart. "I am glad Zakar is on the mend and now I should take my leave." She headed toward Firah.

"Emlyn do not hasten away. Pray, collect yourself and I will escort you home," Dyfen said, seeing her mood shift and trying to settle her.

"Nay, do not join me. I am well enough and can travel on my own." She was firm. "I am not the child you see me as." She pouted.

He forced a chuckle, "How could I see you as a child? You are soon to be wed and bear your husband children." His voice became serious, "I can well assure you, Emlyn, I see you not as a child."

He continued, "But, if you cannot bear my company then Cydryn will go in my stead. He will protect you and make certain you arrive without harm. Do not fight me in this regard Emlyn. It is the only way I will allow you to ride unescorted." He was adamant. "Your father would wish it and your future husband will be ill humored when he learns you have traveled without escort," he chided, "Especially with the Duc de Marche still in residence."

"Why do you speak of the Duc de Marche?" Emlyn looked at him sharply with a strange look on her face.

Dyfen was casually examining the bridle and patterned blanket upon Firah's back. He did not want to scare her regarding de Marche. Instead, he said, "I know he puts you ill at ease. You told me as much. I trust your discomfort."

She grew agitated with the topic. "I thank you for Cydryn's protection. I gratefully accept it."

She moved next to Zakar and began stroking his mane. "True soul," she gently spoke to the stallion. He nickered in response as if he understood her words. Firah pushed into the huddle placing her nose onto Zakar's who softly nickered again with happiness. Emlyn let out a soft laugh. Her joy was evident. "I dare not separate these two. I will not take my leave just yet." She wanted to linger in this happiness a bit longer.

He watched her as she stroked Zakar's neck and gave gentle pats to Cydryn's large head which the dog had rested against her hip.

"Emlyn, when do you wed?" he asked with interest. "Have you marked the date?"

"I know not when," she said uncomfortably, feeling guilty about her secret yet upset that he had not confided in her about his own betrothal. "Why do you ask?"

Dyfen had come to a decision in his mind. He answered her, "I am surprised you accepted. I was of the mind you did not care for Hugo in that way." He tested her. Maybe she was in agreement with the arrangement and it was not the ruse her father thought it was.

"I see no reason not to marry a man who loves me," she answered.

"I am sure there are many who love you, Emlyn," Dyfen responded. Looking at her levelly trying to gauge her honesty.

"If I am loved by others, they have not spoken of it to me," she countered."

Not all who love, speak of it," Dyfen said. He had turned his back busying himself organizing bottles of medicine on shelves.

Emlyn watched him work, his strong back toward her with his long brown braid resting between his muscled shoulders.

"Why do you speak to me so?" she asked with curiosity.

He did not answer right away, focusing on the job at hand. Finally, he turned toward her and said "You should only marry the man you love, Emlyn. My mother and father have such a marriage and it is the flame that fires the soul. It is what I hope for myself."

Emlyn became angry. How dare he say such things to her while being secretly betrothed. That anger made her lash out, "I do marry the man I love, Dyfen."

He stopped talking not knowing what to say in response to her angry words. He looked up at the position of the sun. He wanted to make sure Emlyn returned home well before it set.

"Emlyn, it is time for you to take your leave. 'Your fiancé'," he stressed the word, "will raise an alarm, and begin a search. He will most certainly be worried by your absence."

She turned toward him, still annoyed, and spat out, "Hugo is at sea."

It took a second for him to understand the significance of the words.

"Oh, your fiancé is at sea?" Dyfen exclaimed irritated. "So, you were able to find the time to come to us. I understand now. Well, my thanks for thinking of us."

"Yes, his father had need of his service," she stated. "Why do you always strive to be so contrary? Must you take delight in my distress?"

"You speak of your distress? You clearly are not in distress. Many days have passed since you last saw me. Although a few days ago, I witnessed you with your betrothed walking your mounts side by side a short distance from this very spot. I took note you did not stop by to ask after Zakar's health," Dyfen stated flatly looking her squarely in the eye for a reaction.

"Dyfen, you are most despicable. Spying upon me? Accusing me of I know not what. It is past time for me to take my leave of you."

She was flustered now and turned to leave but knew she would not be able to mount her mare alone. "I require some assistance mounting. If you would be so kind." She would not look at him.

Dyfen walked over and extended his strong hand for her dainty foot to rest in, without speaking. Better she be gone, he thought upset.

She sprung off his hand and pushed her right leg over Firah's back. Her long hair swept by Dyfen's face as she mounted. The old familiar scent wafted past him sending him backwards a bit. He closed his eyes and breathed her in. It went unnoticed by Emlyn. Once settled, she looked down at Dyfen and curtly nodded her thanks and started to ride off.

"Cydryn," Dyfen commanded him. Cydryn stood at attention.

"Cydryn, travel with Emlyn."

The huge hound understood what was asked of him and started after Emlyn and Firah with his long loping stride.

Dyfen watched them go, walking back to Zakar. He leaned his head against the stallion's face. "We leave in two suns my boy. We have important business to attend to in Jaffa."

Chapter 23

Onboard to Jaffa

Two days later, the docks were busy with activity. Men were leading horses up a boarding ramp and onto the ship. Provisions were being loaded. Dyfen, Isley and Dover stood on deck with Tyber and Osyn.

Both crew and crusaders alike gave them a wide berth. Tyber had his nose up scenting the air. He and Osyn were watching with keen interest as the horses were being brought onboard by one of the ship's stable hands accompanied by Cydryn, Avak and Aubryn.

The two dogs were sighted by Arazi and Zakar. Arazi let out a loud neigh in recognition of them and stopped midway up the boarding ramp waiting for the missing two to join the pack. His handler was unable to make him step forward. Once Tyber and Osyn arrived, the horses moved on without further issue, all disappeared below deck.

Isley saw Kellis on the dock with a large basket in his hand. He waved at Isley who made his way down to the dock. "Is all well, Kellis?"

Kellis handed him the basket. "From Mim. She wants to make sure the dogs have a proper meal. There is food there for you as well." He smiled at the joke. "She does well admire your dogs."

"Give her their thanks and ours as well," Isley smiled. "Cydryn and his brothers greatly appreciate the kindness."

Kellis grinned and nodded his head and started back to Kyrenia Castle.

Dyfen headed to look in on the horse, "I will see to the horses to make sure all is well below."

Isley and Dover cast each other questionable glances and hung back. "He seeks solace with his four-legged family," Isley commented dryly.

Dover's blue eyes squinted, and his mouth turned down. "I hope father's wisdom is in the right."

Isley returned the look. "Father is at ease with it although mother does not seem to agree."

"Did she speak of this with you?" Dover queried.

"She did speak of it," Isley nodded slowly. "She asked my mind, but I could not give it. In normal times I would say it would be of no consequence to him. Dyfen has not taken a serious interest in a woman ever since…, you know…". His voice trailed off as he met Dover's eyes.

"Agreed. Dyfen has been indifferent when it comes to maidens these years past. So many have gazed upon him with high regard, but he has never returned more than a thin politeness His current behavior has me perplexed though. He has been decidedly preoccupied just of late," Dover mused. "Father would be concerned if he knew, and I know mother has been from the start."

Isley leaned back against the gunwale with one boot tipped up behind him. His long, brown hair blew back from his face and his green eyes were leveled at Dover. His face was serious as he spoke, "The shipwreck has him turned about." He looked down at the deck, studying it.

"He most assuredly is not himself," Dover answered quietly. "One of us should speak to him."

Isley nodded his head, "I will do it." Letting out a huge breath as he pushed off the rail and walked towards the hold.

Dover watched him leave and let out a sigh, shoulders slumped. "This does not bode well," he murmured looking out over the water.

Chapter 24

Heart to Heart

Isley stepped down into the hold. He stood at the bottom of the stairs to let his eyes adjust to the light. It smelled of horse manure and fresh hay. Dust hung suspended in a beam of sunlight coming from the top deck.

He spotted Zakar and Arazi in loose stalls with Dyfen standing between them talking softly. Isley walked slowly over to them and stopped. Stroking Zakar he looked at Dyfen. "You have seemed troubled since the shipwreck. What is it that weighs on you, brother?"

Dyfen's eyes were watery. He took a deep breath. "I am well, Isley. No reason to worry yourself."

Isley did not accept that as an answer. "Dyfen, it is beyond question to Dover and to me that of late you are most unlike yourself. We are concerned. Pray, share what has you so."

"Isley, there is nothing that needs to be known. I am well and yet overwhelmed with all that is now and what will soon be. I have much to ponder and to remedy. I have written to father."

"If all that occupies you is setting things to rights because of the shipwreck I understand but if you have doubts regarding future commitments then share them with us, with me. You are not alone. You know that."

"Isley, there is naught to tell. Pray let this lie. There is something I must attend to, and I must attend to it alone. My duty, my responsibility. Mine only," Dyfen said, eyes flat, and posture tightened.

"Dyfen, you are my brother. I desire your happiness, as you do mine. It has been years since Ell …" he turned his head and looked down, "Ellette." There, he had said her name. He looked to Dyfen for a reaction.

None came.

For Dyfen, hearing her name sent him into a reverie. He was silent and meditative. No one had spoken the name, 'Ellette', in his presence for two years... Ellette.

He pictured her standing in the wood at home, surrounded by her five young dogs. Long, light-brown hair blowing out away from her slender, young body. Her large, almond shaped, tawny colored eyes smiling up at him from her pale face. Giggling as the dogs licked her hand as she stroked them. So innocent. Older looking than her fifteen summers of life.

Ellette! He called to her. She smiles back at him as he approaches on horseback riding Shariff, his magnificent, black Friesian stallion.

He remembered the deep, earthy smell of the forest. The breeze in the air. The fluttering of leaves above. So peaceful. Such a happy time in his young life. He was a young man of seventeen. Deeply in love for the first time and never since. Ellette.

Isley saw that Dyfen had become lost in his thoughts. He decided to let the matter lie. He went to stroke the muzzle of each horse, pat the head of each dog and then headed toward the steps to return above deck without saying another word, leaving Dyfen to his introspection.

Chapter 25

Jaffa

Dyfen, Isley and Dover stood on deck watching the city of Jaffa rise before them in a pink smokey haze. The gold, burning sun radiated visible circles of heat that hung in the air. Muslim domed masjid jamis, with their towering minarets, punctuated the hazy skyline. Robed men crowded the wharf shouting in Arabic and Crusader knights walked together with their retinue behind them. The air smelled of sea water and sweat.

The horses were brought above deck and the dogs escorted them down the ramp onto the wharf, parting the crowd before them as they moved.

Dyfen had sent word to Lord Dove of their coming.

"Let us slake our parched throats," Dover said in a mock croak, contorting his face, "There is an alehouse across the way. We can leave the horses in the company of the dogs."

"I second that. I could use ale to quench the dryness from the sea wind," Isley said in agreement.

"We are in accord then," Dyfen smiled. "I have felt the sea wind slap against my face enough for my lifetime. At least this last voyage we managed to stay out of the water," he joked.

"Thanks be to Our Lord for that bit of luck," Isley quipped in agreement.

They all headed toward the timbered building with its mullioned windows standing across from the wharf and entered through a heavy oak door leaving the horses under the protection of the dogs. No words were necessary. The hounds knew their duty. Cydryn laid down in front of where the horses stood. The others laid down behind and along the flanks keeping a watchful eye over their charges.

Many by passers stopped to admire the beauty of the stallions, some perhaps with ill intent, but upon seeing the dogs, moved past.

Dover led the way into the dark, crowded interior and headed toward an empty trestle table with lit lanterns stationed down its middle. Isley sat down at the end while Dover and Dyfen took a seat on the benches at each side.

The surrounding tables were filled with sailors from all ports. Turkish, tribal tongues and Frankish patois phrases were heard throughout the dark, smokey room.

An attractive, young woman with dark eyes, long dark wavy hair and an ample bosom approached their table. "Hail, sires. What refreshment do you desire?" She leaned slightly into Dyfen as she spoke brushing her body against his arm. He did not appear to notice so she leaned in further making sure her bosom was level with his eyes.

Isley and Dover glanced at one another with a knowing look. The serving maiden looked somewhat bemused since this was not a reaction she came to know as common.

Dover spoke first, "Ahhh, urrr, brother, I think she is awaiting your answer."

The girl looked at Dyfen expectantly.

"Ale, then," Dyfen spoke seemingly preoccupied in thought.

"Isley, what say you?" Dover turned to face him.

"Ale will be fine," Isley answered.

"Three ales then. With the hopes it will dislodge my brother's tongue," Dover told the serving girl jokingly.

She appeared unwilling to accept Dyfen's indifference and was still at his side as he examined the tabletop. After a few seconds, she brushed against his arm making sure of his notice and then departed the table with their order, letting out a long sigh.

"Isley, I think our brother's mind has left him," Dover stated.

"In truth, Dover," Isley returned. "He is not present although he sits but inches from us," Isley said in mock amazement.

"And yet, again a fair maiden seeks HIS attention and he withholds it."

He threw his hand into the air in exclamation, "I am offended by their lack of discernment. Are we not as handsome and as well made as our brother?" Dover swung his black hair back from his face, his eyes dancing in merriment with the joke.

Isley started to speak, "I…".

Dover cut him off pushing his hand backward thru the air. "Nay, the answer is plain. We ARE; but his lack of interest seems to deepen his appeal. It is all I can imagine in answer to why this occurs repeatedly."

"In the name of Our Lord! Stop your torment of me," Dyfen was back to himself. "I have no need of your try at humor. It is a full failure."

"Oh, the handsome knight rouses from his reverie," Dover teased.

The serving girl returned with their ale. She set them down one at a time on the table, giving Dyfen one last look, she started to turn away as a voice boomed from behind her.

"Fille, ici! Peu importe ces paresseux sans valeur. Je viens de rentrer d'un mois en mer." ("Girl, here! Never mind those worthless sluggards. I have just returned from a month at sea.")

A heavy French accent emanated from a middle-aged sailor with long plaited hair of numerous braids varying in thickness. His face was deeply tanned, tinged with red from being abraded by the wind. His brown eyes held a smokiness suggesting he was not sober, and a wide grin exposed a gold tooth at the top corner of his mouth. At each ear hung a thick gold hoop earring to assure his body a decent burial on land when the time came.

The left hoop had a big red glowing gemstone embedded within it. He was dressed in a foppish linen shirt with black leggings and a broad leather belt studded in silver. His left-hand middle finger held a huge gold ring that rested upon a large dagger kept on his belt. Highly crafted, tall, Spanish leather boots completed his rather flamboyant ensemble.

The serving maiden moved in reverse as his large, outstretched hands moved towards her. She jumped backward into Dyfen who looked up to see why the serving maids bottom was now resting against the back of his head. His eyes followed hers.

Tottering toward them was the drunken sailor, his braids flying about his face which was composed into what could only be called a leer. His bearded face with open mouth was bending into hers. The gold tooth prominently displayed.

"Jeune fille, J'ai besoin de too!" ("Maiden! I have need of you!") he was bellowing. His friends back as his table were laughing and calling encouragement to him.

"Captain Eustace! Show er your need! That is sompen she will not soon be forgettin." They were falling into each other with mirth.

The sailor had reached the girl who was now cowering behind Dyfen.

Dyfen stood up and turned to face Eustace moving the frightened girl toward Isley behind him. The sailor's face dropped the leer and became confused for a moment trying to take in what was happening. Then it quickly became menacing as he approached Dyfen pulling a large dagger from his silver studded belt.

"Stand aside you fop doodle. A man is here with needs." He brandished the dagger at Dyfen. "Near thirty days at sea aboard the Dolphin Chase, the best vessel to sail these waters. Me, being without the comfort of a woman the entire time. The first days we were a carrying priests and holy sorts to mostly the Holy Lands and the last day's sail had me delivering a maiden of rare beauty. She was something to look at and look I did but she was naught but cargo. Keeping that cargo safe took quite a bit of effort, lad. Keeping myself in check as well as me crew. Took it out of me, it did. Now, stand aside," he roared at Dyfen.

"Hold your tongue you lout and go back to enjoying the company of your companions. This maiden has no want of you," Dyfen raised his voice to be heard above the din. He was shielding the girl with his body.

Isley and Dover had stood up which triggered all the men with Eustace to rise and start to move forward with weapons drawn. Isley grabbed the tavern maiden by the arm and pulled her further back from the fray. She stood watching the encounter wringing her hands on the apron tied at her waist.

Eustace's friends formed a half circle behind him and were roaring for a fight. Dover looked at Isley and then started scanning the room for an escape path. Dyfen had pulled his dagger as Dover and Isley did the same as they slid behind him ready to engage.

Something large, brushed past them. Dyfen heard a familiar low rumbling growl next to him and saw Eustace's eye grow large with fear.

Cydryn was standing on top of the table staring down on Eustace whose face had turned a sickly shade of green. Cydryn's charcoal hackles stood rigid on his back, lips pulled tightly to show gleaming fangs dripping with saliva. The dog's eyes glowed in the dim tavern light with a yellow intensity focused on the threat at hand. Tyber and Osyn stood behind their brother, echoing Cydryn's posture, growling in support, ready to spring into action. The crowd wisely removed themselves a safe distance from the dogs.

While outside, always attuned to listening for commands they had heard Dyfen's shouts prompting Cydryn and two of his brothers to push their way into the alehouse as someone was leaving the tavern. The ragged sailor's eye widened as the three dogs passed him in the doorway. He arched his body away from them as they went by. None dared try to stop them as they strode toward their master. Now, the dogs stood in position waiting for Dyfen to signal his command.

"Vous comprenez, la première action qu'il fera sera de vous arracher la gorge?" ("You understand that his first action will be to rip your throat from you?") Dyfen casually asked in French, as he looked at the sea captain.

All eyes focused on Eustace whose face had fallen into alarm, initiating sobriety. Silence filled the room. As he looked into the yellow eyes of Cydryn, seeing no pity there, he decided on a different tact. A slow smile spread over his craggy, windburned face. He began speaking to the dogs, "Calmez-vous bêtes mordues de puces." ("Calm down you flea-bitten beasts.") "Je parle à mon ami, cet homme ici. Vous le connaissez, oui?" ("I am speaking to my friend, this man here. You know him, yes?")

He smiled at Dyfen and then looked back at the dogs. "C'est mon cher ami. J'ai même eu un chien à bord une fois, jusqu'à ce qu'une vague importante l'emmène une nuit d'orage". ("He is my dear friend. I even had a dog on board once, until a sizable wave swept him away one stormy night.") As he spoke, he moved his hand with a flourish.

"Le meilleur ratier que nous ayons jamais eu. Il me manque toujours." ("The best ratter we have ever had. I miss him still.") He bent his head in reverence.

Cydryn was not impressed and neither was Dyfen, but he saw that Eustace was asking for a way out and he decided to give it to him, "We are late for an appointment, let us take our leave brothers." He flattened his hand, palm facing downward signaling a cease command, and spoke the word "cease" and turned to go.

Cydryn, Osyn and Tyber relaxed and turned to follow Dyfen, Isley and Dover outside. All in their path moved quickly aside to allow them passage.

As the dogs turned to leave, Tyber swung his large, black furred body into Eustace as if by accident. The sailor fell backwards with the force of the impact but regained his footing. "Clumsy, stupid beast," he muttered as he caught himself from falling. He brought his head up to cast the dog a frigid glare and found he was staring into Tyber's piercing yellow eyes. He imagined he saw a smile cross the animal's grizzled muzzle before he moved after his brothers.

The serving maiden who had been standing terrified, approached, and grabbed Dyfen by the hand and kissed it. "Thank you for your protection my Lord. None has ever done as much for me. I will remember you always." Dyfen looked embarrassed and gently pulled his hand away sliding money into hers to pay for their ale along with a generous tip. "You deserve a better life my lady. I pray Our Lord, you receive it." She blushed at his use of the honorific referring to her.

She watched silently as the men and dogs walked out the tavern door out into the blinding Jaffa daylight.

Avak and Aubryn stood up to reunite with their brothers. The dogs all touched noses and generally checked to see that the other was unharmed. The horses finished drinking from a trough and stood ready to leave. Dyfen grabbed the ropes encircling their necks. They started toward the covered alley when a shout came from behind him.

"Sire!" A male figure was running toward them waving an arm.

"What is Kellis doing here?" Isley said recognizing the lean youth who was fast approaching.

Dyfen looked towards the running form and started to speak, "Kellis… what brings you..."

Before he could finish a turquoise stone on a leather cord was swinging before his eyes. Kellis began again, out of breath… "Sire, Lady Emlyn sent me to fetch you," he gasped from the effort.

"Kellis, pray what has happened to Lady Emlyn? Speak!" Dyfen said with alarm by the sight of his turquoise pendent. Realizing what it meant. "How did you find us?"

"I saw the dogs, the horses," Kellis gasped with his head down and hands on his knees.

"Kyrenia has been seized. I did not see the men. They took us unaware. Most all of our men at arms left for Limassol hours before they arrived."

"How did you reach us?" Isley asked.

"I brought him," they heard a voice that sounded familiar behind them.

They turned and saw the figure of Hugo Rend dressed in a navy-blue coat with gold buttons at the cuffs, a navy with white bandana wrapped around his head. He was leaning against a building looking hung over.

"Uhhh, yes. I sailed on the Wild Boar," Kellis mumbled looking down.

"Hugo, has a ship?" Dover asked, raising his eyebrows.

"Captain Rend, yes, he has a ship," Kellis affirmed.

"Well, I am astounded. The devil's own son, a sailor," Dover commented.

Kellis looked at them in an extremely agitated state.

"Sires, please we must take our leave now. There is not a minute to waste. I was barely able to escape before the entire castle was overrun by armed men. I know not who they were. The lords of the castle were summoned to the south and left with their noblemen and good men. Emperor Komnenus had left before them and headed towards Limassol to face Richard who has come for his sister and fiancé. Other than that, I know no more."

Dyfen looked at Hugo who was now looking down, apparently examining his boots.

Isley eyed Kellis and asked, "Who is Richard?"

Kellis struggled to regain his composure. "Richard," he took a breath, "Lionheart," another breath, "Of England," he panted stopping to regain his breath before he started again, "He has taken up the cross and was on his way to Acre by sea.

"The same storm that caused your ship to founder blew four of his off courses to southern Cyprus. Three sank in the harbor. The one still afloat contains his sister and fiancé. Emperor Komnenus has denied them food and water." Kellis was exhausted and his tunic was dripping with sweat.

"They refuse his entreaties to come ashore with his promise of shelter. No doubt they have witnessed survivors from the other ships taken captive and their valuables seized from them," he finished.

"The very ships he spoke of at the feast. Although he couched it in a very different light." Isley was stirred. "He has the boldness to insult the King of England. Emperor Komnenus is wholly misguided in his confidence."

"The man has a definite 'unworthiness' about him," Dover said. "He has good reason to fear the people of Cyprus, so much harm he has wrought upon them."

"You can discuss all of this while we sail," Hugo cut in impatiently. "To catch the tide, we leave now. I will be on the Wild Boar. Kellis knows where. We will be sailing in a mileway. I'll not wait any longer." He turned and walked away with a long, purposeful stride completely preoccupied.

"Dover, grab the horses. Isley, have our sea chests brought to the ship. Kellis lead the way. We sail," Dyfen commanded and moved in the direction Hugo left in. Kellis took the lead and they all walked behind. Cydryn and the pack trailed behind the horses.

A short way down the wharf, Kellis halted where a midsized cog with a large, tusked boar figurehead was anchored. 'Wild Boar' was burned into its gunwale. Dyfen noticed pigeons perched on the yard. Its sail was being raised by three sailors. It was considerably smaller than the ship they had arrived on and would be substantially faster.

Hugo was standing on deck speaking to a tall, dark, barefooted man wearing gold rings on all his fingers. His long, black hair was held away from his sculpted face by a wide, silk, bandana encircling his forehead. He was looking down at the deck nodding his head in understanding as he listened to Hugo. He wore a long, dark brown velvet oriental-style robe which opened down the middle. The bottom front had been cut away below the waistline for ease of movement, exposing a bare, thin but steely frame where a King Cheetah was tattooed in full profile across his chest. The three stripes running down the cheetah's back were very visible. Heavy silver chains hung around his neck partially obscuring the tattoo. One held a prominent large silver cross resting against his naked chest.

A wide band of fawn colored fabric bordered the robe's collar, ran down both sides of the center front and encircled the cuffs. Decorative brass buttons set on dark colored strips punctuated each side of the center front opening. The tails of his robe fluttered away from his body in the hot, dry breeze. The effect was wildly dramatic in an unplanned way.

Dyfen could see that Hugo was not hung over, that his face was lined with stress and worry. He was pointing to the ship next to them when his companion raised his head and looked up for the first time. Dyfen was startled by the bleu de France color of his eyes, around which kohl was heavily smudged into his dark olive skin. The set of his gaze, his dark stubbly beard and taut skin gave him a certain intensity. A serious man.

"Rend, sa'uqabiluk plus tard, mon ami." ("I will meet you later, my friend.")

"Martel," Hugo acknowledged by flicking his eyes upward in agreement silently answering him.

Dyfen heard the exchange. Martel spoke a combined French and Moroccan Arabic that he had heard before by sailors in Cilicia. The French having a large presence and in turn influence, in the region. He lithely jumped over the side of the Wild Boar onto the smaller vessel anchored next to it in the harbor that Hugo had been gesturing toward. Martel turned and bowed gracefully toward Hugo sweeping his left palm outward to his side.

Hugo turned back and shouted, "Start loading the horses so we may set sail. We have no time to waste. Let us pray that the wind picks up." "And keep those mangy curs below deck and out of my sight," Hugo added.

Kellis grabbed the horses and moved toward the loading ramp with the dogs trailing. He wanted to waste no time getting back to his mistress.

Isley and Dover were right behind them and looked over at each other rolling their eyes at Hugo's attitude toward the hounds.

"He will never take heed," Dover said shaking his head.

"He is a mulish fool," Isley returned.

Dyfen had heard Hugo's remark and chose to ignore it, his mind too full of getting to Kyrenia. He walked up to Hugo and said curtly, "Rend, tell me what went on in Kyrenia. Is she safe?"

Hugo held up his hand. "In truth, I do not know. I only know that I did not wish to come here that my duty is in Kyrenia protecting my fiancé."

He leaned over the gunwale squeezing with both hands tightly, wondering aloud, "Why am I here? Why! She maddens me beyond all reason. Why does she never pay heed to my counsel?" His frustration was evident. "If she should suffer harm while I am here fetching you...." his voice dropped off.

Dyfen cut him off, "Rend, get to the point. Tell me what happened. I need to know." His body was tense and muscles taut. He looked intently at Hugo expectantly.

Hugo was looking out over the water. "We sailed into port late eve after nearly a fortnight asea. I came across Kellis hiding near the beach half-starved and shivering in the dark. The castle was being overrun by men at arms and those not put to death were being held captive. He told me that Emlyn managed to smuggle him out of Kyrenia sending him to fetch help. He barely escaped with his life. Kellis made it to the docks on foot. All ships anchored in the northern harbor had been commandeered by Komnenus' men and were ordered to sail south to engage Richard's fleet.

"Kellis told me he had an urgent message to deliver in Jaffa and that he had express orders to deliver it in person. My first thought was to go to her, but Kellis was frightened out of his mind and convinced me that this message was vital for Emlyn's safe rescue. That only after he delivered this message would it be possible for him to return. If I did not bring him here, he would find another way. He did not mention the message was for you or I would have never come. But here we are wasting time. We have to set sail for Kyrenia."

The Wild Boar headed out of the harbor with Martel's smaller ship, the Black Trident, sailing behind. The men hoisted the main sails which slowly filled with mild wind off the coast of Jaffa. Rend stood at the helm, one leg resting on the rail. His blond hair and clothing fluttering gently backwards, away from his lean muscled torso. His face was unreadable while he looked out over the water. The sun burned down as they sailed through the brilliantly blue sea. North back to Cyprus. Back to Emlyn.

Chapter 26

Richard

The three guardant lions of England's royal arms billowed outward into the unconfined space of the clear blue Cyprus skies. King Richard Plantagenet in his thirty-fourth year of life stood on the deck of his ship, squinting his blue eyes, intently watching the activity on the beach.

Standing six foot five inches he towered over the men beside him. His naturally ruddy complexion was heightened by the wind. He reached his long arms back to affix his long, wavy hair from his face. It glinted golden red in the morning sun, his beard and mustache impeccably groomed, slightly darker in color. Covering his broad chest was a red Spanish, tooled leather, battle vest studded in overlapping silver crescents burnished to rival the sun.

Staring out over the water, his mind turned back to two year ago, when he and Phillip Augustus, King of France, vowed to take up the cross following the failure of Guy de Lusignan's campaign to retake Jerusalem from Salah ad-Din, Sultan of Egypt and Syria.

Richard immediately began raising money to finance his army by selling titles, offices, castles, land and imposed the Salah ad-Din tax on his subjects. He claimed he would sell London itself if he could find a buyer.

By September the following year, he had enough wealth to finance his crusade and headed to the Holy Land by sea, stopping at Sicily on a secondary mission to rescue his younger sister, Joan, the Queen of Sicily. She had been married to King William ll and imprisoned for the past year by her dead husband's illegitimate nephew, Tancred of Lecce.

Tancred had seized the throne, imprisoned Joan and stolen her inheritance. Richard demanded the release of his sister, return of her wealth plus fulfillment of the pledge King William had made to the crusade before his death.

Tancred refused all requests resulting in Richard seizing his lands. In the end, Tancred wisely decided to relent and fulfill Richard's original demands as well as donate nineteen ships to support his crusade. In return, Richard recognized Tancred as the rightful King of Sicily and ceased all hostilities.

In March, Richard's mother, Eleanor of Aquitaine, arrived at Sicily bringing his 21-year-old fiancé, Berengaria of Navarre, whom she entrusted to her daughter, Joan, before returning to Aquitaine. Marriages were forbidden by the church during the April Lenten season so Richard sent Joan and Berengaria's ship on ahead resulting in the current situation on Cyprus. No way in hell would he accept such insult to family and himself.

Richard's mind returned to assessing current events. His fleet had grown to over one hundred ships. Twenty-five of them were errant, blown off course by the storm. The remaining had weathered the storm and waited at Rhodes ten days to rendezvous, reprovisioning while they waited. All but four were accounted for. Upon finding Joan and Berengaria's ship one of the missing, he had dispatched several of his fastest galleys out in search of them.

All four ships were found several hundred miles away on the southern coast of Cyprus stranded or sunk. Of the three ships that sank, treachery and betrayal had been perpetrated upon the survivors who had reached shore. The wrecks sunk in Limassol harbor including the remains of Richard's treasure ship that had carried the wealth which financed this army. His Vice Chancellor was found dead. His seal of office taken from his neck and currently in the possession of Emperor Komnenus of Cyprus.

The fourth ship which carried Queen Joan and Princess Berengaria was damaged and unable to sail. Emperor Komnenus had been sending invitations for them to become his guests on shore but they had refused after witnessing the treatment of survivors. In retaliation he cruelly refused them water and provisions.

King Richard had only just arrived with his two swiftest galleys armed with his best soldiers. He was not in a mood to be trifled with. The others would join them shortly but he would not wait.

Emperor Komnenus and his army were scattered up and down the beach. Komnenus himself mounted on a comely gold Arabian stallion stood on a high point while his men covered the shoreline. Some mounted and armed but many more without either, so confident were they in their numbers.

"Your Grace! Thrice upon your orders we have petitioned Emperor Komnenus to restore to us our shipwrecked survivors along with possessions and cargo seized, yet he has refused each time. Not only is he defiant he is insolent as well. He mocks and challenges you to come forward to mark your claim. He refuses to speak to a 'mere king' and boasts no fear of you or any threats you may avow," Unwin, his personal assistant, declared in a mild tone. For he knew what would happen. Richard was an adventurer who loved the glory of battle, and he did not suffer insult unanswered.

Richard turned his head to Unwin and spoke, "They are best prepared for fleeing rather than fighting. He insults God, by his interference with we who go to battle for the Holy Land. He further insults my sister, my fiancé, England and with that me as their protector. Against us, is against God. We will settle this matter presently. Komnenus shall pay dearly for his insolence. This self-proclaimed Emperor."

The destriers they had brought with them were the horses in the best condition after the long sail, the others being overly sore from their travels and lack of exercise. Only fifty proved fit enough to make the journey to the island. This did not deter Richard in the least.

His squire, Winthrop, assisted him to put on his coif, pulling it down over his head and arranging the chain mail over his shoulders. Battre, his favorite war horse, had already been loaded. By this time, additional galleys had reached them. Richard pulled his sword from its scabbard and turned to face eastward. Kneeling on one knee, he held the sword hilt upward in front of his face and made the sign of the cross as he spoke to God:

"In the name of Our Lord, the one true God, his beloved son Jesus Christ and the Holy Comforter, hear our prayer. God everlasting grant us victory over Thine enemies as we enter battle for Thine own glory.

Steel our hands, strengthen our resolve and lead us to victory in Your sacred Name.   Amen"

Making the sign of the cross again, he stood and turned to face his men in galleys, raising the sword above his head.

"To arms and follow me! Let us take vengeance for the insults which this traitor hath put upon God and ourselves, in that he oppresses innocent men, whom he refuses to surrender to us. But truly, he who rejects the just demands of one armed for the fray, resigns all into his hands. And I trust confidently in the Lord that He will this day give us the victory over this Emperor and his people."

A great cry rose up from the men as they raised their weapons into the air. The galleys headed toward shore. King Richard's boat at the fore. He stroked Battre, the Spanish stallion was dressed in barding for battle, softly speaking into the great stallion's ear, "Battre, my old friend. We go to battle once again as you and I have done many times before. You are my bravest warrior, Battre." Battre whinnied softly and turned his head into Richard rubbing his champron on his chest. The metal clinked against Richard's plated vest. The level of trust between horse and rider was obvious. A warrior entrusted his very life to his horse and his horse did the same.

King Richard galley was the first to land along with his bowmen. They leapt into the sea and waded ashore. Winthrop led Battre through the cool waters and once they reached the sandy beach, held him still while Richard mounted. He handed him his ax and waited while Richard collected himself. The bowmen began losing a shower of arrows into the sky crippling the attack from Komnenus men and giving the following galleys safety to land. The knights dressed in hauberks, came ashore riding their horses.

Speaking quietly to Battre, Richard pushed the stallion forward holding his ax high and charged into a group of mounted Cyprians, sending them scattering in all directions. Meanwhile, his men were close behind, riding up and down the entire coast, meeting Komnenus' army at each point. The Cypriots were ill-equipped and no match for the skill of Richard's men. His English bowmen and mounted knights had been drilled as a unit and proceeded to slaughter all in their path.

Richard sighted Komnenus and turned Battre toward his target racing down the beach. He called to him, "Komnenus! Let us finish this battle between ourselves. I challenge you man to man."

The Emperor hesitated and then started riding toward Richard as if to meet him in single combat. Richard watched him approach and spurred Battre forward toward horse and rider.

Suddenly Komnenus turned his mount and flew in the opposite direction, running from the challenge. Five mounted, armed mercenaries saw their Emperor flee and retreated after him. The remaining army scattered in all directions in their panic at the desertion of their leader.

Richard gave chase. Upon reaching a highly treed valley he pulled up Battre and held up his hand to stop further progress by his men. "We know not this terrain and dusk is quickly falling. I fear we must resume our chase on the morrow when day's light provides us with safe passage through the woods.

"That we capture our prey is certain, but it may wait. Unwin, tell the men to strike camp while we refresh ourselves. Have the horses taken care of and send the men into the woods to find whatever food we can forage." With this King Richard, attended by Winthrop, started to strip himself of his armor and then did the same for Battre.

"We can do without this for the time being can we not, Battre? On the morrow we ride again. If this Emperor proves himself to be as brave as he displayed himself today, we may have no need of armor. Naught a one of us," Richard quipped. "Unwin, I want three scouts to track our good Emperor and report back this evening whence ever he has settled."

Richard's men chuckled as they broke up. Some of them returned to the town of Limassol, with their captured men and goods. The townspeople were told of Richard's issued edict that all who supported his cause would be treated fairly and allowed to keep their homes and possessions. Those who did not, would lose all. The townspeople did not hesitate to side with Richard, happy to be rid of their cruel Emperor.

Back at camp, the horses were grazed and watered while the men took rest.

Now that the town was secured, Richard sent a ship to escort his sister and fiancé to him. "Unwin, send men to bring my sister and fiancé to shore and see that they are well attended to. I intend to wed my bride within the days to come as soon as we resolve this matter with Komnenus. Set all to prepare for a celebration in the meantime. I will have my wife and England will have her Queen."

Hours had passed when one of the scouts rode into camp and reached Richard with news.

"Lord King," he panted out of breath. "The Emperor has camped but a mile or so from where we stand, along the river, near Kolossi. Only a few men are still with him. The rest must have kept moving north. He was overheard to tell his men that he intended to destroy you and has no fear of the English King."

"I see his bravado has traveled with him, as he flees my presence," Richard said dryly. The men surrounding him snickered. They were used to their leader's dry wit.

"We will pay the Emperor a visit before daylight strikes. He will be provided with the opportunity to extinguish me," Richard jested.

"Only one thing may well prevent his ambition, Your Grace. He will also need to be present! I wager the bastard will piss himself and run before we even arrive," one of the men shouted and they all laughed.

After they had eaten and slept a few hours the King arose before daybreak and sent word to his men to ready themselves. They rode to Komnenus' camp with the scouts leading the way through the woods. When they reached the encampment, the moon was still in the sky but morning was near.

The plan was at the count of ten, to ride through camp emitting shrieks to disorient the sleeping enemy. As they rode and screamed the camp came alive with men running out of their tents. The naked Emperor Komnenus among them.

All ran leaving everything behind so frightened were they. Komnenus fled without arms but managed to get to his horse much to Richard's disappointment, for he coveted the Emperor's golden, Arabian stallion. Tents and wealth were left behind.

Richard pulled up and leapt from Battre. "We can catch them later, no need for us to scurry after a bunch of disrobed men without mounts," Richard said dryly. "Let us see to what the good Emperor has left for us." He grinned.

Word of Emperor Komnenus cowardice traveled fast. When daylight broke all manner of Barons and Lords of Cyprus begged to enter camp to swear their allegiance to Richard. All pledges were accepted.

Three days later, Guy de Lusignan, the King consort to the kingdom of Jerusalem, arrived coming directly from Acre, where a great battle was taking place in the Holy Land. He was a distant cousin to Raoul de Lusignan, the Duc de Marche. He brought with him three ships and one hundred and sixty knights as well as certain Princes of the Latin Kingdom: Gaufrid of Lezinant, his brother, Anfrid of Turun and Leo, brother to King Rupin of Armenia. All four men swore allegiance to the English King and would be present for Richard's marriage to Berengaria planned for the next day.

They had come to Cyprus to aid the King of England in a bold political move to weld Richard in their support of Guy de Lusignan whose legitimacy to the throne after the death of his wife, Queen Sybilla , was being questioned. Opposition to Guy, as ruler, came from Conrad of Monteferrat, supported by King Phillip of France who had already landed in Acre.

Seeing that fortune was against him, Emperor Komnenus sent ambassadors to King Richard to sue for peace and ask for mercy. Richard was ready to accept so that he could continue to the Holy Land but required the following conditions be met:

- Twenty thousand marks of gold, as recompense for money taken from Richard's ships and to surrender the survivors he had imprisoned.
- Emperor Komnenus would accompany King Richard to Syria and bring one hundred men at arms as well as four hundred Turcopole horsemen to further the cause of the crusade as long as Richard stayed there.
- He will surrender all his castles to the King and deliver his daughter, Mareya, into the King's hands to be married to whomsoever Richard selected.

Upon hearing of these conditions Komnenus became outraged. Especially the last which gave him pause. To turn Mareya over to Richard was an iron through his heart. He thought of his innocent young daughter whom he had protected from all manner of harm and dearly loved. To see her become a pawn in the games of men... He winced.

"Who does this King Richard think he is to dictate such terms to an Emperor of the Byzantine bloodline?" he railed.

"Your Excellency," his aide reminded. "You have little choice in this matter. An Emperor is naught without his head."

"Very well, then," Komnenus snapped. "Agree to the terms." He was buying himself time. He had no intention of honoring such tripe.

Word was sent to King Richard.

And shortly afterward, Komnenus arrived in Limassol to meet with the English King and swear fealty to him as prescribed in the treaty agreement.

Afterward, the men retired to their tents for their midday rest. While all slept Komnenus escaped into the forest. He sent word back to Richard that he was reneging on the treaty and would not honor one word of it. Komnenus had called for his horse and was headed toward his castle in Nicosia further northeast with the few men who remained loyal. He would keep ahead of Richard until Salah ad-Din sent help to rid his island of the English pestilence.

Upon hearing that Komnenus had reneged on his word, Richard smiled. He was not at all surprised and welcomed the chance to dispense with treaties and engage in open warfare. Komnenus had abandoned his honor and would be treated as such.

Komnenus was now a fugitive. Thus, his mercenary forces abandoned their positions guarding strongholds of the State and retreated into the Toros mountains. Komnenus was alone. All towns yielded to King Richard as he entered unopposed. To the betterment of the day, the rest of the King's fleet were arriving in the harbor.

"Your Grace, there will be many more wedding guests this day!" Winthrop exclaimed.

"Good fortune abounds this day, Winthrop. God's blessings. They have arrived in time to celebrate my marriage day," Richard proclaimed in a jovial manner, well satisfied with how events were unrolling.

On Sunday, Richard was in a very expansive mood. It was the feast day for St. Pancras and his wedding day to his betrothed, Berengaria, Princess of Navarre, the sister of his old friend Sancho, future King of Navarre.

Berengaria had sailed with all the accoutrements for her wedding day. She and Joan, along with the ladies of their court, spent the day preparing for the ceremony that was to take place in Limassol castle's chapel. Richard's personal chaplain would be officiating at the ceremony.

The castle kitchens had been busy for days nonstop in anticipation of the feast day. Now, that same energy was transferred to including wedding fare as well.

The cooks that had traveled with Joan and Berengaria were directing all activity. Aromas wafting from the kitchens permeated the balmy sea air, stimulating all appetites and creating excitement for the evening's events.

With the arrival of the fleet, thousands of additional men needed to be accommodated. Most would have to retire to their ships for the evening due to lack of housing. They were happy just to be reunited with their King and friends as well as in the anticipation of a lavish meal.

The castle was a constant buzz of activity that extended to the surrounding town. The air was filled with excitement everywhere, even the stables were busy bathing horses and braiding manes.

All would look their best on this day. Even the guards, who guarded the perimeter around the castle and the village, were dressed in their best.

When early evening came, Richard, attired in his red and gold regalia, stood quietly at the altar with Guy de Lusignan. Soft strains of music filled the air.

Joan appeared dressed in blue and gold silk and behind her was the bride dressed in silk dyed a deep violet with silver and gold roses embroidered upon it as well as seed pearls throughout. Her veil was a sheer silk of the same color with silver and gold threads running through. The veil was fixed with a simple gold circlet embedded with sapphires and ruby cabochons. The effect against her pale skin and long, wavy, dark hair styled in heavy braids was stunning.

The neckline was scooped baring her white bosom. The long train of the dress made it quite heavy so that she had no choice than to walk at a slow, measured pace resulting in an elegant gait.

Wedding attendees were transfixed. No one more so than the groom.

Richard was totally focused on his bride as Berengaria walked slowly toward him to meet him at the altar. He reached out with his large hand and took her small one before it was even offered. The two faced forward with bowed heads before the chaplain who held the cross over them in a finely embroidered linen cloth. He spoke the words of marriage and commitment over the two royal heads.

Richard looked at his bride and leaned down, placing his forehead upon hers and whispered his own sentiments under his breath to the beautiful woman next to him, "Berengaria, you are my wife and Queen. I will honor and protect you from all in this world. You may rely on that as long as I draw breath." His blue eyes sparkled and the red-gold tint of his hair glowed in the dim candlelight. He placed his lips softly on her forehead as he drew himself back to full height.

Berengaria looked up at the pleasing face of her new husband. "You honor me, my husband and King. I place my hand and fate in yours without hesitation. I bind my life to your life this day and for all days to come as long as I draw breath," she responded, smiling up at him. Her sweet lips gently upturned at the corners and her eyes gleamed in happiness.

After the wedding ceremony, the Archbishop of Evreux crowned his new wife, Queen of England, as Richard had requested. He would be riding off to war in a few days and he needed to attend to such details now.

Chapter 27

Castle Whetherly on Moon Isle

Lord Braxton Whetherly was staring out of a window in his well-appointed bed chamber as his wife combed her long, dark hair getting ready for the day. The walls were hung with green and blue, paisley brocade silks from the Orient. The cold stone floor was covered with thickly woven wool carpets from the Caucuses decorated with the same tribal patterns used throughout centuries.

The massive stone fireplace was set on the inside wall across from the bed and together with the fabric covered surfaces, created a cocoon of warmth and comfort. The warm glow of alabaster lanterns and suspended mosaic lamps lit the room.

 Outside, the sky was a cornflower blue with white puffs of clouds dotting its canvas over a Saxe blue sea. His intensely blue eyes squinted as he stared out over the treed countryside. Tanned skin crinkling at their corners, a long, thin scar ran down the left side of his face from his temple to the top of his jaw.

Graying brown hair waved over his strong shoulders which heaved as he let out a long sigh while he considered the three missives he held in his hand. They had arrived the same day hours apart. The first from Isley, the second from Dover and third from Dyfen. "There is something here for your eyes," he said as he turned to face his wife.

He stared into her large, brown eyes set into her lovely, sculpted face. She wore her thick, naturally wavy black hair the way he liked it best, loosely, tumbling past her small waist. Her dusky skin tone softened the angles of her face and made her look as if she glowed from within.

He wished for them to undress, get back into the bed they shared and forget all current events as he nestled against her soft body, nose pressed into her scented hair. He considered it seriously for a few seconds and then instead said to his wife, "Fairkene, we may have a problem."

His wife stopped combing her hair and eyed him guardedly.

Chapter 28

Ellette

Dyfen stayed below deck. Dover was resting in the straw. Isley stood leaning against a stall post looking down at Kellis who had passed out from exhaustion and was sleeping soundly in the neighboring stall. His young face relaxed as slumber wiped away the strained and tired look born of the heavy burden he had carried. The scent of fresh, sweet hay mingled with the earthy smell of manure hung in the air. Familiar and comforting.

Isley placed a stable blanket over the boy. "Poor lad. He has had a fair measure of adventure these past days."

Dyfen was silent as he knelt amongst his dogs, moving his hands over their coarse hair. Talking softly to each of them. His mind wandered back to their prior owner two years hence.

They had been Ellette's constant companions ever since, finding them whimpering in the woods feeding upon the meager remains of a deer carcass. There was not much left, but the severely underweight pups chewed on the hide trying to stave their extreme hunger.

Upon seeing her arrival, they fled into the brush. She dismounted and bent down, pushing branches aside to gain a better look. She spoke to them in a soft manner, trying to coax them out. Finally, she went to her horse and pushed her hand into the saddle bag she normally rode with to find fragments of the midday meal her cook had packed for her.

She hurried back to the brush, stooping down once again and held out her delicate hand, holding the coarse bread for them to scent. She counted at least three pups and could see only one plainly. He was dark grey in color and on the smallish side compared to the other two but a commanding enough presence to prevent the others from moving past him while he remained suspicious of her intentions.

Toward him, she pushed the bread placing it down then backing away. The pup waited for her to settle before investigating what she had left. He started to nibble, and the others came forward to join him. Five in all. Colored shades of white to black. Fur matted, wet from the dew. She could see their ribs so thin they were. Their tails a wag, thin bodies wriggling, each filling their empty little bellies with the scrap of hardened crust.

She sat on the hard ground silently watching them, a gentle smile moved over her delicate features. She took great pleasure in their happiness. The small one suddenly stopped and looked at her. Studying her with his drowsy eyes. Finally, he came to a conclusion and padded towards her. He reached her outstretched hand and licked the crumbs that still idled around her fingers and climbed into her lap. She slowly moved her hand over his thin, boney body. The puppy emitted a tired sigh and settled against her. Shortly after, the others followed once they had finished the crust she had left them. They surrounded her body and settled themselves against her while they took the rest they sorely needed.

She dared not move a muscle for fear of unsettling them. After twenty minutes the littlest one in her lap stirred and yipped, awaking the others. Ellette slowly stood and took her horse's bridle, looking behind her to make eye contact with him and started walking at a slow pace. She turned again and could see the dogs following her in a group. Ellette smiled to herself all the way home.

The distance was short, but it took an hour because she wanted to make sure they could keep up. When they arrived the band behind her huddled en masse as she asked the stable boy to gather meat from the kitchen and bring it to the stable. Ellette grabbed a shallow feed bowl and filled it with water from the well. The stable hand had returned with the food which he placed next to the water. "Now then, a proper meal for my sweet ones."

The small dark grey puppy once again approached first and the rest overtook him and surrounded the bowls. While they were eating, she lifted each up from behind and discovered that all five were male. "My lads!" she exclaimed. The smallest she named Cydryn. The largest was completely black. "Tyber" she called out. She looked at the other three. The medium grey color, "Avak", the white, "Osyn" the last one, "Aubryn" the lightest grey.

Once they had finished eating, she took them on a short walk so that they may relieve themselves before taking them into the manor house. Her father, Bishop Brassard encountered them on the way in as the pups ran past in hot pursuit of imaginary prey.

"Ellette, my dear daughter what have you here? Who are your friends? And so many," he observed.

"Father, I found them starving in the wood. I could not leave them to perish. It would not be Christian," she said smiling at her father.

"Yes, it would not be Christian my daughter. We do God's work in many ways. Have they no mother? They do not appear very old, a couple of months or so. I should think they would still be with their mother," he queried.

"They were alone, abandoned but they have a home now," she stated. "They are our family, father."

No one could refuse Ellette, and so the pups became her faithful friends, wherever she did go, the pups also went. None more devout than Cydryn. Even though the smallest, he was also the most fearless. His brothers followed him without hesitation as they wreaked havoc throughout her home to Ellette's delight and the dismay of the seneschal. Dyfen chuckled to himself while remembering.

Dyfen continued stroking the dogs. He could feel the scar tissue on Cydryn's chest where the fur no longer grew. It was invisible to the eye now. Covered by his longish fur. It triggered a more sinister memory from that time.

The sun was high and clear. The air, warm and sweet. His heart filled with joy as he and Shariff headed to meet his love at their arranged meeting place.

When he arrived, his heart fell to his feet. In the clearing, her back against a tree was the lifeless form of Ellette. Her legs were splayed outward and her gown pushed back above her knees. Blood covered her thighs. Still in her abdomen rested a dagger. Dyfen rushed over, but her dogs, witness to the tragedy, had surrounded her prostrate body. The smallest sat between her outspread legs growling at him as he approached. Cydryn, still a pup, valiantly guarding his mistress even though his small chest had been pierced, blood still streaming.

Dyfen started to bend down toward her, Cydryn lunged for his arm. Dyfen caught him by the scruff and gently cradled him in the crook of his arm. Cydryn finally recognizing him, collapsed in relief against his arm. The leaves shuddered on the trees as if they knew the horror that had taken place there. Silent observers.

Dyfen grasped the dagger hilt and pulled the steel from her thin body and dropped to his knees, clutching her lifeless form. Rocking back and forth. The wind picked up and a howl went out through the forest. Bone chilling in itself as it rose and carried the sound around each tree. He could see the five puppies huddled together with lifted heads yowling, telling the world of the misery they shared.

Dyfen pulled her skirts down to cover her and pulled the fabric up over her small breasts where her material had been savagely torn. There was a scratch running down her chest.

The turquoise nugget they had found together in a streambed was still there. Ellette had said the color reminded her of his eyes. It had pleased him to hear those words, so much that he had put the stone on a leather cord which she wore around her neck. Now the stone was pushed around to her back, the leather cord in a tangle. Dyfen gently lifted it over her head and placed it round his own neck.

Then his fingers went to his own right shoulder where he removed the garnet brooch he always wore, a gift from his mother. Grabbing the top of her gown, he shoved the pin through layers of fabric pinning it closed.

Gently lifting her slight form in both arms, he placed the still body over the broad back of Shariff who could sense the tragedy and stood very still. Ellette's long wavy hair scraped the ground. Dyfen lifted the injured Cydryn with one arm while he remounted Shariff and started slowly walking back to the home of Bishop Brassard.

The pack followed in the same slow motion. A funeral procession.

As he rode, he could hear the dogs howl as they traveled through the silent woods, carrying the defiled and lifeless form of fifteen-year-old Ellette Brassard back to her home.

After his daughter's death, Bishop Brassard could no longer bear to be near the dogs. The pups grieved her loss, losing all interest in food and drink. Dyfen saw them wasting away, Cydryn near death. His chest wound was infected and he had refused to allow anyone near enough to treat him.

He gathered the pups and took them home, placing them in the stable where he slept with them. At first, Cydryn would only allow Dyfen to treat his injury and after a time, began to trust Sarkis as well.

He, with the help of Sarkis' hand, fed all five pups until they regained their health.

Dyfen's mind came back to the present. He squeezed his eyes closed as a tear traveled down his cheek. He wearily leaned his head down beside Cydryn's long muzzle for comfort as they sailed back to fulfill his obligation in Cyprus.

Chapter 29

The Search

Almost two days had passed. Dyfen, Isley, Dover and Kellis stood on deck and sighted the cliffs that held Kyrenia castle visible in the half-moon light. The castle was dark except where the moon cast light upon its towers. They could see the pale outline of the Esper crested flags flapping in the breeze.

The Black Trident, smaller, faster had arrived first and was already anchored fifty yards offshore awaiting the Wild Boar. A small rowboat with Martel and a few of his men were waiting for Hugo onshore.

Once in sight of the shore, the Wild Boar dropped anchor and lowered a small boat into the water with some men, staying away from the docks in case any of Komnenus men lingered there. Another boat was lowered containing Kellis and Dover, who were taking the dogs. There was no way to unload the horses this far out so Dyfen and Isley decided to swim to shore with them after encouraging Zakar and Arazi to jump from the cargo doors closer to the surface of the water.

The horses were strong swimmers and with Dyfen on Zakar and Isley on Arazi they were met on shore by Kellis, Dover and the dogs. The stars shone bright in the night sky accompanying the pale half-moon.

On shore, Dyfen mounted Arazi, whose dark coat was less visible in the night. "I will take Isley with me and the rest of you stay here until we return," he commanded. Arazi somehow sensed the seriousness of his mission and stood quietly as Dyfen spoke. So dark was the stallion that he appeared to be a shadow in the dark night. His muscular form and flowing mane presented a powerful image of strength as he stood in the wet sand of the beach.

"No Lord, that will not do," Kellis blurted out. "I know the castle better than any here. You need me to guide you."

"Kellis, lad. You have already risked your life for your lady. It will not be safe for you to come. We only have two mounts," Dyfen's voice was flat.

"I will accompany you," Isley said strongly. "Kellis you will stay here on the beach."

"I must come, and I will come even if I must walk," Kellis stubbornly stated. His eyes challenged Dyfen. "Afterall, she is my Lady and she put her life into my hands." He placed his right hand to his chest.

Dyfen stared back at the youth and finally spoke, "Very well then lad, mount Zakar. Stay far behind me and out of the moonlight so not to be seen. Do not dismount until I tell you to," he relented.

"Thank you, my Lord, I will do as you ask. You will not be sorry," Kellis stated solemnly.

"Ready?" Dyfen asked him. Kellis shook his head in the affirmative as he pulled himself onto the silver stallion. Zakar gently whinnied in recognition of Kellis as a friend. His silver coat gleamed in the mild light and his long mane and tail flowed with the breeze creating a ghostly specter.

Hugo, overhearing the conversation, began to object but before he could speak the two were headed off towards Kyrenia castle.

They took the path Dyfen had used to travel down to the beach for his evening rides. The dogs and horses knew the way. The horses having better eyesight in the dark were able to find their way easily as they traveled upwards through the trees and wild brush.

Once at the top of the hill, they saw no sentries posted but still moved with caution. When they reached the gatehouse both portcullises were up. Dyfen put his hand up to stop Kellis from going further, while he thought through what it could mean. No sound or activity came from within. Looking up he could see no men at the parapets.

Dyfen dismounted from Arazi and slowly crept towards the opening staying close to the wall. The shadows of the surrounding trees fell on the ground before him moving with the blustering wind. Tree limbs soughed in the night and the air smelled of sweet dew. The silence from within created an eerie atmosphere. Dyfen caught the stench of rotting flesh every so often as the wind shifted.

He froze in place as he considered the best way forward. He nodded to Kellis to dismount and join him in the shadows. The dogs stood silently waiting for direction from Dyfen as they had been trained. Their heads were up, and their tails were still in anticipation of action.

"Kellis, is there a hidden entrance, a postern, we can gain access? Most castles possess such an escape as do we on Moon Isle," Dyfen asked speaking softly to Kellis.

Kellis hesitated for a moment and then nodded affirmatively. His tired eyes had shadows beneath them. "There is such a way. I traveled through it but days ago to escape. It is near the western turret and leads down into the dungeons of the castle. We need to follow the wall. Let me lead."

Dyfen nodded to confirm the plan and pushed his back into the wall to allow Kellis to pass. Shadows crossed his face and hid the look of fear that rested there. Fear at what he expected to find once they had breached the walls. The smell of rotting flesh was heavy in the air. He could barely intake a solid breath without feeling sick to his stomach. He felt fear at the thought of failing to be in time to save her whom he had vowed to protect.

Kellis was moving at a brisk pace and stopped at a vine-covered section of the wall. He shoved the vines away and grabbed an iron ring imbedded in a thick wooden door hidden there. Dyfen pushed him to the side and leaned into it with all his might until he felt movement. The door was very heavy and swung slowly open on its heavy hinges to display narrow stone steps leading downward. An unlit rushlight torch was anchored to the wall.

Kellis jumped into the lead and started moving quickly down the steps, feeling the wall as he moved forward. Dyfen followed closely behind so not to lose sight of him in the dark. They reached the dungeons where all the cells stood empty. The torches were still burning faintly flickering in the musty, stale air.

Kellis turned left through a short passage and started climbing steps upward. He pushed open the door at the landing and stepped out into the castle keep. Dyfen recognized where they were now. To the right was the map room and straight ahead was the great hall. Stairs nearby led to the private chambers.

"Emlyn!........ Emlyn!" He began to shout, searching wildly for a sign of her presence.

"Kellis, where did you last leave her?" Dyfen asked with urgency.

"I left her at the dungeon steps, my Lord, after providing me with the path to escape. Her stride was still somewhat labored, so she refused my urging to accompany me to freedom. She did not want to slow me. She sent me to fetch you. I did my best my Lord. I swear it," Kellis' voice broke a bit. Dyfen put his hand on the back of Kellis' neck in affection, trying to comfort him.

They both turned their heads when they heard a scraping noise from the left. It sounded like metal against masonry. Dyfen traveled down an unlit passage toward the noise with Kellis close behind him. Something glinted in the darkness.

Kellis ran past Dyfen and fell to the ground next to a form propped up against the wall dragging his dagger back and forth across the stone floor. It was Eston.

"Eston! Eston what transpired here?" Kellis exclaimed shaken at seeing this unconquerable warrior bleeding from his chest and a significant gash in his left thigh. He had lost a considerable amount of blood. His face was pale and swollen and his eyes were glazing over. Dyfen feared he was close to death.

"Eston, what befell your lady?" Dyfen asked gently.

"Sire" …" sire," he began again. "He returned for her. I tried to stay him." He looked down at his wounded leg. "I failed."

"Who was it? Who dare lay a hand upon her?" he asked Eston in a low tone. His blood was up.

"He set out first but circled back. Serpent that he is. While all men were away, he returned."

"WHO? WHO dare do this?"

"The Devil's own son, the Duc de Marche, my Lord. It was de Marche," Eston's breath was ragged now, he was barely breathing. "That evil viper has my lady."

"What of Lords Esper and Eryk? Where are they?" Dyfen queried.

"Gone, Lord. To join with Richard Lionheart who battles on our southern beaches. They answered his call to rise up against Emperor

Komnenus, ruthless dog of Satan that he is, and free us from his oppression," Eston said with labored breath.

"Sire," he had reached out his large, deathly pale hand to grab Dyfen by the wrist. "Lady Komnenus remains. Her father left her in my care and du Marche had not the nerve to trouble her. She remains in the east tower behind locked doors," he was struggling to touch his belt.

Dyfen saved him the trouble and unfastened a ring of keys, showing them to Eston who was fast fading. "The largest," he panted. Dyfen understood.

Looking up at Dyfen Eston took a short breath, his body slumped forward, barely breathing. Dyfen set the noble servant down so that he was flat on the floor.

Kellis was stooped against the opposite wall with his head lowered into his hands. "All is lost," he murmured his drawn face streaked with dirt.

Dyfen looked at Kellis' slumped body and grabbed him by the arms and shook him; hard. "Kellis! We need to return to the beach. At once. But first you must lead me to the east tower so that we may make certain Lady Komnenus is well enough. Come to your feet and take us there with haste. Then we will return to the horses."

Kellis stood up and pulled himself together. He led Dyfen up the stone stairs that kept winding upward until there were no more. They were in a tower with a window on one side and a heavy wooden, iron studded door on the other. Dyfen began banging his solid fist against it shouting, "Lady Komnenus, Lady Komnenus! It is Dyfen Whetherly. I am unlocking the door. Do not be alarmed."

He inserted the largest key on the ring into the large lock and pushed the door open. In the moonlight he saw a comely maiden calmly sitting in a chair. Mareya. There was an ewer and a plate of bread and fruits on the table next to her.

"Lady Mareya, how do you fare?" he asked with concern.

"I am well enough, Lord Whetherly. I was pushed into this tower and kept here under lock. I could hear men's voices and realized the castle had been breached. Where is Lady Emlyn?" she asked. She looked from Dyfen to Kellis.

Kellis' face told her the answer was not a good one.

"She was taken, my lady," Kellis related.

"Taken by whom?" she asked concerned.

"Taken by the Duc de Marche, the vile scoundrel," Dyfen responded.

"I cannot say I am surprised. Even I could see his ill intentions. I know not where he fled, but I am sure my father would know. They were as thick as thieves. If he had no fear of my father to stay his hand, who knows what would have befallen myself."

"Lady, forgive us but we cannot spare a moment more here. We must go in search of your father to find where de Marche has taken Emlyn."

"Be off, then good sir," Lady Mareya urged. "I will be well enough left here. I have my man servant and maid to look after me. Each has been at the door trying to secure my freedom but could find no key. I will seek them out and we will be well."

Dyfen placed the large key into her hand. In case she had need of it and then spoke to Kellis, "Kellis let us take our leave."

They rushed down the stairs and out through the castle's main entrance. Not a single soul was about. They headed toward the kitchens and discovered a man and young woman seated at the wooden table with Mim fussing over them. There was bread and cheese laid out with the aroma of pies baking in the oven and meat roasting on the spit wafting in the air.

"My word, Kellis! Lord Whetherly!" she cried, happy to see them. "Thank Our Lord you are here. That devil took my angel," she moaned half falling. Dyfen braced himself to take on her weight. He gently pushed her back to her feet.

"Mim, we leave to find her. Lady Komnenus is free from the tower and will need her servants." The two seated people rose to their feet and rushed out the door.

"Mim," he said solemnly. "Eston has been mortally wounded. We left him near the entrance to the castle undercroft," he said gently. "I do not believe he was still in this world but send the doctor in any case."

Mim looked near fainting with the shock of the news. Eston was a long and trusted friend to all. Their perception of his strength made him indestructible.

She slid into a chair nearby with tears rolling down her chubby cheeks. She looked old and tired. "Dr. Chikaris has been searching far and wide for him. You mean to say he has been in the castle injured all of this time? Eston has been a champion for all. I cannot grasp that he may be gone." Her voice trembled as she addressed one of the kitchen boys, "Run like the wind and find the doctor."

She came to herself. "Lord Whetherly! Make haste and be gone to find my sweet Lady. I will take care of all here," she promised. "Take what fare I have at hand." She began ordering her staff to pack victuals for them to take. She handed the packages to Kellis and kissed his cheek. "Return my Lady to me and be mindful of yourselves."

Dyfen and Kellis flew from the kitchen and back from whence they had come. Dyfen let out a shrill whistle and could hear the immediate response of hoof beats. The horses arrived with all the dogs at the portcullis. Dyfen and Kellis mounted and sped off with the dogs running at their side.

They made their way down to the beach. The sea air smelled damp and salty as the wind blew gently in the moonlit night. They could hear the Cypriot Scop owls eerie call echoing in the nearby forest trees. It was hard to imagine tragedy had taken place this day.

As they rode down to the water's edge, Hugo spotted them. "Where is she?" he called out, not seeing Emlyn with them.

"The Duc de Marche has taken her," Dyfen responded. "That bastard Komnenus will know where. We must find him."

"Agreed," stated Hugo, looking levelly at Martel. "Let us go, Francois. We sail."

"We will need to leave Zakar and Arazi here, there is no way we can board them from the water. Kellis can stay behind with them until we return," Dyfen ordered trying to organize his thoughts.

"I think not. We go alone. These being our ships," Hugo returned evenly.

Dover grabbed Hugo by the shirt ready to object.

Martel had a large cuirass drawn and was holding it against Kellis' throat. The King Cheetah tattoo was moving as he breathed. "Release my friend," he hissed. "And take care your puppies do not come to play with me." He smirked. "My hand may slip."

Dover dropped his hold on Hugo and backed up. Isley held both hands up and slowly moved away while Dyfen ordered the dogs to stay. The pack looked at him questioningly. Sensing the present danger, the command to stand still made no sense to them but they did as told.

Pleased at Hugo's release, Martel said with narrowed eyes and customary smirk on his dark face, blue eyes glowing in the dim light, "Now we know each other."

His face shifted as he remembered something. "Bon Ami," Martel exclaimed to Hugo. "When we sailed south there were but two galleys moored outside Limassol harbor. One bearing sail marks of the Lionheart of England. In the distance, there were tens of sails moving toward the harbor. They will be here within a day's sail, deux at the latest in poor winds. He comes for his fiancé and sister. He comes for Komnenus. But there was one ship headed north, toward us," Martel finished and looked to Hugo for a response.

"Let us not waste a minute more. We must encounter Komnenus to discover where de Marche has taken her before Richard captures him," Hugo realized. He shouted out the command, "Weigh anchor."

The men scrambled to the galleys that had brought them ashore.

Martel kept his hold on Kellis and forced him to board the closest vessel. "You will be returned when we are safely away." He kept his blade so close to Kellis' chin that the boy could feel the cold from the steel.

The men picked up the oars and pulled away. Hugo sat aft looking towards the anchored ships with a pensive look on his face. Two furrows rested on his brow.

True to his word, about thirty yards from shore, Martel removed the blade from Kellis' chin and gave him a hard push backwards sending him over the edge of the galley into the sea water. Martel waved his cuirass grandly in the air at Dyfen and bowed. He then turned back to the task at hand, yelling obscenities in French at his men.

Startled by the chilly water temperature, Kellis began his swim back to shore. The dogs were racing up and down the beach when he stumbled onto the sand. They all surrounded him with concern. Cydryn put his cold nose onto his shoulder. "I am well my friend, do not blame yourself," Kellis told the dog chuckling as if he understood. The pack resumed their joyous celebration chasing one another into the shallow water and back.

Kellis squeezed the water from his clothing and came to stand by the group of men in time to hear Dyfen respond to Isley's question, "What of Lady Emlyn?"

He recited what Eston had told him, "Komnenus left to meet Richard taking the Duc de Marche and his men at arms with him. Shortly thereafter a messenger came to Lord Esper with word that the countryside was rising up against Emperor Komnenus. Richard was calling for support, support to finally rid the country of the malady that had overtaken it years before. He and Eryk rode out to answer the call to defeat the Emperor and take back the land. Lord Rend offered his ship to transport them south and they accepted his offer."

"They left Eston and a few men behind to safeguard the women thinking that Emperor Komnenus and the Duc de Marche had left. They were not expecting the Duc to circle back as he did. The devil abducted Emlyn, severely injuring Eston. The castle is virtually empty except for servants."

"Women, meaning who exactly?" Isley asked.

"Lady Komnenus also stayed behind with her servants," Dyfen answered.

"What! Mareya?" Isley cried in surprise. "She is to remain here without protection? This is not acceptable. She must travel with us."

"No, Isley. She is safest here. She has her maid and man servant to look after her and there are few left in the castle. If we take her with us, she will slow our pace and require protection as well. Protection she deserves and that I am uncertain we can afford her. It will not be safe for her with us. Better she remains behind," Dover reasoned.

Isley looked as if he would argue but weighed Dover's words in his mind. After a couple of minutes passed, he spoke, "I will agree, only after I have seen her for myself and am well satisfied of her safety." He did not await an answer. He mounted Arazi and rode toward Kyrenia castle.

Dover, Dyfen and Kellis watched him ride away.

Dover spoke first, "I know you are not well pleased brother, but do not blame him."

Dyfen just sighed and pulled his hand across the right side of his jawline. Dover knew the habit. His brother was in thought.

"If we do not find Komnenus fast and first, she will be lost to us," he said visibly upset.

"Isley knows this and will soon return," Dover tried to comfort him.

Before he could respond, Dyfen became distracted. "What ship sails in our direction?" he exclaimed, sighting a familiar sail in the distance.

Isley and Arazi flew over the road reaching the castle barbican in minutes. He jumped from his mount while still in motion, not waiting for Arazi to fully stop. He ran into the main hall calling out Mireya's name.

He heard footfalls coming from the staircase and a slim figure in a blue gown saw him and smiled. She was radiant even in the dim light. Her dark hair shone like a dark sun and her dark eyes were glowing, alight at the sight of him.

"Lord Standen!" she cried.

"Lady Komnenus, I had to see with mine own eyes that you were safe."

"I am safe and well, Lord Standen. Do not trouble yourself for my welfare. I am ably looked after. It is Emlyn who must have our thoughts. That beast, Raoul de Lusignan, has absconded with her. Rush to find my father. He will know where she was taken. He knows that wretches mind."

On impulse he hugged her against his strong chest before remembering himself. He backed quickly away, turning red. "Forgive me, my lady," he said with some embarrassment.

She smiled up at him to let him know she was in no way offended. She lightly touched his face with her hand and then gave him a gentle push to start him off, understanding he could not stay. He grabbed her small hand, placing his lips gently upon it, just grazing her skin. His heart leapt at her touch.

He let out a low whistle for Arazi who appeared as if magically. His green eyes took in the vision of her just before he turned to run for his horse. Soon they were on the way back to the beach to begin the search for Emperor Isaac Komnenus.

Chapter 30

The Sea Stallion

Isley returned as dawn was breaking. Dover and Dyfen were watching the slowly rising sun above the ocean horizon. In the distance, a familiar sail moved toward them.

"Father! Its father!" Isley shouted excitedly. There was no mistaking the saffron colored sail of the Sea Stallion with its blazing white cross next to the rearing black stallion and the motto, 'Deus antecedit', (God goes before us) in Latin underneath.

"Denisot Febrelle! What in the God's name has brought him here?" Dover cried.

As the ship came closer, they could see a long, black mane flowing back in the wind, on the bow. "I think I recognize Shariff on deck as well as Arka and Seert!"

There was no mane like that of Shariff. Long, wavy, black and shining. He was a magnificent Friesian stallion, a destrier of seventeen hands. His sons, Arka and Seert, were very similar in appearance, stood next to their sire.

They all hurried to the north wharf waiting for the Sea Stallion to dock. As the ship approached, they could hear Shariff calling out to them from the deck. Arazi and Zakar in turn became excited and called back to their friend.

The Sea Stallion was a unique horse transport vessel that possessed an equine friendly design created by Captain Denisot Febrelle with input from Dyfen. It had the normal slings below deck used to keep the horses footing stable while under sail but also had a specially designed ramp used to bring the horses on deck, allowing them to disembark more easily and eliminating the more stressful methods used by other ships.

Captain Febrelle came barreling down the gangplank on top of Shariff. They pulled up in front of the group on the wharf. Denisot jumped off the stallion and came rushing up to Isley and Dover.

The men all slapped each other on the back in greeting.

Shariff pranced impatiently waiting for his sons to disembark.

Dyfen came running up with Kellis behind him. "Denisot! God's eyes I am overjoyed to see you. What brings you here?"

"I am here at the behest of your father; he received your missive Isley and sent me in answer."

Captain Febrelle turned toward Dover, "And here is a missive from your mother, Dover. She told me you await a reply."

Dover looked at the sealed parchment, broke the seal and opened it as he stepped away from the others. It was a short note and he could tell it had been hurriedly written with the words,

'Warmest greetings my handsome boy,

Your news was unexpected! I understand your concern and know that you will act as you see best, my son. I will see to your father. Continue to look after your brothers.

I send my deepest affection,

 Mayrik (mother)'

He shoved it into his pouch and rejoined the others.

"And Dyfen, your father sent this for you," Captain Denisot gently shoved the folded parchment sealed with the Whetherly crest into Dyfen's hands.

Dyfen recognized his name written in his father's script. He tapped it against his thumb a few times before reading it. He unfolded the paper and read the few words that were scribed there then tore it in halves and let it fly to the wind.

Denisot explained his mission, "Isley, I brought the horses as your father instructed. He intended to come as well but at the last-minute set sail on a separate journey."

"Isley, you wrote father?" Dyfen turned to look at Isley who was in the process of straightening his sash.

"I did. I sent a messenger while arranging for our chests to be brought to the Wild Boar before we set sail from Jaffa, as a precautionary measure. Father acted quickly I am glad to see," Isley said with a tired smile on his face.

It took a few seconds for Dover to realize what the arrival of Denisot and horses meant. "Sarkis!" Dover shouted. "Where is he? We have missed his misbegotten self sorely."

As he spoke the words, a tall, lean, deeply tanned, shirtless, figure with long, tousled, dark hair came on deck leading the two magnificent sons of Shariff, Arka and Seert.

"Sarkis!" they all called.

Sarkis stopped and held his hand up in greeting. He had a big smile on his face as he came walking down the gangplank with his charges. His white teeth flashed against his olive skin.

Sarkis hugged and held close the three men who he had known since boyhood with clear affection.

"Kellis, come join us and meet our good friend, Sarkis," Dyfen called to Kellis who reservedly approached the group.

He held out his arm in greeting. Sarkis grasped his wrist and pulled him in for a hug as well. "Kellis, I hope these three have not been the burden to you that they have been to me," Sarkis joked with a big smile, displaying his bright teeth. "It was a good day when they all sailed away leaving me behind to rest for a change."

"You sluggard, resting is that what you have been up to when you are supposed to be feeding and watering?" Denisot laughed, turning to the others. "Your Uncle August has not needed to stitch Sarkis up since Dover left us. He has learned that raging stallions are safer company to keep." They all laughed at the truth in it, jostling each other. Glad to take their minds off the reality of events and what was to happen next.

Dyfen was the first to return to the problem at hand, "What is the quickest path to reach Emperor Komnenus before Rend or Richard do? Sea or land?" he asked, looking at Kellis.

Kellis pondered the question for a minute. "Lord, from what Martel said, Richard Lionheart's vessels will be controlling the southern seacoast before we can arrive. I advise we ride inland to Emperor Komnenus' castle on the northern border of Nicosia. Komnenus was sure to stop there to collect additional men at arms and fresh horses. It is but twelve miles from where we stand, a two-hour ride over flat land. I have family there, where we can stay. My Uncle Ouras."

Isley slowly nodded his head in agreement. "We need to get the horses ready for our ride south. We will squeeze Emlyn's whereabouts out of that devil's bastard, Komnenus. He will know where she has been taken. Kellis, how far is it to Limassol in case Komnenus is not in Nicosia?"

"Fifty or so miles from Nicosia, my Lord," Kellis told him looking anxious.

"How familiar are you with the terrain to reach the south?" Dover asked.

"I have travelled south many times with my Lord. From Nicosia, it's two day's ride but can be done in one if we ride hard. I can lead us there," Kellis said with determination on his face.

Dyfen turned to the captain and spoke, "Denisot, you might as well stay here and await our return. If you do not hear from us within five days' time, set sail for home. It is too dangerous to stay any longer," he directed.

Captain Denisot gave his head a nod in understanding.

Dover spoke. "All of our armor and accoutrements are still on board the Wild Boar which Hugo has so inconveniently fled with."

"I have armor for the dogs and horses on board," Denisot said with a worried tone in his voice. "But sixty miles is far too long for them to travel outfitted in body armor and it is too heavy to carry and still make good time. I fear you must go without it."

Dyfen had the same worried look on his face. "I agree. It would be too much to ask of them to travel so far wearing battle dress and then expect them to do combat at the end of it. Leave it all behind."

They started to tack the horses up for the journey. They threw rugs over their backs and used simple rope halters. The less burden on them the better, to keep them fresh.

Dyfen turned to prepare Shariff while Dover and Isley took care of Arazi and Zakar. He spoke to the stallion in a soft whisper, "Shariff, "Shariff, so good to see you once again my mighty man." Shariff's eyes softened when he heard his master's voice and his ears pointed straight forward attending to his every word, "You sense we are about to face conflict. I can see how you gather yourself my brave steed. Father chose well sending you to us." Dyfen stroked the huge stallion's forehead moving the longer black hairs aside to uncover the white ones that formed a cross hiding there. Shariff's identifying marking. Concealed from the world, Dyfen had only discovered it while bathing the young colt after convincing his father not to sell him to a farmer.

He completed his preparation and swung his leg up and over, gathering the reins in his right hand. The eastern saddle rug he sat upon was his father's favorite design. He smiled to himself. Father is represented if not here in the flesh, he thought to himself.

Sarkis handed a rope to Kellis and said "Arka has hooves the size of bucklers. He is a sure-footed steed." Kellis mounted Arka and could feel the power beneath him. Arka's muscles rolled against his legs as he and the horse moved as one.

"This is his brother, Seert, it means, heart, in Armenian. He has the heart of a warrior and never falters in battle." Sarkis mounted the dark stallion with little effort. They walked up front next to Kellis on Arka.

Dyfen, Isley and Dover brought up the rear. Kellis turned his head to look behind him. Saw that all were ready and started trotting out over the fields heading south, picking up speed as they went on. The dogs followed.

Later, when they had reached the outskirts of Nicosia, capitol of Cyprus, the seat of Emperor Komnenus' power, they took rest. From the edge of the wood, they could see the mighty castle towers rising in the distance with penates fluttering in the breeze. The castle seemed to be abuzz with activity as they saw men on horseback enter and depart.

Dyfen stopped Shariff and whistled in a short burst. All the horses stopped. Kellis turned to look back with a puzzled face as Arka stood still. Sarkis could not help but laugh. Kellis looked at him unable to understand. "They are trained," he laughed. "They are all trained to respond to ques." He was smiling at Kellis. "The Chaverdian family has been training horses for generations back. There are none better," Sarkis said proudly.

"Who are the Chaverdians?" Kellis asked.

"We are the Chaverdians," Dover answered. "Our mother's family name is Chaverdian, and her family has bred and trained horses many centuries back. My father and mother were given land and breeding stock by my grandfather as a wedding gift. Father is very close to all of my uncles. They have had a deep affection and appreciation for him ever since he rescued mother."

"Rescued your mother?" Kellis looked even more bewildered.

"That tale will keep for a less serious time," Dyfen said soberly. "I am more interested in the amount of activity at the castle? Does this mean we have found Emperor Komnenus at home? "

"Allow me to ride ahead," Kellis suggested. "I will seek out my uncle and find what is afoot here to make sure it is safe for us to enter the city." He looked at Dyfen who nodded his head in approval.

"Take Avak with you and send him back when the time is ready for us to follow," Dyfen instructed.

"We should dismount and rest the horses," Isley stated. "Allow them respite while we wait for word to move forward. The dogs can use some rest as well."

Everyone started to dismount while Kellis rode on taking Avak with him. The remaining four dogs laid down in a group but were still vigilant. They knew that Avak separating from the pack meant he was still on duty, and they would not rest until their brother returned. Cydryn laid near Dyfen who unconsciously stroked the hound's large head as he stared at the ground before him, lost in thought.

Finally, he rallied from his revery. "Sarkis, I need a word with you," Dyfen spoke quietly.

"Yes, my Lord," Sarkis responded, smiling at his friend.

"In your employ as arrow boy, did you ever come across such an arrow?" he asked, showing him the shaft and arrowhead he had removed from Emlyn's leg, for him to examine.

Sarkis took the two pieces and turned them over in his hands. "Yes, I have seen this work before. It has been many years, but I recall the four, eagle feather fletching, the aspen wood shaft, the thickness of the nock. Quite unique. Of course, it has been years since I was in service to my Lord Lanfryd. We came under attack while we rode through the forest. These very arrows were loosed at our entourage. Compliments of Lord Clement de Lusignan. An evil man by all accounts," he finished. "Where did you come across this one?" Sarkis asked curiously.

"It landed in a friend," Dover responded, seeing Dyfen falling back into thought. Lord Clement de Lusignan was the father of Roaul de Lusignan, the Duc de Marche.

Sarkis knew that focus and fell silent allowing Dyfen his privacy. He sat down next to Dover and the two of them spoke to Isley about events from the time they shipwrecked near Kyrenia. Sarkis listened intently sighing deeply as the story unrolled. "Seems I missed the excitement," he commented.

"Surely, you did," Dover grinned. "I managed to survive it all without you. Although, we all admitted that it would have been ever so much more enjoyable if you had been here. I must show myself in the monk's robe. I brought it with me. Damned comfortable garment. I wonder why Uncle August does not wear his more often," he mused.

"He would always complain about the rough fabric and the itch it caused," Isley returned. With that statement Isley and Dover looked at each other with a certain realization on their faces.

"It is not a true monk's robe, too soft for that," Dover stated with a curious tone.

He stopped speaking when he witnessed the dogs standing up with erect ears watching a space in the field. It was dusk.

Avak came into view with Arka. The large horse parted the grass with his every stride. The blades moved aside with a subtle whooshing sound. The other hounds ran towards them in reunion. Avak touched noses with each of his brothers in greeting. Kellis gestured for the men to mount and follow as he turned Arka around heading back to where he had come from.

"Apparently, the time is right to enter Nicosia," Dyfen said while rising from the ground. He headed toward Shariff who had been grazing with the other horses a short distance away. Mounting Shariff, he did not wait for the others to follow. Cydryn, seeing Dyfen leave, ran after him. Seeing Cydryn leave, Avak knew his job and stayed back with the pack as stand-in leader.

The small group quickly mounted their steeds and were off riding to catch up with Dyfen and Kellis, Avak and the pack bounding after them.

Dyfen and Cydryn had reached the verge of the city where Kellis on Arka awaited to escort them to his uncle's home. Seeing Sarkis and the others close behind, they stood silently waiting for them.

Sarkis reached them first and clasped his new friend's wrist as Kellis did likewise. Big smiles on each face. The dogs had their usual reuniting ceremony touching noses, smiling, and panting. Happy to be together again no matter how short the separation had been.

Nicosia castle, home to the Emperor, was alive with activity.

They moved them through the city streets of the village where the citizens seemed to be watchful.

Kellis updated Dyfen, "We are met with luck, sire. The Emperor rode in late this afternoon but with many fewer men than he left with. Word is that he had been captured by King Richard but managed to escape into the night, fleeing for his life. The Greek and Armenian nobles who had supported him are meeting to decide how to proceed. My uncle says that the majority want to abandon the Emperor Komnenus and support Richard. They never really favored him as Emperor but supported him to protect their families from the harm he perpetrated upon those who refused to pledge their fealty. He has brought great suffering and none trust his word," Kellis stated with a sober look on his face.

The small troupe traveled through the town streets following Kellis. Finally, they reached a modest stone building where a tall and sturdily made man was standing outside. His arms were heavily muscled, and his face was covered in soot. Kellis guided Arka to him with the others following him.

"This is my Uncle Ouaras," Kellis told them as he dismounted to hug his uncle.

Uncle Ouaras, a blacksmith by trade, rubbed his large sooty hand over his face smearing his face black. His eyes were smiling even though his face was not.

"Let us move off the street. Follow Kellis into the stable," he advised guardedly.

Kellis directed Arka into the stable, dismounted and started removing the horse's gear. The others followed behind and did the same. Sarkis provided the horses with water and hay. The dogs had a drink from the same buckets and settled down while Dyfen and the others followed Kellis into his uncle's modest home.

Uncle Ouaras had prepared for their coming and led them into a room with a rustic wooden table set with cold roasted game, fresh figs, and cups of Ayran. There were two large flat baskets filled with scraps for the dogs.

Kellis grabbed them and left to take the food to the stable where the dogs stayed to watch over the horses. He returned after a few minutes with a grin on his face. "The dogs are supping," he said. "They have hearty appetites. I nearly lost my arm." He lowered his lean body onto the bench next to Dyfen.

Uncle Ouras spoke, "My nephew has told me of your venture. If it is Komnenus you seek, you have found him. He returned last evening as if fleeing for his life. It is rumored that he was captured by Richard Lionheart while his camp slept. Our Emperor Komnenus was taken wearing nothing but what God gave him," Ouras chuckled.

"To save his cowardly neck, he pledged his loyalty to Richard as well as a promise to supply an army of men to fight in the Holy Land. But then the vile bastard ran off first chance. The treacherous snake fled into the night. Only a handful of his men were willing to follow. Instead, most of them offered their allegiance to Richard who is in close pursuit and will reach here before long."

"Was there a tall lean, dark haired Lord with him? Very richly attired. He is one to be taken note of, Raoul de Lusignan, the Duc de Marche?" Isley questioned.

"Hard to tell who was with him. The party rode like the devil was chasing them out of hell," Ouaras stated. "I only know this much because one of his men's horse threw a shoe and came banging upon my door. They will rest little this eventide. All are gathering provisions to escape to the north before Richard reaches Nicosia. I was attending to his horse when Kellis found me."

Uncle Ouaras rested his head on his hands as he finished speaking. He dragged his hands back over his long, rumpled hair and sighed with weariness.

Isley spoke excitedly, "Whatever occurs, we need to get to Komnenus before he is harmed and unable to tell us where the Duc is. Circumstances makes that seem imminent."

"The man does tempt God at every turn," Dover added. He put down the cup he was drinking from and wiped his mouth on his arm. "What a cowardly sort he is. Betrayal is second nature to him."

"He has caused harm to so many on our island. It is a wonder he has not been murdered in his sleep long before," Ouaras noted. "He is a menace to all who encounter him. The devil's own, that he is."

"I am going to find Komnenus and beat the Duc's where abouts from him," Dyfen said with a dull, emotionless tone. "Before someone else claims that pleasure."

His focus was on getting to Emlyn. His promise to come to her in time of distress weighed heavily upon him. He was a fool to leave the island. He remembered Komnenus and the Duc de Marche in church. He must have been planning to abduct her even then. I am such an enormous fool, Dyfen thought to himself. Such a fool not to anticipate these events and where the hell was Hugo in all of this? Was he not charged with protecting her? His betrothed!

Why was Hugo not here protecting his fiancé? He was at sea even before he came across Kellis hiding on Kyrenia's wharf. What was so important that he would leave the fiancé he had sworn to protect while the Duc, and Emperor remained in residence at Kyrenia castle?" Something seemed wrong here but he had no time to ponder it. He had to find Emlyn.

Then another picture came to mind. Dyfen clenched his jaw in an attempt to shake it off. Ellette. Bloody and limp in the forest. The image lingered.

Isley witnessed his brother's attempt at control. Dyfen's shoulders were rigid, muscles taut. Jaw clenched as he touched his hand to it.

"Dyfen!" Isley called to him from across the table. He saw the slight quiver in his brother's chest and hand. "Dyfen!" he called again.

Dyfen brought his mind back to the present and looked at Isley. "Yes, no need to shout."

Isley stared at him to make sure Dyfen was listening. "I know what you were thinking and it is better if you focus on what is facing us right now. Let the past sleep now, brother."

Dover seeing the exchange, motioned Kellis over and whispered in his ear. Kellis quietly left the room.

Dover now turned toward Dyfen and then looked over at Isley. They both nodded at each other in a I see the problem, way. Dover cleared his throat. "Dyfen, Zakar needs your attention. I saw him favoring his injured leg. Kellis is waiting in the stable for you to look him over." He knew this would distract his brother from his present thoughts.

An alarmed concerned expression crossed Dyfen's face. "In God's name," he said exclaimed, "I examined that leg myself just a few minutes ago; he should have no trouble with it. We covered even ground for the most part. Nothing that should cause him a setback." He strode out of the room toward the stable.

He found Kellis in the stable kneeling by Zakar's side. "Kellis, is there warmth in his leg?" he said anxiously.

"None, Lord. Dover must have imagined it. He thought it best to let you know for safety's sake," Kellis said relieved.

"I will examine it all the same. Just to be sure." Dyfen dropped to his knees, placing his hands on the horse's leg and moving them up and down to witness the reaction. Zakar stood stock still, unflinching.

Dyfen sighed in relief and stood up. "The leg feels fine. No heat or swelling. He did not react to pressure. I deem him sound. But best that we know he has not relapsed before we start out again."

"I too, am relieved Lord. We have become fast friends, Zakar and I. I would be aggrieved if he suffered," Kellis said, stroking the horse's flank. "Good, strong boy. He has been through so much already. Shipwrecked, a narrow escape from being kidnapped and now a ride through the fields of Cyprus."

Dyfen reached his arm out and ruffled Kellis' hair. Kellis grinned at him through tired eyes. "Giving my hair a good roughing, eh my Lord? I must look a fright."

"You look as pleasing as the rest of us, I dare say," Dyfen grinned back catching sight of Isley walking into the stable. "And if we all appear as fair as Lord Standen, it bodes ill for all," He chuckled looking at Isley.

Isley rubbed his own head and smirked. "Better?"

"Not by far," Dyfen laughed.

Dover walked into the stable. "So, Zakar seems fine," he observed, casting a look around the stalls. "Must be my mistake. He looked as if he favored his bad leg."

Dyfen gave him an appraising look and let the matter drop. He had much to prepare before his planned raid on Nicosia castle. He would find Komnenus and squeeze Emlyn's whereabouts from his miserable soul. The longer they waited the more to worry about. Emlyn may even be here with the Duc de Marche. He had to get to Komnenus. Tonight.

While the others went back inside to discuss plans, Dyfen rifled around in Dover's bag and pulled out the monk's robe. He shook it out and lowered it over his hauberk. The monk's habit was a little tight but all and all, a good fit. Pulling the hood up over his head, he slipped out the door. Cydryn, who always kept him in sight, slunk out behind him, walking a few paces behind. The streets were dark. He travelled down the village main street with his head down as two horsemen road past in a hurry. Dyfen turned down a dark lane, walked up to the small church made from local stone, he had seen while riding into the village.

He pushed open the heavy oak door and found it was empty. He glanced around the interior which glowed from all the candles that sat on a waist level ledge lining the walls. He headed toward the altar. When he reached it, he fell to his knees and dropped his head. His brows were knit in worry. His chin rested on his chest as he made the sign of the cross and pushed his rough palms together in prayer.

Fingertips pointing towards heaven, he spoke the words, "My Lord, in the name of Jesus Christ and the Holy Comforter who You sent to us as Your light. Please Lord, God, protect her and keep her from harm. I beg this of You as Your humble servant. Let me be in time. Amen" His face relaxed as he spoke with the Lord, knit brow now smooth.

Cydryn had rested his big head on Dyfen's shoulder as he prayed and Dyfen felt the weight lifting as he stood up. Keeping his head bowed he made the sign of the cross, patting Cydryn on his flat head. "Always with me," he murmured softly. He opened the heavy door again and walked out into the night onto the still deserted street, Cydryn by his side.

Dyfen looked up to where castle Nicosia was in an obvious state of alert. Fires were lit and riders could be seen moving up and down the winding road toward the castle's main gates. Dyfen headed toward them. He kept to the side of the road, hidden in the brush. Cydryn moved stealthily by his side. Pushing the scrub away, he moved slowly but steadily toward the gates.

They reached the crest of the hill and could see the barbican. Men were riding through it in a wild panic. Dyfen saw that there were no guards and waited until the activity waned. He pulled a bit of charcoal and a scrap of paper from his pouch, scribed a short message, rolling it up and putting it in Cydryn's mouth, instructed the dog, "Carry this back to Isley, Cydryn."

The big dog turned to go, took a few steps and turned back to face Dyfen. Dyfen could see his friend was conflicted about forsaking him and he said again. "Go, find Isley, Cydryn," in a firm voice. This time Cydryn turned and bounded at top speed down the hill.

Without the presence of a dog to explain, Dyfen stepped out into the road. He kept his hooded head down and entered the castle walls without being noticed, blending in with the general panic. Every man was focused on saving himself.

Mounted men were riding to and fro. Many were entering the chapel. Dyfen followed them, entering quietly, leaving his weapons at the door with the rest that lay there on the stone pavers.

Battle ready men were on bended knee, silently praying. The priest dressed in a simple black robe with a plain gold cross hanging from his belt was saying a prayer over them. "May God, Our Father, protect you from harm. May His mercy be showered upon you on this day of tribulation, and may He shelter you from the ills that the devil hath wrought upon you, Amen."

The priest crossed himself bringing his hands up and spoke. "Arise, brothers and go to your destinies knowing Our Father knows your sins and sees your heart."

Dyfen thought to himself, if these men were honest with themselves, they probably received no comfort from such a prayer. The priest knew this. Most of them had wrought pain and suffering against their fellow man by following Emperor Komnenus in plunder and rape. Their hearts regretted none of it. It had brought them wealth, power, and pleasure. They think to fool Our Lord, but Our Lord will not be fooled.

Dyfen rose with the men and stopped one of them who was moving toward the door to leave," I carry a message for Emperor Komnenus. Where may I find him?"

The man barely looked at Dyfen. "His 'Lordship' is busy cowering in the keep. At least that is where I last saw our brave leader." The tone was one of sarcasm and disgust. "Find him there but beware. He is most foul of temper." With that he walked out of the door.

Dyfen made his way towards the castle. Few loyal soldiers remained to guard its entrance, accompanied by a number of Saracens Salah ad-Din had promised to Komnenus in return for his promise to refuse assistance to all crusaders. He turned to leave but found himself cut off from freedom by Saracen archers patrolling the walls. He made sure the monk's hood fell over part of his face, straightened his back, and walked past. The archers allowed him to pass but looked at each other and flitted their eyes his way. Religious soldiers were the fiercest fighters on a battlefield and given religious differences, they had learned not to engage unless necessary.

Back at Ouaras' home the men were gathered round the fire discussing how to proceed when the dogs started spinning in circles in excitement. The door was pushed open by a big paw and Cydryn walked in with a scroll in his mouth and headed straight for Isley. Isley leaned forward and patted Cydryn on his bushy head and stooped to pick up the document dropped at his feet.

"Cydryn, what is this?" he said speaking to the cur, while flattening the note to read it. The dog looked at him expectantly as if the message were from himself.

He skimmed the document and passed it over to Dover who raised his eyebrows and sighed. "He went without us. The churl!" Incensed, he paced a few seconds.

"Dover, Dover...." Isley was trying to get his attention. His face was calm, but his voice was strong. Isley's long hair was tangled in the dark brown leather combat vest he had been tugging into place. The overlapping panels moved with his body as he was tying the side lace.

"Pray tell, What?" Dover barked irritably, turning his head to see Isley's stolid face staring at him. "Once more, gone without us," the frustration in his voice was evident. "Our brother is but a fool who desires to meet his end alone." He was about to continue but at that moment trumpets were sounding outside, and they could hear the rush of feet running about. All were roused from slumber and lanterns were being lit in every home.

"What is happening?" Kellis exclaimed, looking at his Uncle Ouaras who had just come indoors.

"The Lionheart has come," his uncle responded. "Ships are anchoring in the harbor off the north coast. It is but a matter of time before his troops arrive in the city," he said tersely.

"It will be near impossible to find Dyfen now," Isley stated grimly. He was putting on his sword belt. "Come, Dover. Let us mount and ride to meet King Richard's army. We will offer him our arms so that we may gain information of Dyfen."

Dover pulled his hauberk over his long, black hair. He grabbed his hair at the base of his neck and pulled the strands through a leather thong to keep it from flying into his eyes during battle.

He and Isley left to outfit their horses and gather the dogs. Uncle Ouaras followed them out to the stable. "I have light armor for your horses," he said. "I was also able to quickly fashion something for your dogs while I awaited Kellis' return."

He brought out chain mail body armor that fell over the head and tied underneath at the waist with leather strings. "The dogs are not much larger than a small horse, so I modified some ring armor to fit them." The chain mail hung a couple of inches at the bottom with slits at the legs giving them freedom of movement.

He then pulled chain mail caps with holes for the ears. He fitted the first one around Tyber's head and stood looking at him, tying a string under his chin. It was not a poor fit. Tyber proudly modeled his armor and sauntered toward Dover for approval.

"You do look fierce, Tyber," Dover said laughingly. Tyber had always been his favorite. Full of mischief and yet so obedient.

Tyber approached and stood near Dover with an open-mouthed smile on his face. Dover stroked the black dog's chin speaking words of flattery. "You are exceptionally handsome, my lad. Ready to do your part to save our brother." The dog's mouth widened displaying his large incisors and red tongue lolled to the side. He rubbed the side of his face on Dover's hip and stood calmly waiting for instruction.

Ouaras had clad the other dogs in the same battle dress and noted that Cydryn was not among them. "The messenger hound is not here." he told them.

Isley who was now fully attired, was not surprised, "He went back to Dyfen. We will not see him again until we next see Dyfen."

Kellis and Sarkis had kitted the horses in battle gear. All stood in the lantern lit stable looking at Dover. Dover raised his hand and spoke. "Let us join the battle for our brother's sake. We will yeet the devil's Emperor and his men into the dust before this day is done. But we must ensure Komnenus remains uninjured at all costs, until he discloses where Emlyn is, even if we must fight King Richard's own army to accomplish it. May God grant mercy to our souls and may He bless our cause."

Arka whinnied and stamped a hoof, shaking his long, now braided mane. Sarkis had intertwined silver beads to keep the braids from flying up at the canter. He had a padded saddle rug on his back in the Moon Isle stable colors. Leather stirrups hung down at the sides, set at just the right height for Isley. Arka looked quite impressive with his enormous stature and chain mail clinging to his muscled haunches.

The dogs let out yips in response to the stallion's whinnies.

Kellis and Sarkis had donned ring mail hauberks as well. They each sported large pouches with supplies for the coming battle tied to their saddle rugs.

Sarkis had a sword that Dyfen had given him on his twelfth birthday. He had learned to use it while riding, directing the horse with pressure from his legs to keep his hands free. All Moon Isle horses were trained to respond to leg pressure and key words in order to keep the hands free to do battle.

Isley mounted Zakar while Dover waited astride Arazi. The coursers were known for their speed in battle, leaving the sturdier horses for Kellis and Sarkis who would stay on the sidelines. Kellis handed them both shields that they each secured to the saddle pad and then pushed himself up onto Arka.

Dover looked at the assembled group.

Sarkis was already mounted on Seert and gave a final nod to Isley and with that the four gave one another one last look before giving their mounts a light kick to the flank. With one strong push, the horses were off in a cloud of dust leaving Kellis slightly behind.

Uncle Ouras stood watching them go. "Kellis!" he yelled out. Kellis reined in Arka and turned slightly to face his uncle. "Be safe, my boy," he whispered to himself while raising his arm to bid Kellis farewell. He nodded his head toward his young nephew who had so quickly turned into a man.

Kellis raised his arm in return, his eyes met his uncle's in a deep understanding of the gravity of coming events. For his mistress he would risk all. He lowered his arm and rode off after the others.

They were stopped by armed guards while approaching Richard's army. Isley had a word with them and shortly after they were escorted to King Richard who was surrounded by his field staff. They had watched the group as they rode into the encampment.

Isley was surprised at Richard's height and observed his self-assured persona. The Lionheart was a striking tower of strength with an absolute will that was reflected in his outward appearance. His eyes held a steely resolve and he was broad across the chest with muscled shoulders. Isley could see that Komnenus never had a chance against such a formidable opponent.

The King motioned for them to come closer. He was studying them with an appraising eye. He was well known for his appreciation of a good horse. "My aide tells me you hail from Moon Isle. It is well known for its war horses," he noted. "I can see that to be true. He evaluated their steeds approvingly. "Tell me, why have you come?"

"We have come to offer you our arms in your conquest of the Emperor Isaac Komnenus," Isley said looking straight into Richard's intelligent eyes. "He has information we seek."

"What information would that be?" Richard asked.

"It is of a personal nature, Your Grace," Dover answered unwilling to offer exact details.

"Of a personal nature, you say?" King Richard eyed him questioningly. "I will accept your assistance but make no promises regarding questions to Komnenus," he stated.

Isley did not argue.

Richard turned to his men. "Komnenus is a cowardly sort. A king should be willing to die for his people. Lead them into battle and fight to protect them. This man is none of that. We will route him from whatever hole he hides in. I have had my fill of that weasel who calls himself Emperor." Grabbing his sword by the hilt, he raised it high in the air before him and turned to his men with raised voice so all could hear. "We fight for God!" Richard shouted.

All the men fell to their knee and pushed the point of their swords into the ground and with right hand on their sword, repeated, "We fight for God!" as one voice.

"Now mount up and let us find this knave," the King finished.

The men scrambled to mount their steeds. The ground troops were already assembled to march in formation once Richard gave the signal.

Richard and Battre led the charge with his top men at arms close behind him. Isley, Dover, Kellis and Sarkis galloped in a line after them. Their four barding attired stallions perfectly aligned, moved toward the castle walls. Once within arrow range of the Saracen archers they slowed and allowed the mounted bowman to pass them.

They could see Komnenus' men run to the safety of the battlement.

From the tower battlement, Dyfen saw the approaching army coming toward the castle. The Saracen archers were on the wall. Richard's mounted archers began firing arrows at them. Once the Saracen's were removed, King Richard's army would be able to ride into the castle unimpeded. Dyfen must act quickly before that happened.

He saw a hunched figure twenty feet from where he stood observing the same scene below. He recognized it. He quickly covered the distance between them in seconds. Dyfen grabbed the figure by the back of the neck and turned it to face him. Emperor Komnenus had no time to defend himself. Recognizing Dyfen, he relaxed.

"Where is she? Where is Lady Emlyn?" Dyfen demanded shaking Komnenus. "Tell me or die slowly, your wart of a man."

Komnenus became incensed. He faced Dyfen without fear. Raising himself up to his full height replied, "How dare you address me in that manner? I am still Emperor here."

Dyfen cast a glance over the wall and replied, "For how much longer? I give your reign twenty minutes more until it ends abruptly. Now you will answer my question. Where is the Lady Emlyn," he repeated?

Emperor Isaac Komnenus' face took on a smirk. "She is beyond your reach, you hedge-born churl."

Dyfen annoyed at the delay, raised Komnenus up, holding him off the ground a few inches, "Tell me now or I repeat, die slowly."

Komnenus face was turning purple from the grip upon his throat and he began to panic. He motioned he would speak. Dyfen set him down but maintained the chokehold upon his neck.

"de Marche has possession of her. He has taken her to his fortress on the northern tip of Karpas, near Apostolos Andreas Monastery," Komnenus choked out.

"Where is that?" Dyfen demanded.

"I can show you," he offered. "You will not be able to find it on your own. First you must help me to escape this castle. You will need me to obtain access to the fortress. The Duc has spent months making it impenetrable."

The Flaming Soul   Doreen Demerjian

"He has done this without the knowledge of Lord Esper?" Dyfen countered.

"Rylan, Lord Esper, is naught but a churl. Knows naught what happens under his very nose." Komnenus had a sly smile on his smug face.

His smugness irritated Dyfen. "Komnenus, you evil bastard of the devil himself. How long gone are they? How much time has passed from their leaving?"

Dyfen's ire was growing.

"Time? Days. Days have passed. How long does it take to lift a hem? By now she is ruined for certain." Komnenus added.

Dyfen became quiet and slowly uttered in a measured tone. "Damn your soul to hell, you evil bastard. That damned demon will pay with his life if he but touches one strand of her hair."

Komnenus returned. "Get me out from here and I will provide you access to where she is. I have no love of de Marche. The bastard, circled back to Kyrenia and left me at the hands of the invading English army.

"The truth is, he would not even have his fortress if not for me. "I. Me." He stood with legs apart and chest out, pointing to it proudly, "I wrested it from that old drooling, donkey, Lord Kostas, and this is how de Marche repays me! His lust will be his undoing, mark my words." It was apparent that Komnenus felt himself the injured party.

With those last words, Dyfen's lower jaw became rigid. He pulled his arm back and slugged the Lord, Emperor in the middle of his extended belly, knocking him to the ground, then straddled his prone body. "Tell what you know," he growled lowering his face down inches above the flaccid sputtering face of Issac. "Your putrid excuse for a man. There is little time before Richard will be here for you."

"Allow me to stand. I tell all freely," Komnenus whimpered. "I owe the Duc de Marche naught. Raoul, that swiving fool abandoned me."

Dyfen backed up and allowed Komnenus to push himself to his feet again.

Komnenus brushed down his clothing and straightened his tunic, and smoothed his hair.

"I will tell all," he began. "We allowed Lord Kostas and his rather unattractive wife to leave with their lives. It really was an act of mercy. I swear my tender heart remains my largest liability." He continued, "The Duc took over castle Kantara. The servants remained, as Raoul had need of a household for his immediate occupancy. Since then, the Duc has had work done on his new abode, fortifying its walls against attack. He claims it is virtually impenetrable.

"As you have probably noted, Raoul is drawn to the maidens, in particular Lady Emlyn. She is a pretty wench, I admit. I had hoped to spend some time with her myself, but Raoul was rather strident in his opposition to the idea. I relented in the interest of peace," He paused. Dyfen poked him with his sword to keep him on track.

"Yes, yes, back to de Marche. Even if you make it inside the castle walls, by this time, he has most certainly deflowered her. Many times, over. You are too late to save Emlyn, Dyfen. You may want to reconsider this rescue. Her innocence has passed. Take my advice and forget her. She is no longer what you remember." He heaved out a deep breath and eyed Dyfen whose ire was reignited.

They could hear echoes of footsteps below. They must hurry.

He gave Komnenus a great push with his hand and sent him flying backwards onto the crenelated wall, almost toppling over it. Dyfen's mind was racing, trying to develop a plan for the two of them to get away. He looked out to the sea.

Chapter 31

Lady Emlyn and Raoul the Duc de Marche

Raoul, Duc de Marche, smiled to himself. He had not wasted time with further threats to Rylan regarding the betrothal. Instead, he had planned to make his move at an opportune time. That time was now and his plan had worked. Its success provided him with immense pleasure and restored him to good humor.

He had circled back to Kyrenia castle where he found Emlyn virtually alone. He knew Eston would remain behind but he had his men dispatch him first upon entering the walls. The brave warrior had stood against ten soldiers, killing all but three. In the end, he had been mortally wounded and left to die.

Raoul raced up the staircase to Emlyn's chamber, which he had made note of the evening of the feast. He pushed open the heavy door and found Emlyn sitting in a large, comfortable chair with her needlework. She was alone.

What he did not know was that Emlyn had just returned from sending Kellis off to seek Dyfen. She had heard the chaos of men's voices below her window and knew something was wrong. She now sat with needlework in her lap trying to regulate her breathing to disguise that she had just rushed back to her chamber. She heard a solid knock on the door and almost immediately, it swung open.

Raoul de Lusignan, the Duc de Marche, stood grandly in the opening seemingly unaware of how dashing he appeared. She could not deny how handsome he was even though she abhorred him. She watched him walk slowly toward her with an easy smile on his face.

"What is the meaning of this, Your Grace?" she asked, confused. "How dare you enter a lady's chamber uninvited? I am without a chaperone!" she was not feigning her outrage. Then she realized that he should not be at Castle Kyrenia.

"You left with the Emperor. Why are you here?" she questioned him.

Raoul changed his manner to one of earnestness. "Your father sent word for me to fetch you. The English are everywhere and for his own peace of mind he requires you to be safe until we know their intentions. I have spent months fortifying my fortress to the north and I have come back to take you there for your own protection. It is his wish."

Emlyn became frightened because she knew her father and brother had left with their armies to join King Richard against the Emperor. She was unsure now as to whether they had reassessed the situation. She tried to sound casual. "Where is Eston?" she asked. "I will do as he advises." She could trust Eston with her life. She would attempt to stall long enough for Kellis to find Dyfen. Once he came… all would be well.

"Eston has been commanded by your father to meet him in the south. He is no longer here," the Duc de Marche lied.

"We really have not time for these questions. We must act. Have your girl pack a few items and let us depart. A ship is waiting in the harbor. I know not how long it will remain safely there and we cannot risk it leaving without us." He conveyed a sense of urgency.

Emlyn was conflicted. Her father would never order Eston to leave her alone and Eston would never leave her no matter what the order. She needed to stay.

"But Jinol, my maid, is not here. She is spending the day visiting her cousin. I must send for her," Emlyn protested.

"We cannot wait, Emlyn. Your maid servant will be fine left here. She is of no value," the Duc de Marche answered misconstruing her protest. "You are now under my protection."

Emlyn's sense of alarm grew. She had done all she could do without putting up a fight she knew she would lose. She slowly prepared to leave when she placed her hand to her chest and swooned. Her hand clutched at the arm of the chair she was near.

Raoul rushed to her side. "Lady Emlyn, are you ill? What is happening?" he exclaimed with genuine concern in his voice. He was supporting her to keep her from falling.

"Sangos!" he yelled in a panic to his man stationed outside the door.

A young soldier entered the chamber from his position outside the entry.

"You called, Your Grace?" the youth asked.

"Find me a physician. Run to the ship if need be. Bring a surgeon back, quickly."

Raoul lifted Emlyn and carried her to the bed. He gently laid her down. He picked up her hand and began rubbing it between his two hands as he peered into her face hoping for a sign of recovery.

An hour later Sangos returned with Dr. Chikaris.

"See to her," Raoul barked at Dr. Chikaris. "I want her restored."

Doctor Chikaris had concern on his face as he bent over Emlyn's unmoving form. He turned to the two men behind him.

"Leave me alone with her. You must vacate the room," Physician Chikaris ordered.

Raoul hesitated and then turned to leave, pushing Sangos out before him. He closed the door after them and stood against the wall waiting.

When she heard the door close, Emlyn sat up. "Dr. Chikaris, the Duc de Marche is here to take me from my home. He says it is father's wish. I do not know where Eston is and I have sent Kellis to seek Dyfen Whetherly. I must stay here until they arrive," she begged.

The doctor looked at her with concern. "Lady Emlyn, you must remain still and allow me to persuade him that it is in your best interest to recover here."

She looked back at him with fright in her eyes and nodded her head.

"Where is Eston?" the doctor asked.

"de Marche said that father called him to come to him in the south," she answered.

Some time had passed when finally, the Duc de Marche could stand no more. He entered the room and strode to the bed. "What is your assessment?" he asked sharply, beginning to become suspicious.

"She is suffering from excessive fatigue, Your Grace." the doctor responded respectfully. "She requires rest."

"She may rest on shipboard," the Duc answered.

"It is best she remain here, Your Grace," the doctor countered.

"Nonsense. Whether she be awake or not. She will ride with me. Even If I need to place her prostrate body over my mount's back. When we reach our destination, she will be seen by my own physician, if need be," he insisted.

"Your Grace, you have asked me as a professional for my opinion. I give it. She must not be moved," Dr. Chikaris insisted realizing the Duc was becoming irritated.

The doctor stood and faced the Duc de Marche. Sangos placed his sword under the doctor's chin. It was then that Emlyn awoke, imitating recovery.

"Excellent!" Raoul remarked when he saw her eyes open.

Doctor Chikaris looked at Emlyn questioningly, shaking his head, 'No'.

"I do not know what possessed me. I feel well enough to travel now," she said softly. She looked at her physician signaling him to not interfere.

"Perfect. Sangos, bring my horse around," Raoul commanded him.

"Where are you taking her, Your Grace?" Dr. Chikaris asked.

"That is not your concern, good doctor. I carry out Lord Esper's wish to protect his daughter."

"Dr. Chikaris," Emlyn addressed him. "Thank you for your care. I assure you I am able to travel. You need not further worry for me," she said to assure him she knew he had done his best to prevent her leaving and he should not press the matter.

In the end, the Duc and Emlyn boarded the ship and set sail. They arrived at a large fortress hovering on a cliff overlooking the Mediterranean Sea. The northern tip of the Cyprian, Karpas peninsula was remote and looked impregnable.

They entered the fortress where Emlyn was escorted to a suite. She looked around. The layout resembled that of her own chambers at home with a solar, a private bath, garderobe and sleeping chamber. The windows were large and south facing to catch the days light. The walls were plastered with beautiful scenes of a rose garden reminiscent of her garden at home. Bowls of fresh pink and white roses were placed throughout the suite, their scent filled the air. If she closed her eyes, she might think she were home in Kyrenia. She walked to one of the large windows and looked out. But she was not home. Instead of a garden below there was a sheer drop to a rocky precipice with white waves crashing against rocks.

She pushed open the garderobe door. The walls and floor were covered in Italian marble the color of rose petals. In a windowed alcove nearby was a freestanding marble tub set on a white marble floor. Sheer silk fabric hung at the windows creating a romantic ambiance.

She grew nervous.

Raoul watched her reaction silently. Finally, he spoke, "Everything you would desire should be here but if not, you only need ask." He paused, "I suggest you rest it has been a stressful day and I will return to you later."

With that Raoul, Duc de Marche, exited the chamber closing the door after him.

Emlyn was very tired from the events of the day and decided to take a short nap to refresh herself. She walked over to the plush bed and laid across it.

Hours later, she opened her eyes. The sun had set and the room was dark. She could sense someone in the room with her. She sat up and found Raoul standing over her. He bent down to gently stroke her hair. Emlyn recoiled from his hand, pushing it from her.

"You will need to get used to my touch, Lady Emlyn. We are to be wed. Your father agreed to our match."

"You forget, I am already spoken for, Your Grace," Emlyn responded trying to remain calm.

"Oh, that," he said dismissively. "What type of man sets sail and leaves his betrothed behind without protection?"

"My father and brother were there to protect me, Sire."

"Well, that has changed. They are no longer near enough to ensure your safety. Let me remind you that this is your father's wish. My family is very powerful and an alliance between our houses will extend protection to your father and brother as well. In the event they do not return from their mission south, you will have me as your husband to shelter you."

Emlyn had little hope that Dyfen and Kellis would find her. No one knew where they had gone. Her only hope was that Dyfen would somehow find Eston or one of the servants who saw them leave. Dyfen may guess the rest. She hoped he would find her. She placed all of her faith in it.

Raoul started to stroke her hair once again. She felt a great discomfort at his touch and pulled away. She walked to the door but it was bolted from the outside.

"Your Grace, you must allow me my freedom. Am I to be held as if a prisoner?" she demanded. "I am betrothed to Hugo Rend; you must know that I cannot wed you."

The Duc de Marche realized she was not fooled and dropped all pretense. With a deadened look in his eye, told her bluntly, "You will marry me, and I will have you or we dispense with marriage, and I will have you. Either way you will be mine. Hugo Rend be damned! I do a kindness saving you from that weasel. Now, you can live as my wife or my whore. Decide."

He then went on to present a deeper threat, which shook her to her core.

"If you refuse me, after I have had my fill, I will reward my captain with you as a prize and he will do the same until every man in this castle has bed you. Some of them are not as kind or clean as I. Men can be such brutes," he warned casually. The tone of his voice and the look on his face lacked emotion. Her blood turned to ice and her body slightly trembled.

Her options were pitiable. If she did not acquiesce, her future would be dim and her father and brother would most likely die avenging her. She saw no escape.

"Your Grace, you leave me no choice but to agree to this marriage," she answered him. With iciness, she added, "I will wed you but I will never love you."

Raoul kept his eyes hooded, and his face expressionless but she sensed her words had struck a blow although his only response was in an even tone, "We wed tomorrow eve." He strode to the door and rapped on it with a closed fist.

"Open," he barked. The normally velvet voice sounded coarse. She heard the sound of the bolt slide and the door open. He was gone.

Early the next morning, two young maidens, came to her room accompanied by several servants with arms loaded with bundles. As they set their burdens down, each person bowed to her and left the room.

Emlyn studied the two remaining girls who were so similar in appearance that they could only be sisters. They were similar in stature; both were dark eyed and dusky complexioned and wore their long, dark hair plaited with ribbons. The most conspicuous similarity being they were no more than fourteen years of age and both were heavy with child. Emlyn attempted to speak to them but neither responded as they busied themselves around her. She gave up trying to communicate once they started removing her clothing. Emlyn sat frozen in disbelief. She knew they were there to prepare her for her wedding.

The regime began with the removal of all body hair as they applied warm honey to her skin and laid cotton cloth over it. The hair was removed with the cloth. At first it was painful but after a while she became accustomed to the pain and it hurt less. Afterward, a tepid bath awaited her. The warm water was soothing to her irritated skin. Its orange scented water wafted throughout the room creating a sense of calm. One of the sisters gently tilted Emlyn's head back as she ladled water over her hair. She felt the weight of the water in her hair as light fingers massaged orange scented soap into her scalp. The circular motion encouraged Emlyn to close her eyes and cast her mind adrift, forgetting her current troubles. Elsewhere on her body she could feel the subtle roughness of sponges on her skin. Her eyes flickered open as her reverie lifted. The girls were holding up large towels to dry her.

She stood up and stepped out of the water while the soft cloth was moving over her hair and torso. The sisters were looking her over carefully to make sure their work was successful. Apparently pleased, they began to rub fragrant oils onto their hands which they transferred onto her skin. Kneading her as if she were bread dough. In the end, her hair gleamed as if it were polished wood. It was plaited and twisted to show her thick tresses off to their best advantage. Pearls had been interspersed throughout. Pomegranate juice was used to add blush to her cheeks and a rich red to her lips. Kohl was smudged delicately at the corners of each eye causing the green in them to become more pronounced.

A finely woven, silk chemise was carefully placed over her head and slowly drawn down over her body. It was beautifully embroidered. She felt a hand on her shoulder directing her to sit while silken stockings where rolled up her legs and tied in place with ribbons.

A silk sky-blue, samite kirtle was lowered over her torso and gently tugged into place. The silver embroidery shimmered in the fading light of day. Emlyn was still numb with disbelief and barely stirred while the two girls moved around her. It was early evening when they finished. The sun had fallen in the sky and torches were being lit in the chamber by the time they were finally satisfied with their work.

One of the girls opened a carved wooden casket and lifted a heavy silver necklace inset with emerald cabochons. She placed it upon Emlyn's neck and then lifted matching earrings from the chest which she placed upon her delicate earlobes. Smiling, the sisters held a rare and valuable Spanish made mirror in which to view herself.

Emlyn gasped. Firstly, the clarity of the mirror was unlike any she had seen before. This must be priceless, she thought. Reflected in its clear glass, was not the image of a young maiden but that of a beautiful woman. Large expressive eyes, sleek dark hair with plump pomegranate-colored lips. The two girls had done their jobs well and moved toward the door to leave. Their knock on the door was answered with the sound of a sliding bolt as the door swung open and a tall, young man entered.

"You will allow me, my Lady," he spoke not altering his expressionless face as he held out his hand for her to place her own upon. She was dazed with the day's ordeal and weak from having not eaten. But even yet, the details of events were crystal clear in her mind.

She was escorted to the chapel doors. When they swung open, she was overwhelmed by a feeling of surreality. The chapel pulsed with color and sound. Its silver gilded walls glowed in the reflection of numerous candelabras. Its high domed apse, covered in gold leaf, shimmered above. Magnificent stained-glass windows were embedded in the apse.

The Duc had thought of every detail. Large sprays of white roses were strewn over the blush pink marble altar, their scent mingling with the incensed air. The black slate floor was covered with a fine, silk caucus carpet with navy and red tones. A musical ensemble accompanied a small choir. Their intertwining notes created an ethereal echo surrounding the room.

Raoul saw her enter and ceased his conversation with the priest to turn toward her. He was resplendent in silver and white brocaded silks, as striking as ever. His dark hair was tied back with a magnificently engraved silver band. He wore black leather boots beautifully tooled and polished to a high gleam.

It was apparent that he was pleased with what he saw. A wide grin split his handsome face. He walked toward her and took her hand, leading her to the altar. "Emlyn you steal my breath with your beauty. Words can nary do it justice," he exclaimed. "I am anxious to have this ceremony done."

They were married in a short ceremony without friends, without family.

Afterward, there was no celebration. Raoul picked her up and carried her to their marriage bed now draped with sumptuous damask trappings in blue and violet colors. Her favorite colors, she noted.

He set her down and stood behind her slowly loosening her hair. He began kissing the back of her neck as he worked.

He lifted a goblet from a nearby table and held it to her lips bidding her to drink. "It will relax you," he coaxed.

She gladly took the cup from his hand and drank deeply, preparing herself for what was to come.

The spirits were strong and because she had not eaten its effects put her off-balance. Recovering herself, she leaned against him for support. Roaul, who after failed attempts at unlacing her gown finally lost patience, drew out his dagger and cut the dress from her.

Removing all of her clothing, he gently pushed her onto the bed. He began to disrobe in haste. Emlyn could see the lust in his eyes as he did; his shaft already erect. He lowered himself next to her and let his lips travel over her body. He was tender, but his excitement was rising. He parted her legs with his hand and positioned himself above her. She felt a slight pressure as he entered her and eased himself more deeply as he moved against her. He climaxed in a few minutes and it was over.

Far different than his past experiences, he thought anxiously. He let out a long groan at the end and closely watched her face. "I know it not to be pleasant at first, but you will grow to enjoy it. I have experience with these things." He reassured her. She barely heard him as her own thoughts were present, I am no longer a maiden. I have lost my innocence to a man I do not love.

After he had satisfied his appetite for Emlyn, a growing pang of hunger over took him. His attention shifted to the wedding feast laid out at a nearby table. The aroma of roast lured him to it. He arose from the bed, picked up his tunic and pulled it over his head as he walked over to the table. On his way there, he lifted an ivory-colored silk robe from a nearby chair. "I had this made for you, my dear," he told her, offering it to her. She accepted it from his hand. He held out for her to slide her arms into it. Its sheerness, as such, did not provide much in the way of modesty and the design lacked a way to fasten it closed. In the end, she held it together. Raoul did not seem to take notice. "Emlyn, I am quite famished as you must be. Let us dine. The fare smells of heaven and difficult to resist." He was lifting silver covers from the platters as he spoke. He escorted her to a chair and then went to his own across from her. She was so famished, she only focused on the food before her.

While they ate, Raoul was barely able to take his eyes from her which resulted in injury to his sword hand while he carved the roast. He had dismissed the servants early on so when he sliced his hand there was no one but Emlyn to aid him. It began to bleed profusely and he was unable to stem the flow. "Damn!" he exclaimed, looking at the blood flowing from his hand making no attempt to tend to it. He merely stood watching blood drip to the floor with a look of annoyance on his face. "Damn," he repeated.

"Your Grace!" Emlyn exclaimed as she ran to his side to examine the injury.

She quickly grabbed his surnap, soaked it in his wine goblet then used it to clean the wound. Shoving the surnap down into his palm with pressure, she ordered him, "Press this firmly down into your palm." Crossing back to her seat she grabbed her own surnap to bind his hand tightly. After the wound stopped bleeding, they resumed their meal.

Raoul was having difficulty using the bandaged hand to cut his roast. She went over to do it for him. He moved his hand to stop her out of embarrassment but she pushed it away and finished the job.

While she did so, he lifted his injured hand and tenderly touched her face. They continued their meal as if nothing had occurred but she could feel his dark eyes resting upon her when he thought she was unaware.

After they had dined, he moved back to the bed. Looking down he grabbed the bed clothes and yanked them from the mattress, throwing them to the floor.

He looked at her with faint satisfaction on his face. Her eyes traveled to the fabric on the floor. She saw the red stain, proof of her virtue. She looked away, uncomfortably.

Raoul pulled off his tunic with his good hand and reached out to her with his other as he moved toward her. When he reached her, he opened her robe and forced it to fall as he started to kiss her neck.

He tenderly stroked her hair with his bandaged hand. "You are most beautiful, my wife," he murmured. He had a gentleness about him that he had lacked before.

Raoul took his wife once more before finally falling asleep. His arm was wrapped around her waist. The amount of drink she had consumed pushed her into slumber as well.

When she awoke, he was gone.

One day was much the same as the one before it. Raoul satisfied his strong desire throughout the day. He left her with only the silk robe to wear. She made sure the servants kept the wine ewer filled.

"Your Grace, when will I be able to leave this chamber? Am I to remain a prisoner?" Emlyn asked him.

"Emlyn, you have no need to address me so formally. I am your husband. I wish you to speak my name, 'Raoul', such as a wife would." He looked at her with expectation.

Emlyn remained silent.

The Flaming Soul   Doreen Demerjian

He sighed, "Emlyn, you must forgive me but I am a besotted groom. I admit I surprise myself. I think of nothing but you no matter how I try to do otherwise. I only leave your side to attend to serious matters that cannot be put off. I have waited months to make you mine. I find you more arousing than I ever imagined." His words trailed off as he undressed and sat next to her on the bed, taking her hand in his. To her surprise, instead of becoming amorous he placed his arm around her tenderly as he settled on the bed and began telling his tale.

"I have waited a long time to wed, Emlyn. I did not choose lightly due to my father's legacy." He went on to explain, "My father has had many women during his life. Their chasteness was not a consideration. My brother and I would see them come and go. His bedchamber was never empty for long."

"His many indiscretions resulted in a pox upon his body. His pain was immense and his hunger for women waned as his shaft became wart covered and lesioned. The disease moved over his body. The curse extended to children born from women he had lain with. All stillborn. He warned me of the mistakes he had made."

"'My son lay not with women who have lost their virtue," he warned.

"Bear witness to my pain. I do not pass water without agony and where I longed to have my shaft buried deep inside some maiden, now I only wish for death to end this torture.'

"I cannot forget the sight of his shaft as he made water. It was disfigured and barely recognizable. In pursuit of a cure, he has seen countless physicians who could only offer a means to ease the pain. Poppies from the Levant only mask his torment.

"In his desperation for a remedy, he moved beyond men of medicine and consulted mystics and religious savants. Many of the men he spoke with were on pilgrimages to the Holy Land and told tales of religious relics that cured ills.

"One of these men caught father's interest in particular. He spoke of a legendary spear that had pierced the body of Christ at the crucifixion. It is called the Spear of Destiny and rumored to heal all ailments. It was originally hidden away in Armenia under the protection of the church. He has made it his mission to find the relic if it really exists," he paused and then continued. "He even has reason to think it may be near Kyrenia." Raoul chuckled softly. "I am unsure if these are ravings of a mad man or the potions he takes daily for his pain."

"My father fell deeper and deeper into the use of drugs until he seldom left his bed.

"That was well enough warning to choose wisely with whom I shared my bed. I have satisfied my needs with a plenitude of caution and decided that after I wed, I would look no further to sate my lust. The maiden I marry must fulfill all of my wants so I must choose carefully. Until then, I have kept myself clean and only lain with maidens who I am assured have maintained their purity, so intent am I to avoid my father's fate."

Raoul continued with contempt in his voice. "Thanks to that devil Komnenus and his accursed men there is barely an untouched maiden in Cyprus that has not known a poxed prick."

He looked down at her. "Your father took great care to keep you out of the grasp of such depraved men. I thank him for that."

"From the first I set eyes upon you my mind has been filled with pictures of you in my bed," Raoul finished speaking and looked to her for a reaction.

She had remained quiet until then. "Untouched. Like the pregnant servants who attended me? Both heavy with child!" she exclaimed hotly.

"Does my new bride suffer with jealousy?" he said with an amused smile, misinterpreting her outrage. His face took on a more somber look. "True, they are with child but not by me," He stated firmly. "Not by me, Emlyn I promise you. But they are not your concern," he spoke calmly.

She wanted to believe him especially after the tale he had just told but she could not resist asking, "by whom then?"

He ignored my question and said, "I am anxious to begin a family of my own. I want a son. A son to carry my name. Our son."

She knew what was to follow and picked up the goblet near the bed and drank deeply from it. He grabbed the vessel from her hand and stared into her eyes.

He could not read them.

"Emlyn, I look toward the day you no longer have need of this when I come to you." He waved the cup before her. "Our union would be so much sweeter if you took your pleasure with me. I want you to writhe with desire at my touch, to hear you call my name as our bodies meet."

"That day will never come," Emlyn answered straight forwardly. She could see emotion flash across his face as she spoke the words. Then it was gone. She could not identify it.

"Very well then, I will love for the both of us." And with that he pushed her down onto their bed. His body upon hers. This time he was not gentle. Even his lips left marks upon her.

The Flaming Soul   Doreen Demerjian

While Raoul made love to her, her mind escaped to another place, another time and another man's body. The memories excited her and caused her to lift her body to meet his, moaning in ecstasy. Raoul groaned back in pleasure.

Then his motion suddenly stopped as he lifted himself from her, rolling onto his side staring hard into her face with his dark eyes narrowed. His hard, muscled body was glistening with sweat. His long hair fell about his shoulders, the brown streak hanging in his face as he studied her. "Who were you thinking of just then?" His voice was quiet but had a hard edge to it. "Was it your husband?"

Emlyn's frightened eyes met his angry ones, afraid to speak. He saw the betrayal in them and quickly arose. Jerking his tunic over his head, he grabbed his outer clothing from the floor on his way out, never looking back. The heavy wooden door crashed closed behind him.

The next morning, a strange old woman came to the chamber and motioned Emlyn to sit in a chair. She was accompanied by the two pregnant sisters who had dressed her for her wedding. They appeared even more pregnant, if possible.

While Emlyn sat there, the girls arranged themselves around her. They plied her with strong drink that must have been drugged. When she awoke, they were gone but she felt a dull pain near her trench. She looked down at her nether region to see a mark in of the form of the House of de Lusignan crest with the initials 'RdL' within it. She had been marked like chattel.

Chapter 32

The Path to Emlyn

The harbor was crowded with ships, with more on the horizon. In his search for Komnenus, the Lionheart had split his galleys into two squadrons.

One he commanded himself and the other he had placed under the control of Robert of Tornham. Each squadron traveled in opposite directions around the isle searching for Komnenus and stationing ships at each port as well as capturing ships, men, and treasure along the way.

Now, all were awaiting orders as they sat calmly on the floating sequined sea. By land, Guy of Jerusalem and the other Princes had taken control of a large portion of Richard's army and scoured the countryside. There was no place for Komnenus to hide.

Dyfen would have to act quickly for them to escape.

While looking toward the harbor, one sail caught his attention. It had a black trident upon it. Martel, Dyfen thought to himself.

He grabbed Komnenus by his gemmed studded collar and dragged him to his feet. "You will take me to where de Marche has fled and you will assist me to gain access. If you refuse, I will practice upon you all that I have learned at my uncle's side," he hissed into Issacs's ear. "While you still breath. I swear this to you. You will yearn for Richard."

While he spoke, he saw a flash of fur behind him. Cydryn was standing by his side. "Lad, you are back. Brave boy, Cydryn, my friend," he exclaimed with gladness.

Cydryn smiled at his master and then looked at Komnenus with a less than friendly glare. He understood the situation.

"Now, on your feet and move before me. Cydryn is close behind, never forget. He will kill you in a trice if you dare to run." Dyfen's face was grim, and Komnenus had no wish to test his resolve. He pulled the hood of his habit back up over his head and moved behind Komnenus.

The men defending the castle had all seen the ships and were in the process of assuaging their fear with alcohol. Many were already drunk.

They came to the broad stone stairway to the first floor. Dyfen gave Emperor Komnenus a little push towards it. Komnenus started down. They were passed by a few soldiers headed up to the battlement to keep watch on the forest. As before none questioned Dyfen's presence.

They finally reached the ground floor and went out a door off the grand hall. Once outside, Komnenus started squirming about leaving the safety of his castle. There was mayhem everywhere. Dyfen cast his eyes around and saw two soldiers walking their horses preparing to flee. He pushed his dagger into Komnenus' ribs and shoved him forward.

The Lord Emperor sucked up his shoulders and in his oily voice fixed a stern eye at the men and spoke, "I require your mounts. You will relinquish your steeds to your Emperor."

The two men did not question the order and handed the halter ropes to Dyfen thinking him the Emperor's servant. Dyfen assessed each horse and instructed Komnenus, "You will mount the black. He is solid but a bit slower than his companion. Get up and do not try to escape me. I doubt you will make twenty yards before Cydryn runs you down and my blade catches up with you. So be forewarned." With that said, Dyfen lithely sprung up onto the chestnut stallion he had chosen for himself. They headed toward the east gate where only six men were stationed. The rest had fled. Dyfen gave a stern look to Komnenus who understood.

"Open the gate and stand aside," He commanded. "I go to meet Richard, to negotiate a truce."

The relief on the men's faces was apparent and they hurriedly pulled up the gate and opened the heavy wooden doors to allow them to pass.

Komnenus started on the main path but quickly cut to the left seemingly riding into a bush. Beyond it there was a trail hidden by the heavy foliage. An escape route. Of course, this worm would have many hidden trails for escape. A ruler as unpopular as he would need to run.

"You will take us to the harbor," Dyfen instructed.

Komnenus looked at him as if he were crazy. "The harbor? Did you not see it is wholly occupied by Richard's galleys? His men are not likely to allow us to borrow one of their ships," Komnenus snapped.

"Allow me that burden," Dyfen replied. "You just keep moving."

Finally, they reached the edge of the forest where the trail ended and a field of scrub separated them from the wharf. Dyfen stopped and ordered Komnenus to dismount. He began to remove the robe and held it out to Komnenus.

"Put this on," he ordered.

"Whetherly, you expect me to wear that rag?" Komnenus sputtered. "That scrap you have been sporting for God knows how long?"

Dyfen just looked at him and waited. Komnenus glanced at Cydryn.

"Well then, hand it to me," Komnenus said resentfully. He held it at arm's length from his gloriously attired person and slowly dragged it over his head, pulling it into place around his considerably substantial body. His face reflected his misery.

They got back up on their horses and rode to the wharf where the Black Trident was moored. Next to it stood the Wild Boar. Dyfen could see Hugo talking to one of his sailors. He looked up and saw Dyfen and squinted at the figure of Komnenus. Cydryn's body became rigid at the sight of Hugo. Dyfen firmly ordered him to stand down.

"Whetherly, is that you? And ... and... His Excellency, Komnenus? What in God's name is he wearing? Has your brother, Dover, started a fashion trend?" Hugo now stood on the dock before Dyfen, eyeing him with suspicion.

"Why are you here? And why does His Excellency accompany you?" Hugo was firing questions at him.

"Hugo, we need to set sail and we need to do it at once. De Marche has Emlyn. He has her and according to Komnenus, days have passed since he took her. Days, Hugo. He has had her for days," He was emphasizing his words. His fear of the significance and weight of what he was saying was evident in his face. His forehead was furrowed, and his eyes looked tired.

"That filth has her in a fortress. He has her alone. She must be very frightened." He added soberly, "There is no telling what condition we will find her in."

Dyfen was looking straight into Hugo's eyes, and he could tell that he was not alone in his concern.

Hugo stood erect and looked outwardly calm. "Whetherly, where is this fortress?" His grey eyes were like steel, not reflecting his inner turmoil.

All this time Komnenus had been standing a few feet away looking bored and considering how to flee. "Komnenus!" Dyfen yelled. "Get you here, before us."

Komnenus started out of his revery. He smirked at them and snidely remarked. "You must miss your betrothed, Rend. Was it not your duty to protect her?"

Hugo's face became flushed at the insult. He started toward Komnenus with the intent of doing him harm. He moved forward before Dyfen could stop him.

He reached for Komnenus who deftly threw his right hand out holding a dagger he must have had hidden in his boot. Komnenus grabbed Hugo by the neck. "Stop, where you stand Whetherly or I kill him."

"Without Hugo, you have no sail. So, I recommend that you listen to me." Komnenus pressed the edge of the blade into Hugo's neck sending a thin trickle of blood streaming onto his shirt.

Dyfen, was taken off guard by his action. He looked to the side and commanded, "Cydryn, attack!"

In seconds, Komnenus was flat on his back lying on the wharf with Cydryn standing on his chest, his gaping mouth around Komnenus' meaty throat. The dagger scudded into the water.

Hugo was wiping the blood from his neck with a bandana he wore around his neck. He looked at Dyfen and then at Cydryn.

"My thanks to you, Whetherly."

"You owe me no thanks, Hugo. It is Cydryn who deserves your thanks. The risk was all upon him," Dyfen stated.

Hugo appeared shaken and was silent, still holding his bandana to his throat. He looked toward the dog who returned his gaze with open hostility. Cydryn turned his head back down at Komnenus who was gurgling screams. "Spare me, spare my life Whetherly. Remove this barrel of mange from my chest. I cannot take breath," he was gasping.

"I will call him off and you will behave. I will not ask again or Cydryn's face will be the last you see," Dyfen said evenly.

"Cydryn, Retreat," Dyfen commanded. Cydryn closed his mouth and stepped back off Komnenus' chest. He remained in close proximity to him just to make sure he understood that there was no escape.

Komnenus was slow to get up. While doing so he kept a close eye on the hound as he pushed himself to his feet.

Begrudgingly, he said, "What will you have of me, Whetherly?"

"Komnenus, you will board this ship," Dyfen pointed to the Wild Boar," and guide us to where de Marche has taken Emlyn. Pray on your life she is there or else you will see once again Cydryn's jaws upon your throat."

Hugo had gone to talk to Martel on the Black Trident and they both were walking down the gang plank to the dock. Dyfen noticed Martel still dressed flamboyantly with great panache, wearing a frilled white shirt with his heavily necklaced chest exposed.

If he had any doubt as to who was approaching, it was confirmed by the King Cheetah tattoo upon his chest peeking through the jewelry. His boot length robe was a dark burgundy embroidered with gold threads. Somehow it made him look more dangerous than ever. His facial expression was flat, and it was obvious Hugo had made his case for the assistance needed. Martel was ready to support their effort.

"Whetherly, we must set sail now. More of Richard's ships keep anchoring and soon we will be unable to leave without being noticed. Have Komnenus board the Black Trident instead and let us take our leave. It is smaller, faster, and will be less conspicuous in its leaving."

Dyfen looked at Komnenus, who looked at Cydryn, who looked back at him in a menacing way. "Pray, make sure your dog allows me to move. I do not want any misunderstandings with him."

Dyfen raised his hand with one finger up and Cydryn backed up a pace allowing Komnenus to move past him.

Komnenus moved up the Black Trident gang plank with Cydryn behind him. Dyfen followed, first removing the halters from the two horses that they had absconded with so that they were free to graze the fields. "Thank you, brave lads," he crooned as he pulled off their halters. The horses emitted low whinnies and ambled away.

All were on board and the captain of the Black Trident issued orders to move out of the harbor. They moved very slowly, making sure they did not draw any attention to themselves.

Once outside the harbor many sails were visibly heading towards the them to join the fleet gathering there. They wind was up, and the Black Trident's sail inflated.

Dyfen left Komnenus under the watchful eye of Cydryn and disappeared below deck. He found an empty berth and walked in, closing the door behind him. He fell to his knees and bent his head, clasping his hands together tightly in prayer.

He spoke into the darkness of the room in a low, quiet, wavering voice.

"Lord, in the name of Jesus Christ and the Holy Comforter, sent to take His place on earth. I ardently beg Your mercy for Your daughter, Emlyn. Please keep her from harm. Allow me to arrive in time," he implored the Lord.

He remained in place for a few seconds, he felt a warmth wash over his body as if the hand of God had touched his soul. "Amen," he uttered and arose from his knees. He returned on deck readying himself for what was to happen next.

They headed north to Andrea Point hugging the coastline to make the best time. The wind was favorable, and they were making good time when Komnenus pointed to a prominent outcropping among the hills and directed them to head for it. "A small cove is there where we can weigh anchor. The ship is small enough to safely sail close to the beach."

"If you are lying you will be ripped asunder. Remember that. Even if we are killed, Cydryn will not fail," Dyfen warned him. "There will be no one to stop him."

Komnenus looked shaken. "I protest your distrust of me. My honor is at stake. I have kept my word," he said with gravity, looking wounded.

Martel called for the anchor to be dropped. He spoke something in French to his crew and the sail was taken down so that the ship gently rocked upon the crystal blue sea.

"Komnenus will accompany me. He will gain us access into the fortress. Hugo, you will remain with the ship until I return with Emlyn."

"I will not remain behind. I should be the one to go. She is my fiancé." Hugo face was fixed, as he stood a foot from Dyfen challenging him.

Dyfen disagreed. "We need Cydryn to control Komnenus and with as much progress as you have made at becoming his friend," he said dryly, "he will not obey you. So, it will be me who goes."

Just at that moment, Cydryn gave Hugo a threatening look as if he knew what was being said. Making it clear to Hugo that he could not dominate the dog.

Hugo looked unhappy but, in the end, relented. "Very well, you go. But I will follow if you are not back within the hour."

Dyfen jumped into the galley that had been lowered for the landing. He gestured for Komnenus to move forward with Cydryn close behind him.

Once they were settled in the galley, Martel's sailors rowed toward the rocky shoreline.

Hugo watched them go with a terse look on his face. "I pray for her safety."

Dyfen turned his head to face the shore, his long hair blowing in the wind. His eyes were heavy with worry because although he hoped for the best, he did not expect it.

Once ashore Dyfen and Komnenus, with Cydryn close behind him, started up a small hill.

Dyfen ordered, "Once we have entered the fortress you will convince de Marche to accompany you to Apostolos Andreas Monastery where you will keep him as long as possible. If you fail, I swear by God's eyes I will find you and allow Cydryn to tear you to pieces."

"What am I to say to him to convince him of the need?" Komnenus asked irritably. "I am cooperating, and you ask for the impossible."

"You will do the impossible or die a horrible death. I doubt they will find all the pieces to bury," Dyfen answered him.

They reached the fortress gates and Komnenus yelled up to the guards on the parapet. "Allow us entre, it is I, your Emperor. I have come to speak with the Duc de Marche."

A guard looked down at him with suspicion. "Who may you be? Our Emperor is not a monk."

Komnenus looked bewildered for a second and then realized he still had the monk's robe on. He quickly pulled it over his head. "I am Emperor Isaac Komnenus. I am traveling incognito because of invading troops that have landed on my shores. I do not have time to waste explaining myself to you. I will speak to the Duc de Marche at once."

Without the habit, the guards recognized the Emperor and pulled up the gate.

The three of them were allowed to pass through. Komnenus was in the lead with Cydryn close by his side. He could feel the dog's hot breath upon his shoulder.

He noted the updated and sumptuous trappings resulting from de Marche's renovations. The plastered walls had beautiful frescos upon them and the floors were of intricate mosaic designs.

Cydryn began to whimper and growl immediately upon entering the fortress walls to Dyfen's surprise. He commanded him to settle.

They followed the guard through grand hallways and finally to a beautifully carved, wooden door. The soldier knocked once and went in. Shortly thereafter, the door opened, and he stood aside to allow Komnenus to pass. Raoul, the Duc de Marche, was seated in a comfortable-looking chair. He raised his eyebrows in surprise when he saw Komnenus.

"Why have you come?" he asked in surprise.

"You wretch, you tricked and abandoned me, your Emperor!" Komnenus spit the words out.

"Let us not pretend who you are. You remain ruler at the pleasure of Salah ad-Din based on your promise to repel crusaders from your shores," de Marche said casually. "They now overrun most of the island. He will be displeased."

"Now, why is it you are here?" de Marche repeated coldly.

"I came." Komnenus looked around. "By God's will," he sputtered, not seeing Cydryn or Dyfen behind him. "I was kidnapped by that upstart, Whetherly. He was right behind me with his accursed dog, and they are now gone."

"What!!!! You bring him here, to me? Inside my walls. Where is he?"

"Guards!" he screamed.

The door opened immediately.

"We have an intruder in our midst. Find him! Slay him!"

De March left the room, leaving Komnenus alone. Komnenus fell into a chair and started planning an escape. He would take sanctuary in the nearby monastery. His only wish was not to be found by that accursed dog.

Chapter 33

Emlyn Found

Dyfen dropped back soon after entering the fortress walls while the guard and Komnenus were headed to see de Marche.

"Find Emlyn, Cydryn. Go to Emlyn," he urged the dog.

Cydryn had picked up her scent upon entering the fortress and his tail was wagging violently. He headed down a narrow hall and Dyfen followed. On the way they encountered the resident Marshal, a tall thin man with a stern face.

"What business do you have here?" the Marshal asked gruffly.

"I am my Lord's newly hired huntsman. This is his prize hound. I have orders to come here to discuss a bitch to breed him with. I have one in mind that will do nicely. I only need his Lordships' approval."

"Very well, third door to the left. You can wait there while I speak to His Grace," he stated as he walked away.

Cydryn moved down a narrow hall past the designated door and up a nearby staircase with Dyfen close behind. He scented the air as he moved.

He stopped at a bolted door and whimpered. Dyfen unbolted it and placed his hand on the lever and slowly opened the door saying a silent prayer to the Lord, 'I pray, Holy Lord, you have watched over Your lamb.'

The room was dim and his eyes adjusted to the light. He saw a maiden looking out of a window and his heart sank. Cydryn ran to the figure.

Her long, dark hair was disheveled and limply hung past her waist. She had a bedraggled look about her.

"Emlyn?" Dyfen whispered hoarsely, asking a question more than making a statement.

The maiden slowly turned and looked down at the dog and then at him standing in the chamber doorway.

Dyfen held his breath. It was Emlyn dressed only in a silk robe. Her slender figure covered by her long tresses. He could see the outline of her areolas through the thin fabric.

"Dyfen. Dyfen, you have come." The relief in her voice was evident.

She was not entirely herself he could see. Dyfen spotted a ewer on a chest with a goblet half full of wine next to it. Drunk he concluded.

He rushed to her side. She had the sour odor of wine about her.

"I pledged to you I would come. Did you doubt me?" he chided her attempting to keep things light.

He pulled his hauberk off and let the heavy garment drop to the floor. He tugged his linen tunic over his head, leaving him bare chested. She saw the blue stone she once wore on her own neck.

He gently took Emlyn by the shoulders supporting her against his chest while he lowered his tunic over her. The silk robe separated in the attempt and he could not help but notice bruising on her breasts and down her inner thighs. His eyes were drawn to the raised scar on her left thigh at the site of the arrow wound. He saw something else as well near her denuded nether part. His body tensed a little at the sight of it.

As the fabric settled, it fell past her knees and hung limply off her shoulders. It was not ideal but it would do for the present.

Still in shock upon seeing her condition, he queried, "Emlyn. What has he done to you?" Dyfen spoke calmly while quelling the anger which had arisen inside him. The image of de Marche with her made him sick. He shook himself to clear his mind.

She stood silent. He gently backed her up, looking down into her soft eyes.

"Emlyn, answer me. What has befallen you? Did de Marche do this to you?" he asked again. He did not need her answer. He knew.

"He has taken what is rightfully his," she answered somberly.

"Rightfully his?" Dyfen looked at her incredulously. "How could this," he was gesturing, "be his right?"

"We have married," she answered. "He is my husband."

"Husband! Emlyn you cannot know what you say!"

" He is my husband and I his wife. We married three days ago."

"As my husband he has rights to, to... "she stammered, "to me," she finished. "We share a marriage bed."

"Emlyn, was this of your choosing?" Dyfen was still in disbelief.

She looked down. "He told me he would bed me without marriage if I refused. I would be forced to become an unchaste woman. I could not bring that shame upon my father." Tears ran down her cheeks. "I sent Kellis to you. I sent him but it was already too late."

Her eyes were lowered as she pushed her head into his chest in shame.

Dyfen stood shocked but tried to hide it so not to upset her more than she already was. He said calmly, "We will leave this place Emlyn. After you are safely away, we will deal with the issue of marriage. You are not to worry. This can all be sorted later. Hugo is waiting for you on the ship that brought us here." Dyfen looked down at her.

"Hugo! Oh my God, no!" she became panicked. "I cannot face him."

"You must, Emlyn. Any decent man will see the fault does not lie with you," Dyfen said reassuringly. "Hugo is not a favorite, but his love for you is real. He will not be dissuaded. As your betrothed, you must allow him to decide." The words were out without thought. He was not sure why he brought the subject up other than he was so rattled he was not thinking clearly.

Dyfen had redonned his gambeson and hauberk. She watched him pull his clothing over his muscled torso in misery. After he had completed dressing, he took her back into his arms, cradling her against his chest to comfort her.

Emlyn leaned crumpled there when they heard a commotion at the chamber door. Cydryn began to whimper and growl once again. The hackles on his back became erect and he placed himself before Emlyn shielding her from what he knew was coming. That is when the heavy wooden door was thrown open and de Marche with sword drawn stood there. His dark eyes blazing. Dyfen noticed a bandage wrapped around his sword hand.

"Remove yourself from my wife, you insolent whelp," he commanded. De Marches' grip was so tight on his sword hilt that blood was seeping through the bandage. The pain that came with it did not stop him from an aggressive attack. He came flying at Dyfen.

Dyfen side stepped him. "Wife, you say? You forced a maiden to wed against her will. Repeatedly force yourself upon her, and call her wife?

She does not want you. But you knew that. She was betrothed and yet you stole her virtue from her family and fiancé. This marriage is but a mockery. A sham to cover up your wantonness."

He looked over at Emlyn who was obscured by Cydryn standing before her as a barrier. He had never seen his dog so ready to kill. His teeth were barred, and ears were flat against his large grey head.

Dyfen drew his sword and had held his dagger in the other hand. He flipped it casually when de Marche lunged at him again. Dyfen barely had time to sidestep the charge. De Marche came up behind him and Dyfen spun to face him. He could hear footfalls echoing down the hallway. He managed to stick his head out of the door to glimpse Hugo running down the hall toward them. He shouted out of the open doorway, "Hugo," he yelled. "In here."

While he was distracted, de Marche flicked his sword and nicked Dyfen on the wrist. Blood was rolling down his own hand, making the sword hard to hold onto.

Just then, Hugo slid though the doorway.

"Hugo, take Emlyn and leave! Get her safely away," Dyfen shouted.

De March became infuriated. "My wife will go nowhere. No man will take from me what is mine," he stated in his smooth deep voice.

"Wife? "Hugo repeated. "What does he mean, wife?" he asked, looking at Dyfen with a puzzled look upon his face.

"Hugo, there is no time for questions. Take her and leave. I will follow. Cydryn and I will handle this."

Hugo looked toward Cydryn with askance before approaching Emlyn. Dyfen called his dog to stand down. The hound allowed Hugo to approach and pull Emlyn to his side.

Dyfen parried with de Marche backing him up and away from the doorway leaving room for them to escape. Hugo pulled Emlyn out into the wide stone hallway.

She started back through the doorway, refusing to leave Dyfen. Hugo reentered the room after her. Dyfen saw her from the corner of his eye, "Take her and go! Now!" Dyfen ordered Hugo.

Hugo, in exasperation, picked Emlyn off her feet and placed her over his shoulder.

At the sight of Hugo lifting his wife, Raoul de Marche's eyes widened, his face became alarmed and he lowered his sword hand. "Emlyn!" he screamed with such anguish that she turned her head to look back at him. She could see the bloody cloth around his hand. She saw the despair on his handsome face as he moved to give chase, ignoring the present danger to himself. Right behind him was Cydryn. The last thing she saw was the large hound standing on hind legs, jaws opened wide, grab Raoul by the neck and take him down.

As Hugo ran with Emlyn over his shoulder down the hall to the east staircase, they were met by two guards with drawn swords. Hugo hurriedly placed Emlyn on the floor as gently as possible before turning to confront the armed men. He drew his sword from its scabbard.

The first man came brashly forward and Hugo parried. The guardsman's sword was too heavy for him, putting him off balance. As his shoulder turned toward Hugo, Hugo stabbed him deeply in the back. The man dropped immediately.

The second man moved toward Emlyn huddled on the floor. Seeing the man heading in her direction Hugo moved to head him off. He angerly pushed the man sideways with a thrust of his foot and brought his sword down into his chest. A fatal blow.

Hugo's breath was deep and labored. He returned his focus on getting Emlyn to safety. He picked her back up and with her clinging to him closely, started to run once more. Outside, he took the castle steps two at a time until he reached the bottom. Gently he set her down on her feet and leaped onto a large bay horse he had borrowed from the now dead guard he had encountered upon arrival. Bending to the side, he picked her up and placed her in front of him and raced off with Emlyn firmly between his arms.

When they reached the Mediterranean shore, he dismounted and pulled her from the horse. He guided her towards the galley anchored at the shore.

"Hugo, we must wait for Dyfen," she protested struggling a bit against him.

"We must leave immediately. Those were his instructions. You heard him yourself. Your safety is paramount. The man is risking his life to save you, Emlyn. Do not make his efforts in vain." And with that he picked her up in his arms and placed her in the galley to row back to the Black Trident.

Chapter 34

After the Battle

De Marche was bleeding from the neck wound Cydryn had inflicted. He had hit the floor hard with the dog still on his back.

The large canine, who weighed over one hundred and fifty pounds, was heavy, making it difficult to breathe. The hound stood poised with jaws opened wide ready to finish him off when de Marche lifted his sword, blindly swiping backwards at Cydryn, nicking him in the flank. Cydryn yelped but refused to move. Even injured he could not be distracted from killing the man under him.

By now de Marche's men were rushing towards the room. Seeing that Hugo and Emlyn were safely away Dyfen yelled to his dog, "Cydryn, come now!"

Cydryn looked at his master, who was moving through the doorway, and leapt off of the still body under him to follow.

The two fled down the hallway in the opposite direction of Hugo and Emlyn, leaving de Marche for dead. Their footfalls echoed as they moved. He stopped behind a large column for a few seconds to examine the injury done to Cydryn.

Once assured it was just a flesh wound of no consequence, they continued onward. "Cydryn, we are old warriors, you and I," Dyfen chuckled with relief.

The hound licked his hand and wagged his tail, eyes shining at his master. Together, they raced up a flight of stairs to the tower parapet. As they reached the top, they were espied by three guardsmen who ran at them with swords held high.

Dyfen backed up a step then ran at them keeping them busy, giving Cydryn time to get behind them. From the rear, the large dog leapt with front paws extended, bringing two men down from behind. As they fell, they plunged forward into the third man fighting Dyfen. The man fell, releasing his weapon as he hit the ground. Dyfen kicked their swords from them and then threw the weapons off the parapet for good measure. He heard them clatter on the stone pavers below and overheard a familiar voice cry from beneath him.

"Damn it, are you trying to behead us all?" Dover cried calling upward.

Dyfen looked down and saw Isley and Dover with the dogs, who started barking when they saw him with Cydryn above. Cydryn, recognizing his wolfhound brothers began barking in response.

"My heart is gladdened to see you brothers. How fare you?" Dyfen called down, catching his breath.

"We are well and I dare say we fare better than you, I can promise," Isley returned. "Even from here I can see your weariness. I told Sarkis you would be so."

Upon not receiving the expected response, Dover looked around behind him. "Sarkis and Kellis are here somewhere," he mumbled.

As he said this, two figures on horseback came riding through the gates pulling up next to the group. Sarkis had a big grin on his handsome, youthful face. Kellis, who followed him, looked so much older now as he sat confidently on Arka, Dyfen thought.

Kellis held his hand up to Dyfen in greeting. "Where is my lady?" he said with a worried voice.

Dyfen did not have the heart to tell him more than, "She is safe with Hugo. They sail on the Black Trident homeward."

He could see the relief on Kellis' face and thought to himself. Let the lad have some peace. He will find out soon enough. I hope he does not place blame on himself.

"How did you come to be here?" Dyfen asked Isley.

"We joined arms with Richard once we learned of your solo mission," Isley said accusingly. "Richard seeks Komnenus everywhere and searches everywhere after the devil somehow escaped from his stronghold in Nicosia.

"The King of Jerusalem, Guy de Lusignan, arrived with ships and knights to assist Richard. They are combing the countryside by land as King Richard and Robert of Tornham each search by sea. They have orders to sweep up all vessels in their path. One of those ships happened to be ours. Denisot and the Sea Stallion are here."

"Richard has our own ship?" Dyfen asked incredulously.

"Richard munificently released it to us once we explained our part in this search," Dover answered. "The Lionheart knows the people of Cyprus want their Emperor captured. He is hated by all and many have come forward offering information on his movements. It was reported that Komnenus was here and has taken sanctuary at a monastery nearby."

"We left Richard with his army stationed outside the monastery. Let us go to witness the surrender of Komnenus," Isley said.

"I cannot," Dyfen responded firmly. "I will find you later, but now I must make haste. I have need of Arazi," He was looking at Isley expectantly.

"Here," Isley dismounted Arazi and let the reins drop. "Remain safe brother. We will wait here. May God go before you."

Dyfen moved next to the stallion and pressed the side of his face against him, whispering in his ear. "We ride again Arazi. Like the wind we will go. As we have never run before!" and with that he hoisted himself up throwing his right leg over the stallion's back, pressing his legs against Arazi's flanks. They took off like lightning, heading toward the shore.

Arazi must have sensed the urgency in his master's tensed body because he galloped so fast Dyfen could barely catch his breath. Cydryn did his best to keep up with them.

When they were within sight of the shore they slowed as they approached the beach. Cydryn suddenly reappeared, joining horse and rider once again. Together they sprinted toward the sandy shoreline. Stallion, dog, and rider were out of breath. Their sides heaved as they slowed to a walk.

When they arrived at the beach, Dyfen could see the distinct sail of the Black Trident a few miles from shore. He dismounted and stood watching, one hand stroking Arazi's muzzle, while the other rested on Cydryn's head. The dog moved in closer to Dyfen so that their bodies touched, reassuring both. As they stood watching the Black Trident shrink in size, Dyfen's shoulders slumped and his face was furrowed with worry.

He watched as the sail moved further away into an orange, setting sun. Sighing heavily, he bent his head in silent prayer. When he looked up again the sail was gone and the sun sank into the glittering, aquamarine Cilician Sea.

Chapter 35

Richard Again

The Apostolos Andreas Monastery was situated on a bluff high over the rocky shoreline on the southern tip of the Karpas peninsula. The opposite side of the peninsula as de Marche's fortifications. Currently, the coastline was filled with nearly a hundred ships that had encircled the island seeking Komnenus based on information the scouts had gleamed from subjects. Events were escalating. King Richard and his men at arms had arrived on shore with their horses and had surrounded the monastery.

Inside, Komnenus was in the chapel kneeling before the altar praying to the Lord to protect him. Afterwards, he traveled through the flagstone hallways and up the steps to the monastery's second story roof. Father Goran came up to him and said, "My son, men have come for you."

"I know, father. Do not trouble yourself. I have no intention of giving them your Emperor," Komnenus told him so self-consumed that he assumed the priest was worried about his welfare.

"Your Grace, you may reconsider that decision," the old man spoke gesturing below trying to be diplomatic.

There mounted on a large, magnificent stallion and dressed in his finest battledress was the Lionheart. Next to him on a grey Andalusian was a woman. The horse looked familiar, and he looked more closely, squinting his eyes to focus. The woman looked familiar. It took him a minute to recognize them. Mareya.

He called down to Richard. "Richard, I do not wish to cause you further trouble. I will humbly surrender myself to you as agreed originally. Same terms," Komnenus spoke with bravado. "I surrender myself and ask one condition. That you release my daughter and allow her freedom."

Richard Lionheart had won the right to decide who she would wed. He was not about to yield on this point.

He looked at the woman beside him sitting quietly on her steed. She had her head down and already knew her fate. "As much as that would please you, Lord Komnenus, that cannot be," Richard told him firmly. "I have decided that she will be sailing under the supervision of my sister, until a suitable union is arranged for her.

"You have betrayed my trust more than once. Now you must surrender on my terms alone. Look upon your daughter, she has wisely honored your own pledge and yet, you refuse to comply? She displays more honor than her esteemed father it seems," Richard spoke. "Come down and surrender yourself. Waste no more of my time," the King commanded.

Komnenus stood staring down at his daughter.

She called up to him, "Father, all is lost. Reconcile yourself."

Komnenus looked defeated. "Well then, I ask, ... I demand," he corrected himself, "that I shall not be placed in iron shackles. It does not befit a man of my station. Afterall, I am the Emperor, and this is my land."

Robert, who was next to King Richard, interjected sputtering at Komnenus' tremendous nerve, "Emperor! Indeed, he jests. He lacks both honor and integrity. For that matter, any noble quality held by a ruler or a man. He has told only lies and failed to uphold any of his oaths. Sire, he deserves not your favor."

"Robert, do not trouble yourself; we can surely accommodate the Emperors request. No iron chains will be placed upon his person," Richard smiled as he spoke. "Take him away. Bind him with ropes for now until I have had chains of silver made for His Excellency."

Richard was smiling and Robert chuckled, "Of course, my King, as you command."

As his men went to retrieve Komnenus, Richard addressed Robert, "I place him in your tender care, do not turn your back on this contemptuous betrayer," he ordered.

"Now that the last of our work is fait accompli, we move forward in the true cause of our journey," Richard said with satisfaction. He turned to his men and shouted, "To Acre," holding up his sword.

"To Acre!" his men echoed back, happy to be moving on. They created a tremendous din as they held their weapons in the air and banged them against their bucklers.

Chapter 36

Hugo and Emlyn

The wind whipped Captain Francois Martel's long robe backward from his lithe body as he stood on the foredeck of his ship facing the coming storm. His gold and silver jewelry glimmered in the failing sun against the darkness of his chest. The waves were spraying over the gunwales. He stood staring out over the sea. It calmed him and put him at peace. The black clouds gathering above shrouded the once blue sky. He set course further out to sea to avoid the approaching gale.

Below deck, in the highly adorned captain's cabin, sat Emlyn, still clutching Dyfen's linen tunic over the silk robe she wore. The cabin held luxurious fabrics and exotic, carved woods creating a cocoon of comfort. Captain Martel was a hard man who appreciated luxury.

Hugo stood in front of Emlyn with his back to her. He was bent over a tabletop with his hands tightly clutching its edges gathering himself to face her shattered condition. His hands held on so forcefully that his fingers were turning white. He struggled to calm himself before he faced her, for her sake.

Suddenly, he straightened up, walked to the wardrobe and pulled out one of Martel's long robes. It was forest-green damask. He gently placed it around Emlyn's slim shoulders, tenderly lifting her tangled mane and settling it outside the garment. The long robe engulfed her completely. She pulled the edges together as if she were cold although it was quite warm below deck.

"Emlyn, this is for now. I promise to provide something more suitable as soon as I speak to Francois. I know he has ladies' things on board here somewhere because I have seen them. Plunder from some of his raids. Presents for his female admirers in port. You observe, he sees himself the dandy," he smiled while speaking trying a jest to lighten the mood and put her at ease. "Dandy he pretends to be, but he is the toughest son of the devil I have ever met. Make no mistake in that," Hugo ended as he scanned her face trying to determine her state of mind.

Now he faced her, leaning against the table opposite her position on the berth. His manner became more sedate as he tried to maintain calm.

"Emlyn, how do you fare? Are you injured?" he said as if nothing were out of the ordinary, fighting to keep his emotions in check.

She raised her head and looked him in the eyes, with her own brimming with tears. "Hugo, my woes are too heavy to tell," she said clutching the green damask robe to her body.

"Naught can be so bad, Emlyn. You are alive. That is the only important consideration at present," he replied. "Remember we agreed you would rest your weight upon my shoulders? No matter how heavy? Let me remind you that you gave your word upon it."

"Hugo, I clearly remember our conversation but neither of us imagined the deadly weight of what I now bear. How can I face my father, my brother or anyone for that matter? How do I dare meet your eyes?"

Hugo fought to maintain his composure, "Emlyn, I see only the same beautiful, young girl I have always loved. That has not changed."

He crouched in front of her, lightly placing his hands on her shoulders to reassure her, "Does this have to do with what I heard during your rescue? You are wed to de Marche?"

He braced himself for the worst.

"I am undone. Nothing can restore to me that which I have lost. I am ruined, no longer a maiden," she said with a choked sob. "Yes, I am his wife. I have acted as a wife these days past. I am stained beyond salvation, Hugo," she responded, hanging her head and placing a hand on her forehead.

He stood and spoke, "Emlyn, I still love you no matter what the circumstances. I still wish to marry you. We both saw de Marche fall at the jaws of the hound. You are a widow and are free to remarry. I wish to marry you, now, today." He watched her reaction.

Emlyn said nothing for a time. Finally, she spoke, "Hugo, I am not worthy of you or any man."

Hugo bent back down before her, placing a hand on each side of her. "Emlyn, look at me. Look into my eyes. I want you to see how serious I am. You are what I want. You are what I have always wanted. I care not what has happened with de Marche. He took advantage of you. Forced himself upon you." He held his breath waiting for her response.

His entire body was tense with anticipation of her answer. He tried again. "You acted as a married woman submitting to her husband. That is all. None can fault you for that."

She stared at him for a minute. Slowly she raised her arms over her head and reached into her thick tousled hair. She brought her arms back in front of her with something in her closed hand. She held out her hand to Hugo and slowly opened it as he looked down into her palm. Sitting there was his mother's pearl studded heart.

"I hid it for safe keeping. Everything I had was taken from me. It was a reminder of my life before," she said shyly. She dropped it into his hand. "I have no right to it."

Touched by her consideration, Hugo had an overwhelming feeling of guilt sweep over him. He grabbed her hands in his. He looked at her with glimmering eyes. "Emlyn, forgive me. I have failed you. If anything, it is I who cannot face your father. I pledged to him I would protect you and I have broken that pledge. I should never have allowed my father to send me to sea. I curse him for doing so and myself for going."

"Hugo, ours was not a real engagement. We both knew that from the beginning. Our betrothal was a shield to protect me and with it you put yourself in danger. I fault you not for any of this," she said to try to settle him down.

"I made a sorry job of shielding you. I need to understand what happened. Tell me what befell you, Emlyn. I must know," Hugo pled with her as he got up and sat beside her.

"Hugo, I cannot speak of it. I am too ashamed to tell it," she said gently, bowing her head.

"I cannot rest until I know what you suffered at the hands of that monster. Now, say it. All of it."

She was quiet for a time wondering if she could say the words.

"I must know," he repeated with more force. "You will tell me. We will not leave this cabin until I have learned all of it. It is better for you to share your pain with another."

Hearing the stubborn edge in his voice, she remained silent for a few minutes while she considered if she would be able to do what he asked. Finally, she raised her head and slowly started speaking with her eyes half closed to make it easier in the telling. She was unable to meet his eyes while she recounted certain events. She began.

"It was just before evening and Father and Eryk had taken our men at arms and sailed to Limassol at the invitation of your father. They went to assess the danger presented to our lands with the intention of committing fealty to Richard Lionheart against Emperor Komnenus. They left Eston and a few men behind thinking us safe as the Emperor and the Duc de Marche had already left for Limassol. But he had not."

Emlyn could sense his inner turmoil and looked at him unwilling to go on but Hugo had to hear the rest. "Continue, Emlyn," he prompted. "I want to know the all of it."

Not wanting to see his face while she spoke the rest, Emlyn turned toward the wall. She made a last appeal, "Hugo the rest is as you probably imagine so let us stop here."

"Emlyn, I do not wish to rely upon my imagination because I assure you if what I imagine occurred, I will insert a dagger into my own heart. Now, kindly continue and do not spare the details. I do not deserve such kindness," he harshly spoke.

Seeing that he would not be deterred, she took a deep breath and resumed her tale. She told him as much as she dared.

After she had finished, she said, "This is the woman you ask in marriage, Hugo. You deserve more than I have to offer."

Hugo was visibly shaken. Duc de Marche would answer to him, he would make sure of that. He leapt to his feet to comfort her, taking her hand in his. "I care not, who has come before me, Emlyn. Whatever marks he placed upon you. You were given no choice. To me you are pure as the palest white rose. If you allow me, I will love, honor, and protect you with my life. I swear it." His grey eyes were fixed upon her hazel ones trying to read her.

His hair was askew and rumpled from unconscientiously pulling his hands through it while she spoke. He was holding out the gold, pearl studded heart she had given back to him only a half hour before. When she did not take it, he slipped it into his pocket.

He tried to reason with her, "Emlyn, consider. He is dead. You are no longer wed. You need a husband to claim and protect you." He added, "I can do that."

"Hugo, I cannot allow you to sacrifice your good name for me."

"My name, if you ask others, is not in such fine standing," he chuckled trying to make light of the heaviness they both felt. He leaned his forehead against hers.

"Hugo, what if I am with child? Raoul's child." There was the crux of her dismay.

"It was only a few days. You may become pregnant with our own child. Who is to know?" Hugo responded, trying to discount her fear.

"I do not want the father of my child to be in question," she returned. "It would not be fair, and the child may suffer as well because we would always be wondering, Hugo, we would.

"If I agree to wed, we will not consummate our marriage until my courses have passed. I will know the father of my child," she was firm.

"As you wish," Hugo resignedly replied. He did have doubts as to whether he could accept a whelp by that bastard de Marche but his feelings for Emlyn ran deeper.

"I will speak to Martel at once and it will be done. He can officiate. I hope you do not mind a rather simple ceremony. I do not wish to wait until we reach the Wild Boar. We will wed here on the Black Trident, then sail to the Wild Boar which is still anchored off the coast of Nicosia. From there we can stay at sea, out of harm's way."

Emlyn nodded her head in agreement, not looking at Hugo. She had misgivings regarding marriage to him. Not only because she did not return the depth of his feelings but because he deserved a virginal bride not one that had been debauched. Remaining wed to de Marche was unthinkable. Thanks be to God she was free. Her father will be none the wiser. She did not want to burden him with defending her honor. Seeking revenge against such a powerful family would bring ruin to her own. He and her brother would surely be placed on a dangerous path.

"Hugo, I think we should wait. Give yourself time to consider what you are doing."

"No, I will not wait. I waited and I lost you. I refuse to take that chance once more. We wed today. I yield on consummating our marriage until after you discover your condition but after that, no matter the outcome we will be as husband and wife. Is that clear? If de Marche were not already dead, I would kill him," he said quietly.

"I understand," she said feeling limp from the events of the past few days. "But Hugo, swear to me that you will not tell my father or brother about de Marche. Swear it," she commanded him solemnly.

Hugo fixed her with a serious face, knelt on one knee, pushing the point of his dagger into the floor and made the sign of the cross raising his right hand to God.

"I swear to you, by all that is holy, in the name of Our Lord. Upon my love for you, Emlyn, your family will not hear a word of this from me." He made the sign of the cross again and lowered his hand while still staring into her eyes.

She nodded her head and turned away. He stood up, grabbing her by the arm and continued.

"Emlyn, there is something I will ask of you."

She looked at him expectantly.

"Once we are bound, you will no longer meet with Whetherly outside of my presence," he stipulated. "I see no reason you will have cause to make his acquaintance again so what I ask should be of no consequence."

Emlyn kept her eyes on his, not knowing what to say. The trauma from the last few days was still with her. It all seemed unreal. Hugo was providing a safe haven for her. Dyfen had never professed any feelings for her at all. He had a keen sense of chivalry compelling him to protect the weak, which is why animals were drawn to him. She loved that about him, but he was pledged to another. He had come when summoned as he promised he would and had rescued her. His duty to her was done and she would most likely never set eyes upon him again.

Hugo deserved her gratefulness and loyalty. He was standing waiting for her response. Finally, she gave her head a short nod of agreement. Hugo smiled back satisfied.

"Excuse me my love. I go to Martel to beseech him for maidens' clothing I know he keeps about here somewhere. I will send them back to you. I will instruct water be brought so you may bathe as well."

He left the room humming.

Chapter 37

The Return of the Duc de Marche

Cydryn was scenting the wind. His rough fur blown gently backwards from the breeze. His hackles were up once more. He started barking wildly, interspersed with growls. Dyfen turned to see what concerned his companion. What he saw made him raise his eyebrows in surprise and gave him pause for a second. Reacting quickly, he grabbed Cydryn by the scruff of the neck to keep him from charging.

Mounted on a night black stallion, a disheveled, haggard looking man, his neck still covered in blood and his normally well-coiffed hair all a tangle, flying riotously about his face, was Raoul, Duc de Marche, his sword drawn, ready for use. He was in a fury. "Where is she?" he screamed as he waved his sword menacingly.

"Where is my wife?" he demanded. He kept one eye on Cydryn and made sure to keep his distance from the dog that had almost ended his life.

"Gone, de Marche, she is gone," Dyfen replied somberly. He himself was exhausted but could not let it pass. "She is not your wife," he countered.

This caused de Marche to become adamant, "She IS my wife. Our marriage was consecrated by the church and has been fully consummated. For all I know, she is carrying my child and I will have her back by my side where a wife belongs." He was now shouting to be heard over the gathering wind.

"You forced her. She did not freely agree to become your wife," Dyfen stood his ground. "The law speaks to a woman being forced to wed."

"She is my wife. She married me freely in church, by a servant of God. We consummated our marriage many times over. She was a full participant in that consummation. Her passion was evident," de Marche stated plainly.

"You lie!" Dyfen countered, "You are a nothing but a liar." His hand involuntarily tightened its grip upon Cydryn, who was struggling to break free.

De Marche smiled at him. "I am many things but I have no need for lies," he spoke plainly then continued, "Why would she not want to please her husband? My wife enjoyed our marriage bed as much as I. A man knows these things." He looked at Dyfen in a conspiratorial way, implying they were both worldly men. "Her trench was as moist as any willing partner I have had. She was wanton and I did please her." His smile turned into a smirk as he spoke. With that, he turned the stallion and raced off.

Dyfen watched him ride away and made a split-second decision. He mounted Arazi and called to Cydryn. They headed south.

Chapter 38

A Means to an End

They ran like the wind until the three arrived at Apostolos Andreas Monastery where Richard's navy was still anchored in a calm sea. All sails were furled. The fleet was enormous having swollen in size with those captured during the search for Komnenus. Finding the Sea Stallion without the benefit of a visible sail was going to be a difficult job.

Cydryn located his pack brothers huddled not far from where Isley, Dover, Kellis and Sarkis stood in a group watching the three of them approach.

"Hail, brother," Isley called to him.

Dover raised his hand in greeting looking nonchalant, while Sarkis and Kellis ran to greet him.

"I am glad to see you all. Where is the Sea Stallion anchored? We must weigh anchor and sail out to the Black Trident. I must be on that ship before the day ends."

"No greeting? No explanation?" Dover asked, feigning insult. Dyfen had not acknowledged any of them.

"Dover, try to be less yourself, if you please," Dyfen told him irritated.

"Dyfen, what possesses you?" Isley asked concerned. He pushed the hair from his forehead.

"It is urgent that I leave as soon as possible," Dyfen answered wearily. "It is Emlyn."

"Emlyn?" Isley repeated. "You said she had been rescued and was with young Rend. What has happened since?"

"Since? You ask me what has happened since!" Dyfen exploded. He was playing with his dagger out of nervous energy. "The man I had thought to be dead has resurrected. De Marche is alive, and Emlyn needs to know. He is hell bent on finding her. She is not safe and I need to find her before he does. Denisot must intercept the Black Trident and place me on it. There are so many ships anchored here. Where is the Sea Stallion in this lot?"

"King Richard, I would speak with the English King," Isley answered. "He is with nobles from the Levant who have sailed here to assist him in the pursuit of Emperor Komnenus. If he is not in his tent, he most likely entered the monastery. His aide will know where Denisot is anchored."

"Give me a moment to speak to Rheda. I will find out for you," Dover told them.

They watched him stride off toward the picket line where the horses were tied.

He came back fifteen minutes later. "The aide went with King Richard but the Sea Stallion is anchored off to the south."

"How did you find out so quickly," Kellis asked him impressed.

"Rheda is the daughter of Marshal of the Horse. She assists her father who is informed of where all horse transport vessels weighed anchor," Dover told them and then went on to say, "We will require a small craft to reach it but I think I know where one can be found." He started off and the rest followed him.

Chapter 39

Dyfen and Emlyn

The Sea Stallion anchored far enough from the Black Trident to barely make out its outline on the horizon. A thin fog filtered the full moon's light to cloak their arrival. The Black Trident sat with a dropped anchor and sails furled. No crew members were visible on deck from where they sat in the small galley they had rowed over in.

Dover threw the boarding hook over the ship's gunwale and it caught on his first attempt. He pulled the small vessel close enough for Dyfen to grab the rope and use the knots to pull himself aboard. Once on deck, he looked down at Isley, Dover, Sarkis and Kellis and waved his hand. They started to row backwards returning to the Sea Stallion.

Dyfen stayed out of the moonlight and looked about before moving. He spotted a few sailors at the stern of the ship laughing with their heads thrown back, stumbling to and fro. Probably drunk on grog, he thought.

He moved stealthily through the mist, towards the bow of the ship. There was movement a short distance from where he stood. He could smell her before he saw her. The faint aroma of Damascus rose wafted towards him filling his senses. He could feel his entire body relax.

He whispered, "Emlyn?"

He saw the figure turn and the pale moon caught her face and hair. Dyfen was reminded of her beauty. Her hair shone like polished leather and her eyes like green chalcedony. She was dressed in a green velvet gown. A far cry different from the condition he found her in at their last meeting. He could see the gentle rise of her breasts as her breathing became labored in her shock at seeing him.

"Dyf...," she began.

He placed his fingers over her mouth to silence her.

"Emlyn, where is Hugo? Why are you here alone on this ship of drunken men?" he asked incredulously.

Before she could answer he had placed his arm around her and put his hand under her chin to tilt her head up at him. "Emlyn, I have been overly worried about you. I had to come see for myself that you were safe. For my own peace of mind."

He looked back at the few crew members on deck to see that they had all sat down with backs to the gunwale, heads resting on the shoulder of the man seated next to him. All were asleep.

"Dyfen," she continued, "I am safe. You need not worry for me."

Her lips held a sad smile. She had placed her hand on his chest to put some space between them. The gesture did not escape his notice.

"Emlyn, I had to come. I must speak to you," he whispered. His tone was urgent.

She tried to speak but he hurried on, "I have come for you. I have business to attend to first but after that we will wed." He did not want to tell her de Marche still lived and that she was still his wife. He had come for her. He would entrust her safety to Isley and Dover and then would leave to kill de Marche and finish what he had started. Kill him for the liberties he had taken and to free her from his grasp. He looked down at her expectantly. Anxious. He had hoped she would be happy but what he saw on her face told him differently. His body tensed.

"Dyfen," she spoke. He could barely hear her soft voice above the waves, "I cannot wed you." She dropped her head and swallowed hard.

"Emlyn, pray do not refuse me. I know you do not love me, but I promise to do all in my power to change that. I willingly lay down my life to protect yours." He tried to pull her back toward himself but she resisted him.

The voice of Hugo Rend responded, "She cannot wed you because she is already wed. To me! You can take your proposal elsewhere and leave my wife alone."

They both turned their heads to the side and saw Hugo walking toward them. Hugo's eyes were fixed upon the two of them, his hair smoothed back. His rigid face fixed like stone. He was garbed in only his tunic as if he had left his cabin hurriedly. He still had his boots on. The night wind blew his linen tunic close to his form displaying his hard, muscled body.

"You have a bad habit of always approaching from behind, Rend," Dyfen observed.

"If I had my sword, I would cut you to pieces and feed the fish," Hugo countered, ignoring the comment.

Dyfen drew his dagger and was ready to force Hugo to retreat when a shadowy figure rushed up and grabbed Emlyn from behind.

Raoul, Duc de Marche appeared from the dark. He had a sword drawn and backed away from them still holding onto Emlyn. The terror displayed on her face made Dyfen want to plunge his dagger deep enough into de Marche's neck to separate his head from his shoulders.

Hugo was about to charge forward but Dyfen caught him by the chest and pushed him backwards, hissing, "He may harm her, Hugo. We cannot reach her in time. You have not even a weapon."

"I care not what he does to me. I will kill that son of the devil. She has told me of things…" Hugo was choking on his words, not wanting to betray her trust in him. He clenched his fists in anger. "I know this man. I know him clear to the bone. I know his ways and I will kill him. Do not think I have forgotten, Raoul," he spat with fiery, rage filled eyes.

The Duc de Marche, who had not stopped to repair himself from their earlier run in, looked at the two of them with hatred. Blood still covered his neck and gambeson, clung to strands of his hair making his appearance even more gruesome and bedraggled than when last Dyfen saw him. The disdain on his face was evident as he looked at Hugo. "You are not good enough for my sister and even less worthy of her!" he spat out at Hugo, emphasizing the word 'her', referring to Emlyn. He turned his face toward Emlyn and spoke with an urgency in his voice, "Emlyn, you know not what a bastard this man is. I tried to convince my sister of his inadequacies but she will not listen but you must listen to me in this. He is a viper and to be avoided at all costs."

Emlyn did not seem to hear him and out of frustration, he grasped her firmly in front of him with his left arm encircling her waist tightly. With his injured hand he held his sword. She could see the bloody bandage still wrapped around it, seeping. He placed his mouth near her ear and whispered, "Now, which of them was it?" he demanded. "Which one had your mind while we shared our bed?" he hissed angerly.

Emlyn did not answer.

Raoul became impatient. "If you resist in any way, I will kill them both to make sure."

The injury to his sword hand made him doubt he had time to kill them both but all that was required is he kill the right man. Then he would take his wife and go. How to decide which one of them it was? He hoped it was not Hugo. Killing him would cause great friction within his own family but he was beyond caring. He could deal with that later. Finally, he decided on a course of action.

As Hugo and Dyfen stood before him, de Marche turned his face toward them and spoke mockingly trying to bait them. "My wife is most beautiful is she not?" he taunted them.

Placing his nose against her cheek, drawing in a deep breath and closing his eyes in ecstasy. To Emlyn he whispered, "I have missed you my dear. When I regained consciousness, you had been abducted. Your husband is here to rescue you and return you to the heat of our marriage bed. You cannot imagine my distress when I realized you had been taken from me, my bride."

She responded out of exasperation, "I am not your bride. You forced me."

Raoul was infused with frustration, tired and spent. He would show her who he was. A man other men feared. Her husband whether she wanted to accept it or not. She belonged to him. He had come to take her home.

"I gave you a choice and you chose marriage," he told her sullenly. "You are my wife and you belong to me. If you doubt that then allow me to prove it to all here."

Out of exasperation, with his arm still wrapped around her waist, he began to pull the hem of her gown upward. He would show them his mark and make his claim clear, not realizing each of them already knew of it. Knew of it and were repulsed by it.

Emlyn grasped what he had planned. She blushed in shame and lowered her head so none could see the tears that were forming. He was goading the two men and punishing her as well.

Dyfen, remembering the tattoo he had seen during her rescue, realized that de Marche was about to humiliate her out of spite and could stand it no more. He tightened his grip on his dagger to the point where his fingers were numb. Hugo, who stood next to him, could barely contain himself.

In great anger, Dyfen propelled his dagger at de Marche with lightning speed, impaling his left shoulder and causing him to loosen his hold on Emlyn. She ran toward them in tears.

As Dyfen moved forward to finish off de Marche, Emlyn ran by him into Hugo's arms. He stood still for a second in conflict but kept moving to complete his mission. Eyes not moving from his target.

Raoul, in shock, dropped his sword and pulled the dagger from his shoulder as he focused on Emlyn standing with Hugo.

The sight of Hugo comforting Emlyn maddened him. So, it was Rend, he thought to himself. He met Hugo's eyes with hatred and screamed, "Rend!" Hugo looked back at him.

"Do you not wonder why your father sent you to sea, leaving your betrothed unattended and unprotected? Why he offered to sail her father and brother to Limassol leaving her alone?" he jeered. "His desire was to join our two families. You were to marry my sister," he spoke emphatically, "Emlyn was never to be yours."

He smirked at seeing the shock on Hugo's face. With his eyes locked on Emlyn, Raoul, Duc de Marche, pushed himself backwards and overboard before Dyfen's outstretched hands could reach him. He hit the sea with a splash and disappeared from view in the mist that hung over the water's surface.

Dyfen ran to the gunwale and looked over the edge. There was no sign of movement in the inky sea waters below. He pounded the rail in frustration.

He turned back seeking to ensure Emlyn was safe only to see Hugo and Emlyn huddled together. Whatever trouble Hugo held; he did not reveal it as they nestled together.

Hugo's arms were around her shoulders drawing her into his strong sinewed body where the swell of her hips and soft roundness of her breasts seemed to fit so perfectly. Her long dark hair was flowing down her slim back and Hugo was stroking it with one hand. His tilted face was resting upon her beautiful head, likely filling his nose with the heady smell of Damascus rose, Dyfen thought. He could see the profile of her beautiful face buried in his chest and through his thin tunic that Hugo's body was responding to her proximity.

Dyfen bit his lower lip, drawing blood. He did not wish to bear witness to their intimacy. He stiffly walked to the bow of the ship without speaking. He picked up a lantern that was tied there and waved it back and forth. He had expected to sail back to Cyprus with Emlyn but now he could not stay. He wanted to be off this ship as quickly as possible and was ready to jump overboard and take his chances if necessary. He used the emergency signal they had arranged beforehand hoping it would be seen through the fog.

He saw a muted light in the near distance move slightly in answer. They had seen his signal and would come.

When he looked back, Hugo and Emlyn had left the deck. He did not want to imagine where they went and what they were doing. He slammed his hand down on the rail giving himself pain. He groaned in frustration. It crossed his mind to go below deck, find her and take her with him. Even against her will. He would be doing her a favor he thought, after all she was not really married to Hugo. Now, they all knew that the scoundrel, dc Marche, still lived when they wed. He just wanted to halt any physical contact between the two before it was too late.

At least he had finished off de Marche. That would ease her mind. It did little to ease his own, remembering her wrapped in Hugo's arms. Witnessing Hugo's physical excitement through his thin bedclothes caused him concern. Where had that bastard taken her? "Damn!" he screamed. He headed for the stairs to go below deck. He would take her with him. Hugo be damned. I will kill him if he tries to stop me.

On his way there, he saw her walking toward him. She had on a dark green cape. The gusting wind sent her long, unbound tresses swirling around her head. It blew her cape apart and he saw that she wore only a thin chemise decorated with ribbons. Through its sheerness, he could see the outline of her heavy, full, breasts. She had been preparing to retire for the evening, he thought. He could feel his own body heat up as if his soul were aflame.

He must take her from this ship and back to Moon Isle, he thought to himself. He would keep her safe, give her time to recover from her trauma and figure out the rest later.

"Dyfen!" she called. He stopped and waited for her to come to him, giving himself time to collect his thoughts. But no thought went into what he said next.

"Emlyn! You married him! You married Hugo! Why could you not wait? You depart one sordid marriage and fall into another?" he said in a harsh, raspy voice. His blue eyes flashed in anger. He roughly grabbed the two sides of her cape and pulled them tightly together. Reaching down, he slipped off his belt and tied it firmly at her waist. He let go, giving her a stern look.

Sensing his anger, she folded her arms, holding herself away from him. "Dyfen, I have little time to speak to you. Hugo will miss me. Do not judge me harshly. I had little choice in the matter. I may be with child. How can I bring such danger and shame upon my family? If father or Eryk knew what befell me, they would move to avenge me.

Battle with the house of de Lusignan would be ruinous to my family. Hugo offered me his name and protection."

"So, now that your marriage to Rend is not valid what will you do?"

He held her by the shoulders. His frustration overflowed and what he said next, he knew to be cruel even as he spoke the words, but he could not contain himself. Before she had time to respond to tell him of her decision not to have intimate relations with Hugo until she knew whether she was pregnant by Raoul, he narrowed his eyes intensifying their blueness and continued. "de Marche boasted that you actually took pleasure with him! But even after hearing that! I still came for you!" he said, raising his voice, his eyes flashing.

"Can you imagine how hearing that made me feel? That wretch. That filth. Telling me you enjoyed his bed! If he had only been near enough to grasp, I would have choked the life from him, I swear it on my father's name," Dyfen's strong jawline had contorted with the words.

"How could you do this to me?" he uttered hoarsely.

"Do this to you, you ask? How could I do this to you?" she was angry now hearing his words. "You left me. You sailed away to your betrothed and left me behind! Randall Dove," she said hotly.

"You think I did not know?" she was looking at him with contempt.

"I had heard and was hoping you would tell me yourself, but you said nothing!" Tears were streaming down her face. Her eyes seemed like green glass with the wetness. "Why do you not ask instead, how I survived my husband's repeated assaults?" she shot back at him.

"Well, allow me to tell you," she said bluntly. "I relived our time in the stable that early morning after the feast. You have probably forgotten it. I mean so little to you." She took his large, rough hand in hers as tears slid down her cheek. "Or I never could have survived it, Dyfen. I swear to you."

The strength of her words dissolved his anger. His face softened seeing her tears. He reached his hand out to caress her wet face.

"Emlyn, I remember. I had already resolved to release myself from my marriage contract after your father told me of your false betrothal and the reason behind it. A marriage my father had arranged. I had agreed to for the sake of my family's name. I carry the duty of a first-born son. I cared not who I was yoked to."

His words now became measured, "I sent my father a letter informing him of my decision before we sailed to Jaffa. I went to tell my future father-in-law of my decision, face to face. I think I owe him that courtesy. I wanted to spare my father the humiliation and make it clear where the fault lies. That is where Kellis found us. We were forced to leave before I was ever able to see Lord Dove."

His voice was calmer now, "I am willing to shame myself and my family name for you. Is it not enough to prove what you mean to me?"

He was standing close to her, trying to shield her from the wind. "When your father confided in me that your betrothal was a pretense to avoid de Marche, I had hope that you would have me," he whispered.

Emlyn stood stunned by his sacrifice. Could she allow this man, she loved so well, bring shame upon himself and his entire family for her sake? Could she be so selfish? She could hear the tinkle of his earring and see its silver glint in the moonlight.

She made a painful decision and finally spoke, "It took me a while to see it but I love Hugo," she said softly.

She looked up at him. "I ask that you accept it."

"What?" he asked in shock. "You love Rend? Emlyn, how well do you really know Hugo Rend? Did you know he is a privateer because if so, you never mentioned it? My senses tell me he is not to be trusted. I do not say this out of jealousy or spite. I truly have misgivings about the man you so freely tie yourself to," Dyfen told her.

It was then Dyfen saw the moonlight fall upon the pearl studded heart pinned to her cape that Hugo had placed there earlier. She willingly wore his symbol of possession, he thought. The familiar brooch symbolizing their pledge to one another. It made him hesitate while his tired mind turned over all that had happened.

He could see how deeply she was tormented. He did not want to add to what already was an avalanche of despair.

Afterall, she had never said that she loved him. She felt gratitude towards him for her rescue assuredly. Yet, she had known about Randall and had never spoken of it and allowed him to believe in her engagement to Rend as truth. Could he be imagining his mistrust of Hugo because he did not want to believe him to be the better man? What of Gracyn Rend's part in all of this? Hugo had not known of his father's involvement, that was evident.

All of these questions spun in his head. He was not thinking clearly so torn and exhausted from events of the day. What his own father must have thought after receiving his letter, weighed on his mind.

She had stated that Rend was her husband and that she loved him. When he had looked into her eyes and she had spoken those words, he realized that they had most likely consummated their marriage. She had not expressed the regret that would have encouraged him to follow through with his plan to take her with him.

The Flaming Soul   Doreen Demerjian

He could hear the oars of the approaching galley slapping the water and went to the gunwale. He swallowed his own desires, pushing them aside and decided to leave without her.

He cared not how many men she had been with, but she had given her answer. "May our merciful God watch over you, Emlyn," he whispered and gently kissed her forehead turning to leave.

Heavy footfalls of boots slamming the hard deck were coming closer.

He saw Hugo, now fully dressed, and armed with a sword, accompanied by Captain Martel heading his way.

Hugo stopped next to Emlyn and began an exchange with her. He could not hear their words but she was shaking her head back and forth. He had her by the arm to lead her away.

Chapter 40

Aftermath

"Emlyn, I asked that you do not see Whetherly without me present," he accused, holding her by the arm. "What then, were you doing alone with him?"

"Hugo, we agreed that after we were bound, I would not do so but we were never rightfully bound," she returned.

"Obviously we must repeat the ceremony. I brought Francois to accomplish just that."

"Hugo, I question if such a sacrifice on your part should be made," she answered.

"You refuse me?" Hugo questioned.

"I do not refuse, I pause. I am tired and only wish to rest," she countered.

Emlyn needed a clear mind to review her options. She needed to ask him about his livelihood but that could wait. She was sure her father had not known that the Rends were privateers.

He let go of her arm and stood still putting a hand on each of her shoulders locking her in place. There was something he had to know.

Hugo's focused face looked down at Emlyn and he swallowed hard before he asked her, "Emlyn, do you recall the name of the ship you sailed upon with de Marche?" he looked directly into her beautiful face, waiting.

She hesitated a moment trying to recall and then spoke, "It was called the Dolphin Chase, I think. Do you know of it?"

Hugo's face looked blank. She knew he had heard her, but he did not react.

His mind was racing. The Dolphin Chase was one of his father's vessels. He thought his father fine with their engagement but could it be in pretense? What plans had his father made with the Duc de Marche behind his back? He had to return home and face him. When he arrived, he wanted it to be with Emlyn as his wife. How to make that happen was the question. She was resisting with more vigor than he expected.

Witnessing the exchange, but unable to hear the conversation, created conflicted feelings once again. Dyfen, who had been putting his leg over the side of the ship to leave, turned and reconsidered pounding the life from Hugo and taking Emlyn as originally planned. He struggled internally as to what was best for her. As he twisted his leg back over the gunwale, he glanced her way again. Hugo had his hands on her shoulders and they were conversing. She seemed at ease.

They were together. He pushed the picture from his mind, unable to endure it, and went through all of the events once again, bringing them to the present in an attempt at understanding it all. She was abducted and forced to marry a man she loathed, then to conceal a possible child from her father she rushed into a union with Hugo, a man her father had promised her to as a means of saving her from de Marche. She wed Hugo and then discovered their marriage was not lawful. She must be overwhelmed with emotional trauma, he thought, weary with worry and exhaustion.

If only he had arrived a few hours sooner before de Marche's arrival and Hugo had so much time alone with her. Now, he would give up the hope of Emlyn. She seemed to prefer the love and protection another man had to offer.

Emlyn saw that he was leaving as he grabbed the rope he had left in place and lowered himself into the galley waiting below. He had not looked back at her.

She could not blame him. He had saved her from Raoul yet again and by this time he must feel the burden of their friendship to be too heavy. Hugo had come to convince her into repeating their marriage vows. He had even brought Martel with him, but she was resisting. She needed time to recover and think about her options. Her father and brother must be protected at all costs. She knew that they would defend her honor with their last breath. She was left alone on this ship with only Hugo for protection and he was unhappy at present. Martel made it clear by his demeanor that he was fed up with both of them. She might be in greater peril than even before, she reflected.

Out of the corner of her eye she watched Dyfen disappear over the gunwale and whispered into the wind, "May you sail fare."

As Dyfen settled into the boat, he looked upward to see Martel's face hanging over the side watching him leave. He had a grim look on his dark, handsome face, and was shaking his head in disbelief as he disengaged the boarding hook and casually flipped it over the side. It fell into the water with a large splash.

Dover, looking up at Martel, saluted him with his hand in thanks while Sarkis reeled the hook into the boat, coiling the rope onto its floor.

They all could see Dyfen's fixed expression in the pale light. His eyes were closed.

Kellis, stationed at the back looked over at Dyfen with expectation in his eyes, "Lord, where is my lady?"

The Flaming Soul   Doreen Demerjian

"She loves him," came the answer.

None dared speak as they quietly rowed.

The sound of Martel kicking his drunken crew awake, cursing them in French for being useless dogs, echoed across the water as they moved through the night.

The wind was rising and the Black Trident was fading into a shadow as the small boat moved away into the night's blackness.

Chapter 41

Leaving it Behind

The rearing black stallion danced against the bluest of skies as the saffron colored canvas billowed out toward the south. The white cross in its foreground shone brilliantly in the midday sun. The Sea Stallion glided through the Mediterranean waves on its course to the ancient port of Jaffa.

They were all in a somber mood. Without Lady Emlyn at Kyrenia castle, Kellis chose to follow the visitors who had become like family to him.

He stood absently stroking the grey head of Avak standing next to him on deck. His large canine mouth opened in a smile as the cool air blew through his fur. He was the only dog beside Cydryn above deck. The others were with the horses below.

Denisot was at the stern smelling the sea air, sensing coming weather. His brown hair was blowing back and away from his face. The cool air smelled clean and fresh. The sky was blue with a few white and fluffy clouds and the weather would continue to be calm and easy for a smooth sail. Best weather for the horses below deck in slings.

Dolphins were swimming next to the ship, leaping with joy out of the blue sea water in play. A good sign. It was a glorious day.

Isley observed how their sleek bodies cut through the waves. He was anxious to reach the Levant. King Richard and his retinue had set sail a few days before them. Mareya went with him under the protection of his sister and new bride. They were headed for Acre, sixty miles north of Jaffa where Isley would land.

He was making plans for when he reached shore. He stood with his face to the wind looking out over the beautiful blue sea, deep in thought. His long brown hair was loose and blowing. His face tanned and chin rough with the beginnings of a beard.

A short distance away, Dyfen stood with Cydryn at the bow looking back at the breaking waves as the Sea Stallion cut through the water at an easy clip. He could see the cliffs of Kyrenia in the far distance. Cydryn moved closer to his leg and leaned in against his body.

Dyfen smiled down at him. "I miss her too, Cydryn. She was a good friend," he spoke as if his dog understood. His hand touched her blue and ivory kerchief tied around his left wrist.

Sarkis shirtless, approached the two and put both hands on the gunwale bracing his body. He shared the moment without speaking, understanding the conflict within his friend.

Finally, he broke the silence, "Your father, set sail for Jaffa before we left Kyrenia."

Dyfen came out of his reverie and turned to Sarkis. "What?" he asked with a puzzled look on his face, not understanding, eyes intensely riveted on Sarkis' dark face.

"Lord Whetherly, set sail for Jaffa soon after receiving your letter," he repeated.

"For what purpose?" Dyfen asked.

"I know not, Lord. I was told by captain Febrielle. Lord Whetherly spoke to him about finding another ship as the Sea Stallion was set to leave for Kyrenia. That is all I know. He was in the company of your Uncle August."

The Flaming Soul   Doreen Demerjian

Dyfen looked at Sarkis with troubled eyes. There could only be two reasons why his father and uncle would undertake a voyage to Jaffa at this time. He recalled the words his father had written him and wondered if the Sea Stallion would reach the city's shores before it was too late.

Dyfen,

To the point, I instruct you to await my visit before moving forward with your plan.

Father

He would soon know which as they sailed toward the ancient port.

The End of Book One

Made in the USA
Columbia, SC
17 September 2024